Praise for
Sailing Lessons

"If you are a fan of sisterhood-themed beach reads by Nancy Thayer and Elin Hilderbrand, then McKinnon's latest engaging standalone needs to go on your summer to-be-read list."

—*RT Book Reviews*

"McKinnon writes with such imagery that you can almost smell the salt in the air."

—*Booked*

"Books perfect for Summer Reading."

—*Book Trib*

Praise for
The Summer House

"Completely absorbing. . . . Sure to appeal to fans of Elin Hilderbrand and Dorothea Benton Frank, *The Summer House* is an intriguing glimpse into a complicated yet still loving family."

—*Shelf Awareness*

"Charming and warmhearted."

—*PopSugar*

"McKinnon bottles summer escapist beach reading in her latest, full of sunscreen-slathered days and bonfire nights. Fans of Elin Hilderbrand and Mary Alice Monroe will appreciate the Merrill family's loving dysfunction, with sibling rivalries and long-held grudges never far from the surface. This sweet-tart novel is as refreshing as homemade lemonade."

—*Booklist*

Season offers a compelling tale of family secrets, letting go, and the unbreakable bonds of sisterhood."

—Lisa Wingate, nationally bestselling author of *Before We Were Yours*

"Hannah McKinnon's lyrical debut tells the story of a pair of very different sisters, both at a crossroads in life. McKinnon's great strength lies in her ability to reveal the many ways the two women wound—and ultimately heal—each other as only sisters can."

—Sarah Pekkanen, *New York Times* bestselling author of *The Wife Between Us*

"Charming and heartfelt! Hannah McKinnon's *The Lake Season* proves that you can go home again; you just can't control what you find when you get there."

—Wendy Wax, *New York Times* bestselling author of the Ten Beach Road series and *The House on Mermaid Point*

"Hannah McKinnon's *The Lake Season* is a pure delight. It's a bonus that the setting on Lake Hampstead is as enticing and refreshing as McKinnon's voice."

—Nancy Thayer, *New York Times* bestselling author of *A Nantucket Wedding*

"Charming, absorbing and perfectly paced, *The Lake Season* is as full of warmth as summer itself. Don't blame Hannah McKinnon if this cinematic tale has you glued to a beach chair until it's finished!"

—Chloe Benjamin, *New York Times* bestselling author of *The Immortalists*

"An emotionally charged story about returning to yourself."

—K. A. Tucker, *USA Today* bestselling author of *Keep Her Safe*

Other Books by Hannah McKinnon

Sailing Lessons

The Summer House

Mystic Summer

The Lake Season

For Young Adults
(as Hannah Roberts McKinnon)

Franny Parker

The Properties of Water

The
View from
Here

— *A Novel* —

Hannah McKinnon

EMILY BESTLER BOOKS
—
ATRIA

New York   London   Toronto   Sydney   New Delhi

EMILY
BESTLER
BOOKS

ATRIA

An Imprint of Simon & Schuster, Inc.
1230 Avenue of the Americas
New York, NY 10020

First Emily Bestler Books/Atria Paperback edition June 2020

EMILY BESTLER BOOKS/ATRIA PAPERBACK and colophon are trademarks of Simon & Schuster, Inc.

For information about special discounts for bulk purchases, please contact Simon & Schuster Special Sales at 1-866-506-1949 or business@simonandschuster.com.

The Simon & Schuster Speakers Bureau can bring authors to your live event. For more information or to book an event, contact the Simon & Schuster Speakers Bureau at 1-866-248-3049 or visit our website at www.simonspeakers.com.

Interior design by Wendy Blum

Manufactured in the United States of America

3   5   7   9   10   8   6   4   2

Library of Congress Cataloging-in-Publication Data has been applied for.

ISBN 978-1-9821-1450-3
ISBN 978-1-9821-1452-7 (ebook)

For John, who is graciously writing the second chapter with me. These handscribbled, dog-haired, messy pages are sacred stuff. I cannot wait to fill them.

"I only went out for a walk and finally concluded to stay out till sundown, for going out, I found, was really going in."

—John Muir

The
View from
Here

Perry

Perry Goodwin rang his parents' doorbell and inspected the high polish on his shoes. It was his grandmother Elsie's ninety-seventh birthday, and in lieu of putting her in a nursing home they were throwing her a party.

Already he could hear the thrum of voices inside. But no one came to the door.

Perry did not like crowds. He most certainly did not like parties. He barely liked his family, if he were to be honest. They were just so . . . unshakably themselves. But he adored his grandmother Elsie. And the rest of them needed him, so here he was. He checked his watch. "Be on time!" his mother, Jane, had said in her falsetto hosting voice when she'd called. Which was almost an offense, really, because Perry was never late. Take now, for instance. He was still three minutes early, and yet his punctuality would go unnoticed because no one was there to let him in.

If his wife, Amelia, had been with him, she would've already pushed the door open. Amelia was like that. But she was not here, and so Perry rang the bell again and waited. Finally, the door swung open.

"What are you doing standing out here like a stray?" His

younger sister, Phoebe, grabbed his wrist and tugged him inside. "You were supposed to rescue me. Everyone's here."

"Not everyone," he said, removing his coat. "Amelia is picking up Emma at school. And besides, the party just started." Phoebe could be so dramatic.

But she was not listening. She was suddenly distracted by her reflection in the hall mirror and had begun raking her hands through her hair in some attempt to change it. "So, did you hear about Jake's new girl?"

Perry glanced across the marble foyer at the ripple of gray-haired guests overflowing from the living room. It figured. The elderly were always early. He scoured the crowd, hoping that his parents' neighbor Eugene Banks was not in attendance. Mr. Banks had the distasteful practice of cornering Perry at family parties, clapping him loudly on the back and asking him how much he'd earned in the past year as a car insurance agent. Perry was a risk analyst for one of New York's premier entertainment firms. He did not insure cars. He most certainly did not discuss personal finances.

Phoebe gave up on her hair and spun around. "We finally get to lay eyes on her. She's coming to the party!"

Perry followed the brisk swish of his sister's yellow skirt into the crowded living room. "Who's coming?"

Phoebe glared at him over her shoulder. "I just told you. Jake's new girl."

Perry was about to ask if this new girl of their younger brother's had a name, but he was suddenly clapped on the back. "Perry!" He cringed. Thankfully, it was only his father, Edward, his eyes glimmering with pleasure. "Good to see you, son."

Perry let himself be pulled into a hug. If overly demonstrative, his father was the most reasonable member of the family. "Looks like quite a party. How's Nana doing?"

Edward indicated across the room where Elsie was neatly folded into a damask wingback by the window. "Holding court."

Indeed, his grandmother looked pleased. Her eyes traveled about the room locking every now and then on her twin great-grandsons, Jed and Patrick, who galloped through the sea of trouser pants and skirts with confections in hand.

Spying Perry, they headed straight for him, pushing and shoving to get to their uncle first. Phoebe's sons were a handful, but Perry adored them. "Who got into the sweets already?" he asked, as Jed leapt up to be held. Perry held him a safe distance away from his white dress shirt and inspected the boy's chocolate-dotted lips. The four-year-old still clutched a half-eaten cookie, and once ensconced in the safety of his uncle's arms he leaned down and swiped at his brother's hair with his free hand. Below, Patrick yelped. "Grandma said we could."

Edward shook his head. "Of course she did. Now come with me, I think we should wash those hands." Perry set Jed down and watched him and his brother reluctantly trail their grandfather to the bathroom. Meanwhile their parents were on the opposite side of the room chatting and laughing with guests, champagne in hand, completely checked out. Why not, when everyone else in the family could watch your kids?

Perry helped himself to a cup of punch and made his way through the crowd to Elsie. "Happy birthday, Nana." He leaned down and kissed her cheek.

"Oh, Perry my love," she said softly, her voice barely a whisper. "Look how handsome."

As eldest, Perry had always felt a special bond with his grandmother. He had been the first grandchild, and as such she'd fussed over him. Since his grandfather had passed away last year, she'd come to live with Perry's parents, a move that both heartened and concerned him. The house was hardly suitable for a ninety-seven-year-old. There were steep stairs and laquered wooden floors. He also worried about the toll on his parents for having to care for Elsie. Just as it pained Perry now to feel the tremor in her fingers as she pressed a hand lovingly to his cheek.

"Are you enjoying your big day?" he asked.

"It's just another year," she said. Elsie glanced up at him, her cloudy blue eyes searching his own. Perry felt something inside him shift. Growing old had begun to frighten him.

"Pray tell, where is that bony wife of yours?" his grandmother asked.

Perry was used to this commentary, and yet he still flinched. Amelia was thin, but he liked to think elegantly so. His grandmother did not share that sentiment.

"Now, Nana. Amelia might be hurt if she was here to hear that."

"But she's not. That's the risk of arriving late to a party—you'll find yourself the topic of conversation." She shrugged, a mischievous smile fluttering across the soft folds of her face. "What is that you're drinking, dear?" she gestured to his cup.

"Punch."

Elsie frowned. "Virgin?"

"I believe so. Would you like some?"

She pursed her lips. "What I'd like is a little bourbon."

Perry glanced at the bar cart across the room. "I thought your medications weren't to be mixed with alcohol."

Elsie pointed in the direction of the cart. "Double finger, dear."

"But Nana."

Elsie placed her hand on his own and squeezed. "Perry, my love. You must learn to have some fun. Or at least allow the rest of us."

Perry sighed. "Be right back."

Phoebe found him at the bar cart. "We need to talk."

"In just a minute. Nana insists I get her a bourbon." He shook his head. "I guess one won't hurt."

Phoebe laughed. "One? That's at least her second. She made Dad fetch her one earlier."

Perry set the bottle down. "That minx."

"Relax." Phoebe took the glass from him and resumed the pour. "How many ninety-seventh birthdays does one get?"

Perry watched her march off in the direction of the birthday girl with the drink in question. "There won't be a ninety-eighth if she keeps it up," he called after her.

Amelia and Emma had still not arrived. When he finally made it to the punch bowl, it was empty. He lugged it into the kitchen.

"There you are!" His mother, Jane, stood at the counter scraping something dry and blackened off of a tray and into the farmhouse sink.

"Hello, Mother. What have you there?"

"It *was* a tray of Brie and apricot tarts." She shrugged. "But Nana can't chew very well these days, so it's not like she could've eaten them anyway."

Perry helped himself to a cup of punch and observed the momentary slump in his mother's posture. She turned to him, straightening her apron. "So, how are *you*?"

"Fine." He held up the punch bowl.

"You think of everything." She nodded toward the pantry. "Two bottles of seltzer and one of cranberry juice. You didn't happen to notice if Jake arrived yet, did you? He's bringing his Olivia."

Olivia. So the new girl did have a name. Perry glanced out the kitchen window at the circular drive. What could be taking his wife so long?

"She's a doll, this one. Have you met her?"

He had not. But that was clearly about to change. "Do I have a choice?" It was tiring. Every special occasion, a new girl.

Like the rest of the Goodwin offspring, Jake was sharp and handsome. But unlike his more reserved siblings, he possessed a flirtatious streak that coursed back to their high school years, the likes of which had managed to attract the attention of the cutest girls in Perry's junior class the first week of Jake's freshman year. Although Perry aced his AP courses and swept the CIAC track and field championship that year, he'd regrettably remained unable to engage in any meaningful interaction with a member of the opposite sex, and so it was young Jake who'd lobbied (and then landed) his big brother a date two days before prom. "There's room in our limo," Jake had added.

Perry had been flummoxed. "You're going to prom? Wait—you have a limo?"

Little had changed in the years since.

The last Perry had heard, Jake was seeing the multipierced blond rock climber from Colorado he'd met at Burning Man. The one who'd lasted almost the whole of the previous year, leaving the family to wonder in not-so-quiet whispers if this one would stick. But then there was the redheaded accountant, at Christmas. If Perry wasn't mistaken, she was the one who'd giggled so nervously at the dinner table she snorted spiced eggnog out of her nose. Or maybe that was the blonde.

His mother ignored his question and continued scraping at the burnt tray in the sink. "There's something about this one. You'll see."

Perry found the seltzer bottles in the pantry and emptied them carefully into the bowl, considering his mother's choice of words. "There's always something."

"Oh, and I suppose you heard, I've asked your sister and Rob to move in with the kids while their new cottage is being renovated. I fear she's taken on too much, and they really can't keep living like that."

"Is that wise?" Phoebe could be so selfish. It was too much to ask. Let alone of aging parents who already had their hands full with their Nana. He lifted the punch bowl gingerly, measuring the distance between himself and the dining room table where a clutch of women of a certain age hovered in orthopedic shoes, a group his mother referred to as "the biddies." Mrs. Lorenzo from next door was laughing loudly and gesturing a bit too exuberantly. He and the punch bowl would have to take a different route.

"Well, I can't exactly send my grandchildren out on the streets."

"The streets?" Perry had been thinking more along the lines of a hotel. Or better yet, telling Phoebe to grit her teeth and live through her self-imposed house renovation like most people did. After all, it was Phoebe and Rob's choice to sell their perfectly good house, buy a falling-down shack on the lake, and then tear it apart. It was hardly the cottage's fault it was a hundred years old. "It might not be as temporary as you think, Mom. Renovations always take longer than planned. And the boys are great, but they're a real handful. When you combine that with everything going on with Nana . . ."

There was a sudden clatter. His mother dumped the tray into the sink, and plucked a single cigarette out of her pocket. If she'd pulled out a switchblade, Perry could not have been more surprised.

"Mom?" The punch sloshed dangerously against the sides of the bowl.

Jane Goodwin did not smoke. Had never smoked. His father, Edward, enjoyed the occasional cigar, but Perry had no recollection of ever having seen his mother smoke, even in the haze of the early seventies when just about everyone seemed to. She reached for a high cabinet, ferreted around behind the sugar jar, and produced a lighter.

"Mother. What are you *doing*?"

Jane blinked. "Oh, please. It's just one." Her heels clicked as she headed for the patio door and flung it ajar.

Perry watched in horror as she leaned out, lit up, and inhaled. "When did this start?" he asked. Then, "Do you understand how toxic that is? Your lungs!"

Jane Goodwin was a portrait of health. All his life Perry's mother had been fit and trim. She played tennis. She ate salad. In a corner of their manicured lawn she tended an organic herb garden.

She took a deep drag and closed her eyes dreamily. "Take the punch out to those biddies. And not a word to your father."

Perry navigated the small sea of guests precariously. Phoebe swept up beside him, and again he had to steady the bowl. "Watch it." Then, "Since when does Mom smoke?"

"What? I don't know. Listen, Rob is going to ask you about joining the Club. I want you to talk it down."

"My Club?" Had she not just heard what he'd said about their mother?

Phoebe trailed him to the dining room, fidgeting with her bracelets. "Jesus, Perry. It's not *yours*."

Technically, perhaps. But Perry was the president of the Candlewood Cove Clubhouse, a rustic but exclusive enclave on the western shore of Candlewood Lake in his gated community. Residing in the Cove did not guarantee membership. It had taken him four years, since buying his two-million-dollar home, just to be sponsored. And several more to work his way onto the board and up to presidency. Phoebe may have just bought a cottage on the lake, but it was across the way. Outside the clubhouse community. And though he loved his sister, he did not exactly relish the thought of sharing his private escape with her and her boisterous young brood.

"Relax," she told him. "The house renovations have been more involved than we planned, so joining the Club isn't exactly in the budget. He might as well buy a pony. Will you tell him that?"

"That he should buy a pony?"

Phoebe waited until he set the bowl down and then socked him in the arm. "I'm serious."

"Ow. All right." Perry was used to this. As much as his siblings ribbed him for being uptight, they never failed to queue up when things went down. To ask advice. To borrow money. To try and twist his arm into approaching one family member or other to twist *his or her* arm about one thing or other. Though this time he was secretly impressed by Phoebe's unusual demonstration of financial restraint. Having bought the cottage was one thing, but the gut renovation was a whole other financial misstep. He couldn't imagine where they'd come up with the initiation fee for the Club.

"Have you tried telling Rob this yourself?"

He watched his sister's gaze land on her husband, who was standing by the window, talking to their father. The boys were back inside chasing each other in a hazardously widening circle around the guests. Phoebe's eyes narrowed. "I'm a little over budget on the renovation."

He knew they would be, of course. What he wondered was whether Rob knew. As with many other things in their marriage that struck Perry as unusual, Phoebe had taken the reins of the entire building project. "How much over?"

Phoebe flicked her head. "Doesn't matter."

"That bad?"

"Just forget it, Perry." Now she was upset with him.

He scratched his head. "Listen, I wouldn't worry about the lake Club membership. You guys use mine quite a bit anyway."

"No, we don't."

They did. Every summer, in fact, but Perry did not say this. His bicep still smarted. Instead he said, "Just tell Rob that you want to wait until the house is done. That you want to keep a buffer." He watched his sister's eyebrows rise and fall, as they did whenever she was concentrating.

"I just ordered a three-thousand-dollar bathroom vanity. He won't believe that."

Three thousand? "Then blame it on me. Say it was my suggestion."

Phoebe uncrossed her arms. "Well, that he'd believe."

The doorbell rang and as he watched little sister trot toward the door, Perry found his hand involuntarily pressed to his pants pocket where he carried his wallet. It was only a matter of time, he feared, before she would be asking for more than advice.

Amelia and Emma flurried across the foyer in his direction. "I was starting to worry."

"Hello to you, too." Amelia pecked his cheek. "The car was low on gas. I was on the other side of town, near the Exxon."

Perry flinched. "Three forty-nine a gallon?"

Amelia held up her hand. "I know, I know. Which is why I drove over to the other one, but it was closed. Which meant I had to drive farther south because at that point I was on empty."

Perry closed his eyes. Amelia always did this. Ran the car until the gas light went on, then drove around without a care in the world, coasting on hope and fumes. With Emma, no less.

She smiled up at him. "Relax. We're here."

He knew better than to remind her of the hour. "I'm glad," he said instead. And he meant it. By comparison to his family, his wife was a Zen temple.

Beside her, Emma gazed across the crowd shyly, unlike her

flagrant cousins, who galloped by once more, so involved in their horseplay they didn't even notice her arrival. Emma watched them, with a faint smile. Sometimes Perry wondered if they'd done her a disservice as an only child. "How was school, honey?"

"Fine."

"Anything fun happen today?"

"Nope."

He should've asked an open-ended question. That's what the article in *Parenting* magazine had advised. "Coping with Teens" had been the title. Perry needed some coping strategies. He looked to Amelia, who hadn't even seemed to notice Emma's curt replies. But she wouldn't have noticed. Emma still talked to her, if in exasperated tones. Perry could have settled for exasperation.

"You're here!" Phoebe joined them, and Emma burst into a smile at the sight of her aunt. Perry couldn't believe the trans-formation. "How's school?" Phoebe asked.

"Pretty good. But I can't wait for summer. I'm working this year as a counselor at our clubhouse camp."

Emma had gotten a job as a counselor? He'd heard nothing of that. Perry spun around to his wife, who seemed to already know all of this. Why had no one told him? When Phoebe lifted her hand and Emma high-fived it, Perry's heart gave a little.

"That's awesome! I worked at a theater camp when I was your age. I studied drama in college, as one of my minors."

Phoebe was still studying drama, as far as Perry could tell.

"I can't wait. My campers will be in first grade, so that should be fun."

"They'll love you!" Phoebe gushed. Perry had to agree. But before he could ask Emma about her summer job, there came a small commotion by the front door. His father waved a hand. "Everyone, Jake's here!"

With that, his family abandoned him and joined the stampede for the front door like lemmings. Perry would stay right where he was, thank you very much, and watch from a civilized distance.

It was then he noticed his grandmother creeping up behind the outskirts of the crowd. Elsie held her hands out to her sides, shuffling unsteadily as she went. "Nana!" he called.

Just in time he got to her and guided her back to her chair. "I'll ask Jake to come to you," he promised. How typical of Jake to make a scene of an entrance, with no thought to its consequence. Perry was just about to find his little brother and tell him just that, when he heard his name.

"You must be Perry." He turned.

Perry had only ever taken one art class in the entirety of his comprehensive education, a required and impractical elective. But for the first time in all the years since, it made sense. The woman who stood before him was a subject stepped off the canvas of a Baroque painting and into his parents' living room. Perry exhaled.

"I'm Olivia." She extended her hand and Perry found himself taking it. He glanced down at their entwined fingers. Hers were diminutive in his own. When he looked back up, she was studying him curiously. Quickly, Perry let go.

"Excuse me," he stammered. "You're Olivia."

"I am." She laughed and swept her dark hair back. Perry had never cared for short hair on women, and yet he found himself fighting an urge to reach out and tuck it behind her ear for her. "And this is my daughter, Luci."

An elfin child peeked out from behind Olivia's knees then hid behind her mother again. The spell was broken.

No one had said a thing about a child. It was then he saw the dog.

Behind the two of them stood an oversized mongrel of a dog.

"Oh, and that's Buster." Buster gazed up at him, a viscous trail of drool dangling from his cavernous mouth. "He's our therapeutic rescue dog."

Perry blinked. "I'm sorry?"

"Well, he's a trained therapy dog. But first he was a rescue dog. From Texas." As if that explained what the giant canine was doing in his parents' Connecticut living room, at his grandmother's ninety-seventh birthday party. Olivia bent to rub its floppy ears fondly. "Though I'm not sure who rescued who."

Ah, she was one of *those*.

"So, you rescue dogs?"

"Just this one. But I'd rescue them all if I could. I could own a hundred! They're just so grateful."

Perry cleared his throat. The new girl was an anthropomorphic soon-to-be canine hoarder. Flustered, he glanced about for his family. Had no one noticed the four-legged intruder in the living room? But true to form, Phoebe and Jake were huddled together by the door, chatting away as if nobody else in the world existed. His parents, having already welcomed this circus, had twirled off into the gray-haired crowd, probably to pour more champagne. Just what the seniors needed.

Thankfully, Amelia rescued him. "Olivia! We've heard so much about you."

They had? Perry focused on keeping a smart distance between himself and the encroaching dog. He was allergic to dogs. Already he could feel the ominous tickle at the back of his throat.

But Emma was besotted. She kneeled beside Luci. "Your dog is so big. And so cute!"

Luci ducked behind her mother's knees.

"Thank you!" Olivia said proudly. She apparently thought nothing of the fact that she was standing in the Goodwins' formal living room surrounded by a sea of guests, any of whom could be allergic to or afraid of dogs. Like himself, for instance. "He's Luci's therapy dog. We take him pretty much everywhere we go."

So the dog attended more than just birthday parties.

"And what kind of dog is . . . Buster?" Perry inquired.

Olivia turned to Luci, but the child said nothing. "Pure mutt," Olivia answered.

"Huh." Perry was no expert, but he would've guessed wolf-hound mixed with mastiff. Or some kind of Rottweiler jumble. Impossible to insure. High incidence of bites.

Emma—unaffected by the fact that whatever the beast was, it had pressed itself against her—stroked its head absently. "We were just about to sing happy birthday. Do you like cake?" she asked Luci.

The child glanced uncertainly at her mother.

"Who doesn't?" Olivia answered, again for both of them. She turned to Luci. "Go ahead with Emma. Mommy will be right there."

Perry watched in horror as his wife and daughter whisked the child to the dessert table, as if there was absolutely nothing amiss leaving him standing alone with the new girlfriend and her un-insurable dog. "Would you like some cake?" he asked Olivia, unsure of what else to say. "Or would he?" Perry gestured to the dog.

Olivia seemed to find this wildly funny and tossed her head back. The trill that followed was crisp and girlish. Again, Perry was momentarily entranced.

"I'm sorry Luci didn't answer you or Emma. She has a con-dition that makes it hard for her to talk in public places." She glanced down at her shoes, which Perry saw were poppy red.

"Oh. What kind of condition?"

She glanced back up at Perry. "Selective mutism. It started

when she was two. We have a counselor who specializes in speech pathology, but it really comes down to time and practice. And me." Her voice drifted, and Perry found himself leaning in.

But suddenly there was Jake, blue eyes gleaming. He took the leash from Olivia's hand and slid his arm around her waist. "Perry! How's it going?" There was a lightness about his face. He turned to Olivia. "My big brother is boring you to death, isn't he? Should I get you coffee to keep you awake?"

Again, there was that trill of laughter from her throat. "Perry and I are doing just fine, aren't we?" She grinned at him.

"Just fine," Perry echoed, though he wasn't so sure. He glanced around. Amelia was so much better at these things. "You know, Nana was trying to get to the door to greet you. She almost fell." He paused, aware that he was saying this in front of Olivia and perhaps best not. "Have you said hello to her yet?"

Jake's tone flattened. "She was the first one we said hello to." Already Perry could feel his little brother pulling away. He hadn't wanted to start things off like this, but it had always been the way of their relationship. Jake did what Jake did, and Perry was left to sweep up behind him.

Olivia put her hands together. "I'd better go check on Luci. Perry, it was nice to meet you, finally."

To Perry's dismay, she did not take her dog but instead glided toward the dining room, where everyone seemed to be gathering. As if on cue, a large glowing cake was carried out, illuminating the faces around the table. Upon seeing Olivia, Perry and Jake's mother waved her over, pulling her into the family fold.

Jake shook his head. "Isn't she something?"

Perry didn't know where to begin. "Is that an accent I heard?"

"Her father is French."

"So she's from France?"

"Yeah. She was born there. But she's lived in New York for most of her life." He frowned. "She's American. I think."

"You think? And her daughter . . ."

"Luci. Isn't she cute?"

She was, no doubt. But that wasn't what Perry was getting at. Before he could say anything else, Jake grabbed both his shoulders. "You can't tell the others. But I'm going to marry her, Perry."

"Marry her?" Perry choked.

From the dining room voices rose in a lopsided rendition of "Happy Birthday."

"Why not? She's the best thing that ever happened to me," Jake shouted over the singing. He tossed back the remains of his beer, handed Buster's leash to Perry, and set off for the dining room with a look of foolish love plastered on his face.

Phoebe

I
t was her fault that they'd bought the musty fixer-upper. It was probably also her fault they were two months behind schedule and already squeezing the budget. And yet she'd do it all over again. If only she could get her paint samples and get the hell out of the hardware store in time to pick up the boys from preschool.

The woman in front of her in line at the paint design counter would not shut up. Phoebe checked her watch. Five more minutes—that's all she could afford. She glanced at the color strips in her hand, trying to channel the soothing mood of her blue-and-gray palette. All right, maybe ten more minutes.

"I just love orange. Such a cheerful color. With all the horrors on the news these days, everyone needs a pop of color, don't you think?"

Phoebe eyeballed the woman in front of her. Tan pants, gray shirt. Even her sensible shoes were of the sand-colored variety. Hypocrite.

The sales associate ignored Phoebe's pointed gaze and nodded encouragingly at the "greige" woman. "Have you looked at our Aura line? The right shade of orange or red can be positively galvanizing."

Phoebe would have liked very much to galvanize the woman

right out of line. She could not be late again for the twins' pre-school pickup. Sweet, smiling Mrs. McAllister had not been pleased when she showed up late last Friday. Listening to Phoebe's convoluted excuse for her delay, Mrs. McAllister had distractedly twisted her alphabet necklace until Phoebe feared it would burst. "I'm sorry, Mrs. Riley. But our school policy is that if parents are later than fifteen minutes, we have to place the boys in the extended hours program."

Upon hearing that, the boys had leaned against Mrs. McAllister's pillowy side and glared up at their mother. How quickly toddler alliance shifted. And from her own offspring. "I'm sorry." Phoebe groveled. "It won't happen again." The problem was, she knew it would.

Finally, the woman in front of her paid for her orange paint and vacated her place in line. Phoebe surged forward. "I'd like some samples, please."

The saleswoman smiled as she ticked through Phoebe's choices. "Sea Salt. Tranquil Moments. Healing Aloe. Classic colors."

Phoebe beamed. Her favorite was Healing Aloe. It conjured something warm and gooey Phoebe could smear across her face while she sprawled in a hammock.

"I love the names," her mother, Jane, had said when Phoebe shared her paint chips the evening before at her grandmother Elsie's birthday party. It was after all the guests had left, and the family lingered in the kitchen, picking at the remains of the hors d'oeuvre trays. Perry had winced. "*Tranquil Moments?* Sounds like new-age voodoo nonsense, to me."

"Now, *that's* a paint name," Jake had said.

Perry wasn't totally off the mark. Phoebe's life was so chaotic, it was no longer recognizable to her. She knew how ungrateful that sounded. For starters, she had the twins. Two healthy boys whose legs pumped beneath their sturdy frames as they careened through the suburban square of their Connecticut backyard. A husband, whom she'd not only met and fallen in love with in college, but whom she remained deeply in love with, something her friends routinely commented on. Before starting their family, she'd worked as a copy editor for a local printing business, and Rob still worked for a marketing group. They'd bought their starter home, had kids, and unlike many of the couples they socialized with on the rare occasion when they weren't too burnt out or busy, they were still stable and solid. But something had been missing, something that left Phoebe feeling edgy and itchy. It wasn't being a stay-at-home mother, though that was exhausting and, in her opinion, far harder than her day job had been. It wasn't anything about the boys, who were thriving. Or the husband, whom she adored. It was something else. Something that she needed yet could not name until that fateful fall day she stumbled across it while driving with the boys. It was a house.

In truth, she had not exactly stumbled across it. The lakeside cottage was a thing she'd admired since childhood. Back then, it had been the crisp white of new-fallen snow, its slate roof and cherry-red door bestowing upon it the air of a storybook cottage. Her childhood friend, Jessica, had lived three houses up on the same windy lakeside lane, and Phoebe had spent the better part of her elementary school years passing the house without giving it much thought. Until one summer day when the girls pulled their bikes up alongside the mailbox, which was teeming with soft pink balloons. "They just had a baby," Jessica said. "Looks like a party." Indeed, guests were arriving, arms laden with frilly gift boxes and wobbly Jell-O molds. A man in a seersucker suit walked by toting a giant stuffed giraffe. And there, on the front step, stood the young mother with the new baby swaddled against her floral dress.

Phoebe had stared at the couple in their lush green yard, welcoming their well-dressed guests amid the haze of pink balloons, and thought to herself, *That. That is what my future looks like.*

Of course, she had forgotten the house and the party over the years, but not the feeling it had filled her with that summer day. So, on one dark drizzling autumn day when the boys were both sick with head colds and she'd been driving her Jeep Cherokee up and down the hills of Lenox in a desperate attempt to usher them to sleep in their car seats, she'd crested the hill and seen the *For Sale* sign, she'd slammed on the brakes. Both boys jerked awake, wailing in sleep-deprived protest. "It's okay," Phoebe had cooed as she stared back at the house from her childhood memory. Because, suddenly, it was.

The cottage was no longer crisp or tidy. It had the sad appearance of having not been lived in for some time, its lawn overgrown and its paint weathered. But still—there was the stone chimney. And the faded red door. And the sweeping view of the water. The memory of the beaming new mother clutching her bright new baby rushed back to Phoebe as she stared through the swish of her windshield wipers at the house. *All it needs is a family*, she thought. *Like us.*

She'd raced straight home and called the Realtor. While Rob and the boys were traversing the soccer field at practice the next morning, unbeknownst to him, Phoebe was exploring every inch of the creaky old cottage. By the time he came home, she was waiting for him in the kitchen, with a shy smile and a copy of the listing in hand.

"I've found our dream house!" she announced.

Rob halted in the entryway, one hand on each boy. All three were knee-high in mud splatters. "I didn't know we were looking for one."

"Before you say anything, please take a look. It's a big place that needs a little work." In truth, it was a little place that needed big work. She thrust the listing under Rob's nose.

Rob's eyes had skittered right past the image and down to the listing price, where they widened with amusement. "Did you win the lottery?" He laughed. "We don't have that kind of coin."

"But we do!" Phoebe insisted. She'd done her homework and prepared a small speech. "The Realtor says the market has improved. If we sell our place, we'll have plenty to deposit on the lake house. And extra to fix it up. Just the way we like it!"

"But I like this house," he said, tugging Patrick's wet uniform over his head.

"No, you don't. You just don't realize it because you're always at work. I live here with the kids day in and out. We're busting at the seams."

Newly freed from their soaked soccer gear, the twins bolted away and up the stairs. There was a thundering overhead and the kitchen ceiling shook. Phoebe gritted her teeth.

"Is this about the Warrens?" Rob asked.

Phoebe prickled. Don and Victoria Warren lived next door. Not to be confused with Vicky. Or Tori. "Vic—tor—ee—uh," she'd told Phoebe the first time they'd met. "As in the queen. I don't do nicknames."

Don and *Vic-tor-ee-uh* had recently remodeled their entire house, from foundation to chimney top. Even before their long and noisy renovation Phoebe had struggled with what Rob called "neighborly bonds" with the Warrens. They were the kind of people who had their house decked out, within a twinkle light of being visible from space, for Christmas. And all before midnight on Thanksgiving. The decorative extravaganza kept Phoebe and Rob's bedroom illuminated like a Walmart parking lot. But only until the twelfth day of Christmas, Victoria assured her. Which only served to piss Phoebe off further. What kind of person kept track of when it was the twelfth day of Christmas?

They hosted lavish parties with ridiculous themes. Like their annual Kentucky Derby party ("*A soiree!*" Vic-tor-ee-uh had trilled), where they served only mint juleps and made everyone don fancy little hats. Phoebe liked wine. And she loathed hats. What she loathed most was attending parties where people were required to do anything other than shower and show up. For her, as the mother of toddler boys, those two things, themselves, were reason to celebrate.

Rob, being the better sport, felt otherwise. "Come on, honey. Surely you can put on a hat for one party."

"No. No, I cannot." Phoebe was more from the Robert Frost school of thinking. The whole "Good fences make good neighbors" thing was written for people like the Warrens. She doubted Robert Frost ever had to don a Kentucky Derby hat for a "soiree."

"They have a thing for holidays," Rob had said, with a resigned shrug. "Think of them as jolly."

Phoebe had rolled her eyes. "Jolly assholes."

Just last weekend the Warrens had hosted an elaborate open house. A "Welcome Summer!" gathering, they'd called it, which just happened to coincide with the completion of their renovation. The handsome Dutch Colonial had been completely gutted, along with, in Phoebe's opinion, much of its original character. The old brick fireplaces had been covered up and replaced with a floating gas wall insert of turquoise glass and metal. The antique hardwoods were ripped out, replaced by a cold gray tile meant to look like driftwood. Phoebe had dragged her best friend, Anna Beth, with her to the party.

"Doesn't it feel coastal?" Vic-tor-ee-uh had crooned, as she led a gaggle of nosy neighbors room to room. Never mind that they were a hundred miles from the nearest coast. Anna Beth had grabbed Phoebe's hand as they detoured sharply from the planned route and into a brass and marble–appointed powder room that was more befitting a czarina than a stay-at-home mother. "Welcome Summer gathering, *my ass*," Anna Beth hissed as she slid the pocket door closed behind them. "This is a smug ride on a show pony."

They'd spent the rest of the "tour" doubled over in giggles, try-ing to flush the hands-free smart toilet by wiggling their rear ends over the bowl, until someone knocked on the door.

Now Phoebe gazed back at Rob with what she hoped was masked ire. What was he insinuating? The Warrens' house was ridiculous. All Phoebe wanted was a house with a separate bed-room for each boy and a yard to play in. And maybe more room. The lake house would afford them all of that. Plus the lake.

"Honey. Hear me out. Our lives are crazy busy. School, kids, work. Forget paying bills and mowing the lawn and trying to keep up with cleaning this dump."

"Dump?" It was Rob's turn to prickle.

"This house is our hub. It has to function, or we can't."

Rob stood up slowly. "Maybe we can work on the kitchen a little. I know it's dated, but it still works. Mostly."

"Right. And the last thing you cooked in here was . . . ?"

Rob held up his hands. "All right. But I don't think now is the time."

"You're up for that promotion," she reminded him. "You've been groomed and waiting your turn in line for years. Dan said so."

Dan was Rob's boss at the marketing firm. He'd been hinting at moving Rob up in recent months, and a position had finally opened. Interviews were already underway, but Dan had told Rob off the record that it was just a formality. The job was his if he wanted it.

"Then we should wait until I get the job."

"The house is a steal. It won't be there if we wait!"

"Phoebe, I love your gusto. But this feels rushed. Maybe we should let things unfold and see what happens."

Phoebe glanced around. At the boys' artwork obscuring the dated fridge. At the coats spilling out of the hall closet. The tiny living room, crammed with toys.

"I'm not built like you," she said, fighting back tears. "I've loved this house since I was a little girl. I can't just sit back and let things unfold according to the goddamned universe."

Rob went to her and pulled her against him. "I know. Indeed, you are your own force within it." He sighed into her hair, and she felt the mix of exasperation and warmth in it. "This house is really the one?"

She pulled back to see if he was serious. "It is." Then, "Wouldn't it be nice to host the family at Thanksgiving?"

Rob's nose twitched. "Your family?"

She kissed the tip of it. "Never mind. Friends. Neighbors."

"You hate the neighbors."

She smiled. "I hate everybody."

The next day they went to see it. Rob loved the view. He did not love the improvements that would need to be made. Or the fact they'd have to sell their house quickly to make it work. "It's virtually the same size as our current home," he argued.

"Yes, but it has one more bedroom for the boys. And look at that." She pointed out the picture window at the lake below.

He couldn't argue that. Phoebe made an appointment with an inspector and a contractor. Rob made an appointment with their financial advisor.

On paper it could work. But only just. "You don't have any wiggle room," the advisor warned, as he reviewed the proposed cost spreadsheet with them. He set his pencil down. "Look, renovating an old house can be like opening a can of worms."

Rob didn't like the sound of this either. There were too many opportunities for things to go wrong.

Phoebe did not share the same fear. "Let's not forget, I banked my last year's salary before the boys were born. We've been able to live largely off of your salary without touching mine. We'll create a budget and stick to it. If things go awry, there's always that cushion."

It was true. In five years they'd only dipped into Phoebe's set-aside work income once, and that was when the Jeep needed repairs. But it didn't mean Rob wanted to lean on it.

"Phoebe, we're financially secure. Remember the years of lying awake wondering how we'd pay off grad school loans and buy groceries? I don't ever want to go back to that."

"Neither do I, and we won't. Worst case, I go back to work. Don't you see, this is what we've been talking about. Getting out of our starter and into our forever home. This is the house we'd have for the rest of our lives."

Rob groaned, but she went on. "Picture it: Birthday parties where the kids can swim with their friends right out of their own backyard. Christmases with the whole family over, followed by ice-skating on the lake. Then graduations. Who knows, maybe someday a wedding . . ."

Rob looked at her then, at the stars in her eyes. He couldn't deny it. This was what he loved about his wife. He was pragmatic, and she was the dreamer. Between the two they struck a balance. "So, we're really going to do this?"

It was a question she'd never forget being asked. Because Rob was in. Despite the risks and the unknowns, he was on board. For the briefest moment she waffled.

"If we don't, I think I'll always regret it."

"All right, then."

They'd spilled the good news to her family over their weekly Sunday night dinner. Rob let Phoebe do the talking. To her consternation, only Jake seemed to like the idea. "I get it," he said. "It's your little place in the big world. Why not love where you live?"

Predictably, Perry had shaken his head over his plate of chicken piccata. "You're flipping a house? Do you know the financial risks associated?"

Phoebe rolled her eyes. "No one's flipping anything. We're buying a fixer-upper."

At which Perry mumbled, not quite under his breath, "No risk there."

Phoebe was grateful when Amelia elbowed him. Twice. "We'll live in the cottage as we renovate it," Phoebe explained.

Their mother, Jane, went straight to the kids. "What about the boys? All that dust and debris! Just think about the mess. Can you really live in those conditions?"

Phoebe had pushed her plate away. "This is *for* the boys. And it won't be forever. You guys have to see it. You'll love it."

But the family wasn't done.

"Have you had it inspected?"

"What if you tear off the siding and find rot?"

"Or mold?"

"I've heard slate roofs are harbingers of mold!"

"Have you even checked the roof?"

All the while, her father sat back in his chair, withholding comment. Phoebe locked eyes with him, waiting. Edward almost always championed her ideas.

Finally, he cleared his throat. "What about the foundation? Now, that's the first place you should look. I know a good contractor . . . Honey, what was the name of the boy who went to school with Jake whose father had a Rottweiler he used to let roam the golf course? You know who I'm talking about? I think his name was Rudy."

"Yes, yes. But wasn't that the dog's name?"

And then everyone started in again.

Phoebe looked around the table at all the uncooperative faces that belonged to her.

"I don't know why I tell you people anything." She pushed her plate away.

Grandma Elsie, having finished her soup, set a trembling hand atop Phoebe's and gripped it. "Old houses are a lot of work. But . . ." She turned to the rest of them, as if to impart some gold thread of wisdom.

Everyone quieted.

"But what, Nana?" Phoebe prompted.

Elsie narrowed her eyes. "But I don't see dessert. Where did that cheesecake get to?"

Now, having sold one house, bought another, and survived six months into the renovation, Phoebe squealed into the preschool parking lot in the nick of time. The boys were in good spirits, each clutching a wet finger painting. Phoebe set the paintings on the backseat as she helped the boys into their car seats and held back a curse when one painting slipped, leaving a trail of blue across the black leather.

"I'm hungry!" Patrick announced.

"Macaroni?" Jed asked.

Phoebe hopped in the driver's seat. "Don't forget the cheese," she said, and both boys cheered. Ah, the simple victory of two toddlers climbing into the car with smiles instead of tears!

As she pulled into their driveway, Phoebe smirked with pleasure. The cottage was under renovation, she was still speaking to her family, and just as she'd predicted they'd thus far survived the deadly dust and debris. She swept through the door on the heels of the boys, dumping her paint store samples on the entryway table. Past the original fieldstone fireplace and across the honey-hued pine floors. (No matter that they were mottled with scratches and stains from the years, her contractor Dave had assured her they could be salvaged!) The contractors were done for the day, having finished replacing the windows on the back of the house. But the smell of freshly sawn wood still lingered in the air, and Phoebe tipped her head back with pleasure. Was she the only woman who wished it could be bottled and worn as cologne?

In the kitchen she pulled a saucepan from the cupboard and set a box of macaroni on the orange Formica countertops. The room was a screaming homage to the seventies, a visual onslaught of dated appliances and peeling floral wallpaper that clung as stubbornly to the decade as it did to the walls. But Phoebe could imagine a family crowding in there, reaching for a pitcher of Kool-Aid in the fridge, grabbing some Jiffy Pop off the stove before racing down to the beach. She had plans to make their own twenty-first-century family memories. Walls would be knocked down. New cabinetry installed. Fresh paint. Sparkling stainless steel appliances. All while salvaging the original character—the leaded glass windows, the exposed beams, and one of her favorite touches: the rear Dutch door. She opened it now, stepping out to the stone patio. The macaroni and cheese could wait.

"Come on, boys," she said. "Let's go see if we can spot that mother duck and her ducklings." Phoebe trailed her children down the steps to the edge of the lake and stood squinting into the high sun. Both boys bent down and began splashing. From somewhere out on the lake came the thrum of a motorboat. It was the cusp of summer. The possibilities were endless.

Olivia

When she stepped outside, she found that the late-day haze had lifted, and the June humidity had given way to a gentle breeze. She tilted her face to it. Summer had barely begun, and it was teasingly moody. Rainy mornings sizzled away beneath a vibrant sun. A perfect afternoon could be interrupted by a thunderstorm, driving unsuspecting boaters off the water, only to lure them back to the dock moments later with a dewy rainbow. Olivia liked this about the New England lake region. It was temperamental. Just like her father in his New York kitchen, she mused. One's patience was almost always rewarded when the storm ceased.

The old barn door squeaked on its rollers as Olivia slid it ajar. In the cool recess of the studio, she hesitated, allowing her eyes to adjust. She'd been working as an apprentice and assistant for only the past year, but already this place felt like home. Her boss, the famous sculptor Ben Rothschild, had renovated the barn interior so that it operated as a four-season studio, and though it was still rustic in aesthetic and composition, the space was lofty and welcoming. She strode across the concrete floor, where jute grass rugs defined the separate spaces. Along the sides of the wall were work benches, which had been converted from horse stalls back when Ben and his wife, Marge, bought it in the 1970s. Then it had stalled eight horses, a tack room, and a hayloft. Now the only tools of trade were hand chisels, cloths, and sponges. The loft had been converted to an open-air office space. Downstairs housed the work area, large tables holding various works in progress. Ben's medium was clay, though he also dabbled in bronze sculpture. At the moment, he was preparing for an autumn gallery tour with his latest series, a study in colonial-era farm animals, titled *Beasts of Burden*. As such he was finishing two large pieces. One was an equine sculpture, a mare poised in a swath of grass. Her neck was arched and her ears were pricked forward, inquisitively. Even in stillness, she looked flexed, as if she could flee at any moment. Ben understood horses. Marge was a lifelong dressage rider. Ben had told Olivia that before he attempted the sculpture, he'd tagged along with her to the equestrian stable in Roxbury where his wife boarded her horse, Hercules. "You cannot capture a living creature in sculpture until you are familiar with the way it moves. Watching Marge ride Hercules is like listening to music in three dimensions."

Olivia was not familiar with either riding or horses, but she could see the truth in his sculpture. She stood beside the mare, noting the ripple of muscle through her bowed neck. The flare of her nostrils. There was life captured in that clay. It made something inside Olivia ache with an urge to create. She glanced across the room to the table in the corner by the window. It had been a gift from Jake. Sweet, soulful Jake who did not know a thing about sculpture or cooking or children. The three things that had thus far defined and shaped her world. Olivia still smiled when she recalled the afternoon when Ben had beckoned her out here suddenly to assist him with something important. As soon as she stepped into the barn and her eyes adjusted to the dim light, she saw Jake. Standing in the corner, beside the oak table, with that shy smile. With Ben's permission, he'd set up an entire work space just for her, "by the window, so you have both light and shadow." Beside the table there was a metal stool, for when she wasn't standing, an assortment of sculpting tools, and a bucket. A bronze desk lamp arched its neck over the rough-hewn surface. But she had been unable to take her eyes off of Jake. "Happy birthday," he'd said, softly.

Now, on that very table, beneath a white canvas tarp, her most current project waited. But there was no time for that today.

Upstairs in the loft, Olivia seated herself at the desk and opened the laptop. There were sixteen new emails. Most were inquiries about the upcoming September show. Two were from galleries updating Ben about sales. The last one was a message from the manager of a world-class resort on Cape Cod. Ben had sold a seal sculpture from his previous year's maritime collection, titled *Salt Works*, to the seaside hotel. They'd sent a picture of the new installation in their main lobby. Ben would be pleased. Included with the manager's letter was an invitation to stay at the resort for an evening of his choice, free of charge. Olivia sighed. She would have jumped at such a chance, but she knew Ben would never accept. He'd ask her to thank the gentleman, and leave it at that. Ben was too private, too humble. It was something she loved dearly about the man.

Olivia could still not believe her good fortune in landing this job and living in this place. It was a far cry from the day she'd learned she was pregnant, in her final semester of graduate school at NYU just six years ago. Her then boyfriend, who wanted everything to do with acting and nothing to do with a baby (*this was his life! his chance at making it!*), made it painfully clear to Olivia that she would be on her own. She'd walked graduation with her belly burgeoning through her gown, wondering if she were the only art student to have spent her final semester alternately covered in clay and bent over the toilet bowl with morning sickness. Her father, Pierre, stood in the audience, clapping and shouting alongside Celeste, his restaurant partner who'd also largely helped to raise Olivia since her mother's death. Afterward, they'd had a small luncheon and cake back at the restaurant.

Olivia had been frightened, but she'd had a plan: she would have the baby in the fall, and the two of them would move back to Brooklyn and live with her father, just like old times. But two years after making that plan, Olivia felt stifled. It was hard having a toddler in the city, alone. Gone was her access to the luxury of the NYU art studio and all its conveniences and inspiration. She could not afford to share an artist co-op space in any of the available buildings in and around the city, unlike some of her former classmates. For a while, she worked as an office assistant for the NYU art department, but it was mostly clerical work. Each time she put together announcements for student art shows, she felt a pang. With every grant or internship that came across her desk, Olivia grew more restless. A bitterness crept into her voice when she made small talk with the art students waiting outside the professors' office doors, their brimming portfolios in hand. Yesterday she had been that aspiring pupil. Today she was an exhausted single mother awash in fresh resentment.

Worst of all was the guilt of being away from Luci. Juggling single parenthood with a creative life was nearly impossible, and eventually she gave up and returned to work at the restaurant. There her days were free to be with her daughter, and come nighttime Luci could be put to sleep in the back office. But it was draining, burning the candle at both ends and always having Luci in tow. And despite having secured some sense of routine and a small income, Olivia felt the calendar days peeling off the wall without really getting anywhere. Indeed, she had gone backward. She was single and back working at her father's restaurant, only now with a child to support. Any aspirations of her own seemed laughable.

It was during that second winter since graduation that Olivia received an email from a former professor. A well-known sculptor from Washington, Connecticut, was seeking an apprentice. He worked out of a restored barn on his property. The pay was not much, but Olivia would have a small carriage house in which to live and access to studio work space. It was a ticket out of the city. And perhaps a ticket to a new life.

Olivia replied immediately, keeping the news and the new hope that flushed in her chest to herself. There was no need to involve her father. At least not yet. He would not support the notion, of that she was sure.

Pierre's temper was legendary; at the restaurant he terrified as many sous-chefs as he inspired. And fired twice that number in any given month. But still there was an ever-present line out the door of green young chefs wanting to work with him. For those in the industry and in the know were aware that clientele had been flocking to Bon Coin for years. Reservations were not accepted. You obtained a seat only if the chef knew you; or if you were the honored guest of someone who knew him. His crème fraîche was a full-cream cloud. Between courses you cleansed your palate with tiny ramekins of pomegranate sorbet or flat water with a lemon twist; a shot of apple brandy served as a digestif. On the rare occasion he was in a whimsical mood, Pierre sent out an amuse-bouche: a single seared scallop, a frosty shot of cucumber soup. There was no menu. Patrons ate what he felt like cooking, all of it artfully plated, its minimalist presentation designed to surrender to one and only one sense: the intoxicating pleasure of taste.

Olivia was often asked, "Did you ever work with your father?"

"No," she was quick to reply. "I worked *for* him." Though he loved his only child with a singular focus otherwise reserved only for his cooking, in his kitchen even she was not spared his temperament.

"*Zut, Livi!*" he'd bellow, whisking a cutting board of diced onion out from under the blade of her knife and tossing it into the well of the sink. "*Émincer l'oignon!*" Pierre expected perfection at every turn, from the uniformity of minced carrots to the gleaming reflection of a freshly scrubbed sauté pan. Precision, attention, and the sourcing of raw ingredients—those were the hallmarks of a successful restaurant. That his employees simultaneously loved and loathed the man was not his concern; food critics were the only ones who had Pierre's ear, and even they not all of the time. In her father's kitchen Olivia learned to keep her head down, her knife sharp, and to persevere. Indeed, they were the skills of life.

In a way, working for her father had probably been what most helped her to secure her new job. Pierre was an artist, as well. Olivia understood temperaments and idiosyncrasies. Working for an artist was intimate. Olivia knew how Ben took his coffee, not that he'd ever asked her to get him one. She knew that when starting a new project he required complete solitude. Marge had explained these things during the interview. Olivia had borrowed her aunt's car and driven out to the Connecticut countryside for the occasion, intent on meeting Ben Rothschild, the famous sculptor, and impressing him with her portfolio. But she'd been surprised to not even lay eyes on the man that first meeting. Instead, it was Marge who swung the front door ajar in her bare feet and a sweeping white tunic and invited her inside. She led her through rooms of antique rugs and Stickley furniture, which were otherwise stark white. She poured tea and pulled out a Windsor chair, motioning for Olivia to sit. What followed was a conversation more than an interview. What kind of training had she had at NYU? What was her medium? How did she feel about working closely with another person, who might just as soon request she leave him alone when he "caught the scent," as Ben described his muse, as he might ask her to dig through dusty attic boxes in search of a long-lost photograph so he could study the lines of the family dog, who, by the way, was buried under the red maple in the backyard—should she want to visit him.

What was clear was that there were boundaries, but the lines were not of the usual pedestrian nature. The hours varied, as did the work. Which was why the two of them liked to keep their assistant in residence. "We all have our gifts and quirks," Marge had said that day. That was just fine with Olivia. She had her own, foremost being Luci.

Luci should be treated as any other child. Olivia needed her to live in a space where people let her be herself. "She speaks to four people in her life," Olivia had confided in Marge that day. "Me. My father, her *gran-père*. Her speech pathologist. And our Brooklyn neighbor, Celeste."

Marge had listened deeply, nodding over her cup of tea. "Well, that must be a challenge for both of you," she said, finally. "We know all about those, here."

As Olivia would learn, after she accepted the job, Ben was a gentle man with soft watery eyes. He was as practical about his artistic success as he was about sleep: he needed nine hours exactly, many of which took place during the afternoons, and none of which were consecutive. And he had a complicated relationship with alcohol.

"Art consumes a person, if they're good at it. When he's working, Ben doesn't touch a bottle. But when he finds himself between projects or feeling down, there are times he climbs into it," Marge said.

Olivia didn't know what to say. She was not used to such honest disrobing from someone she'd just met.

"He's a quiet drunk, sticks to the property like an old sheepdog and sleeps it off." She took a sip of her tea and looked at Olivia over the rim of her cup. "At worst, you'll find him snoring in the barn. And that's when you come find me. Will that be a problem?"

Olivia shook her head. She knew too well the lure of alcohol, and the ways people flirted with it, from years in the restaurant. It was common, on both sides of the table. There were business clients who were day drunks. Kitchen workers who got hammered after their shift. Waitresses who did shots, and much more, in the dingy staff bathroom, before heading downtown to clubs. She did not judge. But she was also not foolish enough to harbor anything but a healthy respect for the reality of it.

"I've dealt with it in the restaurant," Olivia confided. "As long as it doesn't impact me or my daughter."

Marge regarded her appraisingly. "Good answer. It won't, I can assure you. Mostly Ben manages it. Sometimes it manages him. You'll come to understand the difference."

What Marge was asking of her, Olivia realized, she was desperate for herself. Respect and space.

Growing up in the city, Olivia had never realized what effect space would have on her. She was used to storing pots and pans (and toilet paper!) in her galley kitchen oven. She and Luci had shared one cramped bedroom, her child-sized cot squeezed in against the foot of Olivia's bed. They walked up three flights of stairs with groceries, which they crammed into the two tiny cabinets above the stove. There was no space to work, to stretch one's legs, to spread out. Certainly not to sculpt.

Until then, Olivia had used a rear corner of her father's restaurant kitchen for her work. He allowed her to keep a small table by a slop sink in what had been a prep area. She'd arrive early in the mornings, when Luci went to school, only hours after the last of the kitchen staff and servers had gone home for the night. The kitchen was quiet and empty; she would work until the afternoon shift arrived to set up the dining room and stock the bar. It was not ideal, but it was what she had.

Here now, with the vaulted barn ceilings and plated glass windows and the overhead loft, Olivia had a new concept of space. Not just in which to work, but in which to envision. To flex her ideas as surely as she stretched her limbs on her morning walks with Luci through the wooded trails that ran behind the house. To sleep beneath the velvety sky, an uninterrupted stretch of dark ribbon and bright star that simply did not exist in the city. To steal an hour here or there at her worktable when Ben took his daily nap. This was what it meant to take up space.

But space was not enough. What Olivia struggled with now was time. As a single mother and studio assistant, there wasn't much left. Something that frustrated her deeply given that the ideal artist's space and boundless inspiration were mere steps away from her cottage. Now she hurried through emails. She gathered the outgoing mailings for the September show to drop off at the post office, and jotted down a list of messages to leave for Marge on the desk. Marge would only involve Ben in communications with the outside world if she felt it necessary. He did not occupy any office space in the loft; his domain was strictly the barn floor, where such distractions would not interfere with his work.

Sometimes Olivia wondered at the devotion Marge gave Ben. At her selfless contentment to manage his world, so that he could manage his art. It reminded her of her father, of how he threw himself into his culinary creations. Of the years it took for Olivia to understand that her father loved her as much as, indeed *more* than, his restaurant. And how she'd struggled to understand it as a child, when other fathers rose early in the morning to take their daughters to soccer games, and were home at night to read to them and tuck them into bed. Love is love, her aunt used to tell her when she brought Olivia home from the restaurant at night to tuck her into bed. Don't question its form.

Back inside the cottage, Olivia lined up the bounty from the farmer's market on the butcher block counter. Yellow summer squash and zucchini. Fresh corn. Four fragrant heirloom tomatoes. The sight of them pleased her more than she could explain, and she smiled to herself as she ticked through the possibilities: sausage-stuffed squash with Gruyère, roasted tomatoes on hunks of crusty sourdough, tomatoes caprese. No additions, beyond a sprinkle of sea salt and zest of lemon. Summer made cooking so easy.

Luci, who'd been hovering nearby surveying the goods, tucked something quickly behind her back and bolted for the stairs, Buster on her heels.

"Just where are you two going?" Olivia called after her.

Luci halted. "Nowheres."

"You wouldn't happen to be going *nowhere* with that lovely chunk of cheddar, now would you?"

Luci slumped. "But it's *sooo* good, Mama."

"Indeed. Come help me set up a cheese board." Olivia sliced the cheddar into fat ribbons, which she set atop grainy crackers and handed to Luci. She selected a Cantal she knew Jake liked for its familiarity to farmhouse cheddar and a bleu. Jake claimed he only liked cow's milk varieties, but she was secretly determined to turn him on to the ripe goat's milk of Montchevre.

"You need to be more adventurous. When my five-year-old has a more sophisticated palate than a grown man, there is work to be done," she teased him. She ran a knife through a ripe pear, licked the juice from her fingers, and fanned the slices artfully on the board.

"Is Jake coming?"

It was still strange to hear Luci say his name, given that she'd never once spoken to him. Olivia often wondered how that made Jake feel.

"Would you like that?"

Luci nodded. "I want him to stay for dinner."

This was unexpected. Olivia was sure Luci enjoyed Jake; it was clear by the way she trailed after him around the house. By how close she scooted next to him on the couch when the three of them watched a movie, or the way she tipped her head back and covered her giggle with her hand when he joked around at the dinner table. But Olivia was in love with him, and it was hard to love two people who did not yet speak to each other.

"It must be your lucky day, because I already invited him." Outside there was the sudden crunch of gravel in the driveway as his Wrangler pulled in. She wiped her hands quickly with the dish towel. "And look—here he is!"

Luci thundered to the door, hopping up and down until Jake appeared on the other side of the screen. "Salutations." Something was hidden behind his back.

Olivia pulled him inside. Jake's face was ruddy with sun and vigor, his two-day-old stubble rough against her cheek. "You smell good. Like the beach."

"I was out earlier on my bike." He pecked her on the lips, something he'd only started to do recently in front of Luci, and produced a small bouquet of wildflowers from behind his back. "For you," he said, holding them out to Luci. "I picked them this morning on my ride."

Luci hesitated before gingerly accepting them, and Olivia feared her heart might burst.

Jake kneeled down, naming the flowers in the scraggly bunch. "This one is called red clover, and the fancy purple one is chicory. But best of all is this one." He pointed to a frilly yellow flower. "Can you guess its name?"

Luci said nothing, but at least this time she shook her head.

"Cat's ear!"

This elicited a shy smile.

Olivia gasped. "Cat's ear. Does it meow?" She bent and tickled her daughter's ear. "What do we say to Jake?" she prompted.

Luci ducked her chin and stared at her bare feet.

"Lu Lu?"

"It's okay," Jake said, but Olivia ignored this.

"Just like Miss Griffin taught you in speech. What do we say when someone does something nice for us?"

After a long silence Luci looked up at Jake and made a small noise in her throat, like a squeak. "Good girl." Olivia kissed her head, trying to conceal how much this meant to her.

"You're welcome, Lu," Jake said.

Later, after a quiet dinner and when Luci had been tucked in for the night, they sat in the weathered Adirondack chairs overlooking the backyard. Jake leaned back and exhaled, contentedly. "So, it went okay with the speech pathologist today?"

Olivia shrugged. "I think so."

"Did she say anything else about starting kindergarten?"

"Just what everyone says. That it will be good for her, having to communicate for herself. Miss Griffin says I am her crutch." Olivia pursed her lips.

Jake did not comment on this. He knew better. There had been times when he'd wondered aloud what would happen if Olivia would only pause instead of answering on Luci's behalf when someone asked her a question. Perhaps that might encourage her to speak for herself. It had ignited Olivia's indignation that he should question her, Luci's *mother*. As if he possessed some knowledge about mutism that she did not, after years of reading every book or article she could amass, and questioning every doctor she could seek out. From pediatricians, to neurologists, to therapists. They all arrived at the same conclusion: ultimately, Luci would speak when she was ready.

Jake's casual suggestion had irked her, causing an argument. Jake was not a parent; he had no meaningful experience with kids beyond his niece and nephews. But on the other hand, Jake was very much a people person. Quite the opposite of her, he sought out large groups and stimuli with the same zeal with which she avoided them. His social appetite was adventurous in ways hers was not, accommodating of things she would not tolerate. Like some of his bachelor friends who came to visit for a night, and ended up "crashing" for two weeks. Like the lifestyle he'd led up until they'd met, happy to wander from place to place and see what kind of work he could find. Untethered and unafraid.

Olivia was very much tethered and, since becoming a single parent, often afraid. She had no time for staying out drinking all night, as some of his old high school friends often invited them to do. Olivia did not desire to go for a drive through the hills of New York, *just because*, on a fall day. When she wasn't working for Ben, she was taking care of Luci: taking her to the library, toddler music classes, speech therapy. Her days were carved out by routine. The very thought of seeing a non-Disney movie in a theater was foreign. Even her bed was not her own space; most nights she was awakened by Luci clambering across the blankets and slipping beneath them against her. Since giving birth, Olivia had not had autonomy over her time any more than she'd had it over her body with Luci's pregnancy. From the beginning, there had been no reason for Olivia and Jake to come together as a couple. And yet they did.

Although their differences had been challenging, Olivia was beginning to learn to embrace them. Jake was the first man who listened intently, no matter what she was talking about, whether it be the curve of a clay bird's wing she was sculpting or the daily concern she held for her child. Every day she reminded him of their differences, and every day he reminded her that in spite of them, his instincts were telling him to let things unfold between them. To give it a shot. And his instincts had been good, so much so that Olivia had eventually allowed him to meet Luci. Never before had she introduced a man to her daughter. What was the point?

Now life had brought her to Washington, Connecticut, a rural hamlet of artists and families. Just outside of New York, but oh how far outside it felt amid the greenery and the hills and the lakes. Jake turned to her and squeezed her hand. "Is that the Big Dipper?" He pointed up at the sky and she followed his gaze.

"I think so. The north star is just above it."

"My father used to point out the constellations to me from the boat. On warm nights we'd go out to the middle of the lake, turn off the engine, and just float beneath the sky. He could name them all."

Olivia pictured it. "That sounds nice."

"Will you do that with me this summer?" Jake asked.

She smiled at him gratefully. "I might." Right now she relished the thought of going in to bed. Not of making love, something they'd often done, but of something they so far never had: falling into the cool, crisp sheets together, with her resting her head against this wonderful man's broad chest. She relished the thought of him staying overnight so that they'd wake up in the morning together, when Luci could come bounding in and jump into bed with them. Like a real family. She blinked in the growing darkness.

"There's something else I need to ask you," he said.

"About the constellations?"

"About us."

And before she understood what was happening, Jake rose from his Adirondack chair and promptly knelt beside her own. He took her hand. "Olivia Cossette. You are more exquisite than any of the stars in the sky. I have fallen in love with you, and I don't want to spend another summer without looking up at the stars by your side. Will you marry me?"

Olivia gasped.

From his shorts pocket Jake retrieved a ring that sparkled in the light from the firepit. He slid it onto her finger.

Olivia stared at the man kneeling before her in the firelight. Then back at the cottage, where Luci was tucked in her bed sleeping, then back at Jake. She started to cry. "Yes!"

Jake pulled her up onto her feet and she threw her arms around his neck.

"I can't wait to tell our families," he whispered.

Tears slid down Olivia's cheeks. Luci would have cousins. And aunts and uncles. A big boisterous family for holidays and birthdays. Who sang Christmas carols and argued at the dinner table and played board games and went boating on the lake. Finally, she and Luci would have a family.

As she stood in Jake's arms, she recalled the day she told her father that she was moving to Connecticut with Luci. Pierre's expression had crumpled.

Leaving the city was unthinkable. "Why would you leave New York?" he cried. "Here, there is everything! Everything a person could need. And me." His sharp brown eyes had softened with sentiment.

She'd taken his hands in her own, large calloused hands dotted with Band-Aids from kitchen work. "Connecticut is just next door, Papa. This job will be good for me. And for Luci. Think of the things she can do in the country."

"Bah." He'd pulled his hands away, crossing his arms and staring across the stainless steel expanse of the empty kitchen. It was late afternoon. Soon the prep workers would file in to start on the evening's menu.

"I will come back," she promised. She retrieved her apron from the back of the meat locker door and tied it tightly around her waist. "You'll see."

Pierre shook his head wistfully. "*Non, ma chérie.* You will fall in love."

Fall in love? She had not known if he meant with the Connecticut countryside, or the job, or a man. Indeed, she had gone and done all three.

Emma

The school bus lumbered down her neighborhood road, and Emma glanced up reluctantly from her book. Almost home.

She gazed out the window. Stately white colonials sat atop grassy rises, their pillared entrances flanking Belgian block drives. The lawns were all the same: blunt-edged and freshly shorn, with sharp rows of boxwoods sheared into submission beneath gaping picture windows. Up the street, her own house was just as unyielding in its bland conformity. Across the aisle Laura Brentwood cleared her throat for at least the tenth time, a nervous tic that Emma tried to ignore. They were the only two sophomores riding the bus. A handful of freshman boys had staked out the back-row seats and inhabited them loudly, probably relieved to flex their muscles in an upperclassman-free zone. Emma got it, but she was also over it. You wouldn't catch an upperclassman dead on the bus; every junior or senior in this neighborhood had a license and a car, or friends who did. Emma sighed. Next year she'd escape it, too.

Outside the bus window she caught glimmers of her lake peeking out from behind the waterfront houses and foliage. She was still staring out the window when she heard the horn. Amanda Hastings's silver BMW roared up alongside the bus in the opposite lane. The top was down. There were two girls in the backseat, their hair blowing behind them in a tangle of brunette and blond. Courtney Alcott and Jen DeMaio, two of Amanda's groupies. Emma couldn't make out the boy seated between them, but she had no doubt who was up front in the passenger seat next to Amanda. Sully McMahon glanced up at the bus windows, his expression cool. Emma ducked.

The horn blared again.

"What the . . . ?" The bus driver slammed on the brakes and the BMW blew past and cut in front of them. One of the girls waved.

"Assholes!" yelled a freshman from the back. Emma pulled her knees up against her chest. Amanda Hastings *was* an asshole.

Across the aisle, Laura Brentwood sputtered in disgust. "The speed limit is twenty. And it's illegal to pass a bus."

Emma thought the strict community speed limit was a joke. But it was a jerk move of Amanda's, who lived a couple of houses up from Emma, by the clubhouse and tennis courts. Emma wondered what they were all doing. Probably sneaking Mr. Hastings's beers from the pool house fridge and hanging out at the pool. Not that Amanda had ever invited her. Emma had only seen the sprawling setup last summer when the Hastings family hosted a neighborhood BBQ. Back when they were little, the two girls had been somewhat friendly, riding bikes with other kids on the road. But these days Amanda kept to a tight circle of upperclassmen who clogged the hallway around her locker, and sat at a head table with the football and lacrosse players in the cafeteria. Her parents always seemed to be traveling, and Amanda made good use of their absences by throwing keg parties, though that was something Emma learned of after the fact through the rumor mill. To be honest, Emma didn't care what Amanda Hastings did. But she couldn't help but wonder about Sully.

Sully McMahon was also a sophomore, and he sat in front of her in geometry. Emma had spent the better part of the school year staring at the soft dark curls at the nape of his neck. On the rare occasion he turned around to pass back a paper, or borrow a pencil, her cheeks burned. Other than that, Emma was sure he had no idea who she was. As the BMW sped out of sight, she slumped back in her bus seat. Why would he?

As soon as the bus dropped her off, she walked up the circular driveway and punched in the keypad code. Her mother would be at her office for another hour at least, and her father wouldn't be back until dinner. She was used to being home alone. As long as she had her book, she preferred it that way. What she didn't like was surprises, and just as she was reaching for the door handle it opened.

"How was school?" Her mother held the door ajar. Emma forced a smile. She was pretty sure Amanda Hastings's mother wasn't greeting her at the door.

"Good."

She dumped her backpack in the marble foyer and kicked off her tennis shoes.

"Just good?"

"Pretty much," she said, pausing at the kitchen island to grab a plum from the fruit bowl. "Just end-of-the-year boring stuff." She was eager to get down to the dock, where she could dip her toes in the water and hunker down with her book.

"I got an email from your band teacher today about the spring concert. I'm planning to come, and I forwarded it to Daddy, too."

"He won't make it."

Her mother sighed. "It's his firm's busy season with summer concerts, honey, but I know he wants to. Maybe it will work out."

"Sure." It never did. Her father was always working, which

he liked to remind them allowed them to live the way they did. It wasn't that Emma didn't appreciate their nice house or their gated community. She liked both. She knew other kids at school thought she was lucky; her family had money. She could buy whatever she wanted at Abercrombie & Fitch or Hollister. Her parents had taken her in to see Broadway shows even as a child." They ate out at nice restaurants. They had a boat. Not just any boat, but the boat her father had longed for since childhood: his Chris-Craft. Which he had finally bought last summer, and they'd maybe used all of three times since. But there were vacations: they skied in Utah, scuba dived on St. John's, rented a house on the Vineyard every summer. All nice. But the thing was, Emma didn't really care about those things. Except for the lake. It was her escape.

"What about a snack? I can make cheese and crackers or something," her mother called after her as Emma slipped through the patio doors barefoot.

"Not hungry." Free at last, she trotted across the backyard and down the steps to the lake, two at a time. Weekday afternoons on the dock were sacred. It wasn't just the lake, which was serene in a way it never was on weekends. It wasn't just the warm weather, or the sun that dappled the shore in molten gold. Nor was it the fact that she could swing her legs over the edge of the dock and drag her toes through the water, a sensation she longed for all winter. It was that she had the lake to herself. And once there, she could curl up on the sun-warmed wooden boards with her book and be alone. The same dock that her father had painstakingly stained that spring in preparation for the summer he would barely enjoy. But he'd be darned sure it would be in pristine condition. Emma didn't understand it. Her father worked so hard to afford things he never even got to use.

Never mind, the dock would be well used by her, she thought as she set down her blanket and book. Voices carried from up the shoreline. Emma groaned. She'd hoped to steal at least one afternoon of peace. The voices grew closer, coming through the grove of pine trees that separated her house and the neighbor's. Everyone on the lake side of the street had sweeping backyards edged by woods, for privacy. Small beach paths wound through them to the water. Her father liked to remind her that when he was a kid, the paths were simple dirt trails worn down by bare feet and flip-flops. Nowadays those paths were handsomely crafted wooden stairs that angled down to the water, like her own. Some were fussy stone steps and pavers set by masons; others had contemporary posts and metal railings. She liked her own, which was more rustic.

Now Emma glanced up the lake as the voices grew louder. Two docks north of hers, a group of people emerged at the waterline and began walking down the pier. Amanda Hastings and crew.

Emma squinted in their direction, shielding her eyes. Sully and another boy held a large red cooler between them. Amanda, who'd changed into a white bikini and cutoff shorts, stepped out on the dock first. Emma watched as she moved around the boat, unsnapping the cover and rolling it back. Eventually everyone hopped into it, and Amanda settled herself behind the wheel. The purr of the engine carried across the water, and Emma watched them reverse away from the dock. Everyone had taken a seat, except for one of the girls. The boat idled briefly and then Amanda took off, causing the girl to tumble backward onto the seats. Everyone whooped and laughed as they sped off into deeper water.

For about an hour Emma tried to ignore them. The engine whined in the distance as they cut across the lake in large arcs. For a while, they took turns waterskiing. Then they cut the engine and floated. Probably drinking or getting stoned, Emma thought. She wondered what they talked about. She wondered if Sully and Amanda were a thing.

By that hour, the sun had moved to the western edge of the sky. Soon a shadow fell across her reading spot, and Emma stretched, rubbing her eyes. Her mother was right—she was getting kind of hungry. She had just begun gathering up her towel and book when she heard a sharp voice. Up the shore, to her right, Mr. Hastings stood at the edge of his dock, hands on his hips. He stared at the ropes strewn about the floorboards and threw his hands up. *This* was interesting.

He pulled his phone from his back pocket and began barking into it. Moments later came the purr of a boat engine from her left. Emma watched the Hastings boat taxi around the rocky peninsula, this time at a much slower speed than when it had left. Impatiently, Mr. Hastings waved it in.

As they neared her dock, Emma cracked her book open again, and stared into her lap. There was no reason for them to hug the shoreline so close to her, but they were. Emma glanced right toward the Hastings's dock, then left toward the approaching boat. Amanda stared straight ahead, her mouth fixed in a thin line as she navigated the water and kept her father in sight. It was the boy leaning over the side of the boat who caught Emma's attention. Was he waving at her?

Emma drew her knees up as the boat nosed its way closer. "Hey!" Sully McMahon was dragging one hand in the water, but his eyes were on her. Emma watched in disbelief as the boat drew up sharply alongside her dock. Amanda didn't even glance her way, but Sully was definitely trying to communicate something. She narrowed her eyes.

Just as they pulled up, Sully lifted his hand from the water. He held out a brown bottle.

"Take it!" he hissed. The boat drew up so sharply, so close, she feared it might hit. In slow motion it glided past, mere inches away. Emma sucked in her breath, and Sully thrust the bottle in her direction.

Suddenly Emma found herself reaching. As he glided by, Sully pressed the bottle into her hands, their fingers bumping together. She looked up and Sully smiled. "Good girl." And then they were gone, taxiing up the lake toward Mr. Hastings, who was now pacing.

Emma clutched the wet bottle to her chest, watching as they tied off the boat and disembarked. Amanda was waving her hands in explanation, talking loudly to her father. The others scurried past them, eyes down. Emma watched in disbelief as Sully stopped and offered Mr. Hastings a handshake. For a beat, it seemed to break the tension. She was even more surprised when Mr. Hastings actually took it.

Quickly, she stood and gathered her things, keeping the bottle concealed in her blanket. Amanda Hastings was in trouble, and as much as she loathed her, Emma actually felt a pang of sympathy when her father resumed his vocal chastising. She wondered if he'd seen them hand off the bottle to her. At the bottom of the stairs she risked a last look in their direction. From across the way Sully McMahon hesitated at the edge of the dock. He glanced back at her, before he, too, disappeared into the thicket of woods.

It wasn't until she was halfway up the stairs that Emma paused and looked down at the sloshing bottle in the folds of her blanket. Wild Turkey. A lake breeze stirred the leaves in the treetops; Emma shoved the bottle of Wild Turkey behind a thick bush, snagging her fingertip on a pricker, and then ran the rest of the way up to the house.

Perry

I t had finally happened. His whole family had lost their minds. First over Grandma Elsie, whom they let roam unsupervised throughout the house and gardens like some kind of aged toddler on the loose. Who could at any minute roll one of her well-heeled feet on the edge of an over-mulched rosebed and topple to her death. Well, more likely to a broken hip. Followed by indeterminate bedrest, followed by subsequent pneumonia, thereby guaranteeing convalescence. Same thing as death, really. It was all there in the insurance statistics, documented warnings available to millions. But not his family. They kept to a strict diet of euphoric ignorance.

As if that weren't bad enough, now Jake was engaged. To a woman from another country whose citizenship was a complete mystery. Who was a single parent of a child who did not speak, yet another puzzle that his family seemed perfectly happy to add to their flourishing do-not-ask list. A child who may or may not have a father lurking in the wings, and for whom Jake would now be financially responsible. There was a term for this in Perry's line of work: damage offset. There was still time for Jake to employ it.

Their mother, Jane, had called that morning as Perry rode

the train to work. The family knew better than to bother him on weekdays. So he'd taken the call, wondering if something had happened to Elsie. "Can you believe it?" his mother had cried.

Perry had slapped his laptop shut, straining to understand her through the tears and hiccups. "What is it? What happened?"

"Jake and Olivia. What else would I be talking about?"

Leave it to his mother to start the conversation with a greeting inducing cardiac arrhythmia. "No, Mom. No, I cannot believe it."

Jane paused. "Now, Perry. This is good news."

"Is it?" Then, "What do we even know about her? For that matter, what does Jake know? Haven't they been dating mere months?"

"Six months. I'll grant you that. It's not long. But Daddy and I knew each other less than a year."

"That was another time," Perry reminded her.

"Oh, please. It was hardly the Dark Ages."

"Mom, my train is approaching a low-signal area. I'm afraid I'm going to lose the call."

"Hang on, I just need a moment." As if Perry could signal the conductor and slow the train. "I'd like to host a party for them. Just a little engagement shindig this weekend. Are you and Amelia free?"

Perry did not understand the posthaste urge to celebrate a union, one half of whom his family had met only twice. Himself, just once. But he understood all too well the nature of his mother's invitations. They didn't require RSVPs. The fact was, they didn't allow for them. You were summoned: if you weren't dead, you came.

"I'm working on the Super Bowl contract, and it's due that following Monday. But I'm sure Emma and Amelia will go."

"Perry. You work too much. It's a Saturday. Spend time with your family."

"I know, Mother, but you see . . ." Perry hesitated. There was no winning this conversation. "I'll do my best to make it."

"Wonderful. And Perry—a simple request, darling."

Perry sighed. "Yes?"

"Jake is excited. He's finally come home. He's landed a job, and he's got a great girl. Let's not shit on his parade."

Perry was used to his mother's profanity, if he tended to avoid it himself. A cultured and elegant woman, she was also not afraid to be direct. She'd recently emailed him an article from the *New York Times* that claimed people who cursed with gusto were intelligent. He'd not bothered to read beyond the headline. According to that criterion, Jane was pure genius. "All right, Mother. I'll fetter the urge."

"Thank you. And honey? Try and be fun. It'd be good for you."

Didn't she mean *have* fun? As the train hurtled south toward the city, Perry stared out the window. Fun was well and good, but it did not make a successful man. Just look at him and Jake. Perry was stable, accomplished, productive. Jake was immature and given to wanderlust and impulse. A victim of his own inertia who still rented an apartment and probably had less than one hundred dollars in his bank account. And yet people flocked to him. Soaked up his silly stories about ridiculous trips he took, like the one Perry must've heard a hundred times about hitchhiking across the Australian outback by car and camel, a two-day trip that turned into two weeks because he had not yet captured the perfect shot of a red desert sunrise. A place where he had to inspect the tent for snakes at night and shake scorpions out of his boots in the morning, but *it was all worth it* to see the Southern Cross constellation rising over the ebony horizon. The words were lost on Perry, who excused himself from the telling each time, but not before noting the expressions on people's faces. Jake drew people as effortlessly as Perry seemed to bore them. It was a fact that irked him today as much as it had when they were kids.

Still, he would do as his mother asked and show up at the party. Hell, he'd even bring a good wine. That was the kind of man Perry was. He still had a gorgeous bottle of Three Rivers Shiraz from his and Amelia's Barossa Valley trip last year to South Australia. But he would not put a cork in voicing his opinions or trying to protect Jake. Because that was also the kind of man Perry was.

What he needed was to get Jake alone. Had he any thought of adopting the child once they were married? Had he even consulted a lawyer? What if Olivia was just using Jake for a green card? Perry did not concern himself with where this woman heralded from, or what the estranged father's status was. That was her concern. What *was* his concern was the legal and financial responsibility for his brother that came with marriage and a child. And in that vein, what on earth did his little brother know about parenting? Jake was no more than a large kid himself. Who after years of wandering about the country, working as a bike messenger in LA, then a ranger in Yosemite, then an IT consultant for a friend's startup, had finally stood still in one geographic location long enough to land a real job. If you counted working for a nonprofit nature center as real work. Even so, he'd barely sat down at his new desk at the Audubon and was already talking about squandering his limited vacation time on a honeymoon.

Perry sniffed. What Jake needed was a girl in finance who was allergic to pets and exotic travel. The kind of girl to squelch the worst of his impulses and keep him on the straight and narrow. And what did he do but dig up a woman with a young child. A starving artist who rescued even hungrier dogs. (Come to think of it, perhaps Olivia fancied herself as rescuing Jake? Perry had read once that people who rescued strays identified with the urge to be rescued themselves. Sort of like hoarders trying to fill a void. He'd have to share this with Amelia later.)

And what did their family do upon being gobsmacked with the news? Why, throw another party! Perry could not abide it. But that would have to wait. His train was pulling into Grand Central, and he headed to the 6 train.

At exactly 8:55 Perry strode through the front doors of McElroy, Greenspan, and Luxe. In his tenth-floor corner office he flipped through the folders on his desk that Maura must have left for him to review before she went home for the night. First, the World Figure Skating Championships at TD Garden in Boston. He grabbed a green Post-it off his desk. Green was the color for "green light": file progressing as expected. Next was the country summer concert series held at Foxwoods Casino. Perry grabbed a yellow Post-it. He'd reviewed the expected ticket sales and show details. But country-western events were famous for high intoxication numbers and arrests. He needed to go over those figures again. Last was his baby, the gig Perry had helped to secure for the firm three years ago and helmed ever since: the halftime show for the Super Bowl. No one but he and his select team had worked on it this year. He ran his hand across the folder front. Super Bowl shows were the crème de la crème of risk analysis. Pyrotechnic accidents. Drunk and disorderlys. Inclement weather. Ticket fraud. Crowd control. Perry had amassed a team of talent in the firm to cover all the bases. They were still in the process of writing up the final draft.

By the time Maura arrived, Perry had reviewed the music festival file and emailed the others his updates. "Good morning, Mr. Goodwin."

Despite their having worked together for eleven years, Maura had never taken him up on his repeated invitation to call him by his first name. Others in the office, even higher-ups, she referred to as such. Like his manager, Charles Glenelg, whom Maura mystifyingly called Chuck. As if they were neighbors!

When they first started working together, Perry had considered Maura a rather formal person. Indeed, she was older than him by at least fifteen years. She was fond of tailored suits and sensible square-heeled shoes, unlike some of the other assistants who dressed far more casually. Some of the younger ones in jeans!

She maintained a sense of order that extended beyond her wardrobe and desktop. She didn't flinch over $50 million umbrella clauses or the grainy naked image of a drunken pop star who'd fallen offstage during his after-party. Maura was as unflappable as the starched collar on her blouse. Perry sometimes wished he could take her home to talk to Emma. He imagined Maura setting a piece of Bundt cake between them on the dining room table and leaning in conspiratorially to dissect the dresses worn at the homecoming dance, like a grandmother would.

Now she set his cup of tea on his desk, another thing he knew none of the other assistants did, and waited for him to run through the morning schedule. "Thank you, Maura," he said. "I emailed you that draft I was working on yesterday for De Beers, if you'd please give it a once-over before finalizing. And I've got a claim from underwriting I'd like you to review before mailing out."

"Certainly. You have a ten o'clock conference upstairs, don't forget."

He reached for the file on his desk to hand her, then hesitated. Her dignified air was what he'd always liked about Maura, in addition to her no-nonsense attitude and the lemon she added to his herbal tea. But lately he'd begun to wonder if it was something about him that had triggered the formality between them.

"May I ask you something, Maura?"

She nodded curtly.

Perry was not accustomed to asking Maura anything outside of the realm of office business. But he realized he spent more time with her than he did his own family. And he trusted her judgment. "Am I fun?"

Maura blinked. After a moment, she recovered. "Mr. Goodwin, I have enjoyed working with you for many years. You are always punctual and fair."

Perry considered these two traits. Both positive. "Anything else?"

This time she did not hesitate. "You are predictable."

Perry sat back in his chair. "So, *no* to fun?"

Maura gave a brisk shake of her head before sweeping the file from his hand.

Perry waited until she had left to spin his chair around to the large plated windows. His office afforded him a sliver of a view.

Perry worked hard in the city so his family could live well in the countryside. He thought of his lake club, where Emma could have a wholesome childhood. There he knew all the members and their kids. He knew where Emma was, and who she was with, and what she was doing. How often did he hear his colleagues complain about their teenagers; how distant they were, how mixed up. Theirs were at boarding schools, unseen and doing God knows what. Or they were loose in this city of strangers, free to roam the boroughs like little adults; riding subways, sneaking into nightclubs, and growing up too fast. The world was a crazy place to be raising a young girl. Thank God Emma didn't have access to that nonsense. Despite the fact they were only a little oa little under a two-hour drive from New York City, his life back home on the lake might as well have been a world away. Sure, he had little free time to enjoy much of it. Or the Chris-Craft he'd finally bought last year that his family liked to tease him about. He couldn't remember the last Club event he'd attended outside of a board meeting. But you couldn't put a price on peace of mind, and he'd happily make those sacrifices all over again, no matter what his family thought.

Outside the sky was a vigorous blue between the buildings. Cars crossed the Brooklyn Bridge. Perry let his gaze rest upon the bridge. Over the years he'd heard it referenced in different respects: *A symbol of unity. An engineering masterpiece. The longest journey in the world.* But at the end of the day, Roebling's creation was just that: a bridge. An unshakable structure built to span obstacles. Perry sat back in his chair and sighed. No one expected it to be fun.

Phoebe

The cool recess of the dimmed Fairfield Designs interior was a balm to the hot summer day outside and the trail of perspiration snaking its way down her back. Phoebe entered the foyer and breathed in relief. The sound of rippling water emanated softly through the showroom, though she could not locate the source of it even as she meandered through the sleek displays. Dave, her general contractor, had sent her there on a mission to get kitchen design ideas. He'd called her that morning to say he'd scheduled the kitchen design guy to come out to the cottage later that week. Phoebe had balked. "But we don't know what we want to do with the kitchen yet! Rob and I haven't agreed on anything beyond the fact there will be one."

Dave let her finish, pausing for her to catch her breath. "Well, it's time. I suggest you visit some local showrooms."

Immediately she'd thought of Fairfield Designs. Her best friend, Anna Beth, had redone her master bath with many of their fixtures, and the finished product was jaw-dropping. But Phoebe didn't have that kind of money to spend on just one room; she had an entire house to renovate. Dave concurred. "You're just there for ideas! I know you. You're going to drool when you see the displays, but remember we're on more of a *big-box-store budget*."

Phoebe was up for the challenge. Her aesthetic may have been out of proportion to her budget, but she'd watched enough HGTV to have a few tricks up her sleeve.

She passed through a farmhouse kitchen, slowing to admire a deep apron sink. Oh, the dirty pots and pans she could hide in its ceramic depths. The backsplash over the Viking range caught her eye: a wall of creamy subway tile dotted with diminutive square bas-relief tiles. Phoebe leaned in for closer inspection. Dragonflies and bumblebees! She traced their glazed wings with her finger and something inside her fluttered like the winged creatures themselves. When the twins were babies, she'd decorated their nursery in bumblebees. This had to be a sign. She snapped a photo.

A small display rack on the counter showed the different glaze finishes with which the insect tiles could be customized. They probably cost a small fortune, but the charm was irresistible. She picked up a crackle-finish bee tile and continued on.

The quaint farmhouse display spilled into a gleaming contemporary in absolute black. Phoebe snorted to herself. The tiny handprints that would show! She continued on into a spacious commercial-grade kitchen with stark industrial contrasts. Here she could breathe. Phoebe meandered between the alabaster-white cabinetry and towering appliances, seduced momentarily by the gleam of stainless steel. At the Calcutta island Phoebe halted, running the palms of her hands over its veined surface. So inviting, so clean. So un-lived-in! She considered the sweeping island top, and her Friday night family routine flashed in her mind like a small detonation: How could anyone in their right mind deign to roll out sticky pizza dough and splatter this pristine surface with marinara sauce? But she did like the commercial-grade faucet atop the sink. She was about to snap another photo when a salesperson appeared.

"May I help you?" Phoebe hadn't noticed her coming, but the salesperson had already noticed the bumblebee tile in Phoebe's hand. "Ah. The Summer Flight series. One of my favorite custom pieces."

Phoebe examined the tile in her hand. Custom was good. Personal. Meaningful. More expensive, probably, but this was where Rob failed to understand her approach. Everyone was doing the white subway tile he favored, and she was happy to go that route, too. But it needed something unique to make it hers. *Theirs*, rather. Poor Rob. She had to stop doing that. "So, these are custom tiles?"

The woman nodded. "It's one of our best sellers." She was pencil thin, dressed head to toe in black. Even her hair was dark, pulled into a sleek low ponytail. The effect was monochromatic. Phoebe wondered if the store had a dress code: "Dress like a curator in a gallery. Blend in so that the custom tiles stand out. Let their tiny ceramic voices be heard!"

"Would you like to step into our design center?"

Phoebe glanced at her watch. She didn't have much time, but she also didn't want to leave the showroom. The lighting was dim and sexy, and that waterfall sound was as lulling as an Ambien. Surely they had some kind of leather chaise she could curl up on while she perused finishes. But she had to focus. "Well, I'm on a tight time frame."

The woman tilted her head and extended her hand. "My name is Thérèse. Would you like a cappuccino?"

Would she like? Phoebe scurried after Thérèse like a lamb to slaughter.

An hour, thirty minutes, and two cappuccinos later, Phoebe was sated. Thérèse had skipped right over granite and gone straight for her jugular with gorgeous samples of hazy gray marble. Rob had already weighed in on marble: Too porous. Too pricey. Too easily stained. Well, now she had three squares to bring home and show him.

In addition, Thérèse had steered Phoebe away from the traditional subway tile they'd had in mind and suggested a crackled glaze. "Much more textural interest."

Phoebe nodded. Indeed.

"What you also need to think about is finishes. Since you're going for more of a contemporary farmhouse kitchen, I'd suggest more stainless steel."

This time Phoebe hesitated. Was contemporary what she was going for? No, they'd decided on a more rustic look. The cottage was lakeside, after all. And her family was . . . well, messy. An image of a thousand grimy fingerprints flashed in her mind. Followed by an image of her on her knees with a bottle of stainless steel spray and a rag. But before she could protest, Thérèse thrust a brochure across the table.

"This is my recommendation. Make your kitchen island a centerpiece. We just love this Amish company who does stainless steel island tops."

Phoebe blinked. "Oh, okay." The Amish had gone contemporary? When had that happened?

"But of course, that all depends on appliances. Have you chosen them yet?" Thérèse indicated the display behind her, where a sixty-inch Viking dual fuel oven rested in the center like a sphinx. A behemoth appliance with an even larger price tag. Rob would die. "Of course, I also recommend Wolf. If you'd prefer."

What Phoebe would prefer, she suddenly realized, was to get out of there. In mere discussion alone, she'd likely amassed a financial tally that toppled the entire house renovation budget. And Thérèse hadn't even gotten her out of the kitchen yet.

"Um, no. We haven't. Yet." She glanced at her watch. The boys! She had thirty minutes to drive the forty minutes to the preschool. As overcaffeinated as she was over budget, Phoebe leapt up. "I'm terribly sorry, but I'm late to pick up my kids."

The serene stretch of Thérèse's forehead wrinkled, but only for a second. "Of course. Let me print out your cost estimate sheet, and we'll set up a time to reconvene." With a few quick clicks on her laptop, a gentle hum from a nearby printer alerted Phoebe to the incoming assessment of damage. Thérèse disappeared around a corner and returned with a stapled sheaf of papers. Phoebe tucked it in her purse, but not before she glanced at the bottom line. *Sixty-eight thousand dollars.*

"Of course, this is for floor, counter, and backsplash finishes only. We'll have to reconvene to make appliance selections." She nodded at the amassed pile of samples between them. "Can I help you carry these out?"

Phoebe balked. To take these samples meant she had to come back. *Reconvene*, as Thérèse said. The thought of which was almost as dreadful as showing all of this to Rob.

This had been a terrible mistake. Her phone vibrated in her pocket, reminding her she had to go. And that she hadn't taken one damn photo for her "idea board." "I so appreciate your help, this has been very inspiring. But I'd like to take a day or two and think about what we discussed, first." She stood.

Thérèse looked stricken. Phoebe didn't blame her; she'd spent almost two hours with her and the woman probably worked on commission. "But what about your samples?"

"They're all lovely. Like you!" Phoebe forced a smile. Too far, that last comment. "But I'm late, so I'll call to set up another time."

She swept her purse over her shoulder and offered Thérèse a harried wave before making her escape. Alone, without her samples, she dashed through the maze of display kitchens, a faint sweat of relief breaking out on her forehead. Back through the contemporary, on past the farmhouse and the industrial, halting only briefly to run her hands a final time over the cool gray surface of the Calcutta. It was cold to the touch. Like the look her husband would give her when she shared the cost estimate sheet with him.

Shuddering, Phoebe hurried out of the marble oasis and for the front door, still clutching the bumblebee tile against her chest. Before hurtling through the door into the heat of the day, she had a final thought: Where *was* that tinkling waterfall sound coming from?

After the wasted trip to Fairfield Designs, Phoebe realized she needed to set some boundaries when interacting with tradespeople and salespeople. "It's all business," Rob reminded her. "Salespeople will try to distract you and sell you more than what you need. It's their job." But the boundaries also applied to herself. The possibilities of any given choice were endless. Take tile: Stone or ceramic? Glass or porcelain? Traditional or contemporary? God help her when it came to patterns, sizes, colors. She spent hours on Pinterest, Houzz, and building sites. Eyes glazed over, she'd stumble into bed past midnight, her brain awash with blue light and the noise of a thousand different options, not one of which she'd decided on. Rob, due to the frustrating mix of his easygoing nature and unavailability, deferred to her. Which was no help at all. "Look at it this way," her friend Anna Beth said. "You like to be in charge. This way you don't have to compromise."

She was right. But Phoebe would've welcomed some input. At this rate it could take her years to design one kitchen backsplash, let alone a floor plan for the entire first floor. The renovation was not even halfway complete, and each day there were more decisions to tackle. Moving forward, she'd have to limit herself if there was any hope of managing the decisions coming her way.

When the electrical bids came in later that week, Phoebe was determined to get it right. She would not repeat the Fairfield Designs field trip disaster.

Dave steered her toward John Glazer, who ran a second-generation family electric business. He was about her age, handsome, and rather shy, but within mere minutes Phoebe had gleaned that she knew his wife from a Mommy and Me music class. When she asked after his youngest child, John warmed up immediately.

Phoebe trailed him through the house nodding and listening as he explained lighting choices. He advised that she only do a few can lights in the kitchen, as they were the most costly. Before leaving, they reviewed the time frame and budget.

"How much do we have to work with?" John asked. Phoebe liked that he turned to her, not Dave, as many of the other subs seemed to do.

She referred to her notes. "Ten thousand," she told him.

John raised his eyebrows. "Wow. For fixtures? That's healthy."

Phoebe was ecstatic to hear this. She'd only done a little research on fixtures so far, but that amount should stretch far and wide. She might even have something left over to put into the kitchen.

"Let me clarify. I mean including labor," Dave added. He turned to her. "Which only leaves about three thousand for fixtures."

Her face must have fallen.

"We can make it work," John assured her. He gave her the name of an electrical supply wholesale store two towns over. "They're reasonable and they know their stuff."

But when Phoebe had driven the forty-five minutes to get there and stood in line behind a slew of loud contractors (all men), her hopes dwindled. Apparently it was a contractor wholesale store, and everyone in line (in work boots) was there to pick up large orders. As she stood in front of a guy who she was pretty sure was checking out her rear end, she tried to focus on her list. Schoolhouse-style nickel pendants. Flush-mount fixtures for the hallways. She glanced around uncertainly. There didn't seem to be a showroom anywhere in sight. When it was her turn, the guy at the cash register took one look at her with her Starbucks coffee cup and handwritten list and instantly looked put out.

Phoebe stole a peek at his nametag. "Hi, Ron. My electrician sent me here. I'd like to look around the showroom at options."

"For?"

"Lighting?" As soon as the word left her mouth, she flushed deeply. The guy behind her chuckled out loud.

Ron stared back at her impatiently. "I kind of figured that."

"What I mean is, I need to pick out fixtures. I'm renovating a house. Is there a showroom I can see?"

"Look, we're not Home Depot, honey. We supply electrical to licensed contractors we have service relationships with, not private customers."

"I'm sorry, I was told you have a showroom."

Ron glanced impatiently at the clock. "We do, but it's in the next building. And as you can see we're pretty busy filling orders this morning. Maybe you can come back with your electrician."

"But he's the one who sent me," she said hopefully. "John Glazer from Litchfield Electric?"

"Doesn't ring a bell."

Phoebe could feel the snickering expressions around her, and she had the urge to flee. It was the inverse experience of Fairfield

Designs. She'd gone from a sleek cappuccino-pushing saleswoman who wanted to sell her the Taj Mahal of kitchens, to a surly chauvinist in scuffed Timberlands who didn't want to sell her a damn thing.

Ron looked past her at the next guy in line. "You should probably come back when you know what you need."

But Phoebe did not budge. She set her list down and waited until Ron looked her in the eye. His eyes were flat with indifference. Phoebe had not sent the twins to school for an extended day and driven almost an hour for this. "I know what I need, Ron. I need eight LED can lights for my kitchen ceiling, which is ten feet tall. But not the new construction variety. I need the remodel type, which I understand is for a prebuilt ceiling. It needs to be IC, insulation contact. Wouldn't want to risk an electrical fire." She glanced at her list, trying to keep the quake out of her voice. "And I'd like all that with a baffle trim. Better to reduce the glare. Did you get all that? You may want a pen."

The guy behind her let out a low whistle. "Guess she knows what she wants, Ron."

Ron narrowed his eyes. Five minutes later, Phoebe was in the showroom with a smiling gray-haired woman named Ruth. Together they selected recessed lighting for the kitchen and a nice-looking bronze semi-flush-mount ceiling light for the hallways and common spaces. But the feature lighting, like bathroom sconces and kitchen island pendants, were well out of her price bracket.

Back at home, Phoebe pulled her desk chair up to her laptop. Three hours later she'd found a discount chandelier on one popular home design website she'd discovered and a set of brushed nickel industrial-style pendants for the kitchen on another site. At a box store site she found outdoor lighting, from gooseneck lanterns over the garage to floodlights. Even after one splurge on

Restoration Hardware for a cast-iron sconce set for the master bath, she still had three hundred dollars left in her budget. The next morning she proudly presented her printed orders to John and Dave.

Dave scrutinized the tally. "Are you sure you got everything? What about the bedrooms? And the upstairs bathrooms?" Phoebe pointed to her selections for both.

John high-fived her. "Not bad."

Dave, whose reserve Phoebe was used to by now, offered her a smile. "Bravo."

Phoebe was thrilled. It wasn't just the outward progress on the house that she relished. There was something about doing the work, herself, that invigorated her. When she wasn't on-site to meet with the revolving door of contractors, or at Lenox Town Hall applying for permits and scheduling inspections, she was in her car driving up and down the corridor of Fairfield County in search of fixtures and finishes. It was endless. But she loved the pace and the change of focus that came with each day. Even the setbacks were invigorating: the snap decisions that had to be made, the sense of accomplishment when something gone awry had been wrangled back on course. Construction was a lot like motherhood: ripe with unknowns. There were sky-scraping highs that made you giddy and breathless, and avalanche-like lows that left you buried. And somewhere in the middle that maternal scrap of hope that it would all prove rewarding. For the first time since leaving her career in copy editing and staying home full-time with the boys, Phoebe felt the whir of her old self humming to life beneath her skin. She could do this. She *was* doing this.

Olivia

The farmer's market was her favorite part of the weekend. She wasn't sure if it was because she was the daughter of a chef who'd taught her to eat foods in their peak of season, or the vibrant vegetables arranged on wooden tables, or perhaps the calloused soil-stained hands of the farmers who stood behind them, but Olivia found the Saturday morning market a feast of the senses. She paused at an organic vegetable stand where she was a regular. Mr. Waters, the farmer, was handing out crisp green sprigs as samples. "There she is! You must come to the asparagus festival at the farm," he told her. "It's next weekend." The lush stem cracked with a satisfying snap as she popped a sample into her mouth. "Heaven," she said. "I'll take two bunches."

Mr. Waters smiled appreciatively. "And how about this little one? Does she love asparagus like her mother?"

Luci stared back at him, and the speech pathologist's advice echoed sharply in Olivia's mind. "Encourage her to use her signs and gestures around others." She took a deep breath and nodded at Luci. After a long moment, when Luci still had said nothing, Olivia prompted her. "Do you like asparagus?" Luci averted her gaze, but just as Olivia's heart sank she lifted her hand shyly and gave Mr. Waters the thumbs-up.

"That's right, darling!" Olivia gushed.

If Mr. Waters wondered at the tears welling in her large brown eyes, he gave her a reprieve, instead reaching for a sunflower. "For you, my little asparagus eater," he said, handing it to Luci.

The small interaction boosted Olivia so thoroughly she stopped for fresh-squeezed lemonade and didn't even balk at the price, three dollars per cup. She bought two. She even lingered at the animal pen under the maple tree where Goatboy Soaps set up their stand each weekend. Luci loved to pet the goats, Matilda and Bee, even though the day was sticky and Olivia needed to get home to the studio to finish up some work Ben had left for her. Best of all, today held the promise of what would be just an ordinary thing for most people: they had been invited on a playdate.

"Come! Your friend Ruby is waiting. Let's get home and get ready."

Ruby was not exactly a friend, but Olivia held out hope. They'd met at the library during story time, and though Olivia had explained Luci's quietude to the parents during snack time, Ruby's mother, Helen, was the only one who went out of her way to encourage her daughter to include Luci. She noticed when Luci looked hungrily at a tube of purple glitter across the table. "Ruby, make sure you pass the glitter to Luci," she'd trilled during craft time, and when Ruby not only did but also told Luci that she liked her drawing, Olivia had wanted to kiss Helen.

From the beginning, playdates had seemed impossible for a child who did not speak. Luci could not express herself for either socialization or her needs. If she was hungry or thirsty, she could not tell the hosting parent. Or if she wanted to pet the dog or ride a bike. When it came to playing, it was heartbreaking for Olivia to watch. The teachers reported that she parallel played at school. When a child was building with Legos on the rug, Luci would watch and then set up her own little spot beside her. But she did not interact. Sharing didn't happen. Luci might glance at a toy she wished to play with, often in a yearning way. But she could not express it vocally. Worse, when other kids wanted something she had, they might ask her for it. But after getting no response, they would lose patience and often take the toy from Luci, leaving her breathless with hurt feelings. Or they'd give up and seek a play-mate who chimed in, who shouted, who sang out loud and asked questions and shrieked with laughter. That child was not Luci. It was soul-destroying for Olivia.

But today, a rare invitation to play was on the calendar. Luci was beside herself. "Did you know she has two cats and a hamster?" she asked her mother, eyes wide. "One of the cat's names is Herman. I can't remember the other." People were always amazed that Luci knew so much about her "friends" when she interacted so little. She can hear! Olivia wanted to cry out. She can see, too! Indeed, Luci was always gleaning information from her classmates. Storing away anecdotal facts that she shared as openly at the dinner table with her mother at night as any other child might. Sarah Pratt was going to Rhode Island for vacation. Dylan Havens snuck his father's car keys to school and the nanny had to come pick them up because Mr. Havens was late for work and couldn't find the spare. The teacher, Mrs. Mandler, cried when she read a story about an old dog. Luci knew just as much about her peers and their lives as anyone else in the class, probably more. What she didn't know was what it was like to have a friend.

"Just pull around the circular drive to the front door," Helen had said on the phone.

Olivia glanced up at the sweeping contemporary as she got out of her car. Sleek black metal roof, commanding glass walls, a pea gravel drive that looked like it had been hand-raked. Olivia paused and tucked her hair behind her ears, smoothed her shirt. She smiled at Luci, who was already tugging her toward the front door. "Ready?"

Luci nodded.

Helen and Ruby answered together. "Hello! You found us out here in the woods." Indeed, everyone in this neck of Connecticut was in the woods.

Helen ushered them into a grand room, minimalist in both design and color. "Your house is lovely," Olivia told her.

"Thanks! My husband, Merrit, and I moved here from New York when we had Ruby." Helen gave them a brief tour of the downstairs, which was every bit as pristine and kid-unfriendly as the exterior. Olivia noted the white furniture and area rugs. How did Helen keep it so clean? Though she realized that job was likely not Helen's. "Ruby, why don't you take Luci up to your room? Ruby has a Victorian dollhouse she wants to show you!" Helen said, bending to Luci.

Ruby did not exactly look like she cared to show Luci the doll-house, but Olivia appreciated Helen's effort.

"Luci would love that, wouldn't you, honey?"

The two girls glanced uncertainly at each other and to Olivia's relief headed upstairs.

"So how do you like Washington?" They settled in the living room on the white couches, and Olivia tried to relax.

"It's been great," Olivia said. "The countryside is so lush, and we love all the lakes in the region: Candlewood, Waramaug, Lilli-nonah. I grew up in the city, but this is where I want to raise my child."

Helen nodded appreciatively. "When we first moved here I remember looking out the patio door at night and all I could see was darkness. No cars, no lights. Not a single house in sight.

Just when I stepped outside I heard a coyote howl. I raced inside, slammed the door, and asked my husband what the hell we were thinking. Now I can't imagine going back."

Olivia's eyes widened. She'd not yet heard the coyotes at night, but Ben and Marge had mentioned them.

"So, what's it like living with Ben Rothschild? His work is amazing."

"Well, I don't exactly live *with* Ben and Marge. Luci and I have a cottage on the property. But he's wonderful to work for. Very kind. Down to earth."

"Did I hear from one of the other moms that you're a sculptor, too?"

Helen wanted to know all about Olivia's own work, and what medium she worked in. It was refreshing, being able to sit down with another woman and talk. Not about speech therapies or objectives. Not about Luci's condition. But ordinary things, like her move to Connecticut and her work as a budding artist. Olivia settled back into the couch, her thoughts less interrupted by every pitter-patter or sound from overhead. The girls were fine. She could relax.

"You know, I have a friend who runs a gallery in Washington Depot. She's always on the lookout for fresh talent. I should put the two of you in touch."

Olivia leaned forward. Granted, it was perhaps friendly small talk. But she was touched by the thoughtfulness. "Really? That's so nice of you. You haven't even seen my work."

Helen stood. "Then you'll have to invite me over and show me." She smiled. "Next playdate at your place?"

Next time. It was something Olivia rarely heard as a mother of a child with special needs. She stood and followed Helen out of the kitchen, grateful that she was able to brush away before Helen saw the stray tear that was threatening to spill down her cheek. "How do you like your tea?"

Olivia was about to answer. About to say, "Cream, no sugar." About to suggest they get together again for a playdate at her place on Saturday, when there was an alarmed shriek from upstairs.

Both women pivoted toward the staircase. "Ruby?" Helen called. She glanced back at Olivia reassuringly. "I'm sure it's nothing."

But Ruby screamed again.

By the time they'd run upstairs, Ruby was already standing outside her bedroom door in the hall, her hands balled in fists. "She did it!" Ruby cried.

"Did what?" Helen rushed into the room, Olivia on her heels.

Stuffed animals and dress-up clothes were strewn across the rug. Olivia spun around, taking in the four-poster princess bed, the pastel tea set on a table, the dollhouse in the corner. Luci was nowhere in sight. "Lu Lu?" she called.

Ruby grabbed her mother's hand. "Look what she did!" Olivia watched in horror as Ruby dragged Helen to the bed and pointed to the chenille duvet. That was when she saw it. The large round stain in the center of the blanket.

Helen stiffened. "Is that . . . ?"

Ruby whirled around to face Olivia. "She peed my bed! She ruined it."

It was then Olivia heard it, a muffled sound coming from the closet. She yanked the doors open. There, pressed in the corner in a little ball, was Luci.

"It's okay, baby." Olivia reached in and scooped her up. To Ruby, she said, "Luci and I are so sorry. It was an accident."

Helen was watching them both with concern, but also something else. "No, no. I'm sorry, too. I assumed she was potty-trained."

Olivia closed her eyes, holding Luci to her chest. She could feel the dampness through her daughter's pants. How long had she sat like that? "She is," Olivia blurted. "But she must've had to go and didn't know where the potty was."

"She should have asked," Ruby sputtered.

"Ruby," Helen said. "You know she can't!" Then, turning to Olivia, "I'm sorry. I didn't mean she can't. What I meant was . . ."

Olivia shook her head. "It's okay."

It was all her fault. Helen knew about Luci's mutism, but Olivia had forgotten to ask Helen where the bathrooms were located. It was her job to make sure Luci knew. To show her. To avoid disaster, like this. But she was so busy talking about herself and her art and her new life in Connecticut, she'd forgotten.

"I need to take Luci to the bathroom, and then I will help you clean up," Olivia offered.

Helen looked at her sympathetically. "The bathroom is down the hall on the right." Then, "Don't worry about it. We can clean up."

"Not me," Ruby said, pulling her stuffed animals off the bed to safety. She glared at Luci, who was still in Olivia's arms. "She's gross."

"Ruby!" Helen said. "That's not nice."

"I think we should go." Olivia was not going to subject Luci to another second of this humiliation. Her wet bottom had already gone cold. Helen didn't offer a change of clothes and Olivia wasn't about to ask. All she wanted was to get out of there as fast as she could. "Thank you, again, for the invitation. I'm sorry about your bed, Ruby."

She was halfway down the stairs when Luci whimpered into her ear. "I tried to ask, Mama. I tried."

Olivia blinked back tears. Miss Griffin's advice rang in her ears. Stay calm, address the situation with Luci in private. "It's all right, baby girl. I know you did."

This was what always got her. Just when Olivia let her guard down and began to enjoy herself like any other mother on any other playdate, something like this happened. Olivia pressed her lips to Luci's temple, and they let themselves out into the blinding light of the afternoon. That was the thing Olivia could never let herself forget. They weren't like everyone else.

Phoebe

S he was not the kind of person who skipped dentist appointments. Every six months Phoebe rounded up the family and dragged everyone in for a cleaning. It was her least favorite day of the year.

So when the phone call came from the dental office, Phoebe was mystified. "You're more than a year past due for a cleaning," the receptionist said.

"A year? But that can't be. Patrick just had a crossbite X-ray." She had the bill to prove it.

"Yes. Your husband and children are all up-to-date. But we haven't seen you in a while. Fifteen months, to be exact."

Fifteen months! Phoebe scheduled her appointment with her tail between her legs, and also made a mental note: she was becoming one of those statistics. The mother who takes care of everyone in the family except herself. What was next? Would she be like that woman on Oprah who was so busy planning and packing for her family's Hawaiian vacation that she boarded the plane and waited until she was in the middle of a surfing lesson before she admitted she was in full coronary distress? Phoebe was pretty sure Perry could supply her with all kinds of statistics on *that* woman.

So there she was, dutifully seated in the waiting room flipping through *Architectural Digest*, when she saw it. The claw-foot tub she'd been dreaming of. Phoebe held it out to the hygienist. "I'm in the middle of a house renovation," she blurted.

She followed the hygienist to the chair in the back room, all the while holding the magazine. "Master baths are one place you can secure a hefty return on your investment," she read aloud. The hygienist smiled and affixed her bib. Was she even listening?

"Do I want a walk-in shower? Or a soaker tub? What I'd like is to have both, but because space is an issue, should I just surrender and do a combo?"

The hygienist shook her head. "Not the combo." So she *was* listening.

At that point Phoebe's dentist, Dr. Kane, walked in. "How are we doing?" Then, seeing the bathroom design spread, he leaned in. "Ooh. Very nice."

"I'm renovating our new lake house," Phoebe informed him. "This is the tub."

Dr. Kane squinted. "It's an impressive tub." Then, as the hygienist whisked the magazine away and the doctor turned to riffle through his set of tools, he asked, "What's that going to cost you?"

Phoebe stiffened in the chair. If it was in this magazine, there was no chance it was in her budget. If she had time, she could stop at one of the box stores and see if there was something similar. She already knew that was a cool chance in hell.

At that moment, her phone buzzed. "Excuse me," she apologized. "Just need to make sure it's not the boys' school."

Dr. Kane nodded patiently.

It wasn't. It was Dave, her general contractor. "Phoebe. Sorry to bother you."

"No bother." She winced, ignoring the audible sigh from the hygienist.

"You need to come out to the house."

"Is something wrong?"

Dave didn't reply right away. Phoebe imagined him glancing up at the sky, and her chest did that pitter-patter thing. Yep, coronary affliction for sure. "We came across something regarding the foundation."

"Oh? What was it?" Let it be a rat. Preferably dead.

Again, Dave paused. "This is something you should probably see."

Two minutes later, Phoebe was trotting across the dentist's parking lot, the copy of *Architectural Digest* shoved in her purse and an appointment card for her reschedule in hand.

When she pulled into the driveway, it was obvious something was wrong. The driveway was empty. Except for Dave, who stood on the front step like a sentinel.

"What's going on? Where did everyone go?"

From the beginning, Phoebe had been glad she'd picked Dave for her general contractor. He didn't mince words. He stayed calm in times she considered crises, like the day the roofers didn't show up and they later learned they would not be showing up, ever. Which set them back a week. Phoebe was all too familiar with domestic mayhem. She had driven babies to the hospital in the middle of the night with 104-degree temperatures. She'd handled blown-out diapers in five-star restaurants (don't bring a newborn out to your anniversary dinner), and she'd nursed their last dog through a case of bloat two years before. What she did not possess was the endless reservoir of patience that Dave seemed to draw upon when things went awry with the house. "What is it?" she asked again, hurrying up the path.

Dave smiled, but it didn't quite reach the corners of his eyes.

Phoebe liked Dave's eyes when they did that. "I'll show you. Why don't you come down into the basement with me?"

Reluctantly, Phoebe followed him to the side of the house where the Bilco doors were located. They were flung open like the cover of a book.

"Watch your head," Dave warned as she stepped down into the darkness behind him. The air was cold, and there was a slightly earthen smell that made Phoebe nervous. Had there been a flood? Some kind of burst pipe?

Dave flipped on his flashlight and the overhead beams came into dim view. "We're right underneath the living room," he explained. "When we began removing the clapboard siding around the front door, we noticed some rot. Which led to us discovering this." He reached overhead and placed the flat of his hand against a giant square wooden beam. It had to be at least eight by eight inches thick. But as Phoebe looked closer she could see it was much thinner in some places, as if it had been chewed into.

"I don't understand," Phoebe blurted. "We had the house inspected."

"Yes, but this wasn't something an inspector would've been able to see until we removed the doorframe and exposed this section." Dave pointed a screwdriver at the beam. "This is your front sill plate," Dave told her. "These beams run all around the base of the house and rest on the foundation. They're an integral part of your home's structural integrity." Phoebe watched as he tapped the length of the beam, jabbing the tip of the screwdriver along its length, to demonstrate its solidity. "From down here, the bottom of the beam looks pretty good. Notice how the screwdriver can't penetrate? But when we removed the doorframe and exposed the top of this beam, I'm afraid we found evidence of pest damage and rot."

"Pest damage? Rot?"

Phoebe shivered, listening as Dave explained what the beam did (supported the house), what was wrong with it (termites and decay), and what had to be done (tent the structure, spray it, jack up the house, rip out the rotten beam, replace it with a new beam, lower the house). Dave studied her carefully as he delivered the news. If she wasn't mistaken, Phoebe was pretty sure he didn't blink once during the delivery.

"This sounds expensive."

Dave nodded toward the steps. "Let's talk outside."

"This is not reassuring me, Dave." Phoebe trailed him out, her thoughts spilling. "Oh my God. I can only imagine what this is going to do to the build time frame." Then, "Is this going to kill my budget?" Followed by, "Rob is going to kill us both."

She followed him up the stairs and out into the fresh air again. Phoebe blinked in the daylight.

"Here's what I was talking about," Dave explained, as he led her around to the front of the house. The siding and doorframe had been removed, leaving a cavernous opening. The front of the house looked like an unsettled face, its mouth hanging agape. Which was exactly what Phoebe's was doing as she watched Dave jab the end of his screwdriver into the newly exposed beam. The tool sank through the dark wood, and the surrounding area crumbled like dust. Phoebe pictured her budget doing the same.

"So, what is this going to cost?"

Dave let out his breath. "To treat for termites is only about three thousand."

"Only?" Phoebe sputtered.

But Dave wasn't done. "Your house runs thirty feet across. To jack up the house and replace the sill, plus labor, we're going to be looking at about five."

"Five thousand?"

Dave nodded.

"On top of the first three?"

"Correct. Around eight thousand in all," he said.

Phoebe exhaled. "Excuse me," she said, straining to keep her tone somewhere in the range of what her mother called her "good company voice." "I'll be right back."

What Phoebe really wanted to do was run. A good scream would work, too. Instead, she pivoted toward the car. She swept her phone out of her purse and pressed Rob's number. Then, thinking better of it, she hit cancel. Rob would have to know at some point. But to tell him now would mean also telling him that she'd borrowed money from the window budget to apply to the kitchen budget, both of which were already at the top. The man could shoulder a lot. But this would just be cruel.

Thinking better of it, she spun back toward the house. "Dave."

"Yes, Phoebe."

"Is there an alternative to the sill beam?" She paused, her thoughts spinning. "Perhaps some kind of different material? Or structural approach?"

Dave shook his head matter-of-factly. "You can't have a house without a sill beam unless you want to all end up in the basement. And you need to spray for termites or you'll have the same problem again down the road."

"But we don't have those numbers left in the budget," she said. "I'm sorry, we just don't." She could be matter-of-fact, too.

Dave held her gaze. "Well, I realize that, based on our discussions of late."

Was he raising an eyebrow, or was she just imagining that?

"This has to be done, but I suppose we could review the budget and try to make some cuts in other places. Though that means you'll have to adjust accordingly."

Phoebe brightened. Of course, they could adjust. She would have to let go of the claw-foot tub.

Dave was thinking out loud now. "We can try to whittle down the bathroom and kitchen tile. And the fixtures. But remember, we were hoping already to borrow from those for appliances."

Damn, the appliances. Those, too, hadn't made it into the original numbers. She figured they'd pick those up somewhere along the way. Maybe a bonus at work, or an unexpected savings in another line item in the house budget. After all, at Rob's insistence they'd allowed an extra 10 percent to start with. But they'd eaten into that as surely as the termites had the beam.

Dave was waiting. "Should I go ahead and call the exterminator, or do you want to talk to Rob and call me after? Either way, the subcontractors can't come back until it's taken care of, and every day we lose them is a day we risk losing them to another project at another site. They get paid by the day, and they're not going to hang around waiting if we don't move fast."

Phoebe's stomach began to churn. "How long will all this take?"

"Spraying, about three days before the crew can safely return. Then the sill—probably two days. Three max."

"So, about a week in all?"

Dave looked almost sorry to say it. "At best."

Phoebe envisioned a paper calendar hanging on the wall, the days whipping off and blowing somewhere out across the lake. Just as her money was doing. Doing the sill repair and spraying the house were unavoidable, it seemed. Delaying things wouldn't change that fact.

"Go ahead," she said, staring at the cottage. How was it that all her careful planning could go so far off course? They'd done an inspection. They'd even had a structural engineer come take a look. And yet every board they pulled off of the siding or pulled up from the floor was like opening a new can of worms. Everywhere, worms.

To her further consternation she realized it was what Perry had said from the beginning: an old house is a Pandora's box.

"Is there anything else you want to ask about?" Dave asked.

Phoebe shook her head. She tucked the issue of *Architectural Digest* she'd pilfered from the dentist's office under her arm. There was no point asking Dave about the claw-foot tub. Though she could really use one now. Not to take a relaxing soak in, no. To climb in and sink beneath the surface.

Perry

"This is classic Jake. Jump first, don't worry about the rocks in the water until you hit them." He was sitting in bed, propped up against the pillows, a small laundry basket of socks beside him. The housekeeper had folded the socks the wrong way again. He rifled through the basket, looking for pairs that needed refolding. "This whole marriage idea is ridiculous."

Amelia stepped out of the steamy master bathroom, her hair swept up neatly in a towel. She glanced over as he tipped the basket of socks across the bedspread without blinking. "I think it's romantic."

"You can't be serious."

He watched as she sat down at her vanity and unwrapped the towel. Her long dark hair spilled across the back of her bathrobe. Amelia had always been attractive, if in a slightly staid way. From the first time she joined his study group in graduate school with a sheaf of color-coded notes tucked under her arm and her hair pulled tightly in a no-nonsense bun, Perry had taken notice. Her nose had the tiniest bump in the center, a feature she later confided her brothers had nicknamed the "mogul" when they were children, but Perry thought it added strength to her profile, like an ancient Greek statue's. Amelia radiated order, from her spartan sensibilities to her conservative attire. But every once in a while, a flicker of romantic whimsy exposed itself. Like now. "Why not?" she asked.

"Because they just met." Perry began unrolling the pairs of socks. All were solid black; it was the only color Perry would wear. But some had gold threads across the toe and some had white. Perry could not stand for them to comingle. The housekeeper, Estelle, however, seemed to embrace such chaos. He had to remind her every time not to mix the two. "What does Jake really know about her? And her child?"

Amelia raised an eyebrow in the mirror. "You mean Luci?"

"And that dog." Perry shook his head. "They're rushing. Jake is too rash."

"He's in love." Amelia sighed. There was the flicker.

"And what does he know about parenting?"

Amelia set her hairbrush down. "Well, that I'll give you. Getting married is one thing. Having a stepchild is another entirely. And Luci has special needs."

"Exactly." To his dismay there were two strays at the bottom of the basket, one with a gold toe and one with a white. Perry flinched. Estelle had done it again. He'd have to unfold the entire pile and find their mates. "Why doesn't she speak?"

"She does, just not to us. It's kind of like an anxiety disorder." Amelia turned to him. "Imagine the strain that places on Olivia."

"Well, she certainly made the rounds at the party explaining Luci's condition. Shouldn't that stuff be kept private?"

Amelia considered this. "I thought that was brave. She doesn't make apologies. I don't know that I could handle having a child with mutism with such grace."

"Luckily we don't have to."

Amelia and Perry were blessed that way. Emma had always

been a healthy, well-adjusted child. Granted, Perry likened much of that to their parenting. Not that that had happened overnight.

If he were being honest, Perry would have said that he'd been paralyzed with fear the moment he learned they were expecting. He'd always wanted a child. But as the months passed and Amelia's belly swelled, Perry began to develop a significant twitch in his left eye. It happened every time they talked about the baby.

"Honey, are you sure you shouldn't go to the optometrist?" Amelia had asked. It was becoming rather noticeable. But Perry knew better. There was nothing wrong with his eye. Perry did not like change. The baby hadn't even arrived, and already everything around him seemed to be changing at warp speed.

It wasn't just the obvious transformation in Amelia's body and demeanor. Gone was the woman who worked until eight p.m. in her office and met him at a restaurant for a late dinner. Instead, Amelia started coming home by five o'clock, bedraggled and exhausted. And starving. They began eating dinner in, earlier and earlier each night. And gone were nice meals, like poached salmon and wine sauce, his favorite. Once Perry arrived home to find his wife bent over a saucepan shoveling boxed macaroni and cheese into her mouth. She'd looked up, her lips tinged orange with powdered cheese, and smiled. "Sorry. I didn't save you any." Who was this woman?

In an effort to restore the slipping sense of balance, Perry responded the only way he knew how. He prepared as if for disaster. During his daily commute to the city, he pored over baby books. Sleep books. Feeding books. Behavior books. At night he and Amelia lay in bed, shoulder to shoulder, paging through them. If the arrival of their child was a black hole of the unknown, Perry would make it his job to fill as much of it as possible with information. His favorite book focused on structure. "Babies thrive on predictable routine. Schedule naps and feedings, and don't deviate. Adherence to routine makes for a happy baby!"

Amelia, reading over his shoulder, had snorted.

"What's so funny?" Perry asked.

"It's like they're talking about you, honey."

Perry was used to this. He felt no shame in his philosophy. Life was all about preparation. Something his brother, Jake, had always balked at.

Now when Perry thought about the time and planning that he and Amelia had put into raising Emma, he shuddered. And that was for their *own* child. A child he'd held since the day of her birth. Who'd known him every day and night since. What about a stepchild?

Perry wondered what Luci thought of all this. What it meant to her to have a strange new man in her life, soon to be in her home. She'd lived the whole of her five years with just her mother. It was all she knew.

How could Jake expect to just stumble into fatherhood? It was the worst kind of foolishness. It wasn't a job you could charm your way into. "I need to talk to Jake," he said, as Amelia climbed into bed beside him. "No one else in the family is going to."

"Just don't expect to change his mind."

Amelia slipped beneath the sheets just as Perry finished the refolding. He held up the last two socks. There was still one gold toe and one white. He sighed.

The next day he didn't get to speak with Jake as hoped for. Thanks to MTA work, his train was behind schedule, and by the time he arrived he was late for a meeting. The day continued as such, and by the end of it he climbed back onto the train and loosened his tie. Just outside the windows, on the dim platform, Perry saw a flash of color. A woman in a bright yellow dress. Like a buttercup, Perry thought.

Her back was turned, but Perry noted her elegant carriage, briefly, before another passenger slid past him and into the window seat. The passenger blocked his view, and the pretty woman standing on the track disappeared.

The whole ride home Perry could almost feel the exhaustion radiating through the car along with the smell of the fumes. It was always like this on the way home, a sharp juxtaposition to the morning train, where voices were crisp, postures erect, and phones dinging the entire ride in. Now, as the train bell chimed and the doors slid closed, Perry allowed his eyes to do the same. The train hurtled toward Connecticut, the only sound the hum of cable on track and whispers around him. Except for the soft voice of a child, a few seats behind him on the opposite side of the aisle.

Perry tried to tune the child's banter out, to let his thoughts wander. He was reminded of when Emma would sit beside him on the train on the occasions he brought her to the city for a day. When was the last time they'd done that? Perry had taken her to see *Wicked*, and they'd gone out to dinner at Keens Steakhouse afterward, lingering over Bananas Foster, but that was at least a year ago. Maybe two. He deflated. In two more, she'd be out of the house and off to college.

The little girl behind him was still talking, her small voice rising and falling animatedly. Curious, Perry peered over his shoulder. The child's mother was the woman in the yellow dress. He could not see their faces, only the curve of the mother's neck as she bent toward her child to listen. At that moment, the child leaned forward and peeked around her mother. Perry found himself looking back at a familiar little face. Immediately she stopped talking. It was Luci.

Olivia turned, her face lighting with surprise. "Perry?"

Perry jerked to attention. "Well. Hello." He'd never heard the child speak before, and felt thrown off. But Olivia played it down.

"You're on your way home?" she asked.

Perry nodded, careful not to stare at Luci, who was now leaning against her mother shyly. "Yes, heading home from work. What brought you girls to the city today?"

"We went to see my father, Luci's *grand-père*." She glanced at her daughter. "Isn't that right?"

Luci stared back at Perry.

"Well, that's wonderful." Perry didn't know what to say. Here was Luci, who only moments before had been chattering away, right in front of him. And the lovely woman in the buttercup-yellow dress—it was Olivia. He felt himself flush.

"Are you all right?" Olivia asked.

Perry cleared his throat, and coughed. "Yes, just warm."

Olivia reached into her purse. "Would you like a drink?" She held out a bottle of water.

Perry coughed again. He had not needed a drink, but suddenly his throat had turned to sand. He could feel the heat rise up around his collar, and indeed into his cheeks. What was happening?

"Here, please." Olivia thrust the water bottle in his direction and he took it, aware that others were glancing their way. Perry took a deep swallow, then another. The cold rush of water revived him.

"Better?" Olivia nodded encouragingly. Perry felt like an idiot; he did not need to be mothered. And yet he was grateful.

"Yes, thank you." He looked at the half-drunk bottle of water in his hand, suddenly unsure of what to do. He couldn't exactly return it to her, having used it. Could he?

"Keep it," Olivia said, as if reading his mind.

The train stopped, and thankfully they were interrupted by passengers disembarking. Olivia returned her attention to her book. Luci, however, kept her eyes trained on Perry; he could feel the weight of her stare. When he looked back, their eyes locked. And then something happened. She smiled.

A signal chimed and the doors slid closed. The announcer came over the speaker: "Next stop, Mount Kisco." Passengers rose, again blocking his view of Luci and Olivia. But when they cleared, there was Luci, still staring.

When the seat across from them vacated, Olivia turned to him. "Care to join us?"

Perry cleared his throat again. He glanced at Luci, then Olivia. Then back at the empty seats. He hated sitting on a freshly vacated seat. They always held the body warmth of the previous sitter. It was so unhygienic, so intimate. Perry cringed.

Olivia, however, pet the seat as if he were her dog. "Come. Chat."

Perry wasn't sure if it was the cool recesses of her large brown eyes. Or the peculiar smile he was certain her child had offered him. Or the liquid-yellow folds of her dress. But he found himself rising from his perfectly good seat, crossing the aisle, and sitting down across from the two of them. The vinyl cushion was indeed still warm. But Perry did not flinch. He turned to Luci. "So. How was your visit to see your grandpa?"

———

That night as he sat in bed, waiting again for Amelia to join him, he did not think about socks that might need re-sorting. Or about his myriad concerns over Jake. Or the Super Bowl halftime contract that was sitting in his briefcase downstairs, unfinished. Overcome by a wash of exhaustion, Perry closed his eyes. The color that flickered behind his lids was buttercup yellow.

Emma

This summer was turning out to be like every other summer. That was the problem.

Emma tromped downstairs, still in her pajamas, and through the formal foyer. The marble was cold beneath her bare feet. On the kitchen island was the usual note from her mother: *Good morning, sleepyhead! Fruit, yogurt, and eggs in the fridge. Have fun at camp!*

She was fifteen, heading into her junior year. And yet, aside from a summer leadership program at George Washington University at the end of August, Camp Candlewood was about the only thing she had going on. The internship had been her father's idea. He was a GW alum, and the fact that his daughter had beat out thousands of applicants from some of the best schools in the country had tickled him greatly. How many times had she heard him mention it to friends and neighbors since the acceptance letter had come in the mail? At first it was sweet. Just stealing her father's attention had been nice. But it was starting to wear on her. And she was beginning to have doubts. How much fun could it be to attend seminars and debates for a whole week in August? At least the camp job would be enjoyable.

When she was younger, she'd been a camper at the community

clubhouse herself. It was where she learned to swim, sail, and play tennis. Now she'd be working there teaching neighborhood kids to do the same.

Emma's position was as a counselor in training, or CIT, which meant she would be doing a lot of the gopher jobs. Craft prep. Walking a kid from the lake to the bathrooms. Lining up the kayaks and helping kids get their life vests on and off. Having been a camper herself, she already knew the ins and outs. And she loved working with little kids. She just hoped she wasn't assigned to Amanda Hastings's group.

She arrived at the clubhouse at 8:45, freshly showered and with her lunch packed. Already most of the other CITs were gathered around the main room. She scanned the area. Alicia came bounding over. "Hey, did you get my text?"

Like Emma, Alicia was in honors classes and did well in school. Also, like Emma, she wasn't part of the cool crowd. But she was sarcastic and funny and had a thing for Adam Levine. "No, sorry. I was running late."

"That's cool. I was wondering if you want to swim after work."

Which meant Emma's house. "Sure. My parents won't be home, though."

Alicia's parents were still of the mind that an adult needed to be around at all times if they went down to the lake. Emma's father shared the same concern, but the thing was he was never around. So he asked that she text before she swam and immediately after. But since he was always in a meeting of some kind, it was another one of his useless rules.

"We can bring our towels down to the dock and do pedis." Emma glanced down at her freakishly pale feet and bare nails. "I forgot to do mine."

Alicia rolled her eyes. "Oh look, the princess has arrived."

Emma glanced up in time to see Amanda Hastings breeze into the rec room. The boys playing Ping-Pong paused. She was wearing the shortest white shorts, and already her skin was a golden bronze. Emma groaned. She couldn't see from there, but she was sure Amanda's toenails were freshly painted. Probably Kiss My A's red.

"Who wears white shorts to camp?" Alicia said.

A handful of girls surrounded Amanda, and they squawked together.

"She can afford to. We're the ones who do the dirty work. I pray I'm not assigned to her."

"Yeah, me too. That'd be a summer killer."

The office door opened and the camp director, Bob Kline, came out. He was a textbook camp director, with a whistle around his neck and his camp hat pulled down over his eyes. Most of the kids had nicknamed him Smokey the Bear.

Bob called everyone in. It was the usual rigmarole of rules, expectations, and safety. Alicia and Emma were not in the same group, but neither were they with Amanda Hastings. Her two CITs were Brandon Fisher and Alex Cummings. Both cute sophomores looked like they'd won the lottery when their names were called out. Alicia whispered, "They think they're lucky. But she will treat them like slaves."

They were about to break up into their groups to head down to the lake for a kayak test when the screen door slapped shut. Emma looked up. Sully McMahon stood in the doorway.

"What's he doing here?"

Like Alicia, Sully didn't live in the private neighborhood or belong to the Club. Unlike Alicia, as far as Emma knew, he didn't have any connections to the Club who would've sponsored him for the summer position. Unless . . .

Emma watched Amanda pop up off the bench and wave. "Sully! Over here."

But Bob Kline beat her to it. "Mr. McMahon?" he barked. "How nice of you to join us."

To Emma's surprise Sully went right up to Bob Kline. "Sorry, Mr. Kline. I got behind a bus and was stuck in traffic."

Bob Kline didn't want to hear it. "Then you need to get up earlier. If you're late again, don't bother coming in."

Emma watched as Sully stood toe-to-toe with the camp director. "It won't happen again," he said. Emma stared straight ahead as Sully ducked past her. If he noticed her or recognized her from the dock the day before, he didn't show it.

Behind her, Emma heard Amanda whisper to Sully. "Bob's a douchebag. Don't let him bother you."

"Nah, I was late."

They spent the morning doing CPR training and reviewing water safety in small groups. For the most part it was focused work, and Emma had to pay attention. But she stole occasional glances across the beach to Sully's group. Sully had been assigned to a senior, Tucker Owens. Tucker was a football player at school and, like Amanda, popular. The two seemed to like each other. The other CIT in that group was Brad Adams. Brad was shy and quiet, and not at all outdoorsy. His freckled skin was untouched by the sun, and he ate lunch alone at a picnic table in the shade with his book. "Poor Brad," Alicia said, as they finished their sandwiches. They were sitting on an overturned kayak by the grass. "I wouldn't want to be in that group."

"Sully seems nice enough," Emma allowed. She tore off a piece of bread crust and tossed it to a little sparrow who hovered nearby.

Alicia eyed her. "Seriously? He kind of loves himself. Like the rest of them."

Sully was standing at the edge of the water looking out across the lake. Emma watched as he bent to pick up a rock and flicked it across the surface. It skipped five times before disappearing into the inky water. "I don't know. He seems okay."

She ignored Alicia's curious gaze. Now was not the time to mention the Wild Turkey under her bed. She'd only taken it out once after retrieving it from the bushes. When she opened it and sniffed, she'd winced. Who would want to drink that stuff? Ever since, it had sat under her bed like a secret. At first, she was scared her parents might find it. But she didn't want to get rid of it, either. Technically it wasn't hers. And what would she say if they wanted it back?

Briefly, she'd wondered if they'd pull into her driveway to get it back. She imagined Amanda Hastings's blond hair whipping out behind her like a flag as her BMW roared up the driveway. But that was ridiculous. So she'd held on to it and waited for some kind of sign. Only now here they were at camp, and none of that group had even glanced in her direction. They probably had plenty of other bottles of booze. They'd probably forgotten all about it. As she watched Amanda laughing with the counselors, a wave of embarrassment washed over her. She'd been a dumping ground for evidence. Sully would never come up to her and ask for it back.

The rest of the afternoon dragged by. They worked inside the clubhouse, in the rec hall, spread out in circles prepping crafts for the first day of camp. Emma was in charge of cutting out triangles from white cotton sheets that would later be used as sails for miniature boats. She was halfway through the stack of fabric when Bob Kline came over and handed her another stack. "Nice work, Goodwin," he said as he walked away.

Emma tried not to groan. Her fingers ached. "How many do we need?" she called after him.

"At least a hundred. Maybe two."

She swiveled and found herself staring up at Sully McMahon. He grinned.

Before Emma could think of what to say, he knelt beside her. "Still got that juice?"

"What?" Then she realized what he meant. Emma glanced around the rec room, her eyes landing on Alicia, who was watching them. She nodded, heart thudding beneath her camp T-shirt. "Yeah, I've got it."

"Good. Bring it down to the dock tonight. Say, nine o'clock?"

So he did want it back. She tried to keep her voice even. "My dock or Amanda's?"

"Yours. See you then."

At eight forty-five, Emma slipped into a pair of cutoff shorts. She stood in front of the mirror in her bedroom. What she needed was a white pair, like Amanda's. Maybe not as short. She took care with mascara and lip gloss, even though she knew it would be dark. At the last minute she kicked off her tennis shoes in favor of a pair of strappy sandals.

It wasn't clear if Sully wanted her to meet them at the dock to give the Wild Turkey back, or if it was an invitation to join them. To be fair, she didn't know which scenario she preferred. The thought of being left on the dock as they motored away was unbearable. But the thought of climbing into the boat with them and having to make small talk, and probably drink, was terrifying. Carefully she wrapped the bottle in a beach towel and slid it into her backpack.

The hallway was quiet, the only light coming from a sliver under her parents' door. She'd said good night to them earlier, claiming she had a headache. Her mother had looked at her funny. "It's so early. Are you sure you're feeling okay, honey?"

"Yeah. I just got a little too much sun today."

Per usual, her father barely looked up from his laptop. "Hope you feel better, Emmy-Bean."

She really wished he'd stop using that nickname. But she was glad they didn't press further, and also glad they went to bed early.

It was alarming just how easy it was to fool them, she thought, as she stepped out into the hall. Quietly, she tiptoed down the stairs and through the kitchen. Moments later, she was sliding the patio door closed behind her and racing across the backyard. Easy as spilled milk.

Down on the dock there was a chill in the air coming off the lake. Emma peered into the darkness, her fingers drumming against her backpack straps. Across the water came the thrum of bullfrogs, a familiar cadence that helped slow her breathing.

Ten minutes passed, then another. After a while, she stopped checking her phone. The illuminated screen drew bugs, and already she could feel the sting of mosquito bites on her bare legs. But still she waited.

By nine forty-five the realization that they weren't coming washed over her like fresh embarrassment. Angrily, she slung the backpack up over her shoulder. What had she expected? It wasn't like she was friends with any of these people. Amanda Hastings didn't acknowledge she had a pulse. As for Sully, she was just the girl who had his bottle of booze. But still—why had he invited her?

Maybe Sully McMahon was messing with her. Or maybe he'd planned to come but things fell through. As she turned away from the water and crossed the dock for the stairs, an even worse thought occurred to her. Maybe he'd forgotten.

Tears pricked her eyes. This summer was going to be exactly like all the rest. She was halfway up the hill for home when she heard a sound. Emma froze, listening. Yes, there were voices coming from up the shore.

A minute later, the rumble of a boat motor broke the stillness. Hesitantly, she headed back down the hill. The motor grew louder and the white shape of a boat sliced through the darkness. "There she is." It sounded like Sully.

Emma made her way slowly across the dock to meet it. Let them think she was just arriving. Someone in the boat had their phone on, illuminating a handful of faces. She could make out Amanda behind the wheel, but neither girl greeted the other.

"Emma. Our Turkey delivery girl."

It was Sully. He leaned out over the side.

A flicker of anger rose in her chest. They'd kept her waiting over an hour, and like a fool, she'd stayed. They were probably laughing about it on the way over.

"Here," she said, thrusting the backpack toward him. "Take it."

Sully took the bag from her hand, and she waited for him to unzip it and retrieve the bottle. He could keep the backpack, for all she cared. Instead, he set it down on the floor of the boat. Then he extended his hand. "Come on."

It was a directive more than an invitation. But she reached out.

Sully's grip was warm. He tugged her forward and she stepped down into the boat, landing roughly on the seat beside him. Someone laughed. The engine sputtered and they turned out toward deep water. As they picked up speed, Sully shifted beside her on the bench, and she could feel the warmth of his leg against her own. The boat surged and she fumbled to hang on to the side. Her hair streaming out behind her, Emma threw her head back. She wanted to scream at the stars.

Olivia

The playdate had been a disaster. "We haven't heard a peep from Ruby or her mother since. I invited them to come over, but Helen declined, saying their schedule was '*terribly full*.'"

Olivia slumped against the speech pathologist's overstuffed couch, playing with her engagement ring. Luci was just outside in the waiting room. "I don't know which is worse, keeping Luci home to protect her from this kind of thing or pushing her back out there to socialize."

Alison tapped the eraser tip of her pencil thoughtfully against her chin, considering Olivia's words. "Neither," she said, finally. "It's a matter of finding a balance between the two. You're doing the right thing by giving her these opportunities. That said, the right thing often isn't easy."

"It's downright brutal." What Olivia most appreciated about Alison was the relationship they'd forged since she'd moved to Connecticut. Leaving New York, where Luci had received therapy through the Brooklyn school district as a preschool student, had been hard. Starting over with a new school district, new therapist, and pediatrician had felt daunting. Olivia always came to Alison's office feeling small and inadequate against the world, ripe with anecdotes of their latest challenges, e.g., the playdate. But Alison sent her back out every time, bolstered with strategies and encouragement. Buster was a great therapy dog. But what Olivia really wanted to do was put a leash on Alison and bring her along, too.

"What about the social group I referred you to? How's that going?"

Alison had suggested that small group interactions with children going through similar struggles might best help Luci. The trouble was, there weren't many kids dealing with selective mutism living nearby, especially in the more rural hills of Connecticut. They'd done a similar playgroup in New York, and the ages and diagnoses of the children in the group ranged from Asperger's to autism to general anxiety disorders. Olivia liked the support of other parents also struggling to provide their children with meaningful social experiences, and the empathy that came with that. But the group Alison had suggested she join was an hour away, in the Hartford area, and getting there with any regularity just wasn't easy. "We tried it twice," Olivia told her. "And there were some nice kids in the group. But Hartford is so far. Which is why I thought it'd be good to pursue some relationships here, within the community." She threw up her hands. "I don't know, maybe I should rethink it."

Alison regarded her with sympathy. "You're doing great, Olivia. When Luci starts kindergarten this fall, there will be more consistent opportunities for interaction. She'll see those classmates every day."

Olivia winced. That was true, but it was also part of the problem. Luci would deal with these struggles and setbacks every single day. And at the end of the day, none of the therapists or doctors could possibly understand what it was like for Olivia. It was she who climbed into bed with Luci and rubbed her back as she said a little prayer for a friend on a good night. Or reassured her when Luci cried that she had none on a bad one. It was Olivia who lingered in her child's doorway, watching her little girl sleep, finally free from her worries if only for a few hours. No bedtime story or session of therapy could change that.

"I have some other news. I'm engaged."

Alison brightened. "That's wonderful! How did Luci respond?"

Olivia smiled, allowing her mind to wander back a few days. The morning after Jake proposed, she'd told Luci the news alone. Jake had wanted to be in on the conversation, but Olivia felt that if they really wanted Luci's genuine response, it would be best if she did it.

"All right," he'd agreed. "But when we're a family, we'll be doing these things together, right?" The look in his eyes was not a demanding one. He wanted to be brought into the fold.

To her delight, Luci had shrieked when Olivia told her.

"So we'll live together?"

"That's right. Jake will be here for school days and weekend days. He'll be here when you wake up in the morning, and to tuck you in when you go to bed at night. You, me, Buster, and Jake. We're going to be a family, Lu."

Luci had smiled, the little gap between her front teeth showing in full. "Buster will be so happy!"

After their appointment with Alison, Olivia stopped at the market to pick up some things for dinner.

That night Jake came over after work, and they grilled chicken and squash on the barbecue before taking a long walk with Luci and Buster. After, when Olivia had given Luci her bath and helped her into bed, Jake had climbed the stairs and stood in the doorway with a book tucked under his arm. "May I?" he'd asked, showing them the cover of Paddington Bear. "This was my favorite when I was little."

Olivia looked at him with surprise. Jake often came up to say good night to Luci, but he'd always left them to their story time alone, a gesture she had seen as respectful. The intimacy of this new offer touched her.

And apparently, Luci, too. Instead of looking away when he asked, Luci had scooted over to make room for him. Olivia slipped off the bed as Jake climbed into her spot; then she lingered in the doorway listening as Jake read aloud. His voice was melodic. Luci's eyes were glued to the illustrations, but Olivia couldn't take hers off of Jake. The sight of him propped up against Luci's pink lace pillows, surrounded by stuffed animals, was more than she could bear.

Now, with Luci sound asleep and the peepers singing their nighttime chorus, she and Jake lingered on the back patio in the growing darkness, a bottle of wine between them. Jake looked up at the stars. "There will be other playdates," he reassured her.

"I hope so." Olivia looked for a star to wish on.

"Maybe what you girls need is a break." He smiled. "With some good food and company. And a view."

Olivia leaned over and rested her head on his shoulder. The stars were growing brighter against the darkening sky. "That sounds divine. And where exactly is this magical place?"

"My parents' place. Let's get everyone together on the boat. We'll make a day of it on the lake."

Olivia had heard the stories about Jake's childhood summers growing up on Candlewood Lake. The days spent waterskiing, boating, and jumping off of Chicken Rock. They sounded idyllic, and something she found herself craving each time she listened. But Jake's family was still very much new to her and Luci, and placing Luci in the tight confines of a boat with a big group gave Olivia pause. If she found it to be too much, it wasn't as if she could get off to take a break from all the stimulus.

"I don't know," she said, carefully. "It sounds lovely. But what if Luci gets overwhelmed?" She didn't want to hurt his feelings, but it wasn't as simple as a day out in a boat.

Jake was still learning what worked and what did not. There were times when Olivia thought he understood; when they planned outings together, he was certain to keep the trips short and allow for a stimulus break, so Luci could wander off and have time to herself. Earlier that spring they'd gone on a hike to Kent Falls. The day had been perfect, sunny and blue-skied. Visitors crowded the park tossing Frisbees in the field, picnicking, and climbing the steep wooded steps alongside the waterfall. They could lose themselves among it all. Luci delighted in running around and petting the dogs. She waded in the pools at the base of the falls, watching the other kids splashing one another. And when she needed a break, they could retire to the wooded trails together. It was the perfect kind of outing for her. Now, with this invitation to crowd into a boat in the middle of the lake with all of Jake's family, Olivia fought off her frustration and wondered if she'd overestimated his understanding.

"Do you think it's too much?" he asked.

Olivia shrugged. There was also the matter of not wanting to be burdensome on others. She imagined Jane Goodwin packing an expansive picnic lunch and all the fixings she'd go to the trouble to prepare. There'd be mixed drinks and multiple courses— enough to make a full day of it out on the lake. The last thing Olivia wanted as a soon-to-be daughter-in-law was to be a downer to their outing. And then there was Perry; he was unflappably polite if quirky, but no matter what she did or said, Perry always seemed to be watching her warily. Unlike the others, who were so vibrant in their welcoming, she'd not been able to break through his cool exterior.

"Look, my family understands," Jake reassured her. "And I think it's time we did more together, so that both they and Luci get comfortable around each other. We're going to be a family, right?"

Even in the growing darkness, Jake's brown eyes were bright with hope. He wanted so much to include her in the fold of his family, something she loved deeply about him. He'd only recently returned to New England to settle down, he'd told her when they first met. Never before had he thought he'd come back to sleepy Connecticut to stay, let alone get married. And yet he had, and she was the one he'd chosen.

From the day she'd attended his grandmother's birthday party, it had become clear to her that Jake was the golden boy in his family. All of the Goodwins were startlingly good-looking and bright, but Jake possessed the best qualities of them all. He was sharp like Perry, and yet playful like Phoebe. He was as kind as she'd found his father, Edward, to be in just the few times she'd spent time with him. And as social as Jane, who loved to fill her house and entertain. Since they'd met, Olivia had seen how others were drawn to him, just as she had been. Complete strangers in bars who would be laughing and sharing stories like old friends by the time the evening ended. Beautiful women on the subway, who stole looks across the aisle, despite the fact that he had his arm snug around Olivia's waist. Jake Goodwin was the kind of man who could have his pick. And he'd chosen her and Luci.

"All right," she said, finally. "Let's make it a date on the lake."

Jake leaned over and kissed her. "It will be fun. I'll take good care of you girls," he said. "I promise."

Already, Jake had promised Olivia so much. She tipped her head back, letting her eyes wander across the starry sky. Olivia was the only child of an expat single father and raised in a New York restaurant. Her sense of family consisted of busboys and hostesses and loyal customers. Holidays belonged to the public; her father's job, and later hers, was to host and feed and nourish them. To make their special occasions more so. There had never been cousins to play with, or aunts and uncles to visit; no grandmother to fuss over her. Olivia had never had any of that as a child. And it was all she'd ever wanted for Luci.

Olivia reached over and squeezed Jake's hand, as the wine settled into her limbs. With Jake's family they'd have it all.

Phoebe

Rose Calloway was the bank construction loan officer, and over the course of the seven months the house had been under renovation the two women had had so many phone conversations that Phoebe considered her almost a friend. Almost.

The initial conversations had been endless: the application process, the insurance policies needed (one million dollars for a five-hundred-thousand-dollar house?), the advances, the inspections, the payout schedule. If getting the loan wasn't hard enough, keeping track of the construction loan process was positively mind-boggling. First there was the advance, which initially seemed generous to Phoebe, to get the renovations started. But Phoebe soon learned it would be burned through like fire. Not to worry, Rose assured her; it happened all the time with up-front costs, and she'd get the hang of staying ahead of the budget as building progressed. After that, Rose explained that payouts were determined based on progress inspections. It was up to Phoebe to decide when she wanted to schedule these inspections. When the inspector did come out, he or she would review the progress of the renovation and give percentages of funds according to percentages of work done. Then Phoebe could forward the funds to her contractor to cover costs and dispense them to his subcontractors. There was a good deal of passing large sums of money through hands, and for a girl who loathed math, the management of such funds was daunting. But with Rose's help, Phoebe had gotten it done.

Over the course of those many phone conversations, Phoebe felt like she and Rose had gotten to know each other. During their first call, she learned that Rose had a grandson named Peter who played soccer. During another, when Phoebe lamented the late night she'd spent with two sickly throwing-up toddlers, Rose had clucked her tongue sympathetically into the receiver and said, "Oh, I don't miss those days. But you'll get through it." Commiseration had taken place. A few laughs had been shared. Rose knew that Phoebe was a real person. And surely that would help her to make her case today when she met with Rose to ask for an increase in funding. Besides, Phoebe had always pictured what Rose looked like and was looking forward to seeing how close her imagination had been.

Now, as she sat on the other side of Rose's desk, she realized that her imagination sucked. Rose did not have a soft grand-motherly expression or a sympathetic ear. Phoebe's imagined kinship with the woman vaporized under the harsh bank lighting as soon as Rose opened a file and turned it around to face Phoebe.

"Remember the appraisal report?"

Phoebe did.

Rose pointed to a number at the bottom of a column. "This is what we base your loan amount on. The combination of proposed building improvements with the current value of the building and the value of the land."

She looked at Phoebe. "Have you made any upgrades or additions to the building design?"

Phoebe shook her head.

"And the lot size remains the same."

It was not a question. But Phoebe nodded.

"Then I'm afraid we can't increase the funding allotted since it matches the appraised value of the proposed work to be done." She let out her breath. "If anything, the market has struggled and lakefronts have been slow to recover. This appraisal from over a year ago is higher than what it might evaluate at today. In that case, you're lucky."

"Lucky." Phoebe stared at the chart. What she felt was poor. House poor, to be exact. She fiddled with the collar of her shirt and looked around. Why was it so hot in the bank?

"Well, if we can't increase the amount of the construction loan, there must be something else we can do. Is it possible to advance an advance?"

Rose looked at her levelly. The woman did not look like anyone who'd nursed a sick boy through a night. "As I explained at the beginning of the loan process, advances are based upon percentages of work done." She whisked another file out of the shadowy reach behind her desk. God, there were so many files. This time she ran her finger across a spreadsheet. "See this? This is your total loan balance of the funds paid out thus far. And here is the percentage of work done. If you look carefully, you can see that on your most recent inspection he allowed for one hundred percent release of the siding funds. That includes both materials and labor." She looked up at Phoebe to be sure she understood. "And didn't you just tell me that the siding is only about fifty percent complete?"

Phoebe winced. The siding was only halfway done. And yet they'd blown through all of the funds for it. Which had gone to sill beam and termite repairs. Yes, money had been misallocated. But wasn't that exactly what Rose had also told her in one of their first phone conversations? "I remember you saying that I could allocate funds accordingly. That just because the inspector released funds for siding, for example, it didn't mean I couldn't apply those funds to something else."

Rose nodded. "Correct. How you channel those funds is ultimately up to you, because we recognize that the building process isn't exactly linear. As you've discovered, there are all kinds of unknowns."

Phoebe sat up. "Unknowns! Yes. That is what I've been dealing with." Perhaps Rose understood, after all. This was Phoebe's opening.

"However," Rose interjected, "that doesn't change the end number. When all is said and done, you still have the funds you started with. Maybe you save money on the roofing budget, but maybe the septic goes over. We allow leeway."

"Leeway," Phoebe repeated. She smiled at Rose. Now they were talking.

"But unless something major changes to the plans or property value, we don't loan more money than the value of the project as a whole."

Phoebe felt herself deflate. "So, I can't get more, and I can't get it any sooner."

Rose shook her head. "Unless there is a compelling reason, some sort of crisis." She sat back in her seat. "Is there a crisis?"

The back of Phoebe's neck prickled. Why else would she be sitting here practically begging for a fund increase? "I wouldn't call it a crisis, exactly." Phoebe paused.

"If there is, we should review your books."

Books? The closest thing Phoebe had to books were a Thomas the Tank notepad stuffed with receipts, chicken-scratch numbers, and messy handwritten Post-it notes. All in different-colored ink. If she were to hand over her "books," the bank would see it all: the budgeted line values went way over what the original construction estimate sheet allowed for. Phoebe was in crisis, but the crisis was of her making. And the bank might get nervous and step in. What was that nifty little term she'd glossed over in the loan agreement: right of seizure? Phoebe would lose control of the project. Or worse, lose the house.

She wagged her head. "No crisis. Just a little setback with the unforeseen termite and sill structure issues."

"It happens," Rose allowed. "And I'm sorry to hear you're experiencing it. At this stage, we recommend the homeowner and general contractor discuss and try to adjust the cost estimate sheet accordingly." She paused. "However, if it's something you can't seem to resolve, then you should come back to me. I can call for a review and a site visit from the bank."

Phoebe let out a nervous laugh, one she'd intended to sound carefree but which she realized had come more as a squawk. "Oh, no. No, thank you. There's no need for any kind of review. My contractor has helped me adjust accordingly, and I just wanted to come in today to bring you up to speed. Really, I can't believe how beautiful the house looks." She glanced at the inspection file, which she knew held photo updates of the last inspection. "What'd you think of the siding color?"

Rose did not comment on the color. Instead, she sat back and offered Phoebe a mixed look that could at best be called one of empathetic scrutiny. "New construction is a huge undertaking, and we realize that. What's important now is to try to stay on track with the funds. Itemization is your friend."

Friend? Was Rose offering encouragement, or a warning? It didn't matter. The woman was a vault. A vault of funds completely inaccessible to Phoebe. Phoebe needed to get out of there. She gathered her purse and reached across the desk with what she really hoped was a firm handshake. "Thanks, again. It was nice to catch up."

Outside, Phoebe scurried across the parking lot and into her car. Coming to the bank had been a terrible idea. All she'd managed to do was to confirm her fears: she was running out of money. And now she'd probably given Rose Calloway cause to scrutinize the project from here on out. Phoebe glanced around the car, at the crumpled juice boxes. At the granola bar wrappers fluttering between the seats, the uncapped Crayola markers, and a lone shin guard left by one of the boys. She was half tempted to go back inside and pluck Rose out from behind her desk. Bring her out to the car to itemize *that* shit show.

Instead, she sank back in the driver's seat and closed her eyes. Everything was turning into a mess. Her dream house. Her finances. Maybe even her marriage. She looked at the clock and cursed. She was fucking late to preschool again.

Perry

It was a nice enough day to be out on the lake, he'd allow that, but there were more important things to do. For starters, the lawn. The crew had done a royally shoddy job. Perry strode across the front yard inspecting the borders of the garden beds. Cedar-colored mulch was bunched around the base of his box-woods in large uneven clumps. Perry had asked for black cedar, not this artificially charged orange variety. Worse, much of it was piled right up to the edging, which he had specifically stated he wanted to be well defined. He'd have to get down on his hands and knees and rearrange it.

The front door opened and Amelia popped her head out. "What are you doing? It's almost time to go."

Perry kept working. "I wish someone had asked me about the timing of this family boating excursion," he said. "One o'clock is right in the middle of the day."

"Exactly," she replied. "Which is prime for swimming. And fun," she added. She waited until he stood up and brushed his knees off, which they both noticed at the same time were now stained orange.

Perry sighed and followed her inside. Didn't anyone do their job well anymore?

Amelia handed him a wet paper towel and returned her attention to the cooler she was packing. He could see a good bottle of rosé sticking out the top. "Where's Emma?" he asked, as he scrubbed at his knees.

"Upstairs. In her room."

"Still? But why?"

Amelia shrugged and went to the fridge for a wedge of cheese. "She's a teenager. That's what teenagers do."

"I didn't do that. She's spending a lot of time up there lately."

"You worry too much," Amelia said.

Perry supposed his wife was right. She was probably just tired from her long days working at the Club camp. Perry loved that she had a summer job there. He loved most of all the wholesomeness of it all: working outdoors teaching small children to swim and kayak. It was the best part of living in their private gated community, and it made all those years of holding his breath on the membership waiting list worth it.

Getting into the Candlewood Cove Clubhouse had not been easy. It was an exclusive Club that catered not only to those living primarily in the community but also to members who had something *to offer*. Members included bankers and artists, philanthropists and writers. Some of them were legacy members, whose families had long established their place since its inception. In the early 1930s the Club had been a bit of a social enclave of New Yorkers seeking respite and privacy away from the hustle of the city. To this day, the membership was capped at one hundred families, and spaces did not open up with any regularity. Gaining membership required an application, sponsorship by current members, and an interview of the entire family. When he was growing up, Perry's family had known members and had always socialized on the outskirts of the Club, but as much as he loved his parents, they weren't membership material. Jane was too out-spoken, too liberal. Edward was not impressed with the trappings of those who already belonged. But Jake had been the most per-plexed. "Why on earth would you want to waste your money to blow smoke up all those conservative butts?" Perry had not both-ered to explain why. If Jake didn't understand now, he never would.

When Perry and Amelia had finally been admitted, it was an arrival of sorts. The fruition of a dream Perry had harbored since childhood. And today, on the rare occasion he was home, was the perfect day to spend in peace and quiet at the Club. But instead Jake had insisted the whole family go boating on the lake.

This struck Perry as highly amusing since Jake was the only member of the family who did not technically live on the lake or own a boat. Even Phoebe's *shack* was on the water. "So kind of Jake to invite us out on our own lake and to use our own boat with him today," he mused out loud.

"Oh, stop. It'll be nice to be out with the whole family."

Perry had to give his wife credit. Amelia had grown up as an only child and found his vocal and intrusive family both enter-taining and comforting. Perry knew what the day held in store: everyone would argue about where to go and what to do. And once they got to wherever they finally agreed to go, they'd tie the boats together and the kids would hop between the two like forest monkeys, in and out, littering the clean carpeted floor with peanut butter and jelly and juice boxes and whatever other sticky snacks Phoebe allowed her boys to eat. Everyone would talk at once, right over the top of one another. There'd be at least one debate, one spill of something that stained, and at least one howling cry for Band-Aids. Perry cringed just imagining what awaited him.

At least the weather was good. Perry put on his sunglasses, and they taxied out into the shoals to meet the rest of the family. The joke among lakegoers was that it was better to have friends who had boats than to own one yourself. But Perry had grown up in a boating family. When he was growing up on the lake, his parents had owned a motorboat, and all three of the Goodwin kids had learned to water-ski at an early age. It was a rite of passage at thirteen to take the Candlewood Lake water safety course and get your boater's license. Of the three of them, Jake had been the most eager. Phoebe was lazy; she loved the idea of going out on the water with friends, but she didn't like the hassle of the work involved. They could always tell when she'd been the one to use the boat last because the cover was never replaced correctly or the ties were done too loosely. Eventually her social life got the best of her, and she resorted to asking Perry to drive her and her friends around while they sunbathed and gossiped and sipped Bud Light from pilfered cans. For Jake, the boat was one endless summer party. Once out on the water, he'd be gone all day. But he always returned the boat with care, tying it neatly to the dock, snapping the covers tight and never leaving a trace of the fun Perry knew he'd enjoyed out there. The eleven-mile-long lake ran along several town borders, and Jake seemed to know just about everyone from the tip of Sherman's shallow waters to New Fairfield, Brookfield, and beyond.

Perry marveled that just about each teenage boater they passed waved and called out for his sibling. When it was just Perry alone on the water and a boat full of teenage girls drew up alongside him, he couldn't help but feel offended by the disappointed expressions on the girls' faces as soon as they realized it was him, and not Jake, at the helm. Perry recalled the time a group of Phoebe's friends had gone out in the boat with him. Jake was at the wheel, but Perry didn't mind; cute Tricia Schneider in her peach bikini had seated herself next to him. Jake was doing all the talking, pointing out the sights and waving to passersby like he owned the lake. At one point Tricia put her hand on Perry's knee and leaned in close to whisper in his ear. Perry had blushed, eager to hear what she had to say. "Your brother is so funny," she'd gushed. "Is he dating anyone?"

Jake, whom Perry hadn't even realized was listening, had turned around from his position at the wheel and winked at her. "You tell me."

Well, now Perry was the one out on the lake with his beautiful wife and daughter, in their beautiful boat.

"How long are we going to be out here, anyway?" Emma shouted over the whir of the motor. Immediately Perry deflated.

"Long enough to have fun," he said, trying to sound convincing.

In the distance, Perry spotted his parents' pontoon boat creeping along the shoreline. Amelia leaned forward from where she was sitting on the bench and squeezed his elbow. In spite of himself, Perry smiled. Maybe today wouldn't be so bad, after all.

When they pulled up alongside the pontoon, the first thing he noticed was Olivia's crimson bathing suit.

This pained him. Perry was a heterosexual man who'd appreciated the physical nature of female beauty since adolescence. It was science. But Perry had never taken that as license to ogle women. Especially as a devoted husband. Besides, one thing he'd learned in his adult life was that it was fleeting. The most obviously alluring face on a crowded sidewalk could be made ugly by a curt eye roll at the homeless man in the doorway. Just as he now appreciated a different kind of beauty; a loveliness in the hand that guided a shy child into a classroom, or in the doting look of an old man gazing at his wife on the train. As Perry aged, his perception of beauty had altered.

He could hardly blame Olivia's swimsuit, a faded, modest one-piece that suggested little. And yet there was the round swell of her small breasts. Just above which her wide brown eyes seemed to smile, even from a distance. Perry looked away from her smile. He busied himself with the tying up of his boat to theirs, in the passing of coolers and picnic baskets. He did not redirect the kids as they scrambled into his pristine new boat. Nor did he open a beer and clink bottles with Jake and his father and Rob, who looked like he really needed his. *Focus*, he chastised himself, as he climbed onto the pontoon with the rest of his family.

"How's the house going?" Perry asked Rob.

"What's going are the sill beams." He took a deep swig of beer. "Every rotten one of them."

Phoebe wasted no time in chiming in. "Which, as it turns out, is quite common in older houses."

Perry didn't dare comment on the "old" part. The old house was already theirs. Along with its old sill.

"Yikes. What's that going to cost you?" Amelia asked.

Perry shot her a look.

"What?" she said. "We're family."

"Indeed, we are," Rob said. "And getting closer every day. Did you hear we may move in with your folks?" He held up his beer as if toasting, but his expression said otherwise.

Perry's gaze swiveled to his mother. "They're moving in with you and Nana?" Jane, who was holding a mimosa, tipped it back like a spring break tequila shot and feigned interest in a distant shorebird.

"Since it's going to take a few more weeks than we thought. And about ten thousand more dollars," Rob added.

Phoebe looked wounded. "Eight," she interjected. "Only eight.

And no one is moving anywhere just yet. It's merely a backup plan." She slumped against the bench.

"Do you guys need help moving stuff into Mom and Dad's?" Jake asked. Leave it to Jake to keep things moving in the wrong direction.

No one replied.

"What about Nana?" Perry asked. He had a startling vision of toys scattered underfoot and his nephews thundering up and down the hall at the crack of dawn as she tried to sleep. Of the noise, the mess, the extra mouths to feed for his parents. What was Phoebe thinking?

Jane snapped back to attention. "We'll ask the visiting nurse to increase her hours. It's only temporary."

"*If* we move in," Phoebe stressed. "It's not like it's decided."

Perry bit his tongue. They would, he was sure. He pictured the whole thing unfolding. Although maybe it wasn't all bad; if Phoebe ferried her family and all their belongings in, maybe it would be the natural time to ferry Grandma Elsie out to a nice, quiet assisted-living facility that was better suited to her needs, and where she could be cared for 24-7. He was about to suggest as much when he couldn't help but notice that his mother was pouring herself yet another mimosa. At least she wasn't lighting up.

Amelia must've noticed it, too. She glanced at him. "Who's hungry?" she asked. This they agreed on: when in doubt, stuff everyone's mouths with food. Less talk, less opportunity for insult.

Lunch was a feast. Jane had made her signature chicken curry wraps. Amelia had brought a homemade hummus that Perry did not particularly like but ate because he figured it was good for him. Phoebe held up a plastic grocery bag. "Sorry, everyone. Our kitchen was demolished, so I picked up a few things from the store." She plunked the bag unceremoniously on the table, leaving whatever was inside a mystery. Amelia, to her credit, unpacked it. "Oh, how nice. Cookies and cupcakes."

Sugar, Perry thought. Just what all the kids on the crowded boat needed.

Amelia reached into the bottom of the bag and pulled out a soggy box. "And popsicles!"

Melted, thought Perry.

He excused himself and went to gather the kids for lunch.

Emma was leaning over the railing with Olivia, chatting away. He wondered what on earth Olivia could have said that had pulled his daughter out of her funk. Whatever it was, he was grateful, but he had to look away because there was the matter of her crimson bathing suit. He needed a beer.

"Food is out," he said.

Olivia brightened. "Oh good. I brought something."

Before he could answer, she retrieved a large food basket from under one of the seats and carried it over to the table. The family gathered like vultures as she unpacked its contents. She'd brought far more than just something.

"Olivia, did you make all this yourself?" Jane exclaimed.

"She sure did," Jake said. He was beaming. "She got up early this morning to get it all done."

There was a chilled bean salad tossed with a tart vinaigrette. Toasted ham and cheese crostini. A glass container filled with neat rows of endive and herbed cheese. And a tart lemon cake sliced into small squares with powdered sugar. Phoebe snagged one. "Oh my God, this is heaven. What's in it? A pound of butter?"

Olivia bit her lip. "Maybe."

"I have to stop," Phoebe said. She took another and went to check on the boys. A moment later, she was back for more.

Perry had not been hungry at all, but he found himself drawn to the spread. For once the Goodwin clan went silent, sampling all of what Olivia had brought, licking their fingers. Perry tried the ham and Gruyère crostini, and found he was starving. He filled his plate with two more.

"My girl can cook," Jake said, looking around with pleasure.

"You're going to be fat," Phoebe told him. "I can't wait."

Everyone chuckled, even Rob. Lulled by the rocking boat and the good food and the warm sun, Perry felt the family begin to relax.

Sated, he stood and stretched. "Anyone want to swim?" he asked. But to his dismay, the adults all shook their heads.

The children, however, were all in. Phoebe's boys were fearless, flinging themselves into the water from every height the pontoon boat could offer. Perry noted with astonishment at how untroubled Phoebe and Rob seemed to be by it. They sat on the far end of the boat, drinks in hand, as if they had not a care in the world. His expression must've said as much.

"What?" Phoebe snapped, glancing over at him. "The boys have life vests on."

Perry shrugged. "I know. But they can't actually swim, can they?"

"Oh, Perry. Here we go." She got up and stalked off in the boys' direction. "I'll go be a better mother."

"That's not what I meant," Perry said.

Jake, who was the only one still eating, set down his plate and peeled his shirt off. "Let me take a turn watching the kids. I could really use a cooling off, anyway."

And just like that, suddenly everyone wanted to swim. "Good idea," Edward agreed. "It's gotten warm, all of a sudden."

Even Amelia stood and removed her cover-up. "Want to swim?"

Perry shook his head. He had wanted to. Five minutes ago, when he'd asked them all.

Jake positioned himself at the edge of the railing and swung one leg over. "Don't try this at home, kids."

Perry could practically feel the intake of breath on the boat as he rose with barely a wobble and balanced on the narrow rail. "Look out below!" he yelled, and then he executed the perfect backflip.

Perry's eyes went straight to Olivia. When Jake shot back up to the surface, she let out a whoop and everyone clapped. The rest of them jumped like lemmings. His father, Rob. Even Amelia leapt off the back of the boat. Perry had never known Amelia to jump off of anything.

Perry went to sit with Emma, who seemed engrossed in texting. He wanted to ask whom it was with. "Having fun?" he asked instead.

"I guess."

Below them, the boys splashed about in the water with Jake, taking turns wrapping their arms around his neck.

Phoebe shouted down at them, "Careful! You're going to drown your uncle."

"Livi!" Jake called. "Come rescue me." Perry had not heard his brother refer to her as such. To him, Olivia seemed more fitting.

But she didn't seem to mind. "You're on your own," she shouted back.

"City girl!" Jake taunted her.

That was all it took. Olivia turned and grabbed Luci's hand. "Come on, love. Let's show these boys." But Luci shook her head.

Perry tried to avert his gaze as Olivia undid the button on her jean shorts and they slipped to the boat floor. But when she bent and tossed him her cutoffs, he couldn't help but blush.

"Would you please set those on my bag so they don't get splashed?" She flashed him a dizzying smile. Perry coughed.

In no time, Jake had organized a diving competition. Because that was the kind of thing Jake did. Even Emma stopped texting to take a video of everyone playing in the water.

Refreshed and dripping wet, Amelia climbed up the ladder and wrapped herself in a towel. "See who's having a good time?" Amelia said, gesturing toward Emma. "I don't know why you worry so much about her."

Emma had abandoned her phone and was in line for the diving contest. Perry grinned as she cannonballed off the edge. He realized that only he and Luci remained.

Olivia climbed up the ladder and waved. "Lu Lu! Want a turn?"

Timidly, Luci peered down into the water.

"Oh, come on," Olivia coaxed. "Show the boys your stuff."

From below came Jake's call. "What's going on up there? The judges are getting tired of treading water." He'd said it jokingly, but Perry thought he saw a flash of consternation cross Olivia's brow.

"Just a minute," she said, climbing up onto the deck. "She's coming."

But Luci didn't go to her mother. Instead she turned and looked at Perry. Unsure of what to do, he waved. Luci returned the gesture shyly.

Perry leaned forward from his seat. "Can I tell you a secret? Emma used to be afraid to jump," he told her. "And you know what I did? I said I'd jump, too, if she went with me."

Luci glanced over at her mother, then back at Perry.

"What do you think?" Olivia asked. She was smiling encouragingly, but her question came out as more of a plea.

Perry felt something inside him shift. Suddenly, it mattered to him very deeply that Luci answer her mother. That she join in the group, and not hold back, afraid.

"I bet you'd have the best dive," Perry said, softly. "What do you think?"

"Okay." Luci's voice was so soft, the single word so small, that at first Perry wasn't sure he'd heard right. Had she really spoken, or had he just wished it?

But the look on Olivia's face said otherwise. "That's my girl!"

Luci pointed to the water.

"Want me to go first?" Olivia asked.

The child nodded.

Olivia turned to Perry. "Okay, will you stand with her?"

"Of course." He glanced down the boat. Amelia and Phoebe were lounging on the seats, chatting away with Rob and his parents. No one had any idea what they were missing.

Olivia stood at the edge of the boat and waved down to Jake. "Here I come!" she called. Then, to Luci, "I'll wait for you. You go next."

With that, she thrust herself off the edge of the boat and tucked. Perry watched her slip gracefully into the water with barely a ripple.

"Wow," he said.

Luci stood beside him, very close, watching her mother surface.

"Your turn, *ma chérie!*"

Perry looked at the little girl. Her braids were soaked from splashing like two little rat tails. Her thick eyebrows were knit in concern. She was such an odd little creature.

"You can do it," he said.

Suddenly, Luci slipped her small hand into his. She squeezed it. The force was no more than a mosquito bite, but Perry felt it go straight to his chest. He squeezed back. And then she let go and disappeared off the side of the boat. There was a splash. A whoop. Olivia held her arms out and Luci was in them.

Perry found himself gripping the railing of the boat like a drunk.

Below came the joyous burst of laughter and splashing. The sun prickled in the late-day sky. Perry turned away, just in time.

Emma

Alicia was mad at her. Again. "What do you mean you *went out* with them?"

"Hang on, and I'll tell you." Emma was at the crafts table helping one of her campers assemble a dream catcher. The little boy was having trouble with the yarn.

"I can't cut it," he complained.

"It's okay," Emma said, taking the length of yarn from him. "I'll help you."

Alicia stared impatiently across the table. "Like, you went out out? At night?"

Emma nodded. "Here, I'll hold the yarn tight, and you cut it. That's right. In the middle." She held the yarn between her two hands and smiled at the boy, trying to ignore Alicia's outraged expression.

"But I thought you hated them."

This got the little boy's attention. "Hated who?" he asked.

"Keep going," Emma said, redirecting him. She helped him write his name in marker on a piece of masking tape and affix it to the dream catcher. The end result was loosely tied and slightly crooked, but as far as she was concerned that's what made it camp-perfect. "Your mom will love this," she told him, and he beamed.

Alicia waited until the first grader galloped off after his friends before resuming her interrogation. "So what happened? Tell me everything."

That was the thing. Emma didn't really feel like telling Alicia much. It was the double-edged sword of being best friends for so many years. Like a favorite pair of jeans you'd had forever: they were comfortable. Every rip and fray told a story. And on a bad day when nothing else looked right on you, you knew you could tug them on and feel pretty damn good about yourself. But the fact was, they could also be outgrown.

Emma didn't like to think of herself as outgrowing Alicia. They'd been best friends for as long as she could remember, and for good reason. But since high school had started, Emma felt restless. She liked her friend, but sometimes she longed for new ones. Alicia liked to make fun of the more popular kids, dissecting the gossip they heard after a weekend party or mocking the way those kids strutted down the hall.

"Did you hear how much Courtney Jacobsen drank at the keg party? I heard she was literally licking the walls." She and Alicia would criticize their clothes, their predictable inner circle squabbles, their smug expressions. "They're such jerks," Alicia would say, and Emma would laugh or nod in agreement. Emma used to find it funny, but lately it only highlighted for her how much on the outskirts they were socially. Emma watched the popular group sitting together in the cafeteria and wondered what it would feel like to casually set her lunch tray down, laying claim to her seat at that table. Deep down, Alicia probably wondered the same. And now Emma had had a taste of what it was like to sit at that table. If only for a little bit.

"It wasn't a big deal," Emma said now, as she scooped up remnants of yarn and collected glue bottles. "They wanted their Wild Turkey back. When I gave it to them, they sort of invited me out."

Alicia stared at her wide-eyed. "Which one invited you?"

This was where Emma had trouble hiding her smile.

"No. It was *him*?" Alicia's expression darted across the rec room and landed on Sully, who was playing Ping-Pong with two little girls.

There was no denying it.

Alicia narrowed her eyes. "Spill."

It was still so hard to believe. As soon as she'd climbed into the boat, Emma had felt a rush. Like she'd gotten away with something. But that feeling had quickly faded, replaced by dread. Almost immediately the bottle of Wild Turkey was opened and passed around. Amanda Hastings was driving the boat, and going so fast that it lurched against the water, jostling them about and against one another. At first it seemed funny, but after slamming her knee against the side so that she still had a bruise two days later, it was less so. When the bottle was handed to her, Emma was so busy trying to hold on that she didn't even have time to think. She took a deep swallow, and instantly regretted it. The spicy bourbon slid down her throat like liquid heat, making her choke.

Sully leaned over. "You okay?"

She'd wiped her mouth on her sleeve and nodded. He clapped her on the back, and laughed. "You're funny."

The next time someone passed the bottle, she took a deeper sip. After that, an easy warmth spread through her limbs. It took the edge off, made the rocking boat less worrisome. She was able to sit back and listen to the others.

There was Dewey, Chris Dews, who was a junior like Amanda. He was on the lacrosse team with Sully, and known to be a smartass. And Kyle Tiller, another junior, who was dating the third girl in the boat, Courtney Jacobs. Courtney sat next to Amanda at the wheel, the two talking and laughing between themselves, as Amanda steered them around the lake. "What do you guys think? Chicken Rock?"

Emma knew Chicken Rock. She'd jumped off it the summer before with Alicia, something her father did not and could not ever find out about. It was a well-known rock on Candlewood. Boaters pulled in as close as they could and swam the rest of the way in to the base. There was a rope swing about midway up, off a ledge that jutted out into the water. That was child's play, frequented by plenty of kids and their parents. The highest point above it was Chicken Rock.

"Yeah," Kyle shouted over the roar of the boat. "Let's do it."

"In the dark?" Emma asked. But no one answered.

They drew up to the base of the rocks, and Amanda cut the engine. "Are we putting down anchor?"

"I'm staying," Amanda said. "You guys go ahead."

Dewey tugged his shirt off and pounded his chest. Emma could see the pale flash of skin in the darkness. If Amanda was staying put, that meant Courtney probably was, too. Emma glanced around, unsure of what to do. The thrill she'd felt coursing through her moments earlier had chilled, and suddenly she wondered what she was doing here.

"Aren't you jumping?" Kyle asked the other two girls.

"Too cold," Courtney said. She lifted a can of beer to her lips, and Emma wondered where it had come from. Nobody had offered her one.

"Well, I am." Beside her, Sully stood up and took his shirt off, too. There was a general bustle as flip-flops were kicked off and the guys crowded around the bow.

Emma remained frozen in place, feeling more invisible than she had before. The initial buzz from the liquor was now making her feel a little dizzy. Nobody seemed to care if she was going or staying.

The boys took turns leaping into the water, whooping and hollering. The boat rocked violently in the wake of their sudden exodus. And then it was quiet again.

Emma hugged her knees to her chest.

"Did you hear what happened to Jacklyn?" Courtney asked, suddenly.

Amanda was staring off in the distance, watching the boys. She lit a cigarette and inhaled sharply. "No." She didn't seem interested, but Courtney went on anyway.

Emma feigned interest in the dark shoreline, her eyes fixed on imaginary objects. The boys must've reached the rocks by now. She pictured them scrambling up the ledge.

"Her parents found out she went to Glen Robinson's kegger, and they grounded her for two weeks. Can you believe that? Now she's going to miss my birthday party."

Amanda exhaled. "That sucks."

Emma wondered at Amanda's coolness. Was Amanda annoyed that she'd tagged along?

"Glen had a kegger?" she asked. The two turned sharply as if noticing her for the first time, and Emma bit her lip in the darkness, instantly regretting it.

"Last week," Courtney said. Then, turning her attention back to Amanda, "Are we still going to the mall tomorrow? My mom took away my credit card."

Emma sank back against the side of the boat, wondering how long the boys would be. And if they were sober enough to jump off and safely swim back. This whole thing was stupid. Suddenly she wanted to get off the boat and away from Courtney and Amanda's trivial conversation.

"So, you're friends with Alicia?"

Emma looked up. The only thing she could see was the orange glow of Amanda's cigarette tip.

"Yeah," she said, cautiously.

"You know her older brother?"

"Sure." Emma had known Chet all her life. He was three years older, and was kind of like her own big brother, only better. He'd be the first to tease her, but also the first to stick up for her if someone else bugged her on the school bus. When they were kids, Chet and his friends used to play hockey on the frozen expanse of Candlewood Lake, and Alicia and Emma would skate crooked loops around them, begging to be included. The only bone she ever broke was in fourth grade during one of those games. Chet had picked her up and carried her all the way up the steep lakeside hill, across the street and straight to her front door, where her frantic mother took one look at her purple wrist and drove her straight to the hospital. Last year Chet had graduated and gone off to Colgate, so she didn't see much of him. Now he was home for the summer, working at the beach as a lifeguard. The one time she'd seen him, Emma had been surprised by how much older and sophisticated he seemed. God, she hoped college did the same thing for her.

"Is he single?" Amanda asked her now.

So that's why she was even speaking to Emma.

Alicia had mentioned something about a college girlfriend, but that was back at Christmas. "I don't know. I mean, I can find out for you," she added. She wondered if that sounded too eager.

Courtney was staring at her with mild interest.

"You ever hook up with him?" Amanda was so direct. Emma couldn't tell if she was messing with her or just trying to glean more information.

"Sort of. Once." It was a big fat lie. The closest contact Emma had had with Chet was when he pulled her into a headlock and gave her a noogie. She was the kid friend of his kid sister. But Amanda didn't know that.

"Seriously? Like were you two a thing?" Now Courtney was paying attention.

Emma pictured Alicia's face if she could only hear her now. She'd be pissed, because not only was Emma outright lying, but she was using her brother to do it. Not cool.

"It was no big thing," she added quickly, trying to sound casual. "He's more of a friend now."

Courtney shrugged, her gaze already sliding away in the direction of the boys, but Emma could feel Amanda staring right through her. She wondered if she believed a word of it.

From the shoreline in the distance there was the clamor of voices, and the girls turned their attention back to Chicken Rock. "Hey, Amanda! Dewey wants you to hold his junk for him while he jumps." It sounded like Kyle.

Both girls laughed, and Amanda shouted back, "Don't be a pussy, Dewey!"

Emma rolled her eyes, grateful for the dark. Why did some girls feel like they had to resort to that kind of lingo around guys?

There was a peal of laughter, followed by three loud splashes. Moments later their voices drew closer. The boys climbed up the ladder, all three amped from the jump. Amanda started the engine and the boat roared to life. "Turn on the music!" Dewey shouted. He held up a six-pack, and everyone reached out.

Emma sat still, watching Sully out of the corner of her eye. He tugged his shirt down over his wet chest and flopped down next to her again. "Too chicken?" he asked.

"What? No. I didn't feel like it tonight." She'd jumped before.

Though certainly not at night. And certainly not while drinking. "Next time."

He pressed a cold can of beer into her hands. "Here's to next time," he said.

For the rest of the night they drove around, music blaring, until the beer was gone and the Wild Turkey bottle was empty. Emma found her head starting to flood with a strange warmth. Was she getting another buzz? Whatever it was, she kind of liked it. She felt her insides uncoil. Even though the night had started as balmy, it was cooler out on the water and the temperature had dropped with the late hour. She didn't realize she'd begun to shiver in the wind until Sully passed her his towel. It wasn't exactly dry, but she didn't object when he draped it across her shoulders. When she was sure no one was looking, she held a corner of it to her nose and inhaled. It smelled like sunscreen and pine, and she smiled to herself in the darkness. She was pretty sure if she pressed her nose to Sully's neck it would smell the same.

When they finally dropped her off at her dock, Emma's head was swimming with alcohol and fatigue. And something more. "Thanks," she said, as she stepped off the boat and tried to balance herself.

Dewey laughed. "Whoa, better get your land legs, Emily."

"Emma," she corrected him. And then she laughed. Because she was drunk and feeling bold. She was sick of being a dormouse. "My name is *Emma*."

Dewey stood and saluted. "Okay, *Emma*."

She braved a glance at Sully to find that he was watching her. "Next time," he said.

The nose of the boat turned away. Emma waved. To her shock Amanda Hastings lifted a hand. "See ya." It felt like some kind of permission had been granted.

Giggling, Emma stumbled all the way up the hill, her heart pounding. *This was maybe the best night of my life.* The patio door was unlocked, *thank God*, and it slid silently across its tracks. On the stairs, she tripped and fell hard, banging her shin. But no one came out of her parents' room, and no lights went on.

The last thing she remembered was falling onto her bed, and the way her hair smelled as it spilled across her pillow. Like cigarette smoke and lake water. And something else.

Like freedom, she thought, right before she passed out.

Phoebe

Hemorrhage was such an ugly word. It implied blood. Internal workings. Spillage of the gravest kind. The mention of it made Phoebe nauseated. But she had to admit it, there was no other way to describe what was happening to their renovation budget.

The sill work had gone better than planned. Dave was able to get a beam delivered and had the crew working on it the very next day. The jacking up of the house, which could have resulted in other issues altogether, thankfully went seamlessly: there were no cracks or mishaps. Phoebe had stopped by that first morning with the boys and stood at the edge of the lawn watching with grave interest as the house was lifted clean off its foundation and several feet into the air.

"We're going very slowly, an inch at a time," Dave said. "We don't want anything to shift suddenly, or we risk cracks."

Phoebe could barely watch. It was discombobulating, seeing the cavern of light fill the space between house and ground.

"It's like watching surgery," she mused. "The house looks so vulnerable, just hanging in the air like that. All its insides exposed."

Dave shook his head, laughed.

"What?" she asked.

"Can't say I've ever worked with anyone like you before."

"How do you mean?"

He regarded her curiously. "This house. It means so much to you."

"I would think most of your clients feel that way about their houses."

"You speak of it like it's a person."

Phoebe shrugged. "I wouldn't go that far. But it's seen a lot of history, this old place. Surely it has a soul."

Dave didn't say anything.

Normally, Phoebe cared a lot about what Dave thought. Thus far his guidance had been invaluable, and she trusted his expertise. But right now she didn't care if Dave thought she was crazy. She gathered the boys and loaded them into the car. As she backed out of the driveway, she glanced uneasily at the space of lake visible between the stone foundation and the base of the house.

Later that day, when the sill repair was complete and the house was eventually lowered back into place, Phoebe received a text. It was from Dave.

"All buttoned up. The old girl recovered nicely."

As Dave had assured her, it had all gone well. The following termite treatment was nothing to worry about; they'd tent, spray, and air everything out. But the costs were still a punch in the gut. The previous disbursement she'd had from the bank had been earmarked for kitchen work and replacement windows. The windows were done, and the electric started, but none of the kitchen renovation had even begun. She had about fifteen thousand left over, but the remaining work for the next phase of the renovations required thirty-two. Phoebe had kept Rob apprised of the incoming issues and subsequent costs, but she hadn't exactly spelled out the fact that they'd leached into other expense allotments. They at least had personal savings left over from her job, but they had agreed not to dip into it except for emergencies. Did this qualify as an emergency?

At night, in bed beside her husband, Phoebe could feel the burgeoning space between them, not unlike the house being lifted from its foundation. Rob was entrenched with the new marketing campaign his firm was trying to secure, staying late at the office and working into the night at home. And Phoebe was equally rooted in the renovation. It didn't leave much energy for family time. Couple time was an outright joke.

But even though they'd agreed she would take the helm with the renovation, it was time to loop him in. She needed his input and as much as he wouldn't like it, he needed to know what was going on.

She decided to tell him that night after dinner. But the interruptions were endless. For starters, his cell kept ringing. It was his partner, Chris, from work. Then her mother called to ask, again, if they wanted to move in for a while. "All that dust! It can't be good for you and the kids to breathe."

"Mom, I appreciate all of what you're saying. But I don't think it's necessary. Besides, you've got your hands full getting ready for the engagement party."

Jane clicked her tongue on the other end of the line. She didn't like being dismissed. "Still."

"So far much of the work has been external or in the basement. Plus, the weather is great. The house aired out all day." It was true—construction was messy and loud, and it got tiring having crews in and around all the time. Sometimes Phoebe had to scoop the boys up and leave for whole parts of the day, just to get away and also *out of the way*. "I admit it's not ideal, but we're managing." In truth, they were. But just barely. The renovation they'd planned on was much less intensive than the one they were actually now doing. But Phoebe wasn't too worried; she'd heard that was common. Once the workers were on-site and the equipment was there, why not go ahead and tackle refinishing the floors? Why wait to upgrade the plumbing? Better (and cheaper!) to do it now.

Her mother was not buying it. "Well, when it gets to the kitchen I don't think you're going to have much choice. Try going without a sink, stove, or fridge with kids. Impossible! Better to plan ahead and move the boys now before things get out of hand." Phoebe's mother had her there.

But as inconvenient and messy as the construction had been so far, it was also exhausting to even think about packing up and moving. Already, most of their belongings had been tossed into storage. Knowing they'd be renovating, she and Rob had rented a unit—which turned into two—so they wouldn't fill up the house with too much stuff until the work was complete. As it was, she was driving to the storage unit almost as often as she was to building supply stores, to fetch one thing or another. Pots and pans. More of Rob's business suits. The container of beach gear for the boys.

When she hung up with Jane, she was so drained the last thing she wanted to do was cook, clean up, and then start on the budget with Rob. Her head positively throbbed. But Rob was home early, for once, and working at the dining room table on his laptop. Phoebe popped two Advil and pulled taco ingredients from the fridge. "Honey, I was hoping we could talk about budget stuff," she began. Then she dumped a package of ground beef into the fry pan.

Rob looked up. "Tacos? Again?"

Phoebe ignored this. The kitchen cupboards had just been ripped out and the stove stood alone against one bare wall. It was the only one-pan, low-mess meal she knew the kids would eat and she had the energy for.

"Can I update you on the renovation budget, please?"

"Not now," he replied. "Wasn't exactly a good day at work." Phoebe glanced at her husband's slumped posture at the table. He was surrounded by boxes of toys that were in a constant state of being repacked and moved from room to room, as they cleared spaces for the workers. Rob looked like the house: unkempt and beat down. She felt bad for him, trying to work in such conditions and being under pressure at his job. But it hadn't exactly been a great week here at the house, either.

"We can talk after dinner," she allowed. What was the difference?

At dinner the boys were loud and chatty, per usual, seemingly oblivious to their parents' tension. Phoebe was at least grateful for that. She waited until they'd finished and gone back upstairs to play.

"You know, I think we may be getting over what we allotted for."

Rob was pushing the tacos around on his plate, not really eating. As he explained over dinner, the presentation at work hadn't gone so well, and the clients were holding out for a new approach.

"Honey?" she asked, when he didn't reply.

Rob blinked. "What?"

"I was talking about the budget." She regarded him softly, noting the deep recesses under his eyes.

"What about it?"

"Well, the sill work put us back, as you know. But we'd already dipped into the excess funds for the kitchen."

Rob had set his fork down with a clatter. "Phoebe. I can't do this right now. Is there something specific you need to tell me, or is this something you can perhaps figure out with Dave and loop me in on tomorrow? Because I have twelve hours to redo this entire pitch, and I haven't a damn idea how to start."

It was completely unlike him. Phoebe lost her cool all the time. But not Rob. "Forget it," she said, standing up. "You're right. I'll figure it out with Dave." She began gathering the kids' plates.

Rob reached over and put his hand on her arm. "I'm sorry. I didn't mean to snap."

Phoebe stilled. "I know. The timing isn't good."

Rob ran a hand roughly through his hair. "Well, it never really is. So, what is it you need to tell me?"

Phoebe waffled. Rob deserved to know the truth. Besides, it would be worse if she told him later. Just rip off the Band-Aid, she thought.

"Dave called yesterday." She paused. There was a loud thud overhead.

Rob didn't seem to notice. "And?"

From upstairs there was a yelp by one of the boys. Followed by a beat of silence. Phoebe and Rob looked up at the ceiling in unison. Either the boys would return to their play, or someone would begin to howl.

"Mom-*eee*!" It was Jed.

Phoebe groaned. "I've got it," she said, heading for the stairs.

Patrick met her at the landing with a guilty look. "What happened?" she barked. What she really wanted to do was scream. Their timing was without fail.

Jed appeared on the steps behind his brother, holding out his hand. "He twisted my fingers. They're broke."

Patrick scowled. "He took my truck!"

"Broke!" Jed sobbed, waving his hand in the air.

"Time-out." Phoebe pointed Patrick to the bottom step and scooped up Jed. "They're not *broken*, baby," she said, trying to soothe him. "Let's get you some ice." By that point both boys were crying.

Rob didn't even look up when she carried blubbering Jed through the dining room and into the kitchen. He was back on his laptop, his dinner plate shoved aside like their unfinished conversation. "Have you seen my charger?" he called after her.

Ignoring that, she set Jed on the counter, which only set off more howling, and rummaged through the freezer. "Hang on, buddy, I'm looking for the Boo Boo Bunny." But there was no sign of the blue rabbit ice pack. Just as she reached for a bag of frozen peas, the overhead lights flickered. Then the house went dark.

"Fuck." Rob stood up from the dining room table, his face twisting in the blue glow of his laptop light. "I just started a new spreadsheet. If this thing surges . . ." He yanked the cord from the wall. "I'm calling Dave," he said.

Phoebe froze in the dark kitchen. "No, let me."

If Rob called Dave, Dave would have to tell him that Phoebe had paused the electrician's work that very afternoon. Because there wasn't any money left in the current bank installment. And that the electrical subcontractors wouldn't be coming back until there was.

The lights blinked on, then off. And then, to her overwhelming relief, back on. Rob stood in the doorway, holding his laptop as if it were kryptonite. "Never mind," he said. "You call Dave. I've got to get out of here."

Still holding the frozen bag of peas, Phoebe swept Jed onto her hip and followed him out to the front door. "What do you mean? Where?"

Rob snatched his briefcase from the foyer, blew the construction dust off the top. "It's too much, Phoebe. This whole thing has gotten away from us."

"In just a few more months it should be done."

Rob spun around. "And how many more issues will be revealed by then? What's next: asbestos? An electrical fire?"

Phoebe kept her mouth shut. It was not her fault the house was old. Rob had been there for the inspections. He'd signed the same papers she had.

He bent down and pecked Jed on the head. "Feel better, buddy." Then to Patrick, scowling from his seat in time-out, "You owe your brother an apology." To her, he said, "I'm going over to your parents' place to finish up this presentation. I can't work in these conditions."

"But they're getting set up for Jake and Olivia's engagement party. It'll be a madhouse over there."

"It can't be worse than here." He turned on his heel.

"Rob, wait." She trailed him through the door and out onto the lawn, where he stalked across the patchy grass, navigating the piles of lumber, his posture slumped with defeat. She halted unsteadily at the end of the walkway, her toe catching on the crooked edge of fieldstone walkway.

"You know, this isn't easy for me, either," she called after Rob.

He didn't even turn around. "But it's your dream, Phoebe."

She watched irritably as he got in the car and reversed out, her eyes fixed on the taillights as he headed down the driveway.

Jed fussed in her arms. The frozen bag of peas she still clutched was causing her hand to go numb. Behind her, from inside her dream house, the lights flickered again. Phoebe went back inside and slammed the door.

Olivia

"Please, can I go, Mommy?" Luci pressed her lips against her mother's ears. They were cold and wet with lake water, and Olivia giggled and pulled away.

"I don't know, honey. That's a fast boat. Why don't you wait until later and we can go together?"

"But I want to go for a boat ride."

Olivia sighed. She'd just sat down and kicked her sandals off. Amelia and Jane had invited her to join them, and Jane was emptying the remains of a lovely bottle of Riesling into their glasses. The engagement party had ended moments ago, and the last guest was still making his way across the lawn to his car. The remaining family was gathered around the patio table loose with social fatigue, drinks, and sun. Only the kids seemed to have enough energy left to play down by the water. Jane had done a swell job.

"Nothing too fussy," her future mother-in-law had promised from the beginning. "Just us and some good food." And to Olivia's delight, she'd kept to her word.

Initially, Perry had offered Jake and Olivia his clubhouse, with its vaulted ceilings and exposed beams, its sweeping views of the water. Olivia had liked the idea, at first, but Jake hadn't. "Too stuffy," he'd said. "Not my thing."

When Perry pressed further, expounding on the catering staff and the ballroom, where weddings were held, Olivia understood. They had no desire for white linen and crystal goblets. They wanted to gather the people they were closest to. "We're going for more of a rustic vibe," Olivia had explained, after thanking Perry for the offer.

"There's an antler chandelier in the ballroom," Perry said. "The clubhouse is rustic."

"But the members are not," Jake joked. "Thanks, Perry. But we want to keep it simple."

Perry had looked dejected. "Well, maybe for the wedding," he'd mumbled.

In the end, a luncheon at the Goodwins' lake house was perfect. Jane and Edward had hosted a small clambake on the patio by the water. Jane set up one long farm table overlooking the dock and dressed it with a traditional French tapestry tablecloth which doubled as a gift to the couple, something that touched Olivia deeply. It was covered with vases of fresh-cut hydrangeas, arranged simply in silver pitchers. For lunch there were grilled littlenecks with beer and butter, corn on the cob, barbecued steaks, and salmon. An old red canoe filled with ice held bottles of wine, champagne, and cans of Jake's favorite IPA. There was a dessert table with tart lemonade and airy orange zest meringues topped with whipped cream and mint leaves.

Marge and Ben were invited, along with neighbors, and some of Jake's colleagues from the Audubon Nature Center. Childhood friends popped in with their own young families or partners. Olivia was introduced to so many people her head spun, and that was before she'd even had a glass of champagne.

Exhausted by the festivities, she wanted nothing more than to take a nap in the hammock over by the cedar trees. But Luci had other ideas. She wagged her head. "Pleeeeease! Emma is here. I want to go on the boat."

Olivia glanced across the yard at Emma, who was making her way toward them. Jake adored her and was always going on to Olivia about what a bookworm she was, what a levelheaded kid. Luci had taken quite a shine to her. There were several times Olivia could almost feel Luci start to say something to Emma, so much so that she saw the words forming on her daughter's lips. And then Luci would catch herself, and say nothing. It was something she'd not done with anyone new, and Olivia wanted to encourage it. Spending more time with Emma could be good for her.

"You haven't been out on that boat before," Olivia reminded her. By then Emma had reached them. She held up a purple life vest.

"I think this one will fit her," Emma said. "That is, if you're okay with her going."

Olivia smiled. "You're reading my mind. But still . . ."

Luci pressed her lips against Olivia's ear insistently. "Please."

Behind Emma, Jake hollered from the dock, "You want to come, too, baby?"

Olivia did. But not at that moment. She was having her first ever real conversation with Amelia and Jane, and she really wanted to get to know them better. The shade was nice and cool. And the glass of wine was perfectly crisp.

"Jake is an excellent boater," Jane said. "You don't have to worry." She tipped her face toward the sun, contentedly. "The lake is in his blood."

In that moment, Olivia felt her earth shift on its axis. She wanted that contented air Jane Goodwin possessed. Her family surrounding her. A beautiful home on the lake. And the knowledge that everyone who mattered to her was right here, right now.

"Okay," Olivia said to them all. "Luci can go." Then, "Be careful!"

Luci pressed her lips to her mother's and giggled. Then she darted off with Emma, hand in hand down to the dock. Olivia watched as Jake helped Luci into the boat, then checked her purple life vest. She breathed a sigh of relief.

"We're all set!" he called up to her.

The engine purred, and Olivia stood to wave goodbye. "Be careful!" she called back. "You've got . . ."

"I know," Jake said, finishing her sentence. "Precious cargo." As if on cue, Luci turned and waved goodbye.

Olivia watched them back slowly away from the dock, then turn out toward open water. Her stomach rose to her throat as the boat grew distant and Luci's purple life vest grew faint. She would have to get used to this. They were going to live here. They were going to be lake people, like the Goodwins.

When she sat back down, Olivia pushed her sunglasses higher up on the bridge of her nose and sipped the last of her wine.

Jane turned to her. "See? You look like you were born here."

Olivia's insides fluttered. From across the table Amelia smiled in agreement, and poured them each another glass of wine.

Perry

Jake wanted to take Perry's boat out. His glorious still-new Chris-Craft 230 Sport Deck. That Perry himself had taken out only four times since purchasing it. It was parked at the northern point of his parents' dock like a promise of summer, and all through the party Perry had been approached by so many guests who'd admired it and inquired about it that he'd barely had time to tip back a juicy clam, let alone finish his meal.

"Come on. Let's let her stretch her legs," Jake said. Boat talk for heading out into open water.

Perry had imagined this moment with his little brother for a long time. Years, perhaps. Jake wanted what he had.

It wasn't that Perry wanted to show off. Well, maybe, just a little. It was that he wanted a moment on the water with his family that was *his*. All his life he'd driven Phoebe and her friends around, towed Jake as he water-skied with reckless abandon, listened to his father comment on his brother's athletic prowess. How his little brother owned the lake. How, as his mother said, the lake was in his blood. Now Perry was the one with the house and the powerboat on the water. He had a beautiful family, a successful career. It was his turn to take a spin on the lake and take them all with him in *his* boat. That was his plan for the afternoon.

But now, lounging on the patio, his Wayfarer sunglasses hiding the weary expression in his eyes, Perry could not bring himself to stand up and leave. He was overcome by the lavish late-day sun and too engrossed listening to Olivia talk with his wife and mother. About growing up in the restaurant in New York. About her temperamental and fiercely loving father, and the food he made for the people he loved. About what it felt like to sculpt: to stand before a cold earthen square of clay and set the palms of your hands against it, letting the clay choose its form. The lilt of Olivia's voice was an intoxicating accompaniment to the sun on his skin and the wine in his veins. Perry was entranced. Immobilized. And deeply ashamed.

When Jake had found him on the patio and asked if he could take Emma and Luci out on the water, Perry's impulse had been to stand up and shout, "No! I will take them. I will take all of you." But the thing was, Perry was already taken. Down a path he'd had no intention of treading and yet could not deviate from. As long as Olivia Cossette kept talking, he was helpless to stop listening.

"Here." Before he could second-guess himself, he handed Jake the keys. "Be careful."

As he stretched his limbs and listened to the women talk, he thought, *I should really try to follow my own advice.*

Emma

She had always wanted a younger sibling, but given the choice, she'd have picked a sister in a heartbeat. Luci looked nothing like her. Her eyes were dark and curious, just like her mother's. And Luci did not speak. At least not out loud. But as far as Emma was concerned, Luci spoke plenty with her eyes and her toothy grin. With her squeals of delight as she leaned over the boat and pointed. At the blue heron standing on one leg in the shallows of the shore. At the massive four-story Adirondack-style timber house on the hillside that Uncle Jake called Paul Bunyan's mansion. At the water-skiers and tubers skipping across the lake's choppy surface. Because of the good weekend weather there was a lot of traffic out there, and Jake had to concentrate.

Emma was still fiercely hungover from the night before. Bleary-eyed, really. She'd kept her sunglasses on all day so that her parents wouldn't notice. She had not wanted to get out of bed and come on this family outing. She was tired and likely even still drunk from the night before with Sully and Kyle and Amanda and Courtney. But she was glad she'd rallied.

Luci pointed to Jake. "What?" Emma asked, softly. "Do you want to drive the boat?"

The little girl shook her head.

"Do you want to help Jake?"

Luci nodded. Emma wished Olivia were here to see that. She knew it would make her eyes water with hope.

"Hey, Uncle Jake!" she called. He turned, a big smile on his face. That was the thing with her uncle: he was always so happy. Sometimes it was hard to believe he was related to her father. "Can Luci come sit with you and help steer?"

Jake slowed the boat to a standstill. Tentatively, across the rocking boat, Luci made her way over to him. "Come on, Lu," he said, petting his lap. Emma smiled as Luci climbed onto him behind the wheel.

"Hang on," she said, grabbing his phone from where he'd set it down on the seat. "Let me take a picture." She'd have to show Olivia later.

Emma watched Uncle Jake hold Luci on his lap. Pointing out all the sights along the shore. A natural, Emma thought. Luci didn't have a father, but he would make an excellent one. She couldn't wait for Jake and Olivia to get married.

"Hey, Em. I'm thirsty. Toss me a beer, will you?"

Emma reached for the cooler. She was also hot and thirsty, desperate for a bottle of water or an iced tea. But the only thing left in there was beer. She handed her uncle one, relishing the feel of the cold can in her hand. The label was neat, two bright green and blue lizards. Double IPA. She wondered what it tasted like.

She glanced at Jake, whose back was to her. He was always so cool, but she doubted he'd be cool with her having one. Even though the stories about him at her age suggested otherwise. Still. It was so hot out. And her throat was so dry. He wouldn't mind that much, would he?

Ahead of them was a pontoon boat full of people. As they pulled alongside it, several pointed at them and waved.

"Gorgeous boat," an older gentleman called out.

As Jake thanked him and waved back, Emma slipped her hand into the icy depth of the cooler and grabbed two cans. Quickly, she stuffed them in her beach bag by her feet. It was almost too easy.

The sun beat down and her mouth watered. "Let's drive along the shore," Jake called back to her.

Emma tried to keep her voice even. "Sounds good."

As he steered them along the shore, she pulled her beach bag onto her lap and reached inside. Quickly, she popped open one of the cans and took a big gulp. The beer was strong, but cold. With her eyes on Jake and Luci's backs, she tipped the can to her lips and guzzled the rest of it, careful to tuck the can back into her beach bag. A few moments later, she reached for the other one.

As they motored along the shoreline, Emma leaned back against the bench and let the wind tousle her hair. It wasn't so long ago that she was riding the bus home on the last day of school, feeling like she had nothing to look forward to. She closed her eyes. *Summer is looking pretty damn good, after all*, she thought.

Olivia

When the emergency room doors slid ajar, the first thing she noticed was the arctic blast of cold air. It smacked her in the face, stilling the urgent heat that had coursed through her skin since the call from the paramedics had come through.

Olivia had no recollection of sprinting across the Goodwins' yard for her car. She would never recall the drive in, or how she got there ahead of the others. What she would forever remember about that moment was the initial surge of hot panic turning to ice as she stumbled into the lobby of the emergency room. How everything swerved to a sudden frozen halt.

The receptionist looked up. "May I help you?"

"I'm looking for my daughter, Luci Cossette. And my fiancé, Jake Goodwin. They just arrived in an ambulance?"

The receptionist glanced around her desk at paperwork, then checked her desktop monitor. Finally, she typed something into her computer.

"From where?"

"Lenox."

"You are the girl's mother?"

Olivia nodded hastily.

"You need to go to the registration desk." The woman pointed around the corner, to another counter.

Olivia exhaled. The only thing she *needed* was to find her child. "But my daughter just came in by ambulance," she managed, her mouth so dry she could barely articulate the words. Was this what Luci felt like when she couldn't talk? "Can you at least tell me how she is?"

The receptionist regarded Olivia coolly. "Yes, which is why you need to go around to registration first. Do you have your child's insurance card?"

"Her name is Luci, and I just want to know if she's okay."

"I can look up her information after you register."

Olivia grasped the edge of the counter, as if holding on for life. "I will give you whatever information you need. Please, just tell me where my baby is."

The receptionist pointed around the corner. "If you would just head over to registration with the insurance cards, we can complete the process."

"Here!" Olivia flung her purse onto the counter and dumped it upside down. The contents spilled out, a shimmering array of money and pens and small bits of paper. Coins clattered to the floor. She thrust her wallet at the woman and screamed, "Take it all. Just tell me where she is!"

The receptionist rolled her chair back. "I think we need security."

At that moment, Perry materialized at Olivia's elbow. "Excuse me," he said. "My name is Perry Goodwin; my daughter Emma Goodwin was also just brought in on the same ambulance. We are all here together." His voice was calm, decisive. He took Olivia's wallet from her and extracted her insurance card, which he handed to the woman. Then he wrapped one arm around Olivia and directed her away from the counter. "Come sit."

Amelia was already seated in the waiting room, along with Jane and Edward, who were wringing their hands, and pacing, respectively. When had they all gotten here? Amelia patted the empty seat beside her sympathetically. A security guard rounded the corner, and Olivia sat.

Perry returned to the counter and continued addressing the receptionist. Olivia could feel the woman's eyes on her, but she could not make out what Perry was saying, between the roaring in her ears and the crackle of the security guard's walkie-talkie.

"It's okay," Amelia was whispering. "We're going to find out where they are." She seemed calm, but Olivia couldn't help but notice the whites of Amelia's knuckles where she gripped the edge of her own chair.

Olivia put her face in her hands. There was no one to call. Her sweet Jake was somewhere behind the closed doors with Luci and Emma. Her father, Pierre, was far away in Europe. There was no one else, except Ben and Marge. But she couldn't even remember where her phone was. Had she left it on the deck back at the Goodwins' house? An image of spilled cups and half-eaten plates of food left on the deserted patio table came to mind. She pictured stray beach towels and overturned chairs littering the plush lawn. Like a scene from a movie after a mass exodus.

Someone put a hand on her shoulder and she jumped. It was Perry. "We can go now." Amelia also rose, and the two flanked her like bookends as they moved down the hall to a large set of doors. A bell chimed, there was a swoosh, and the double doors to the emergency department swung open. Olivia allowed herself to be propelled inside.

A nurse in pink scrubs met them. "Goodwin family?"

"Goodwin and Cossette," Perry said.

She checked her clipboard. "This way," she said. "Room seven for Cossette, and room nine for Goodwin."

They followed the nurse around a maze of cubicles where doctors and orderlies lingered and laughed, where computer monitors flickered, as if it were any other afternoon in any other office. Why wasn't anybody hurrying? This was an *emergency* room.

But then Olivia's eyes landed on a doorway. "Number seven," Perry said. "That's Luci."

Olivia broke away from them. "Luci?" she called.

There was no reply. She tugged aside the blue curtain. There, in the bed, beneath an oversized blanket was Luci. She was sitting up, conscious and eyes wide.

A sob rose up in Olivia's throat. "Thank God."

At the sight of her mother, Luci burst into tears, and Olivia raced to her bedside. It was then she noticed the brace on Luci's left arm. "What happened?"

When she touched it, a small squawk rose in Luci's throat.

Olivia sank gingerly onto the bed beside her and cupped her small face. "It's okay, baby. Mommy's here."

Where were the doctors?

Gently but urgently, she examined Luci with her eyes and hands. Every finger, every toe, no different than the day she was born. "Does anything else hurt? Can you show me?"

A nurse sailed into the room. "Are you Mom?" Both her voice and smile were bright, reassuring, unlike that awful receptionist. Olivia felt her insides loosen.

"Yes!" Olivia said. Then, "Her arm? What happened to it?"

"Our girl is so brave!" the nurse said, adjusting Luci's blanket and checking her vitals. "Her vitals are all good—oxygen and pulse are both normal, no temperature. But we do have a boo-boo on her arm." She looked sympathetically at Luci. "The paramedics splinted it on the ride here, and the doctor has been in. She'd like to order some images. So, we are headed to X-ray."

"Is it broken?" Olivia asked.

"We don't know for sure, but given the swelling and bruising we want to check." She lowered her voice, turning to Olivia. "We haven't been able to get her to answer any questions. Apparently, the man who came in with her said she doesn't talk?"

Jake. At the mention of him, Olivia felt her eyes well. He'd seen to taking care of Luci, after all. "That's my fiancé. How is he?"

"That I don't know, but I can find out for you. I'm going to check with radiology about this X-ray, so we can get Luci going, and then I'll come find you. Okay?"

None of this was okay, but Olivia nodded gratefully. Right now this nurse was her lifeline.

Olivia turned back to Luci, forcing a smile. "Everything is going to be all right," she told her. But her mind spun, images of Jake and Emma fluttering through it. Now that Luci was accounted for, she needed to find out about the others.

Luci pointed with her good hand at the doorway. Olivia turned, expecting to see the nurse again. But it was Perry.

"How is she?"

Olivia rose to meet him in the doorway. "She seems all right, except for her left arm. They need to X-ray it. What about Emma?"

"We haven't been able to see her yet. She's still in radiology. Amelia is over there now, trying to learn more."

"Did they give you any information? Anything at all?"

"That she is conscious and alert, which is good. But that she appears to have a head injury." His voiced wavered. "We'll know more with the images."

Olivia glanced back at Luci through the curtains, and lowered her voice. "What about Jake?"

Perry's eyes were as wide and blue as his brother's. Had she ever realized that before?

"Perry?" she asked again, dread rising in her throat. "What do you know?"

"Jake is in the OR," he said, softly.

"What? Why?" Again, her heart sounded against her ribs. Luci was okay. But for the first time since giving birth, Olivia realized that it was not just Luci and her father around which her world revolved. Jake was part of that world now, too.

She stepped out of the dim light of the examination room and into the buzz of activity in the hallway. Perry followed. "Tell me what you know," she demanded. "All of it."

Perry told her. About the compound fracture in his right leg. About the blood loss from that injury. And the gash across his head. Unlike the two girls, who were found on the floor of the boat after the accident, Jake had been discovered at the edge of the shore. They believed he'd been ejected from the boat upon impact with the dock.

So, the boat had hit a dock. Olivia felt her knees buckle. She waved Perry's hand away when he reached to steady her. "Go on," she told him.

When he finished, Perry watched Olivia like one watches an injured animal.

He did not attempt to console her, or even put an arm around her. He did not tell her everything was going to be okay. "All right," she said, finally. She would not stand here in the hallway and cry. It wouldn't change a damn thing if she did, except to scare Luci. She took a deep breath. "Thank you."

"I'll come back as soon as I know more," he promised. "I'm sorry."

The engagement ring on her finger flashed under the fluorescent hospital lighting as she twisted it to and fro.

But Perry didn't go. She could feel him standing behind her as she hesitated in the doorway and tried to collect herself. Olivia parted the curtains and sat down in the chair beside her daughter's bed. Finally, there was the fall of receding footsteps.

Gently, Olivia took Luci's good hand in her own. It was so warm and small.

"Baby, can you tell me what happened in the boat?"

Luci winced. She leaned back into the pillows and shook her head. Beneath the blanket one foot began to jig. Then the other. It was what she did when overcome with anxiety, something she used to do when she was younger and less able to articulate. Olivia hated to see its return.

"It's okay, Lu Lu. Everyone is going to be all right. Mommy just needs to know what happened on the boat. Can you tell me?"

Luci looked away, her feet kicking faster beneath the sheets.

"Okay," Olivia said. "It's all right. We don't have to talk about this now if you don't want to. How about I get you a drink?"

She fumbled with a paper cup at the sink and filled it. When she turned back to Luci, she knew it was too late. The blank look on her daughter's face was one Olivia knew well. Luci was shutting down, retreating to that faraway place deep within her. Where she went to feel safe. Where even her mother could not seem to reach her.

Phoebe

Phoebe stood in the middle of Perry and Amelia's kitchen, her arms hanging uselessly at her sides. She'd offered to go back and get things for Emma, a mission that had at first felt extremely necessary and helpful, but Phoebe now realized was a knee-jerk reaction when there was absolutely nothing anyone could do but wait.

None of them had any idea what had happened out on the lake. The perfectly peaceful day had turned to chaos as soon as their cell phones began ringing. Edward had acted first, placing a call to his friend, Clayton Bennett, the head of the Candlewood Lake Authority, to try to get more information. Jane fluttered around the yard like a downed bird, laying her hands on everyone as if it could somehow help: first Amelia, who had screamed for Emma, then Olivia, who had simply gone white and silent. "Come," Jane said, pulling both women away from the water's edge and guiding them like frightened animals up the grassy slope of the yard. "Let's get our things and get in the car." At which Olivia sprang to life and sprinted for her own car, despite everyone's suggestion she wait and *let someone else drive you*! Perry, the most composed, had driven the others.

Thank goodness Rob had shepherded the boys home, herding

them wordlessly out of the water, across the yard, and into the car, trying not to alarm them. "Where is everyone going?" Patrick asked, his little face filling with concern.

"The picnic is over," Rob told the boys calmly. "Time to go home." Phoebe had shadowed him, helping her husband collect the toys and swim bags, the shoes and socks and clothes. Both afraid to look at each other too closely, and neither saying what they both were thinking: Thank God they stayed behind. It could have been them.

It certainly could have been. Jake had asked them to come. Phoebe had been sitting on the edge of the dock with Patrick, helping him cast his little red Mickey Mouse fishing rod. Rob and Jed weren't far off, wading at the edge of the shoreline with a toy boat. The day was uncomfortably hot, and the boys were pink-faced and sticky. How she would've loved to accept Jake's invitation and get out on the water. How heavenly the lake breeze would have felt out there. But when she really thought about it, along came the exhausting reality of taking toddlers out on the boat. The thought of reapplying sunscreen, wrestling both boys into life vests, then inevitably having to take at least someone to the potty was too much. Once on the boat, the boys would not have wanted to sit still. She and Rob would have needed to wrangle them onto their laps and hang on tightly while the boat was in motion. They'd have wanted to go tubing, which would require either her or Rob to put a swimsuit on and go, too.

She'd decided right then and there that there was no lake breeze refreshing enough to convince her to sign up for that amount of drudgery. So, when Jake jogged over and asked Rob, "Want to come out with us?" Phoebe had barked an answer for the both of them.

"Nope! Thanks, anyway." She ignored Rob's pointed look, not

knowing if he'd really wanted to go or whether he'd simply wanted a chance to answer for himself. Saying no had been the right thing to do if she were to get through the rest of the day with a scrap of patience or good humor. Sometimes parenthood was simply about survival.

Now, as she climbed the stairs in Perry's house, she pushed the selfish relief for her good fortune out of her mind. She was here for Emma.

At the end of the hall she surveyed the scene in Emma's bedroom through the doorway. The room was bright and neat, and smelled faintly of shampoo, as if her niece had just showered and walked out the door. There were a few T-shirts tossed on the plush carpet by the closet mirror, probably fashion discards tossed in haste, which made Phoebe smile. She stepped inside. On Emma's dresser were photos, mostly of the family. In one silver-framed picture was Emma in a white dress for her first Communion. There was one of their pet cat, and a dated elementary school class picture—Emma's cheeks still rounded out with baby fat. Phoebe squinted at the placard at the bottom: Mrs. Ainsley's fourth grade. And of course, the most recent Goodwin family photo, all of them squished together on Jane and Edward's dock, everyone having donned their requisite red holiday scarf. It was the insisted-upon family Christmas photo that Jane arranged each year, and all of them grumbled about assembling for with just as much dutifulness. Someone was always sick, and someone always forgot. Yet year after year Phoebe's mother managed to wrangle all of her children and her children's children and spouses for the annual trek down to the dock in their Christmas reds. With the same inevitable result: as soon as it was over, there would be relief that the picture was finally taken (this year in a mere eight tries, unlike the year before, when it took twenty, thanks to Patrick), then Jane would point out that since everyone was there and it was getting dark, why not "stick around, order some pizza?" And suddenly it was a family dinner. Phoebe set the photo down and smiled ruefully. Her mother was a master.

As she looked around Emma's room, it occurred to Phoebe that there were no recent pictures of any high school friends, something she noticed in abundance in other people's houses where teenagers resided. Her friend Anna Beth had two teenage girls, and their rooms were plastered with photos of themselves and what they referred to as their "squads." Sports photos. School dance photos. Photos of them all at the lake. Teenage girls seemed compelled to capture every mundane moment, leaving Phoebe wondering how on earth she would've survived such relentless exposure had she been a teenager in the cell phone age. Now she scanned the bare surfaces and walls of Emma's room, with the unsettling realization: there was not a piece of evidence of Emma having a social life.

Since there was still no word from the hospital, she grabbed a backpack from the closet door and she gathered things she imagined both Amelia and Emma would want: a fresh set of clothes, fuzzy socks. She found pajamas in the bottom drawer. In the attached bathroom, Phoebe found deodorant and face lotion. She plucked a purple toothbrush from its holder. On her way back through the room she halted at the sight of Emma's bed. There, squeezed between Emma's pillow and the wall, Phoebe recognized the old stuffed rabbit.

"Cedric!" she said, aloud. It was Emma's childhood "lovey," the one she'd dragged around since she was a baby. The very same Cedric who once upon a time inspired phone calls that sent the whole family into panic on any given holiday, when Perry would call them shortly after leaving to report Cedric's sudden absence.

Back then, Phoebe had made note and tucked away this important information, pledging that when *she* eventually had her own babies, she would sharply monitor the whereabouts of their lovies and never have to make such calls or rustle the family into such manic searches. A pledge she sheepishly realized, once she did have her own babies, had been made in vain. Now Phoebe grabbed the stuffed bunny off the bed and held him to her chest.

She could not imagine what was going on over at the hospital. Her own boys were back home. They were safe with their dad, probably slipping beneath the plastic construction tarps that hung everywhere, probably trying to touch the numerous cords and tools and building supplies that Dave and the crew neatly removed to the corners of the rooms each time the workday ended, but that were like a magnetic field to little boys nonetheless. All this time Phoebe had felt guilty for the disruption of the house renovation to their lives: the dust, the debris. For all the mishaps she'd not only stumbled into, but leapt into. And all the bad news that she'd kept from her husband, so as to spare him the stress and the worry. She'd become consumed by the house renovation—completely, stubbornly consumed.

Phoebe kissed Cedric between his worn ears and swiped at a stray tear. Then she stuffed the bunny into the backpack, hurried downstairs and out of the house into the bright sun. What a goddamned fool she'd been.

Perry

Amelia was beside herself. Of course, he didn't blame her. He should've been, too. But since his wife was hysterical, someone had to maintain calm and rationality for Emma.

Emma, who had been returned to them and was now sitting up in bed. His beautiful girl looked to him like she had been badly beaten in some kind of fight club. Perry could barely bring himself to look at the misshapen purple contours of his daughter's face. Her right eye was so swollen it was closed shut. Her nose, though miraculously not broken, was the color of an overripe plum.

When they'd finally been allowed to see her, Amelia had let out a yelp so primal Perry had had to take her out into the hall, where she sobbed into his shoulder. Perry would have liked to sob, too. But so far not a single tear had presented itself, and he began to wonder if he were in shock. What he was sure of was his growing anger. Perry pictured it bloodred and working its way through his veins like a brush fire. Though, as of yet, there was no clear target for it.

As they waited for the doctor to return, Perry squeezed his wife's hand. She did not respond. Amelia had not been able to respond to anyone except Emma. And so far Emma had not done anything aside from open her one good eye and hold the side of her head in her hand as if cradling a broken egg. Speaking seemed to cause her headache to worsen, so they had agreed to let her rest for now. This decision made perfect sense to Perry, and yet it was almost impossible to abide by: it forced him to bite back the questions burning the tip of his tongue. *What the hell happened out there?*

To Perry's relief, the doctor, a middle-aged man with a trim silver beard, rejoined them.

"All right, folks. Both her X-rays and CT scans are clear, and there is no evidence of any internal bleeding. What evidence we do have points to a decent concussion."

Decent? Perry thought. As opposed to what? As an analyst he liked hard numbers.

A whimper of relief escaped Amelia's pursed lips. "You're certain?"

"Well, there is never certainty when someone has been involved in an accident with multiple contusions, like Emma's. So we try to measure symptoms and compare them with imaging results. For example, she is complaining of head pain. Which is normal, given the nature of her injury. And there is demonstration of light sensitivity and nausea. Also normal for someone who's experienced a head injury." He pulled a sheaf of papers off a clipboard and passed them to Amelia, who started rifling through them like she was going to be tested on their contents at any moment.

"Are there any further tests you recommend?" Perry asked. As much as he wanted to whisk Emma home, he did not want to step one foot out of the hospital until all bases had been covered. They were not necessarily out of the woods, he knew. Potential for future risks must therefore be managed.

The doctor considered the question. "There are always more tests we can run. For example, an MRI. But at this stage I don't think that's warranted. Despite the relatively low exposure to radiation and the low risks associated, we still want to balance those possible downsides with the reasonability of ordering such tests." He turned to Amelia, who was still devouring the packet he'd shared. "Unless, of course, either of you feels strongly about running them."

Perry liked this doctor. He seemed balanced in his approach. And Perry found comfort in balance. It gave him a sense of control, despite the looming evidence to the contrary: none of them had any control at all. Not over what happened today on the lake, and not over what might come as a result. He glanced up at the wall clock. Jake was still in the OR. It had been almost two hours.

"So, what happens next?" Amelia asked, finally setting the papers aside.

"Emma's pain level remains high, and her dizziness and other symptoms quite pronounced. And though rare, there is a chance some internal bleeding could develop in the next few hours. As a precaution, I think it makes sense to admit Emma for the time being and continue to monitor her."

Amelia's face crumpled, but she did not cry. Perry shook the doctor's hand. "Thank you." The relief he felt was palpable. The doctor went on to say that they'd move Emma upstairs into a private room once they admitted her. A nurse would be in shortly with that paperwork.

After kissing Emma's forehead with the lightest brush of his lips, Perry went out to the waiting room to update his parents. Jane was blanched with worry, her tennis tan faded under the harsh waiting room lights. "What did they say?" she asked, leaping to her feet the second she saw him.

"They're going to keep Emma overnight, just as a precaution. We're lucky. It seems she just has a concussion."

"How is she feeling?" Edward wanted to know. "Is she in much pain?"

Perry realized that they had not yet seen their granddaughter, and he wished there were some way to steel them for it. "She has some contusions, and she's nursing quite a headache. But she'll be glad to see you once they get her settled in a room."

"Let us know as soon as they do, son." Edward excused himself for coffee.

"What about Jake?" Perry asked Jane. "Any updates?"

His mother sat, placing her hands in her lap. Perry had never seen her look so small. She had so many loved ones in the emergency room, he couldn't imagine what it was like for his parents to be out here waiting all that time. "The orthopedic surgeon came out, ten minutes ago. He said they are finishing up his surgery, and he thought it went really well. But they did have to do a blood transfusion." She looked up at Perry with watery eyes. "He has a compound fracture," she said, her voice breaking. "You know how active your brother is. I don't know what this will mean for him."

Perry sat down and wrapped an arm around his mother.

"And poor Olivia," Jane went on, reaching into her purse for a tissue. "She's got her fiancé in one room and her little girl with a broken arm in another. I just can't imagine."

"So Luci's arm is broken?"

Jane dabbed at her eyes, nodding. "What I want to know is what happened out there. I just don't understand it. There was no other boat involved, from what Dad learned from the lake authority."

The brush fire in Perry's chest surged, once more.

Behind them, the ER doors slid open. "Perry," his mother said. When Perry turned around, Amelia was standing in the doorway, motioning for him.

Amelia waved over his shoulder at Jane and Edward, as though everything was okay. But Perry could tell it wasn't. The doors slid closed behind them. "Is Emma okay?" he asked, a bloom of fresh worry burgeoning.

Amelia thrust a paper at him. "The doctor just came back with this report."

Perry blinked. Had they found bleeding? "And?"

"The lab work," Amelia sputtered.

Perry stared at the report, but the codes and numbers blurred.

"They ran blood alcohol tests," she said.

Perry prickled. "Why would they do that? I don't understand. She's just a kid." Then his confusion gave way to understanding. "You mean for Jake." Again, the angry surge in his chest.

Amelia jabbed her finger to the last line on the sheet. "Look at the results, Perry."

Perry stared at the bottom line. "It says point-one-two." He looked up at Amelia. "Jake was intoxicated?"

"Not Jake. Emma." Her eyes flashed. "Perry, our child was drunk."

Olivia

Aside from the Goodwins, she was all alone. Since her mother passed away when she was just five years old, it had always been just Pierre and her. And the restaurant. Which supplied them with a colorful if changing flow of people in and out of their lives over the years. But all through her life, whether she was at her highest or lowest, a winner of an art grant or suddenly single and pregnant in the city, there was one person she turned to: her father. And now, with Pierre away in Europe for the summer, Olivia felt the depth of her aloneness set in.

Luci's arm was broken; she had a fractured radius in the forearm. Olivia had gone with her for the X-rays, during which Luci was stoic and calm. Alarmingly calm, Olivia thought. The good news was that it was a clean break, common in children, the doctor assured her. "Children's bones are still growing. They heal much faster than us adults."

When Luci had been told she could choose her cast color, Olivia asked the nurse to recite the color choices like a menu. When they got to pink, Luci put her good thumb up. In the end they did a beautiful job, and Luci was a trouper. But looking at the plaster cast on her five-year-old's arm, Olivia had never hated anything like she hated the color pink in that moment.

Worn out by the events of the day, Luci drifted off as soon as she was back in her hospital bed. Olivia watched her little girl, imagining all the scary things that must've run through her five-year-old head. The boat had collided with a dock hard enough to send Jake out of the watercraft. How long had Luci and Emma waited for help to arrive? Did they ever fear Jake was dead? And what had Luci thought of the rescuers descending on the accident scene?

Her child had ridden in an ambulance all by herself to the hospital, unable to speak or reply to any of the paramedics' questions. Worst of all, she couldn't have asked anyone for her mother. When Olivia imagined this, tears streamed down her cheeks.

There was so much Olivia wanted to ask. She wondered if the sirens had been turned on for the ambulance ride to the hospital, something she was certain would have scared her little girl even more. But Olivia could not ask Luci any of these pressing questions. Luci wasn't speaking. She was silent and fearful, regressing right before Olivia's eyes. And so Olivia waited until the nurse came back before leaving to check on Jake. "You'll stay with her the whole time, yes?"

Reluctantly, Olivia left Luci for the first time since arriving at the hospital. The nurse had directed her to an orderly seated at a cubicle. "I'm Jake Goodwin's fiancée," she said, breathlessly. "Can you please tell me where he is?"

The orderly looked up at her sympathetically. "He should be coming into recovery shortly," she assured her. "You'll be the first to find out."

It was six hours ahead in Toulouse, and stubborn as he was, Olivia was certain that Pierre was traveling with a cheap cell phone with limited range and even less reliability. She tried her aunt Celeste's house phone, but it rang and rang until the answering machine finally picked up. Hesitantly, Olivia left a message:

Luci had been in a boating accident. She was okay. They hoped to leave the hospital soon, but she didn't want her father or aunt to worry. They could call her in the morning.

Unsure of what to do next, she dialed Marge. As soon as she heard her warm voice, Olivia broke down.

"Oh, honey," Marge said, her voice rich with comfort. "I can be there in fifteen minutes. Let me get Ben."

"No," Olivia insisted. "Please don't bother him. He's got the show deadline. This will upset him." Ben was crazy about Luci. But there was nothing any of them could do now, and Olivia had no idea when Luci would be discharged. The last thing she wanted was to stir Ben and Marge into action, only to leave them waiting around in the over-air-conditioned waiting room.

"Are you kidding? Ben will have both our heads if he finds out I didn't tell him!"

"Please," Olivia pleaded. "I'm here with the Goodwins, and there are plenty of hands to go around. You can tell him, but promise you won't come. Not yet. I just wanted you to know where we were, so you didn't worry."

"Well, now I *am* worried," Marge told her. "Is everyone else okay?"

Olivia had had every intention of telling her about Jake, but as soon as Marge asked, Olivia's throat constricted. "I'm afraid I have to go, but I'll call you as soon as I know more."

She couldn't fall apart yet. She checked on the nurse sitting with Luci. "Do I have another minute?"

"She's still sleeping," she assured Olivia. "Go get yourself some coffee or food—whatever you need."

What Olivia needed was to see Jane and Edward. Ignoring the god-awful receptionist from before, she headed back into the ER waiting area. The moment they saw her, both hurried over.

"How is Luci?" Edward asked.

"She's doing okay. Resting now." Olivia blinked back tears. "Is there any word about Jake?" Out in the bright light of the waiting room it hit her. She could step away from everything happening on the other side of the double doors, but Jake could not. He was alone back there, lying on an operating table. She hadn't been able to kiss him before he went into surgery. Hadn't been able to tell him she loved him. "I haven't even seen Jake yet."

Edward opened his arms and Olivia stepped into them. "They should be wrapping surgery up soon," he told her. "We'll be able to see him in recovery, the nurse promised."

Olivia nodded gratefully. "It's a bit chaotic back there. Will you send word, as soon as you hear?"

"Of course, honey." Jane looked weathered but calm, and Olivia tried to channel the older woman's energy. "Phoebe ran home to pick up some things for Emma. Can one of us run over to your place and get anything for you or Luci? Does she have a favorite doll or blankie?" Her expression was as reassuring and soft as her voice. This was what it was like to be in a big family.

Olivia wiped her nose. "I have her stuffed elephant in my purse, but thank you."

"Well, if there's anything else you need. Food? A drink?" She riffled through her purse and handed Olivia a tissue.

"I'm fine, thanks."

But Edward was already heading to the coffee station. "Cream or sugar?" he called. And she realized it was exactly what she needed.

"Both, please."

"Come sit." Jane guided Olivia over to the chairs. "We can't stop thinking about Luci. Has she told you anything?"

Olivia shook her head, fresh tears springing to her eyes. "She can't get a word out, even to me. She's mostly all right on the outside, but on the inside, I can tell she isn't."

"Give her time," Jane said, rubbing Olivia's back. "It must have been very frightening for her. I just don't understand what could've happened out there."

If only Olivia had gone with them on the boat, this might not have happened. At the very least she would know what had.

When she returned to Luci's bay, the curtains were slightly ajar. Oliva peered inside, hoping to find her still sleeping beside the nurse. But Luci was awake, sitting up in bed. And it was not the nurse who was sitting with her. It was Perry.

"Here you are," he said, standing. It was then Olivia saw the book in his hand. He held it up, sheepishly. *If You Give a Mouse a Cookie*.

Olivia glanced between the two and hurried to Luci. "Sorry, *ma chérie*. I just went to call *Grand-Père*. Did you just wake up?"

Perry stepped aside to make room for her. "When I stopped in to check on you both, the nurse said you'd stepped out. I figured Luci would be bored when she woke up, so I went to the gift shop and found this book. It used to be one of Emma's favorites." He looked at Luci. "I think she likes it."

To Olivia's relief Luci didn't seem as upset. In fact, she appeared more relaxed and alert. "Thank you, Perry. That was terribly thoughtful."

"You're welcome."

Perry looked large and out of sorts standing beside the bed with the mouse book. She almost regretted interrupting them. "Did you finish the story?" Olivia asked.

He held up the open book. The illustrated page showed the mouse drawing with a green crayon. "Not quite."

"That's my favorite part! Keep going." Olivia gestured to the chair.

Perry sat back down, and in his deep voice picked up where he'd left off.

Olivia settled onto the bed beside Luci, her mind a tangle of details. She tried to focus on what was happening in front of her: Luci tucked against her side, alert and safe. The clock ticking on the wall, every second bringing her closer to seeing Jake.

As Perry read on about the little mouse who wanted more and more, Olivia leaned back against the pillows. Luci snuggled in. Perry's voice was melodic. Olivia was taken aback by the gusto with which he narrated; never would she have guessed he had it in him. When he got to the part about the mouse asking for a glass of milk, Luci giggled aloud. Against the buzzing and hum of the emergency room backdrop, it was the smallest sound. So faint that if Olivia hadn't been able to *feel* the laughter course through her daughter, she wouldn't have known. She looked up. Perry had heard it, too. He smiled at Olivia over the book. Then he went on.

Page after page, the little mouse asked for more. And each time the boy gave it to him. *That is love*, Olivia thought, just before she closed her eyes.

Emma

I hope you're okay. What happened 2U?

It was the first message she saw on her phone after the accident. Emma gasped, and set it down. Then she picked it up and reread it, to be sure she wasn't seeing things.

It was from Sully, sent around ten o'clock the night before. Her mother had brought her phone to the hospital that morning, along with a ham and cheese croissant, her favorite thing from Starbucks.

"Where did you find my phone?" Emma asked.

"Grandma brought it over. It was left at her house." Amelia stared at her hands in her lap, something she did whenever the accident came up.

"Grandma?" And then Emma remembered. She had set it on her grandparents' patio table, right before she went out in the boat with Jake and Luci. Normally she'd have brought it with her, stuffed in the back of her shorts pocket, but her dad had noticed her holding it. "Why don't you leave your phone?" he'd suggested. "You don't want it getting wet or falling overboard." Always the risk analyst. Now she realized it had been a stroke of good fortune. If she'd had the phone with her, it would probably be at the bottom of Candlewood Lake right now.

So, Sully had heard about the accident. News on their narrow strip of lake traveled faster than sound across the water. Despite the pain that radiated through her cheeks every time she moved any part of her face, Emma smiled. Sully was checking up on her. She put a hand to her cracked lip. God, she was glad he couldn't see her right now.

There was only one other text, and it was from Alicia. From the night before. "Want to meet at the beach tomorrow?" Apparently, Alicia had not yet heard about the accident. Emma felt terrible. She hadn't hung out much with Alicia, having been so distracted with Sully and the others. She started to text Alicia back, then stopped. Where should she begin? With Uncle Jake driving them out to the cove, or the part where Luci sat on her lap and waved at the water-skiers?

Luci. Sweet little Luci who didn't talk but whose big brown eyes said everything for her. Emma had been pointing out some of the big fancy houses along the shore before the accident, and Luci had seemed so excited. She'd even laughed, out loud. It was the first time Emma had heard her actual voice, and it sounded like what Emma imagined a fairy's voice to be.

She groaned at the memory and put her hand to her head.

Her mother hopped up. "Honey, is the phone screen giving you a headache? Oh God. The nurse said that electronics should be limited. Here, why don't you let me take that for you."

"Mom."

"Are you texting a friend? Because I could type for you, if that helps. I won't even read them, I promise." Emma could see the need in her mother's eyes to do something. Anything. This was one of the worst parts of the accident, aside from the obvious: her busted-up face and the pain. And of course, the worry about Luci and Uncle Jake.

Her stomach turned, and she set down her croissant. "I can't eat," she said. "I feel nauseous."

Her mother swept away the offending breakfast sandwich, and took the phone from her hands, too. What difference did it make? It wasn't like Sully McMahon would ever come here to visit her in the hospital. Would he? Her heart skipped at the mere notion. But oh my God, if he saw her face. Now, *that* would kill her.

Her mom was looking at her with that expression again. That dreadful mix of fear and feigned hope. She dug around in the bag from home and produced a tube of Aquaphor. "Here. For your poor lips." Before Emma could object, her mother was smearing some on her finger and dabbing it on. Her mouth hurt, but her mom's fingers were tender and light, and Emma felt just the slightest bit of relief. Besides, her mother seemed possessed by some visceral maternal urge to fix everything. If a tube of Aquaphor did it for her, who was Emma to deny her mother that?

Her father, however, was not calm. At the foot of her bed, he maintained his slow, methodical pacing. Per usual, he was in what the family jokingly dubbed his "home uniform" of pressed khakis and French-blue button-down shirt. "My dad is so chill, he takes his tie off at home," Emma used to tease him. Now his hands were jammed in the pockets of his khakis as he made slow, steady rotations around the foot of her bed, his eyes trained on the floor. A few more days of this and he would wear a track through the linoleum.

"Honey, please." Her mother motioned for her father to sit down. Apparently, it was starting to get to her, too.

But Emma could tell it took a lot out of him to still his arms and legs. To just sit. He leaned forward and rubbed his eyes. "Emma, we got some blood tests back that we need to talk about."

Immediately her mother shot him a look, but her father seemed to ignore it.

Emma swallowed hard, sinking into the blankets. She did not want to talk about any of it. Already there had been so much talk. There were the nurses, who'd taken her vitals and asked her if she remembered what had happened. Followed by the doctor, who examined her and asked more questions. She'd been wheeled in and out of radiology, where she'd lain on cold steel surfaces as the technician asked her to move this way, then that way, then not at all. At least the cute young orderly had given her a warm blanket. "Franco," his nametag said. He was nice. A couple of times he tried to make her laugh, but each time it made her lip split, and then she cried, and poor Franco had looked like he might, too.

Since the tests were complete and rest had been ordered, the doctors and nurses had come in less and less frequently. Her father, however, remained. As did his overwhelming worry. She could almost see it rippling beneath the surface of his skin as he sat there, chin in his hands in the hard plastic chair. "Do you know what blood tests I'm talking about?" he pressed.

"No." Sweat broke out in her armpits. Her mind flew to her uncle. Uncle Jake, her favorite relative in the whole family. The cool, funny one who didn't ask too many questions and always knew how to make her laugh. Who was just having a few beers and a good time at his own engagement party. Who wouldn't hurt a fly. Whom she'd begged to take her out on the boat. It was her fault they'd been out there to begin with. Jake hadn't meant to put them at risk.

Every time she closed her eyes, she replayed the crash again. The dock swerving into abrupt view. The surge of speed, and Uncle Jake's urgent voice. And Luci. In one moment Luci was there. And then she was gone.

Emma shielded her eyes. "Please. Not now. I feel sick." The lights were too sharp, her father's questions too knotty.

"Okay, that's enough." Her mother rushed for the light panel, then the curtains. Instantly, her father stopped talking. "Let's go. She needs to rest."

Emma curled into the blankets, hand over her face as their footsteps moved to the door. "We'll be down in the cafeteria, honey. Try to get some sleep." Then there was the click as the door closed behind them.

Emma lay in the relative darkness for what seemed like a long time. Eventually her eyes got heavy, and she felt herself drifting off. She was almost asleep when a jarring *ding* startled her. On the bedside table her phone screen was illuminated. Her mother must have accidentally left the phone behind. She reached for it.

There was one more message. From UJ. *Uncle Jake.* Eagerly she swiped it open.

Emmy, are you okay? I want to check on you, but I'm kind of tied up in Room 103. LOL. Luci is all right, and I'm relieved to hear that you are, too.

I'm sorry—you must have been really scared. Love you, kid.

Emma read it through twice, a sense of relief flooding through her. She'd felt so isolated not being able to see Jake or Luci. Her parents had assured her they were okay, but hearing from her uncle was different. Now she could rest.

She was just about to turn her phone off and return it to the bedside table when another message came through.

One more thing . . . don't say anything. Please.

Perry

It was the green light he'd been waiting for: Emma could come home. Despite her fat lip and the blue-green bloom of bruising that spread across her right cheek, he and Amelia could collect their baby girl and ferry her home. Where things could once again go back to normal. Perry craved normal. He hadn't slept in the last two days. He could not remember having eaten a damn thing besides the acrid coffee in the waiting room and a stale bagel that Amelia had forced into his hand and he'd attempted to gum down. Everything about his constitution was off, and the moment they wheeled Emma out into the sunlight and up to the curb where his car idled, Perry thanked God. He did not consider himself a religious man, but knowing what he knew about accidents and probabilities, about risk and result, he knew this: the fact that two young girls were walking away from that boating accident was nothing short of a miracle.

The night before had not been easy. Perry had stayed at the hospital after finally convincing Amelia to go home. Amelia was strong; it was something he admired most about her. She could walk into a sterile conference room and stand at the head of an all-male table and deliver a presentation without faltering. She was also direct. Whenever things concerned them during Emma's childhood, either at school or in her social interactions with peers, Amelia had never hesitated to pick up the phone. Perry had once watched his wife in the principal's office take down the hulking female phys ed teacher, as big in bullying as she was in physicality, for singling out and humiliating in front of the whole kindergarten class a child who couldn't tie her shoe. But sitting beside their daughter's hospital bed, Perry saw a fresh vulnerability in his wife that filled his chest with both sadness and deep affection. Amelia had been scared to her core. They both had. And he was relieved when she finally relented and went home to take a shower and crawl into bed.

The nurses had been kind enough to order Perry a cot, but he was a tall man, and he tossed and turned in its narrow confines. By five a.m., when he could lie there no more, he got up and sat beside Emma while she slept. It reminded him of the hours he'd spent doing so fifteen years earlier when she'd first come home from the hospital as a newborn and he was beside himself with worry. Amelia had plucked her from her crib, put her to her breast, burped her, and changed her with such confidence. But not Perry. He was terrified of this tiny person, this person who had turned his entire world upside down and whom he loved with a biological pull so encompassing that he was almost afraid to touch her. But he could watch her, that is what he did.

To his dismay, Emma had not rested easily last night either. At first she groaned and tossed, until he couldn't stand to watch. Thankfully, the nurses gave her something to help her sleep. Perry wondered if she were experiencing the beginnings of PTSD.

To be honest, he wondered if he were, too. Because earlier that evening Perry had done something he'd not yet told his wife about. He'd snuck off to the scene of the accident.

As soon as Emma was admitted and settled safely under her

mother's watch, Perry had excused himself to get a coffee. Instead, Perry took the elevator down to the parking garage and drove back to Lenox. Perry needed to see it for himself. It was something he had to do alone.

He'd gotten the exact location from the police officers who'd stopped by earlier to file their report. Perry had known the general area of the scene from the calls his father had made to the lake authority and a report from a neighbor who'd called to check on the family. But when the officers appeared at the hospital later that afternoon, Perry had been able to nail it down. To Amelia he'd said, "I'm going to go out for a coffee. I can't stand the cafeteria stuff they're passing off. Can I get you one?"

She had barely looked up. "No, thanks."

Alone in the car, Perry had turned the radio off and input the address to his GPS. It was a private property just north of their Candlewood Cove Clubhouse on the New Fairfield town side. Since he wasn't accessing it by lake, he'd have to go to the property owner's house and ask permission. That could be dicey. But Perry hoped they'd understand, and he was right. The owner, Mr. George Dunlap, met him in the driveway, and told him how sorry he was. He didn't say a word about damages or insurance. He would later, Perry knew. They always did.

Mr. Dunlap walked him down the rear hillside to the water's edge. When they got to the dock, he kindly left Perry alone. Perry took it all in. The splintered pilings jutting out of the inky water. The stray boards, torn from their footings where the bow of the boat had struck. Pieces of wood floated like shrapnel in the shallow water. A single white slice of fiberglass from the boat floated in a tangle of cattails like a lone snowflake against pavement. Perry stood at the shore and cursed. What would have brought them in so close to shore at such a speed? And caused the dock to be ripped apart like this? And thrown Jake from the boat altogether? They could've all been killed.

Sickened, he'd turned to a scrubby patch of bushes and bent over. Perry vomited twice, hands on his knees.

Back at the hospital, when Amelia had gone home and he was sure Emma was still ensconced in the dreamless sleep of the sedative, he walked out. He turned left, passing the nurse's station. Past the darkened rooms of other sleeping patients, to the row of elevators at the end of the hall. Perry rode up to the third floor and stepped out onto the bright white light of the surgical unit. A male nurse standing in the hall looked up. "I'm sorry, sir. Visiting hours don't start until eight a.m."

"I'm staying downstairs with my daughter, in the observation unit. She and my brother, Jake Goodwin, were brought in from an accident yesterday. I'm looking for my brother."

The nurse glanced at his clipboard and flipped through. "Jake Goodwin. Our compound distal femur fracture." He looked up at Perry. "Tough guy."

"They were in a boating accident. I haven't seen him yet."

The nurse let out a breath. "All right, I guess I can give you a few minutes. But if he's sleeping, please don't wake him."

"Thank you," Perry said.

The nurse led him to the doorway of Jake's room.

Jake lay on his back beneath a dimmed overhead light. His gown was open at the chest, and from the waist up he looked as young and strong as he had to Perry that day on his boat. But his right leg was ensconced in an enormous white cast, elevated in a sling. The rest of his lower body was covered in a thin white blanket. Perry approached the bed and looked at his little brother.

Tears pressed at the corners of his eyes, and angrily he swiped them away.

"What happened out there?" he whispered.

Jake did not stir. Perry stared at the IV bag, momentarily lulled by the slow, precise drip of fluid. Unlike Emma's, Jake's face was miraculously clear of any trauma. But then Perry noticed his hands. They were scabbed over and swollen, his knuckles purple and scratched. They rested at his sides, palms up, in a repose that struck Perry as uncharacteristically vulnerable. As if asking for forgiveness. Perry was half tempted to touch them, but he could not bring himself to.

Instead a wave of anger overcame him, and he felt his face flush with it. Jake was an avid boater, a skilled captain who knew the lake better than any of them. He was the only adult on the boat. He should've known better. He should've kept those girls safe.

If there had been another boat, Perry could have made sense of it. In his life he'd passed too many inexperienced boaters out on the water. Teens going too fast. Large parties of adults having imbibed too much. Water-skiers who swung out too far and too wide on turns, crossing dangerously into his path. It was the thing Perry hated most about the lake he loved: people were so damn irresponsible, putting others and themselves in harm's way.

But not Jake—even carefree, jovial Jake would never let that happen. Perry shook his head. It didn't make sense.

But how to explain the alcohol in Emma's bloodstream? Perry remembered that Jake had been holding a beer. He couldn't say for sure how many he'd had that day; they'd all had a drink or two during the clambake. But Jake was different with Emma. She'd always called him her "favorite uncle," even though he was her only one. It wouldn't have mattered if there'd been five more, Perry knew Emma would have preferred Jake to anyone. Because Jake was fun. Jake bent the rules. He understood her. If Emma had pressed, would he have given her a sip of his beer? Clearly more than a sip had been had; her blood tests were evidence of that. Perry's fingers curled around the cold steel of the bed railing.

Jake was out of surgery. He was out of the woods. And so help him, he had questions he needed to answer.

Now, with Emma about to be discharged, Perry needed answers. But Emma was too upset and Amelia was glaring at him like he was some kind of monster. Perry needed to step out. "Discharge will probably take a while. I'll be back in a few minutes," he said. Neither asked where he was going.

Without thinking, he found himself heading briskly down the hall to Luci's room. But he faltered in the doorway. There, resting in the corner chair was Olivia, her head tipped back against the wall, eyes closed. He was about to turn when her eyelids fluttered. She glanced first at Luci, who was curled on her side beneath the blankets. Then at him. Wordlessly, she stood and followed him into the hall.

Olivia rubbed her eyes. "I've been going back and forth between them all night."

Perry knew she meant Jake and Luci. She looked exhausted, her eyes clouded with red. "How is he doing?" he asked.

"He was gray with pain when he woke up in recovery last night. They seem to have controlled it, since he's finally able to sleep. But you know Jake. He wouldn't complain anyway." She sighed. "He's so upset about the girls, I doubt he's gotten much rest." She checked her watch. "Would you mind sitting with her while I check on him again?"

Perry nodded. "Take as long as you need." But there was something else on his mind. The anger had not dissipated on the elevator ride down. Nor in the dark, cool recesses of Luci's room. Not even standing by Olivia, who seemed to have that strange effect on him. "Have you been able to talk to him? Has he said anything at all about what happened?"

Olivia's eyes softened. "No. He was really out of it after surgery. His pain levels were so high they gave him medication that pretty much knocked him out. I barely had time to tell him I loved him and that the girls were okay."

Perry flinched. He had not said any such thing to Jake. The image of the shattered dock flashed in his mind. The police tape. The Candlewood Lake Authority boats. What kind of big brother felt ire for his sibling, who'd narrowly escaped death?

Perry flexed his fingers, then uncoiled them consciously from the balled fists that hung at his side. He forced the words out. "If he wakes, tell him I send my best."

Phoebe

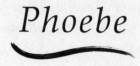

She was losing her mind. She knew it the second she signed into the hospital for her visitor's pass and stepped out of the elevators onto the wing where Emma and Luci had been admitted. *How lucky they are*, she'd thought.

Hospitals were like an alternate universe. Time stopped, the normal push and pull of everyday life ceased. Here you did not worry about the onslaught of news, the mortgage bill you had to pay, the baths you had to give your kids, and the farmhouse sink you've always coveted for its deep recess but realize, come to think of it, the uncanny volume of dirty dishes it can contain might just prove cruel. Such concerns vanished, if temporarily, when you were admitted to the hospital. Here, people took care of you. Nurses strode purposefully between rooms administering to their patients. Trays of steaming food were plucked off carts and delivered. To one's bed! There was staff who mopped, changed your sheets, inquired about your vitals. They even helped you shower if you needed it! As Phoebe walked down the corridor, even the views were intoxicating: the verdant hills of Litchfield rolled between window frames. She could stay here, like one stayed at a spa retreat. Suddenly, she desperately wanted a bed. Yes, she was losing her mind.

Focus, she chastised herself. *This is not about you.*

It was the first time she'd been allowed back to see any of them since the accident. The previous day, she'd felt useless. Only Amelia, Perry, and Olivia had been allowed back in the ER, and eventually her parents. Unable to loiter in the waiting room fielding construction texts from Dave and alerts from the bank, she'd tried to help instead, by running errands. It also gave her good reason to avoid the pressing matter of renovation issues, and she texted Dave just that: *Sorry, but I can't be reached today.* She was needed here! This was her family. And this was what family did when crisis hit.

First, she'd gone back to her parents' house to update Rob and say good night to the boys. Then she'd gone to Perry and Amelia's to collect some things for Emma. She'd just been heading to the hospital when her mother called.

"Where are you?" Jane asked.

Phoebe had initially prickled. She was going as fast as she could. But then she understood why Jane was calling. "Olivia has her hands full here. I know it's a bit of a drive, but might you head over to her place and pick up a few things? I think she could use our help."

Twenty minutes later, Phoebe found herself sailing over the wooded hills of Washington's Route 109 before being deposited into the cozy hamlet of the town center. She slowed as she drove through, soaking in its Norman Rockwell vibe: white clapboard churches, historic farmhouses, rustic red barns. When she pulled into the long gravel driveway of the address Jane had given her, Phoebe was met immediately by a kind-faced older woman in front of the main house. Marge was tall and elegant, her silver hair pulled back in a chignon. But she was dressed unassumingly in a peasant blouse and faded blue jeans. "You must be the sister," she said, leaning into Phoebe's window. "You and Jake have the same mischievous twinkle in your eyes."

Phoebe was pleasantly taken aback. When she'd first heard that Olivia shared the property with an older couple and worked as an apprentice in the barn, she'd immediately felt sorry for Olivia. Not only was the money likely minimal for a single parent, but Phoebe had wondered at the close quarters and how dreadful it must be to live with the person for whom you worked. Like some kind of indentured servant!

But as she looked around, Phoebe was positively envious. Between the large barn and the farmhouse was a sprawling stretch of cultivated yard dotted with flower beds in full bloom. A fieldstone patio hugged one side of the house, and to the other side lay a wooded grove of pine trees. The place was right out of a storybook.

Behind the barn, Phoebe could make out a small cottage, matching the farmhouse in its white clapboard siding and cedar shake roof. A winding stone path led the way to its front door. Phoebe figured if she sat here long enough, Red Riding Hood would poke her head out.

As Marge handed her a carefully packed bag of Olivia's things and asked worriedly about everyone back at the hospital, Phoebe realized her misjudgment. On the way over, she'd imagined the awkward formality of her mission. Having to knock on the door and explain who she was. Having to ask permission to be let into Olivia's cottage, where she imagined herself rummaging through the rooms as Marge looked on proprietorially. How wrong she'd been.

These people were Olivia's Connecticut family just as much as Phoebe's family was hers. "I packed pajamas and fresh clothes for both girls, their toothbrushes, and a couple of Luci's dolls. I figured the poor little thing could use some cheering up."

"Thank you so much," Phoebe said. If Marge hadn't been

leaning into the car, she'd have opened the door and gotten out to hug her.

"Oh, and please tell Olivia not to worry about Buster. I fed him dinner and Ben is out now taking him on a walk. We'll keep him in the house with us tonight so he doesn't get lonely."

Phoebe remembered then about the dog. What a shame he couldn't go to the hospital with them. She had a feeling everyone in the family could use a good dose of therapy dog right about then.

After promising Marge that she'd call with updates, Phoebe drove back down the driveway. What she would've given for a Marge and Ben herself, she thought.

Unfortunately, when she returned to the hospital, she still wasn't allowed back to see any of them. Perry came out to collect the things she brought, and thanked her. He looked terrible, but he assured her the girls were okay. Jake was the one they were most worried about now, and one look at her parents told Phoebe it was wearing on them.

"He's in recovery, and Olivia was able to spend some time with him. The doctor says the surgery went well," Edward told her. He looked exhausted.

"Let's all go home and come back in the morning," Phoebe suggested. For once, her mother did not argue.

By the time she fell into her own bed, beside Rob, Phoebe was too exhausted to lie awake worrying. About the fact she'd barely seen the boys all day. About money. About the fact she lay beside a husband who was too disillusioned to turn over and kiss her good night. Instead of fretting, it had been all she could do to kick off her sandals and crawl into bed in the clothes she'd worn all day. She was out cold before she remembered she'd not brushed her teeth.

This morning, she thought the next day, would have to be different. She vowed to call Dave and make a plan for the house. Rob had gone into work, and she'd convinced Anna Beth to take the boys for the morning. "Jesus," she'd said when Phoebe called to explain why. "How is Jake? I can't picture him laid up for a second."

Tears pricked her eyes as Phoebe realized with a start she did not know if Jake would be all right. The surgery may have gone well, but the fracture was serious and he'd be in traction and then rehab for a long time. And it wasn't just the leg. There still wasn't any clear understanding of what had gone wrong out there. Although nobody dared say the words aloud, she had a bad feeling it involved Jake. And Phoebe could tell she was not alone.

She'd seen it bubbling beneath the surface in Perry, when she'd visited the hospital late the night before. He looked god-awful. She understood as a parent what Perry was already feeling and Jake could not; when your children's well-being was threatened, there was no telling how you'd react. Brothers or not. Even in a big close-knit family, when it came down to a crisis, your children trumped everyone.

After signing in at the visitor's desk, Phoebe stopped at the Starbucks cart in the lobby. She spent almost thirty dollars on coffees, which she could not afford at all. But given how deep she was in the hole, what difference did six more coffees make? In that case, why bother with her usual skinny latte? She ordered herself a mocha Frappuccino, and watched with zero concern as the young barista mixed the creamy confectionery drink. She didn't even blink when the girl dumped in chocolate syrup.

"Whipped cream?" she asked.

Phoebe stared back at her youthful smile. "Drown it."

Now, as she stood mesmerized by the gauzy summery view

outside Luci's hospital room windows, she remembered her tray of drinks.

"Phoebe?" Olivia rose, and met her in the doorway. Luci was sleeping behind her in the bed.

"Hi! How is she?" Phoebe whispered, coming to her senses.

"She was up a bit last night, but she's fallen back to sleep, thank goodness."

Olivia looked exhausted, but Phoebe noticed she was wearing the plaid pajama pants she'd picked up from Marge at the house the night before, and that cheered her. She handed her a cup of tea. "I remembered you like chai lattes."

"How in the world?" Olivia asked. She pecked Phoebe gratefully on the cheek and pulled a chair over next to her own.

Phoebe shrugged. "I noticed Jake drinking them and gave him a hard time. He's normally a boring black coffee kind of guy. You're sophisticating my brother. We didn't think it could be done."

Olivia smiled sadly. "He does like his lattes."

They sat a moment in silence, sipping their drinks and watching Luci sleep. "Any updates on him?" Phoebe asked warily. She didn't know Olivia that well, and she couldn't imagine what it was like to be in the hospital with the two people you loved best.

"I was in with him, earlier," she said. "He didn't get much sleep either. I think they're hoping to move him to a rehab center, possibly as early as tomorrow." Her brow furrowed. "I don't think he'll be out on his beloved lake any time soon."

Phoebe sipped her Frappuccino, eyes trained on Luci's peaceful face. There seemed to be no ire in Olivia's tone. Phoebe wondered if she knew any more than the rest of them did about the accident.

"How are you doing?" Phoebe asked.

Olivia seemed about to answer, but instead, she began to cry. "Luci won't talk. Not even to me."

Phoebe leaned forward and put a hand on Olivia's back.

"I don't want to push her, but this is not good. And then there's Jake. They don't know what kind of mobility he's going to have. Last night the doctors told him that he may have trouble walking again, that they won't know anything for sure until the bones have a chance to set and he gets into rehabilitation." She covered her face in her hands. "Of all the people this could happen to. He can't sit still for a second. This will do him in."

Phoebe scooted closer. "Listen, if there's one thing I know about my little brother, he defies the odds. Always has." She forced a smile. "Did he ever tell you how he got on the football team in high school?"

Olivia shook her head.

"When he was a freshman, he decided to go out for football. Which was ridiculous because he was a track star, and he was short at the time. The coach told him exactly that.

"But Jake showed up, every day. And every day the coach would ignore him. He'd tell him, 'Go home, Goodwin.' But Jake wouldn't. He'd shadow the guys during practice. He'd do every drill they were doing. And after a while the coach couldn't ignore him."

Olivia was listening. "He never told me that story."

"He wouldn't. He's too modest. Eventually the coach let him on, but he never played him. That whole season, Jake sat on the bench. Until one of the last games. One of the running backs pulled a hamstring, and Jake begged to be played. My dad jokes that the coach was so sick of Jake, he was probably hoping to throw him in there, watch him get sacked, and they could all be done with it."

"What happened?"

"The quarterback threw him the ball. And he ran with it."

Olivia beamed.

"I was afraid to watch, to be honest. Jake was a string bean compared to the other players. There's no way he would've survived a tackle. But he was fast, and he got yardage."

"Did he score?"

Phoebe smiled at the memory. "Yeah. He made a touchdown. It was epic." She shrugged. "It was Jake."

Olivia laughed, softly. "I bet he was hard to live with after that."

"Nah. I would've been. Perry certainly would've been. The two of us would've lorded that kind of thing over everyone in the family. But Jake wasn't after that. He usually doesn't care what anyone else thinks. I guess he just wanted to prove it to himself."

Olivia twisted the ring on her finger and stared out the window. "He's so sure of himself. I wish I was."

"Which is why we need to be, too. He won't be down for long. Not with you two girls to come home to."

Olivia smiled and turned her gaze back to Luci. "I just hope the same for her."

"She's had a bad scare," Phoebe said. "Give it some time." Phoebe glanced at her watch. "Speaking of which, I should be going."

"Are you going to visit Jake?" Olivia asked.

When Phoebe nodded, she saw the pull in Olivia's eyes. "Please tell him I'll be in as soon as I can."

Phoebe held up another chai latte. "I'll tell him this is from both of us," she promised.

She took the elevator up to the surgical floor. "I'm looking for Jake Goodwin," she said at the reception desk.

The male orderly directed her down the hall. She hoped the

latte was still hot. Jake could use something sweet and distracting. She was about to round the corner to his room when she heard the raised voices.

Phoebe halted in the doorway. Perry was standing at the foot of his brother's bed, arms out by his sides. Jake lay under a white blanket, one leg up in traction. Her little brother had never looked so small.

"What the hell were you thinking?" Perry asked, his voice rising in anger.

Jake stared back at him, his face dark with regret. "I told you I'm sorry, Perry. It was an accident."

"Sorry?" Perry bellowed. He banged the bottom rail of Jake's bed, and Jake winced. "You let my daughter drink beer to the point she was intoxicated. Then you drove the boat into a dock. Christ, Jake, you could've killed them!"

Phoebe froze. She wanted to run in and yell at them both. At Perry to stop; couldn't he see the pain Jake was in? At Jake to not listen to his brother. They all knew Jake would never have done this on purpose.

"It was an accident," Jake said again. "A terrible accident that I will never forgive myself for."

"It was *you*!" Perry bellowed. "You being reckless, and showing off, like you always do. You will never change, Jake Goodwin. But one thing will: you will *never* be allowed near my family again."

Jake sat up in bed, the blanket falling from his bare chest. His face twisted in pain. "Perry, please!"

"And after what you've done to little Luci, I'm sure Olivia will want nothing to do with you either!"

At that Jake fell back against the pillows, hands to his face.

"Stop!" Phoebe yelled from the doorway. "Both of you, stop it now."

A strangled cry came from the bed, and she rushed for Jake. "He didn't mean it," Phoebe cried. She grabbed his hand, but Jake refused to look at her.

"The hell I didn't!" Perry roared.

A nurse flew through the doorway. She bumped against Phoebe as she tried to get to Jake. "All of you, out," she ordered. "Now! Or I'm calling security."

Perry's face was flushed, the veins in his forehead throbbing. "I'm sorry," he managed, pulling himself together. "I'm leaving now."

The nurse checked Jake's vitals, adjusted the IV bag. "You need to calm down, Mr. Goodwin. We have to keep that leg immobile."

Phoebe's eyes darted between her two brothers. Thank God her parents weren't here to witness this; she could imagine the disappointment in her father's eyes. In all their mistakes and missteps growing up, they'd never known Edward to raise his voice, let alone his fist. Jane would've intervened; she was the shouter. But neither brother listened to her.

When Perry ducked past her toward the door, she reached for him. His hands were still balled in fists, stiff at his sides. "Perry," she said. "Stop."

But he wouldn't. He stepped quickly around her and hurried through the door. Phoebe glanced back at Jake, who was staring helplessly out the window while the nurse spoke with him. "I'll be right back," Phoebe said. Then, to the nurse, "I'm so sorry. This accident . . . it's hurt us all."

But Perry was getting away. Hastily she excused herself and went after him. He was already halfway down the hall, making stiff, sweeping strides toward the elevator. She had to break into a run. "Perry, wait!" she called.

Phoebe caught up to him at the elevator doors. He kept his back to her, stabbing at the buttons.

Warily, she reached for his arm. "Perry," she tried again.

When he turned to look at her, Phoebe saw something in his watery expression she'd never seen before. It looked like fear. "I'm sorry," he managed, and without warning, Perry fell against her. Phoebe struggled to prop him up, to wrap her arms around the breadth of his shoulders. "It's okay," she said, pressing her face to his heaving chest. "Emma is safe, and so is Luci. Everyone is going to be okay."

The elevator doors swung open, but neither Goodwin noticed. For the first time in her life, Phoebe held on to her older brother as he sobbed against her. She imagined herself as a blanket, muffling the pain. Phoebe had never seen Perry cry. And it scared the hell out of her.

This was the big brother. Unflappable, rational, problem-solving Perry. The one they all turned to, and always had, their parents included. What did a family do when their one true rock broke?

Over his shoulder, through the sweeping bank of hospital windows, she could see the horizon, nothing but blue sky and rolling green hills. It shifted with every racking sob that escaped her brother. Phoebe squeezed harder. "We're all going to be okay," she lied.

Olivia

Olivia splashed cold water on her face and regarded her reflection in the hospital bathroom mirror. She hadn't slept, and the evidence stared right back at her.

"There's my girl!" The beauty of a familiar voice sang out and Olivia turned in the tiny bathroom doorway to see Marge sail into Luci's room, arms outstretched. Luci's face brightened and she gasped, but Olivia's spirits sank when she didn't emit a single sound. Marge and Ben were like family, and this was another test she'd been holding her breath for. Sometimes it was possible to snap Luci out of her nonverbal state. If she was surprised by something both familiar and positive, her instinctual reaction might be to vocalize. But it didn't happen. Olivia tried not to show her disappointment as she went to Marge and hugged her.

Marge held up a tin. "I baked blueberry muffins this morning." She turned to Luci and lowered her voice conspiratorially. "I snuck them in just for you!"

Luci grinned and looked at her mother, expectantly. "Go ahead," Olivia said.

As was his way, Ben stood beside his wife, quietly shadowing her exuberance. "Good to see you, darling," he said, pecking Olivia's cheek. "How are you holding up?"

"Still standing. Thank you for coming."

Luci and Marge dipped into the tin of muffins, and Olivia accepted one gratefully. It was still warm to the touch. "Boy, you really did just bake these."

Ben shook his head when she offered him one.

"You've more willpower than I do," Olivia said, tearing into the buttery folds of the muffin. She'd been living on hospital cafeteria food, and as the warm blueberries melted on her tongue she seriously wondered if she'd ever tasted anything so gratifying.

Marge shook her head. "Oh please. You give that man too much credit. Who do you think taste-tested them?"

A small giggle escaped Luci and hope filled Olivia's chest. God, she was so glad to see Ben and Marge.

"Now," Ben said, sitting beside Luci's bed and examining her cast, "this is a lovely shade of pink, but I think it might need a little artwork. May I?" He reached in his pocket and held up a black Sharpie marker.

"I didn't even think of that," Olivia said. "Luci, Ben can sign your cast. We all can."

"Even better," Ben said. "I can draw you a picture. Would you like that?"

Luci's eyes widened. She nodded happily. Drawing was something they did together, Ben and Luci. Whenever Marge and Ben invited them to the big house for dinner, Ben would sit down at the farm table with a big sketch pad and a black marker. Whatever Luci pointed to he would draw; a flower from the garden, their tabby cat, Simon. Then he would hand the marker to Luci and let her take a turn. "He's crazy about that child," Marge would say, as she and Olivia watched from the kitchen. Ben never said so, but Olivia had long suspected it was more than a means to pass the time. It was Ben's creative way to get Luci to express herself. The fact that he'd brought his black Sharpie to the hospital made her eyes water.

Ben uncapped the marker, holding it up like a wand. "All right, then. What will it be, sweet one?"

Olivia watched as Luci considered his question. She turned her eyes on her mother, with a sudden pleading look. There was something special she had in mind.

"You have an idea," Olivia said, moving closer to the bed. "Can you give us a hint?"

Behind her, Olivia could feel Marge holding her breath. Indeed, she was, too. But as much as she didn't want to pressure Luci, this was what their speech therapist usually encouraged. When Luci's brow furrowed in consternation, Olivia wavered. "Is it something here?" she asked, hopefully.

Luci shook her head.

"Okay, Mommy will guess." She ran through the usual objects the two liked to commit to paper. "Is it a butterfly? Or a flower?"

Again, Luci shook her head.

Olivia sighed inwardly. "Tell us yes or no," she encouraged. She wanted Luci to articulate, even if it was just a guttural sound in the affirmative or negative. Olivia might be pushing it, she knew. But this was Ben and Marge. Besides Olivia and her grandfather, they were the safest people Luci could practice this with.

"Do you want Ben to draw an animal?"

Luci brightened.

"Ah!" Marge said with relief. "You love the birds that come to my feeder in the garden. Would you like a chickadee?"

Luci shook her head. She was getting discouraged, Olivia could tell. "We're going to help you to tell us what you want. Can you draw it for us?"

Ben held up his marker. "Excellent idea." There was a fumble as Marge rustled through her purse looking for a scrap of paper. Olivia scoured the room. The only things she could find were hospital forms and a magazine, both filled with text. Meanwhile Marge kept guessing aloud.

Luci was starting to look as if she might cry. This was the problem—when Luci couldn't articulate and Olivia couldn't guess, things unraveled. Olivia wasn't about to let Ben's lovely idea be wasted. Determined, she tore through the drawers in the nightstand. There was a bedpan, a washcloth. Nothing else. Feeling frantic, she turned to Luci. "Hang on, honey. I'll go ask a nurse! We'll find you a piece of paper, don't worry." But as she spun toward the door, she halted.

There, in the doorway, stood Perry. He had a bashful look on his face. In his hand was a rope. "Perry?"

He stepped to the side, but not to make room for her. Olivia's eyes followed the length of rope from Perry's hand to the shadows behind him. Buster lumbered forward. The second he saw Luci and Olivia he barked, and his whole body began to wag.

There was a small shriek from the bed and everyone turned. Luci leapt from her covers and leaned over the railing, reaching out with her good arm. Her face was alight with joy.

"Perry!" Olivia exclaimed.

Perry sneezed twice, then shrugged uncertainly. "I hope you don't mind, but I think Buster missed you." He let go of the rope and Buster trotted up to the edge of Luci's bed, hopping up on his hind legs. Luci threw her arm around his neck and buried her face in his fur.

When she finally looked up, Luci motioned to her mother.

The room had gone quiet. Olivia hurried over. "What is it, baby?"

Luci pulled her close. "It was him," she whispered.

Stunned, Olivia pulled back to take in Luci's expression. Fearful of breaking the spell, she encouraged Luci to go on. "*What* was him?" she whispered back.

Luci pressed her lips to her mother's ear. "Buster. Buster was what I wanted Ben to draw on my cast."

As the words flowed into her ear, Olivia's eyes traveled to the doorway. Perry hadn't moved an inch. His nice navy trousers were coated in dog hair. He dabbed his runny nose absently with a balled-up tissue. He looked more uncomfortable than she'd ever seen a person look. And yet there he was.

Yes, she thought. *It was him.*

Perry

Perry had not planned on the dog. That would have been a terrible plan. Getting the dog meant finding out where Olivia lived and driving all the way over there. It meant locating the dog, once he arrived. Worst of all, it meant securing the beast, without getting a limb torn off, and somehow convincing it to get into his car. His car. With the buttery leather interior and pristine surfaces. Free of food, beverage, and most certainly pet hair. Getting that dog was the last thing he'd ever wanted to do.

He could not say for sure how it happened. First, Emma had been discharged. She was home, tucked safely in her bed. Not that Emma showed any sign of being happy about it. Beyond the obvious trauma of the accident, and the painful bruises and scratches his daughter had suffered, there was a deeper sadness Perry saw and felt, but could not reach. Nor could Amelia. To their combined consternation, Emma had swiftly closed her door and climbed into her bed. Refusing tea or lunch. Declining Perry's offer to make her a bed on the living room couch where she could watch a movie, something that had always worked when she wasn't feeling well. It wasn't good that she'd shut herself away like that. Emma needed to get up and move about a little bit, as the doctor had suggested. Moreover, they needed to talk, all three of them, about the accident.

With all of that going on, Perry's head and heart were still floating somewhere outside his body, a sense that so unnerved him he felt compelled to get up and *do* something, as if that might somehow spark the three to reconnect.

What he couldn't stop thinking about was the toxicology report. Emma had been drunk. To his knowledge, their child had never touched alcohol. And even if she'd tried it, there was no way he could imagine she would drink in front of her family or while out on the boat in the middle of a summer day. She was too smart for that.

Her uncle was another story. It was well known that Jake liked his beer, and any social occasion was an excuse to crack a few open. It was true, he had seemed to slow down now that he was with Olivia. But Perry had seen him with a beer in hand at the party, and come to think of it he could not recall a time he'd seen Jake without one. But was it the same one—or two? Or had there been more?

Then there was his relationship with Emma. Emma had adored her uncle ever since she was a little girl. The two had a bond that, if he were being honest, Perry would admit he envied. Deeply. And Perry was sure Emma would protect her uncle, if she had to. That he could forgive. She was a teenager, and she was loyal. What he couldn't forgive was Jake putting his daughter in that position.

He found his wife in the kitchen. "Amelia, we have to ask her about the alcohol. And what happened out there with Jake."

Amelia looked exhausted. "I know. But we have to tread gently."

"I don't disagree, but the longer we wait the harder it will be. Can we please ask her together?"

"Let me make her lunch first. She's barely eaten a thing."

When Perry knocked on Emma's door and opened it, to his dismay, she was staring at her phone. Something else she wasn't supposed to be doing. "Would you like to come sit outside on the patio with me?" he asked. "The doctor said it would be good for you to get up and get some fresh air. Maybe do some of those stretching exercises to loosen things up?"

Emma kept her eyes trained on her phone. "No, thanks."

He paused. "Want anything special for lunch?"

"Mom's taking care of it. She's making a kale smoothie."

Perry did not like kale, and he did not understand the affinity his wife and daughter held for the viscous green smoothies they sometimes whipped up together. Usually for breakfast, of all things. But at least Emma was eating, if a kale shake constituted such a thing. "Well, that's wonderful."

She looked up from her phone, frowning.

"That you're eating something," he added quickly. Could he say nothing right? "Emma, I was hoping we could talk a little. If you're up for it."

At that moment, Amelia joined them, with the questionable concoction in hand. "Here you go, love." She set the glass down on Emma's bedside table.

Emma glanced at it, then at her father. "Thanks, but I've lost my appetite."

Perry saw the restraint his wife exercised. Her lips parted, then closed. "Well, maybe later," she said, finally. He rested a reassuring hand on her lower back.

"Emma, we want to talk to you about the accident." Emma kept her eyes trained on her phone, but Perry saw his words register in the set of her jaw. "The lab tests showed a blood alcohol level. You were drinking?"

Beside him, Amelia drew in her breath. She hadn't wanted to press Emma about this, but they needed to while it was still fresh. She was home now. It was time to face facts.

"Emma?"

She set her phone down roughly. "I had some beer. Big deal."

Perry flinched. He'd expected her to be remorseful. Not defiant.

"You're underage and you were just involved in a serious accident. This *is* a big deal."

Emma stared straight ahead.

"Have you drunk before?" Amelia ventured.

To Perry's relief, Emma shook her head. Tears filled her eyes. "No," she said, burying her face in her hands. "I'm sorry. I'm so sorry."

Perry sat down beside her on the bed, a lump growing in his throat. His little girl was still in there. "I didn't think so. Neither of us did. Which is why we want to know what made you do it that afternoon. Did Uncle Jake offer it to you?" Perry tried to keep his tone neutral, but there was that familiar pang of anger rising inside him.

"It wasn't Uncle Jake. I mean, it was his beer. But he didn't exactly give it to me."

"What does that mean?" Perry asked.

Emma looked between the two of them. "Is this an interrogation?"

"Okay," Amelia interjected. "Let's move past that for now. How many did you have? Because your blood alcohol level was too high for just one."

Emma shrugged. "I don't know. Maybe two? It was hot out, and I was thirsty. I just wanted to try it. Everyone else does."

Amelia shook her head softly. "It doesn't matter what everyone else does, honey. We're talking about you. And making good choices."

"Well, after what happened, it's not like I'll ever do it again,"

Emma said, swiping at her eyes. It was a small acknowledgment of her screwing up, and it gave Perry a flicker of relief.

"It's not your fault," he assured her. "Your uncle is an adult. He should've been paying more attention out there. To you. To what he was doing . . ." His voice trailed off.

"Can you both please stop now?" Emma asked. Amelia handed her a box of tissues.

Perry wished he could. He wished they would never have to talk about this sort of thing again. But there was one more question. "Honey, I know this is hard, but there's one last thing I hope you can help us with. This is important. Do you think Uncle Jake was drunk?"

Emma hesitated. "No." Then, "I don't know. Maybe." The only sound in the room was her fingers drumming nervously on her phone case.

Perry glanced at Amelia.

"Can't you ask the hospital about that?" Emma was waffling, trying to cover for her uncle. He could feel it.

"The reason I ask is because he went straight into surgery after the accident, and they didn't do a blood alcohol test on him. But we need to know."

"Why?" Emma snapped. "It doesn't change what happened. Luci's hurt. He's hurt. What difference does it make now?" Her face flushed as she struggled to hold back tears.

Amelia went to her and looked beseechingly at Perry. "It's okay, honey. We didn't mean to upset you." She rubbed Emma's back in slow circles, and as Perry looked on he felt whatever had been coursing through him slow. "Why don't you try to get some rest."

Perry followed Amelia out of the room, feeling worse than he had when they'd gone in.

"At least she told the truth," Amelia whispered as they went downstairs.

"Yes, but not all of it. She's hiding something. I think she's protecting Jake."

Amelia went to the kitchen and put on a pot of tea. "If that's true, you know I'll kill him with my bare hands before you have a chance to."

Despite the awfulness of it all, Perry smiled at his wife. He did not doubt this.

She turned to look at him. "Look, we may never know for sure if Jake was drunk. Your brother has always had a complicated relationship with alcohol. But we can't keep pressing Emma," she said. "It's too much."

"Do you think I like this? I hate having to ask her, seeing how tortured this makes her feel. But how else are we supposed to find out what happened?"

Amelia threw up her hands. "I don't know, Perry."

"I had hoped the police would take care of this, but they haven't found out shit. They need to do their job."

"Then let them! Let the police handle it. Stop trying to find out what exactly happened and let's instead focus on getting Emma better." Amelia's eyes flashed. "That is our job!" She was as angry as he was, he realized, but for different reasons.

"I'm sorry," he said, stepping toward her. "I'm trying." He put a hand on her arm, but she shrugged it off.

"Please, Perry. You need to stop pushing everyone."

He let his hands fall to his side. "I don't mean to."

The teakettle began to whistle and Amelia yanked it off the range. "I know Emma's okay and I should feel relieved, but I just feel so . . ."

"Angry?"

She met his gaze. "And helpless."

Perry nodded. He felt it, too. He was angry that their daughter looked as if she'd been mugged, but was clearly far more bruised somewhere on the inside. He was angry that their boat was destroyed, and now he'd have to deal with insurance. He was angry that he hadn't finished his contract at work and that his colleague Spencer Ashe was probably taking it over at that very moment while he was standing in the kitchen. But most of all, he was angry at Jake. Jake, who was not a parent. Who had no idea what it was like to trust someone else with your only child and then get that phone call from the paramedics. To throw yourself behind the wheel of a car that simply could not deliver you fast enough to the hospital, not knowing what you'd find when you got there. The back of his neck prickled at the memory. It was only two days ago, and yet Perry had felt the pulsing course of adrenaline every hour since. He was poised and alert, ready to strike.

Amelia abandoned the teakettle and headed out of the kitchen.

"Want me to pour you that cup of tea?" he offered.

"What I'd like is a little space. I think we could both use some. I'm going upstairs to lie down."

Perry watched her climb the stairs. How he wanted to flop down and give in, too. What he'd have given for a moment's rest. He'd have slept like the dead, if he could. But he couldn't. Just as he couldn't seem to comfort his wife or daughter.

He spied his keys on the far counter, and retrieved them. He was halfway to the door when he heard Amelia call down to him. She was leaning over the railing.

"Where are you going?"

"For a drive."

"A drive." She said it with soft wistfulness, as one does when they name something they love. A favorite dessert. A place they miss.

He paused, his heart hopeful for a beat. "Would you like to come?" It was something they used to do, after a fight: go for a drive together. The destination did not matter, because the place they were aimed at could not be found on any map. It was a space between them. They'd get in the car and stare straight ahead. Mile after wordless mile. Until at some point one would reach for the other's hand. Just like that. And then Perry would know they'd arrived.

Amelia shook her head. "I think we're out of toilet paper."

"Toilet paper," Perry said, trying to hide his disappointment. "Right."

As he turned his car onto the main road toward town, Perry could not think of toilet paper. Or stopping in at the small local market where everyone knew him and would have heard about the accident. This was exactly what Amelia claimed to love about living in a small town, and exactly what he loathed. Instead, he sailed right past the market turnoff and up Route 37 toward New Milford. From there he turned onto Route 7, wound his way through the back roads past the hospital, and continued left on Route 202. For the first time, Perry did not have a plan. What he had was an image. Of Emma in bed. Emma who did not want or need them right now. Who would not even make eye contact with him, and whose fingers drummed anxiously on her phone. Who was not *perfectly fine*, as the discharging hospitalist had assured him. And whom he could not seem to help.

So instead Perry switched mental gears and focused on the next image that came to mind. Of a little girl, smaller than Emma. With a pink cast.

Twenty minutes later, he sailed over the winding hills of Litchfield County that divided his town of Lenox and Olivia's town of Washington. To the big white farmhouse with the shingled cottage in the rear. Where Buster lunged and barked on the other side of the door like a rabid animal. Where Perry was tempted to turn around and get his wits about him, but upon seeing a child-sized pair of polka-dot rain boots sitting on the front porch, he halted. He looked once more through the door. At the dog that little girl loved. Who might or might not take his arm off.

Perry did not believe in signs. He believed life was a string of unpredictable occurrences looming on the horizon. Planning was your only hope against it. There were no signs. But then he spied a length of rope lying on the porch next to the polka-dot rain boots. And when the door handle turned beneath his fingers, he had to wonder.

He knew his behavior could be construed as breaking and entering. It might even have constituted dog-napping. The only thing he could do now was push the front door ever so slightly ajar to give himself ample time for a head start. Then, he grabbed the rope and raced down the porch steps to his car, faster than he had run since his high school track days. To where he flung open the back door and stood behind it, shielding himself. By then Buster had nosed the front door open and galloped down the porch steps toward him. Perry closed his eyes, praying to remain unscathed and intact. Buster stopped short of Perry, who hid behind the open car door, and thrust his nose exactly where he should not. Perry winced, holding his breath as the dog sniffed up and down his leg, his nostrils making quick snorting noises. After determining Perry bore neither threat nor treat, he ambled over to a clump of daylilies and lifted his leg. For a moment Perry feared his mission would fail.

But as he imagined all the things that could still go wrong,

Buster turned his way. He walked up to the open door and stuck his head inside Perry's car. And then with the whole of his hairy being, like a magnificent mythical beast, Buster leapt into the backseat. Perry slammed the door. Before he could change his mind, he hurried around to the driver's side and slid behind the wheel.

In the rearview mirror Buster stared back at him. "Want to go for a ride?" Perry asked in the most nonpetrified tone of voice he could muster. He could've sworn the beast smiled back at him.

In that moment Perry made a decision. In fifteen minutes they could be at the hospital. He would not look back again. Not at the cloud of dog hair rising about him. Not at the pattern of wet nose prints accumulating in viral momentum across his back window. It was too late.

Perry started the car. He sneezed once, and again. Then put the car in drive.

Phoebe

With everyone at the hospital, Phoebe did not want to bother her parents with the realization she'd finally come to: her mother was right. There was no other choice. She needed to move home. The renovations had hit a point where the house was no longer livable.

"Remember we talked about adding a second bath upstairs?" she had asked earlier.

Dave kept working, so at first she didn't think he'd heard. "What about it?" he said, finally.

"Well, you'd mentioned borrowing some bedroom space from the second large bedroom. I don't love the idea of one boy having a larger bedroom than the other."

Dave turned to her, hands on his hips, his gaze even. So even that she imagined him using one of those liquid-filled bubble levels to direct it at her. However he did it, it was effective. She tried to fix him with one of her own. "What I also don't love is all four of us sharing one bathroom upstairs. You know, for resale purposes, as well as livability."

Dave considered this. "Those are both good reasons. But a second bath isn't a budget item."

"I'm aware of that. But is it still possible?"

Dave glanced around the room at the dusty space. "Do you mean humanly possible?" Another of his quirks. No matter, she had her answer. It could be done; it just wasn't going to be easy.

"Good. Because I'd like to tackle it."

"I suppose if you're going to do it, it makes sense to get it over with now. While the house is torn up and the workers and equipment are on-site. Cheaper that way."

Phoebe nodded heartily, but he wasn't done.

"Look, if you're serious about that, we can go up and take a look. But I'd need to know in the next couple days to line up the plumber. And you'd need to check with town hall to be sure the septic is in compliance."

Phoebe loathed going to town hall. There was always another permit to obtain, another inspection to schedule, and then there was the waiting for approvals. She'd become painfully familiar with the Health Department, the Building Department, the Planning and Zoning Board, and her least favorite, the enforcement officer. The woman seemed poised to veto just about every proposed project, citing anything from setbacks to "endangered fern species" on the property. Twice already Phoebe had had to go before the Board at monthly meetings. It wasn't just expensive. It was stressful. She trudged into the town hall with a hastily written script in hand, including several highlighted things Dave had advised she say, and a few underlined things *not* to say. What she really wanted was for him to go in; he was so much better at this than she, but she couldn't spare him at the site.

To her surprise, the news from this town hall visit was good for once! She returned to the site that afternoon and told Dave that the septic was in compliance for an added bathroom. It was almost too good to be true. Rob, however, didn't celebrate the small victory.

"Are you sure we need a second bathroom?" he asked her as he changed out of his business clothes, later that night. The look on his face was anything but pleased. But she could not have timed it better. It was the bedtime hour, and as if on cue the boys came thundering in. Phoebe didn't say a word. She allowed Rob to witness the pushing and shoving, the splashing. The soaked towels on the floor. The smeared toothpaste in the single sink.

"It is pretty tight in here," he admitted, glancing warily at the aftermath.

"They're only going to get bigger," she reminded him.

"If only our bank account was. Where are we going to find the money for this?"

That was the bad news. They'd have to dip into savings. "But a two-and-a-half house is more valuable than a one-and-a-half," she proffered. "Think of the resale. It's an investment."

The next day Jed was moved into Patrick's room, his furniture emptied, and the wall came down. With all the commotion and debris, Phoebe took the boys to her parents' house for the day. She was sitting at the kitchen island eating a grilled cheese sandwich and showing Edward and Jane the adorable Jack and Jill bathroom they had designed when her phone rang. For the first time, things seemed to be working out. Until her cell phone rang.

Half an hour later she was back at the cottage she'd only just left, staring at a newly exposed wall of twisted electrical lines. "I don't understand. The house is supposedly up to code. The electrician rewired."

"He did," Dave said. "Downstairs. But this section of the house was an addition, and whoever did it didn't wire properly."

All of the progress they'd made came to a halt. And the punches kept coming. It wasn't just the wiring. One of the walls, a load-bearing one, wasn't properly framed. Dave called Rob and

Phoebe in to explain his concerns. "See this joist? All of the weight from the roof rests on this, and it runs the entire section of this part of the house. It's a mere two-by-four, attached to another. And they're bowing. We need a new LVL beam."

As Phoebe stood under the eaves, which had been opened up to reveal the skeleton of the framing, she felt like her own insides were also being exposed. Rob stood motionlessly, hands on his hips. She could feel stress radiating from him, reverberating off the pitched ceiling. She wondered, if she opened a window, would it fly up into the sky, allowing them all a little more breathing space?

Dave's gaze traveled from Rob's face to hers. She and Dave had a solid working relationship. They were in the trenches together day in and out, and they knew how to read each other. Rob was only on-site for occasional updates and walk-throughs. Dave had no reason to know how Rob would take this news, and for once, neither did she.

"What kind of cost are we talking about?"

Dave shook his head. "I can't say for sure until I get John Glazer back in here to look at the electricals. But for the beam work, somewhere in the order of five to seven thousand, all in."

Rob raked his hand through his hair. "Look. I understand the wiring is a fire hazard. But what about the beam? What if we just seal it back up?"

Phoebe looked at Rob aghast. He couldn't be serious.

Dave must have been very used to such questions. "Well, the house won't fall down today or tomorrow. But that's where it's headed."

Rob considered this for a long moment. "Well, then I guess we have no choice. I'm just glad it's not a five-digit fix."

Phoebe let her breath out. "Right. Thank God."

As the crew packed up for the day, Phoebe went down to the kitchen to start dinner. At that point of the project, her "kitchen" had been reduced to a corner in the living room. A microwave rested on one of Grandma Elsie's dovetailed occasional tables. Rob had set up a double-burner camping hot plate on the table. She went out to the garage, where the old fridge hummed loudly in the lone bay, and pulled out chicken breasts and squash. She took these to the back patio where she lit the grill. Rob joined her.

"Barbecue chicken," she told him, smiling. "Taking a night off of the tacos." She glanced around. "Though I can't find the new bottle of barbecue sauce. Do you know where we put the boxes of kitchen staples?"

He feigned a smile, and shook his head. Rob looked drained.

"Baby, I'm sorry about the wiring and wall work," she said.

"Well, at least they caught it. If we hadn't opened up that wall, who knows what would've happened."

He was right, and she was relieved to hear that he was seeing the sense this made, despite the blow to their wallet.

"But, Phoebe, this is what I was worried about. There's no telling what's next. Old houses have old problems. And they're costly."

"The inspector should've picked up on this stuff." She drizzled the chicken with olive oil and glanced around for the salt and pepper. Damn it. It must be in the living room.

Rob shrugged. "The sill stuff, yes. But I don't even blame him for this. Unless you tear open walls, who's to say. We just can't do anything else. After this bathroom, that's it. Whatever else we may want or think we need, it has to wait. We can't afford it."

She was glad to hear him using the term "we." Most of the ideas had been hers, even though he'd gotten on board. "I promise," she said, looking up at him.

He watched her set the meat on the grill. "Fuck," she said, looking around her cramped work space.

"What's wrong?"

She gave him a sheepish look. "I don't know where the spatula is."

From inside the house came a crash and a shout. The boys had been cooped up in the living room this whole time. Along with the couch covered in toys, her makeshift kitchen, and what seemed like a hundred boxes, none of which ever seemed to hold what she was looking for.

"Don't you need a platter for the chicken, too?"

She nodded, feeling about ready to cry. "And plates."

Rob looked at her sympathetically. "I'll go look, but, Phoebe?"

"Yeah?"

"It's time."

She knew what was coming.

"We can't stay here. Not with the increase in renovations going on. I want you to call your parents after dinner." Rob waited until she looked up and nodded.

As much as she hated to pack everything up and move, *once again*, she couldn't disagree. She'd lose her mind if she stayed.

When he opened the sliding door, the noise that emanated from the living room was one of toddler disaster. She watched Rob climb over the boxes, bending to scoop up Jed, who was crying. Or maybe it was Patrick; she couldn't tell from the late-day sun reflecting off the glass. Rob had probably already forgotten about the spatula, platter, and plates. Phoebe turned her back and stared out at the lake.

Olivia

The two uniformed officers had their backs to her when she entered the hospital room, but Olivia could tell right away from the look on Jake's face that something wasn't right.

When he looked up and saw her standing in the door, he adjusted his expression. "Oh. This is my fiancée, Olivia Cossette."

The officers turned. The older one, with soft features and graying hair, smiled empathetically. "I'm Sergeant Baylor, and this is my deputy, Officer Cripky." Cripky looked her up and down a moment too long.

"We're trying to gather some information about the accident," the older officer explained, as if her arrival commanded explanation.

"Should I go?" she asked. Though she did not want to. Something about Jake's demeanor warned her not to. Her interest went beyond curiosity, even beyond a mother's need to know. Something about the accident still didn't seem right.

"That's up to your fiancé," Cripky said. He was attractive and direct, but there was a cockiness to his bearing that Olivia didn't trust.

She looked to Jake, trying to gauge his expression. "She can stay," he said, finally, fidgeting with the edge of his hospital blanket.

Olivia took a seat by the window, trying to make herself obscure. While this was likely all a formality, she couldn't help but feel uneasy. Jake looked positively irritated.

Sergeant Baylor continued his line of questioning. "So, from what you're saying, you were driving the boat along the shore just before the accident. Can you estimate the depth of water, or the distance from the dock?"

Jake's brow furrowed. "I'd say we were one hundred feet offshore. Maybe a little more."

"Do you make it a practice of hugging the shoreline, or was there a reason you were close?"

"No, but there were a number of boats out on the water that day, some waterskiing. Since we were just going for a little sightseeing, I figured we'd get out of the way of traffic."

Officer Baylor flipped through some notes he had on a pad. "It says here that it was estimated you were traveling at high speed upon impact. Would you say that was the speed you maintained along the shore, or did you suddenly increase speed for some reason?"

Jake shook his head. "High speed? I honestly don't remember how fast we were going, but I never travel at a high rate of speed along the shore. It can be rocky with shallow pockets." He looked to Olivia. "I had the girls with me."

Cripky cleared his throat. "Do you know what the speed limits are on Candlewood?"

"Forty-five miles per hour," Jake replied. "But there's no way we were going that fast."

"Twenty-five at night, sir," Cripky added.

Jake narrowed his eyes. "It was daytime."

"About how fast would you say you were traveling?" the sergeant asked.

Olivia leaned forward. Every time she and Jake discussed the accident, he got flustered. But he'd sworn up and down that they'd been traveling at a slow clip. That he couldn't account for the sudden increase before the boat hit the dock.

"I don't know exactly, but no more than twenty-five."

"Do you have any idea what speed witnesses estimated you were traveling at just before the point of impact?"

Jake regarded the sergeant with sad eyes. "No."

Sergeant Baylor flipped again to a different page of his notebook. Olivia had full view of his notes from where she sat, but she was too far away to make any of them out. "One eyewitness account guesses you were going at about fifty miles an hour."

Jake looked at him. "Guesses."

"Another guessed sixty-five."

"There's no way," Jake snapped.

Olivia watched him pick at the blanket. She couldn't blame him for being nervous, after all that had happened. But she knew Jake: this wasn't nervousness.

"Mr. Goodwin, no one is trying to place blame. At this stage, we're trying to understand what happened. We have three people in the hospital, and a privately owned dock that's been ripped in half. Insurance will be asking the same questions."

Jake didn't look up. "And I'll tell them the same thing."

The sergeant closed his notebook and Olivia's chest tightened. Jake's attitude was starting to annoy him. "Had you been drinking that day, Mr. Goodwin?"

Jake's head snapped up. "A little. Why?"

Cripky stepped forward, and Olivia could feel the energy in the room shift. "No need to be defensive, Mr. Goodwin. We're just trying to get a picture of that day. How long would you say you've been boating on Candlewood Lake? You grew up on the lake, right?"

"I got my CPWO when I was thirteen." He looked at the sergeant. "Certificate of Personal Watercraft Operation. We've had boats in my family since I can remember."

"And you're how old now?"

"Thirty-two."

"So, let's see. That would mean you've been boating for . . ." Cripky smiled indulgently over his shoulder at Olivia. "Hang on. I was never top of my class in math."

"Nineteen," Olivia replied.

All three men turned around.

"Jake's had nineteen years of boating experience." Olivia looked at Cripky when she said it. "He's a very safe driver." But even as she found herself defending Jake, a flicker of warning lit within her. If what he had told her about the accident was true, why was he getting so angry with the officers' line of questioning?

"So, nineteen years. That's a lot. In those nineteen years, have you ever lost control over a boat before?"

Jake considered the question. "Never."

"Can you account for reasons why someone would lose control over a boat and achieve sudden acceleration, as you did the other day?" Cripky was pushing. Olivia suddenly decided she hated the guy.

Jake looked flummoxed. "I don't know, a few reasons maybe."

"Such as?"

"Such as another boat cuts you off. Or you run into something underwater you can't see. Or snag something in the propeller."

Cripky leaned back on his heels. "Did anything like that happen to you before the accident that you're aware of?"

Jake shook his head. "No."

"Are there any other reasons you can think of that boat operators suddenly lose control?"

"If they were drunk."

"How much did you drink that day, Mr. Goodwin?"

Jake locked eyes with Olivia.

"Answer my question. How many did you have?"

"I don't remember." Jake shook his head. "A few. I really don't remember."

"In how short a time?"

"Maybe an hour or so. I don't know. It was a party. It lasted all afternoon."

Olivia's eyes watered. It *was* a party. For the two of them. And even though Jake had never been a big drinker since they'd met, he'd admitted to having been a bit of a party boy in his past.

She shifted in her seat and Cripky looked her way. "Everything okay?"

"Everything's fine." But it wasn't. This was on her, too. She'd let Luci go out on the boat without her.

Cripky resumed his questions. "Unfortunately, Mr. Goodwin, we can't be sure of how much you had to drink that day. Because you were brought in with serious injuries and went straight to the OR. By the time they ran a toxicology report on you, it was several hours after the accident. All we have to go on is . . . you."

Jake's eyes flashed. "You think I'm lying?"

Cripky regarded him thoughtfully. "It doesn't matter what I think. The truth has a way of coming out. Eventually."

Jake glared back at him, saying nothing, and the two held silent eye contact until Olivia feared she would fly out of her seat.

"Well, I think we're done for today," the sergeant said, tucking his notes away. "We'll be in touch if we need more."

Olivia stood up, eyes on Jake, but he wouldn't look at her.

The officers thanked Jake, then turned to say goodbye.

"Miss . . . ?"

"Cossette," Olivia said.

"Miss Cossette. May I have a word with you, in private?"

From over the sergeant's shoulder Olivia saw Jake's gaze snap in their direction. But she found herself following them out into the hall, anyway. She had her own interests to protect. "Yes, of course."

The sergeant spoke first. "You understand, we're just trying to put together the pieces of the picture. None of us were there. And that means we have to talk to everyone involved."

Olivia nodded. She wasn't stupid. "I told the first officer who interviewed us everything I know. About the barbecue; who was there, what we ate, what we drank." She paused. "I wasn't on the boat."

"That must tear you up," Cripky said.

Olivia ignored this, aiming her gaze at the sergeant instead.

"Even so, you were there before the accident. You saw Jake. You two spent the day together."

"We did."

"With your daughter, as well."

Olivia swallowed. "Yes."

The sergeant flipped through his notes. "Who was also in-jured. Somewhat seriously. A broken arm, I've been told?"

"Yes." But there was more, Olivia wanted to scream. All the invisible injuries, the ones on the inside.

"We understand that your daughter may be suffering from PTSD, and we are very sorry to hear that. But we'd like to talk to her."

"You can't." Olivia crossed her arms.

"I know how difficult this is . . ."

"No, Sergeant. You don't." Olivia glanced down the hall to Jake's doorway. She recalled Perry's condemnation of his brother: "Reckless."

And Jane's insistence that this was all a terrible mystery. A freak accident.

And also the pain in Jake's eyes every time she walked into his room. From the moment he'd started to rouse in recovery, something about him had been different. From the way he wouldn't quite look at her, to the tone in his voice; a wounded tone that she'd been sure would fade. But instead, it had grown into anger. She had anger of her own. At herself. At both of them, for ever thinking it was all right to let Luci out on the lake without her. There was enough anger for both of them. But standing there in the hospital corridor she realized for the first time they were not united in it. Her deepest loyalty lay to her daughter; Luci came first.

"Luci suffers from a condition called selective mutism. At times she cannot talk. Literally cannot talk." Olivia waited for this news to sink in. "But she has always talked to me. And now she can't do that either." Without warning hot tears poured from her eyes. But she wasn't done. "If my daughter is so traumatized that she can't talk to me, her own mother, then she cannot talk to you." She looked fiercely between both officers to make sure they understood. "I won't let her suffer anymore."

Cripky opened his mouth to speak and Olivia felt herself coil, at the ready, but thankfully the sergeant held up his hand. "I understand, Miss Cossette. We don't want to upset your child anymore. If we need anything further, we'll be in touch."

Olivia waited until she could hear the distant echo of their footsteps moving down the hall. Then she returned to Jake's room, and pulled the door closed hard behind her. Jake was staring out the window. He did not turn to look at her.

Olivia cleared her throat. She was a mother, first. "What is it you're not telling me?"

Emma

That saying about kids being brutally honest? Yep. Brutally true. But she would rather endure the guileless gasps and pointed fingers of her campers than the covert glances and whispers from some of the counselors any day. She hadn't been back at camp for more than two minutes, and already her first-grade campers had circled her in one scrutinizing little band.

"Where *were* you?"

"What happened to your *face*?"

"*That* looks like it hurts. Bad."

The morning was bright, and Emma instinctively shielded her eyes. Much of her swelling had gone down, but the bruising had not. The initial purplish blue that had radiated across her cheek had morphed to a greenish-yellow cast that no amount of concealer she'd tried in the mirror could cover. In the end, she'd pulled a baseball cap on and tugged the brim down low over her forehead. As she walked down the street to the clubhouse, she steeled herself against the onslaught of questions she knew would be waiting for her. Candlewood Cove was a small lakeside community within Lenox, and word of the boating accident had already traveled up and down the lake. She'd have to face the music sometime. And seated here, in front of twelve inquiring sets of eyes and gaping mouths, she realized that time was now.

Six-year-old Maisy Barton had curlicue chestnut pigtails that stuck out due east and west. Now they swung back and forth as she shook her head in awe. "Oh, Miss Emma. You look terr-i-ble!"

Emma managed a smile. "Yeah, I know. But it'll get better soon."

"I hope so," another little girl said. "Does it hurt?"

Emma shook her head, even though it still did, a little. "It looks worse than it feels. I'll be okay."

"Were you in a fight?" Taylor Gould asked.

Before Emma could answer, someone else did. "If you think *she* looks bad, you should see the other guy."

All the campers turned, as did Emma. Sully McMahon sliced through their tiny circle and slid onto the picnic table seat across from her. He propped his chin on his hands and smiled. "I hope you won."

Emma couldn't help but laugh.

"I knew it!" Taylor shouted. "Miss Emma was in a fight." Which set off a buzz through the circle, until the morning meeting bell clanged from up the hill and the campers dispersed.

"How are you, really?" Sully asked when they were alone.

Emma touched her cheek again. "We should probably get up to morning circle before our boss loses it."

Sully remained seated. "I texted you." His blue eyes were so intent. She stood up.

"I know. Thanks for checking in. My mom took my phone away." She pointed to her head. "It's a concussion thing. No bright lights or screens."

Sully hopped up and came around the table, matching her stride as she climbed the hill to the clubhouse. "So?"

Emma glanced sideways. "So what?"

"What happened out there?"

She paused. "What did you hear?"

This made Sully shake his head. "Do you ever answer a question directly?" They were almost at the morning meeting spot, and she really wished he'd drop it. She didn't want to discuss this, period, let alone in front of everyone else.

"All I heard was your boat ran aground. You were with your grandfather?"

"My uncle. And his fiancée's daughter." Emma's throat got tight at the thought of Luci and her little pink cast. "And the boat didn't run aground, it hit a dock," she corrected him.

"Okay. The uncle. And the dock. Got it." Sully held up his hands defensively.

Emma halted. It had come out more strongly than she'd meant it to. But she really didn't want to get into the accident. It was bad enough that Sully had already studied every bruise and bump on her face close-up. Maybe her father was right. She should've stayed home.

"Look, I'm sorry. It's just kind of fresh, is all."

Sully's expression softened. "I don't mean to pry. I'm just glad you're okay."

The bell clanged again. The morning meeting was getting started. The camp director was doing his usual last call of the roster, looking for stragglers. "McMahon, get up here!"

"Catch you later," Sully said. He trotted ahead to the circle.

Emma took her time joining them. She could feel Amanda Hastings's eyes on her as she approached the campfire circle, taking her place beside Alicia, whom she figured was about the only person she could take shelter with. But she was wrong.

"Oh my God," Alicia whispered. Her eyes widened as they traveled across her face. "You look like hell."

"Jesus. Thanks." Emma turned away. This was why she sometimes couldn't stand Alicia.

Alicia grabbed her hand. "I didn't mean it like that. It just looks like it hurts. A lot."

"Yeah, well it does."

"Sorry I was late today. I overslept. But my dad had a meeting in the city yesterday, and he brought home Zabar's bagels." She handed Emma a wrapped wax-paper packet. She'd even taped it neatly. "I know how you feel about bagels." And this was why she loved Alicia.

Emma accepted the bagel, but she was still annoyed.

Alicia wiggled her eyebrows. "Extra cream cheese . . ."

"I'm not really hungry," Emma said.

"Liar. Just shut up and eat it."

Being on restricted activity was deathly boring. The doctors said Emma could return to camp as long as she didn't do anything physical. No swimming. No running. No contact sports. Which basically meant Emma was constrained to the craft table and the narrow spit of beach sand, watching as the other counselors and CITs took the kids out in kayaks, played games, and swam. But even that beat staying at home with her parents. Ever since the accident they'd done nothing but hover. Outside her door. Over her shoulder. Did she want tea? Was she hungry? Did she need a Tylenol? She wouldn't have been surprised if her parents were lurking outside the bathroom door as they did when she was potty training: "Do you need help in there??"

Her mom was what she thought of as a typical parent worrier. Like when she went to the mall with Alicia. "Stay together! Don't talk to strangers." Her father, however, was another story. "Don't forget to triple-check the ties on the boat. Make sure they're secure. Put the cover on tight. Did you check the cover? Check it again." He was fastidious. Everything in life had to be done in a certain way, in a certain order. And since coming home from the hospital, he'd turned it on her.

"Is that wise?" he'd asked her mother that morning at breakfast, when he learned that she was heading back to camp. "She hasn't had her concussion release test done yet. The doctor was very specific about that."

Thankfully her mother was ahead of him. "Which is why she isn't doing anything physical. She needs to get out of the house. Get some sun, see her friends. Let her go, Perry."

Her father looked aghast. "But this isn't protocol."

Her mother handed her a bagged lunch. "Here, honey, make sure you eat." Then to her father, "It's just up the street. She'll be fine." And so far, she'd been fine. Mostly. Until lunchtime.

For lunch hour the campers were free to sit with friends from any of the groups, in a variety of spots. Some chose the shade beneath the giant weeping willow on the hill. Others liked the picnic tables on the beach. Emma and Alicia always sat together, sometimes with Brad, beside the kayak stand. It was partly shaded and near the water. And far enough away from others to speak freely.

"So what happened out there?" Alicia asked. Emma had to give her credit that she'd waited until lunch to ask. Alicia was anything but patient.

"My grandparents had an engagement party for my uncle Jake and Olivia. We took the boat out for a spin."

"Your dad's beloved boat?"

Emma nodded.

Alicia snorted. "I can't believe he let anyone drive it but himself."

Brad was listening quietly. "Was your uncle the one driving?"

Emma stared at her sandwich. "Yeah. Why?"

Before Brad could answer, Alicia interrupted, "Was he drunk?"

Emma spun around to face her. Alicia had known her family for years. Had always thought her uncle Jake was cute and fun—for a while Emma suspected she had a crush on him. Most girls did. It was no secret Jake liked to have a good time at family parties and holidays. Sometimes, too much of one. But it pissed her off to hear Alicia say it out loud. And with her mouth full like that. She glared at her. "Jesus, Alicia."

Alicia wiped her mouth. "Sorry. I was just wondering."

"Well, stop," Emma snapped. "It doesn't change anything now, does it?"

Brad looked uncomfortably between the two of them. "She didn't mean it like that, Em."

"I didn't," Alicia insisted. "I said sorry."

They ate for a while in silence, and Emma fought the memories coming back to her. Even here at camp, they flashed in her mind like snapshots: *Sitting on the bench seat with Luci in her lap. Jake at the wheel, reaching behind his seat for the cooler. Emma helping him with the lid, passing him a beer. The look on his face when she reached for another. Twisted off the lid.*

She squeezed her eyes shut, trying to shake the memory away.

"So, does it hurt?"

"What?" Emma opened her eyes to find herself staring up at Amanda. Her gaze was cool, not exactly concerned.

"Of course it hurts," Alicia told her.

Amanda ignored this.

"Not so much anymore," Emma said. She glanced past Amanda to her usual table. Sully, Christie, and a few others were talking and eating.

"I heard your dad's boat was totaled. Bummer."

Emma swallowed. Her father hadn't said anything about the

boat to her, and she'd been wondering when he would. He loved that boat.

"Yeah, it was a bummer." She looked at Amanda. What did she want?

"So, my dad and mom are away. I'm having people over Saturday night." She looked at Alicia. "Is your brother home for the summer?"

Alicia nodded warily.

"Cool. You should bring him."

"My brother?"

Amanda regarded her. "If he's around, you three should come by." It was clear to Emma then. Amanda didn't care about the boat accident. Or inviting them to a party. Emma was Amanda's connection to Alicia's brother, Chet. This was about Chet.

Alicia perked up. She either wasn't getting it, or didn't care. "This Saturday? Yeah, I think I'm free."

Brad, who'd remained silent until now, leaned forward. "What time is the party?"

Amanda flicked her gaze in his direction. "Who are you?" Before he could answer, she returned her attention to Emma and Alicia. "If Chet is around, feel free to stop by." The message was clear. They were invited—if they brought Chet. Amanda didn't wait for a reply. She was already heading back to her table.

"Cool! See you Saturday," Alicia shouted after her.

Emma elbowed her gently. "Chill."

Next to her, Brad stared at his lunch. "You're not missing anything," Emma told him. "I've heard her parties are lame, and it'll probably get broken up by the cops anyway."

But Alicia was too overcome to notice. "Oh my God. We're invited to Amanda Hastings's keg party! I have to come up with an excuse for my parents. What are you going to wear?"

Emma set her lunch down. She wasn't hungry anymore. Amanda probably wanted to date Alicia's brother Chet. She probably wanted to make her boyfriend, Steve, jealous. Emma would have to warn Alicia about all of this before they decided whether or not to go. Did she even want to go?

From Amanda's table across the sand, Sully looked up. Before she lost her nerve, Emma waved. Sully waved back.

She really hoped Chet was free on Saturday night.

Perry

The Metro-North commute back to Connecticut was a sweatbox. Midway between Chappaqua and Mount Kisco the air-conditioning went out. By the time the train pulled in to Southeast Station, Perry's dress shirt was stuck to his back. The car smelled of overheated vinyl and body odor. It was nauseating.

Thank God it was Friday. Emma would have finished her first couple of days back at camp. The family could slow down and relax for the weekend. But not on the lake. Despite the perfect forecast, Perry had no intention of going anywhere near the lake.

The insurance company had come out to assess the damages. Just as he'd known it would be, the boat was declared totaled. But still, it smarted when he had to sign insurance forms. In addition to the boat damage, there was the matter of the repair work to be done to the Dunlaps' dock, where the accident had occurred. Perry had accompanied the adjuster to the site, and again, Mr. Dunlap kindly made no fuss. But he had requested his own assessment, as well. The two quotes would be compared. Negotiations would be made. Perry did not take any of it personally. This was the business of insurance. Still, having the insurance company's official paperwork completed somehow made all of it feel worse. Perry knew he should feel grateful. Boats and docks could be replaced. People could not. But Perry couldn't help himself; with Jake at the helm of this accident, Perry found he was unable to shake a growing ire within him. His only recourse for now was avoidance. Avoidance of the water and of his brother.

But there were others to consider. Emma first, of course. And Olivia and Luci. Perry worried about Olivia being on her own. He had no idea what kind of insurance she had, though, frankly he'd been surprised she had any. Usually those artistic types just didn't. And he still didn't know if she was a US citizen or on some kind of visa, an assumption that only further undermined any confidence he had in her holding good health insurance.

But Perry knew this was not a matter of insurance. He also felt a responsibility for Jake. People had been hurt and property was damaged. And though Perry felt badly for his little brother on some level, he couldn't help but feel that Jake was burdening Olivia further with his own injuries and needs. After all the harm he'd caused, poor Olivia was the one who'd end up taking care of him.

He tried to think of alternatives. Perry didn't exactly want his parents stepping in to rescue his little brother; something they were not only known to do but also famous for. They had Grandma Elsie to take care of, and now Phoebe and her family on top of it. Which only left Olivia and him.

But before he could consider what to do about Olivia and Jake, first there was Emma.

Something wasn't right. It went beyond the obvious fact that she was still in recovery. It also went beyond the explanation Amelia kept circling back to: "She's a teenager, honey. They're surly. They're aloof. She's just doing her job." Boy, was she! But all that was too convenient a package to wrap this in. Perry's gut told him there was something else. Something that kept his daughter distant, if polite. Troubled, despite appearing put together on the surface. Emma was simply not herself.

As he walked across the commuter lot to his car, he dialed Amelia. "Do you think she needs therapy?" he asked the moment she picked up.

"Who?" There seemed to be music playing in the background.

"Emma," he said impatiently.

There was a pause. "Did you have a bad day at work?"

Perry was used to this. Amelia answered questions with questions. But given his commute and the heat, and yes, a not-so-great day at work, he was less patient than usual. "Something is off about Emma, and I don't think we should ignore it. I'm wondering if she might have PTSD." Perry knew plenty about PTSD. A growing claim in insurance suits. Difficult to prove. Difficult to valuate. Which often worked to the insurance company's advantage. Now, on the victim's side, Perry suddenly felt differently.

"Hang on," Amelia said. On the other end of the phone he could hear some activity. Then the music faded. "Emma's here now. With Alicia."

"She has a friend over?" Perry was heartened.

"Yes. They came home together after camp. Emma asked if she could sleep over."

Well. Perhaps he'd jumped the gun. Maybe he just needed to give Emma more time to come around. She had been acting withdrawn, but if she had a friend over and was out of that cave of a room of hers, then this was a positive development.

"Can she?" Amelia asked. "I told her I thought it was fine, but maybe it's too soon for a sleepover. She's still supposed to be taking it easy."

"No, no. Let her have Alicia stay over. She could use a change of pace, and Alicia is a quiet kid. It's not like they're going to be up all night, partying." He was feeling so relieved, he laughed when he said it. Alicia was even more of a bookworm than Emma. She was shy, an honors student, and straightlaced. "Do you have popcorn at home?" he asked suddenly.

"Um, I think so. Why?"

"So the girls can watch movies. The doctor said she could have some screen time back now."

Amelia seemed distracted. "If that's what they want to do."

Perry had reached his car and he fumbled for his key. "Oh— here's a thought! Maybe I can fix the Ping-Pong table in the bonus room, like I've been meaning to. The girls can spread out their sleeping bags and camp out in there like old times." This was an excellent turn of events. Perry and Emma hadn't played Ping-Pong in years. She'd gotten pretty good, before the net broke. And he was working more. And then it just sort of stopped. Tonight he would change that. Maybe he'd challenge both girls to a tournament.

There was silence on the other end. "Well, sure. You can fix the table, I guess."

Perry sensed some disagreement with his idea. "Is that too strenuous for her? Now that I think about it, the doctor did say no heavy exercise . . ."

"No, it's not that."

"Then what?"

Amelia paused at the end of the line. "Nothing. It's sweet. It's just . . . she's older now. So don't be disappointed if you get the Ping-Pong table all set up and they end up doing something else instead. She's not ten years old anymore."

"Okay." Perry knew darn well Emma wasn't ten anymore. The fact that she'd drank beer with her uncle on the boat was proof of that. Which is exactly why he wanted to reintroduce some of the more wholesome things she enjoyed. Like Ping-Pong. What did

Amelia, or American youth over the age of ten, have against Ping-Pong? You could barely get a turn at the table at their beach clubhouse on any given weekend. Once again, he felt that Amelia was being overly critical. But he wouldn't say so. Not today. Today was turning out to be good. Emma was home with a friend. And she wanted to have a sleepover. Perry checked the time. If he hurried, he could stop at Dick's Sporting Goods and get that replacement net on the way home.

By the time he pulled in his driveway, the late-day sun had shifted to an orangey-pink hue, stretching its fingers over the lake. Perry stood by his car and admired the view. "How lucky we are to live here," Amelia often said. Perry appreciated the sentiment. But it had nothing to do with luck.

The moment he opened the door, the smell of sautéed garlic met him. He found Amelia in the kitchen, humming over a skillet of pink shrimp. "Hi, honey!" She turned for a quick kiss. "The girls are hungry, so I started dinner. I was worried you wouldn't make it. Traffic tonight?"

He held up the box he'd picked up at Dick's Sporting Goods.

"Oh. The net. You stopped for it."

"I did. Where's Emma? Maybe she can help me."

Amelia pointed her wooden spoon toward the stairwell. "They're upstairs getting ready."

"Getting ready?"

Amelia poured some white wine into the shrimp, and a cloud of steam rose. Perry's stomach growled in response. He realized he hadn't eaten since an early lunch meeting, and he was starving.

"Apparently there's some kind of camp event tonight. For the staff."

Perry hadn't heard anything about it. "On a weekend?"

"Well, I think it's more of a social thing. You know, the counselors getting together at the clubhouse."

Perry wasn't sure what to think about that. He'd hoped the girls would be home. He'd hoped they'd try out the Ping-Pong table and hang out with him and Amelia. It had been a while since Emma had had anyone over, and he rather liked the thought of hearing them giggling down the hall. When was the last time that had happened?

"Do we know what kind of get-together it is?"

Amelia shrugged. "She didn't really say. But I'm sure it's fine. It's just at the clubhouse. And that closes at ten." She returned her attention to the shrimp sizzling in the pan. "Will you call the girls? Dinner's ready."

Dinner was served outside on the patio, but it was not the relaxing summery evening he'd anticipated. Instead, the girls passed their phones back and forth, whispering and laughing over whatever it was they were looking at. Perry knew they didn't use Facebook—"*That*," Emma had informed him once, "is for old people." He caught Amelia's eye at the other end of the table. "It's the perfect night," he said, meaning the pink sky and the light breeze coming up over the water. But to his dismay it was lost on Emma and Alicia.

"Girls," Amelia said, finally. "Why don't we set our phones aside."

Alicia looked up, embarrassed, and turned hers off. Emma took longer to set hers aside.

"Hey, Mr. Goodwin," Alicia said, as if noticing Perry for the first time.

He smiled. "Hello, Alicia. How's your summer going?"

Alicia was excessively talkative, but for once Perry didn't mind. He liked hearing about camp. After working his way up on the board, to president of the Club, he oversaw the camp program, and it was one of the things he was most proud of. Engaging their community's kids in a safe educational environment on the lake was the quintessential summer experience!

On and on Alicia went. Perry soaked it all in, hungry for every grain of detail she shared, but he couldn't help but notice a few looks from Emma. It seemed she was trying to tone Alicia down. "We should probably go get ready," Emma said, rising suddenly from the table.

"There's dessert," Amelia said. "I have blueberry pie from the farm."

Emma loved the local farm's blueberry pie. But to his surprise, she declined. "No thanks. We're going to be late."

"Hey, honey," Perry said, hoping to grab her attention before they escaped the table. "I fixed the Ping-Pong table. It's ready for you!"

Emma blinked. "Oh. Thanks." Then, "What was wrong with it?"

Perry tried to keep the disappointment from his voice. "The net broke, remember?"

"Right." She nodded. "Okay, so we'd better get ready for tonight."

"What exactly is tonight?"

Perry could tell from the look on Emma's face she thought he was prying.

"Nothing, really. Some of the counselors are hanging out. At the clubhouse," she added.

Perry kept his sigh to himself. Well, maybe she'd at least play some Ping-Pong there.

"They're just excited about tonight," Amelia reassured him once the girls were indoors. "How was work today?"

Perry pushed the shrimp and rice around his plate. It was delicious, but he suddenly didn't feel as hungry. He didn't want to get into the halftime show issues. It was the weekend, and he wanted to leave that behind him back on his office desk in New York. "Tell me about your day," he said, instead.

Perry tried to listen as his wife filled him in on a meeting she'd had, and something else about an upcoming baby shower she needed to purchase a gift for. Instead he watched the endearing thing she did as she spoke. The first time he'd noticed it was on a second or third date, after they'd seen a particularly bad movie together. After, they'd gone to a hole-in-the-wall diner and ordered chocolate shakes and greasy burgers. He had no recollection of what the story was about, only what she'd done when she began to tell it. Amelia had set her hands on either side of her plate, palms down. Then she took a deep breath and leaned in as if she were about to tell him a secret, a small anticipatory smile playing at the corners of her mouth. Perry found himself mirroring her, leaning in, too. Hanging on to her every word. It had endeared Perry to her the very first time, and it had never failed to since. Now, under the growing dusk and the twinkling lights of the patio, Perry found he had no idea what Amelia was talking about. And gone was that special feeling that he wanted to hear whatever it was she had to say.

Was this what happened when parents were on edge about their child? Or was it the inevitable fading of appreciation for your spouse that came with the passage of time? Perry loved his wife, always had. There was no better match for him. And he was pretty sure she felt the same. But somewhere along the way something had gone missing. And whatever it was, in its place was an ache for its return.

Later, they cleaned up the kitchen mostly in silence. Despite his full belly, Perry felt the ache. He glanced over at Amelia, and wondered if she felt the same.

"Would you like to go for a walk later?" he asked. She always enjoyed a stroll through their neighborhood on a warm summer night.

Instead she glided out into the living room and turned on the TV. "Maybe later."

By the time the girls came back downstairs, Amelia was lying on the couch engrossed in a TV show. Something loud and gaudy flickered on the Bravo channel. Something he had zero desire to watch. Perry wiped down the kitchen counters and looked up just as Emma walked in. "Is that what you're wearing?" As soon as the words were out of his mouth, he regretted them.

Emma's smile vanished as if he'd taken a whiteboard eraser to it. She looked down at her cutoff shorts and midriff shirt, then back at her father. Only now there was an expression of ire, enhanced by the rim of dark eye makeup she'd applied. Where was this coming from? he wondered. Alicia was dressed in far more modest attire, he noticed. And her eyes had less . . . black stuff on them. And certainly less ire.

Amelia, who probably couldn't see what Perry saw from her seat in the living room, called out, "What's wrong?"

"I'm sorry," Perry added quickly. "You look very nice, Em. But isn't that a bit revealing?" Emma's slim waist was exposed from the top of her low-rise shorts to just below what he imagined to be her bra line. He winced.

Instead of replying, she stomped off toward the living room. Well, fine. Now it was her mother's turn to say something. Perry waited for Amelia to chime in. But she didn't.

"You girls have fun, and check in with me by ten, okay?" she said. Her voice was downright chipper.

Perry trailed Alicia, who trailed Emma out to the living room.

Emma leaned down and pecked her mother's cheek goodbye. She did not come over and offer him one.

As she was heading out the door, he stopped her. "No swimming yet," Perry reminded. "You haven't been—"

"Cleared from my concussion," Emma interjected. "I know, I know."

Amelia flashed him a look, and Perry held his tongue. He didn't want to ruin Emma's night. After all, this was what he and Amelia had wanted, for Emma to be more social. To spend more time with friends and less time hidden behind her books alone in her room. Besides, Emma was a good kid. A great kid. He trusted her.

"Have fun," he called meekly after them. What else was there to say?

As soon as the door closed, he turned to Amelia. "What was that?"

"What?" She seemed reluctant to drag her eyes from the television.

"Did you see what she was wearing? Since when does she dress like that?"

Amelia shrugged. "It's not like she's wearing it to school, and it is a Friday night with friends."

Friends. Some of whom were boys. Perry knew what effect an outfit like that would've had on him at that age. "I don't think she needs half her torso hanging out just because it's a Friday night."

Amelia put her hand to her forehead, as if she had a sudden headache. "Perry. I know it's hard to watch her grow up, but trust me. It's not a big deal. You should see what other girls wear every day."

Perry didn't care about what other girls wore. He had never liked that argument anyway. Who cared what everyone else did? This was their kid. And it was unlike her, even if it was like everyone else.

Amelia regarded him. "Why don't you go for that walk? You seem tense. It's a beautiful night."

Perry considered this. He didn't really feel like a walk anymore. "Sure you can't join me?"

She shook her head. "I'm wiped out."

"All right." Upstairs Perry changed out of his work clothes. He tossed his shirt in the dry-cleaning bag and cinched it tight. Tomorrow he'd drop it at the cleaners. He set his camel-colored loafers on the bottom shelf of the walk-in closet, between the saddle-brown and the black ones. He scrutinized the row and straightened one wayward pair of loafers, before standing back to admire it. Satisfied, he flicked off the light and shut the doors. On his way down the hall, he paused in Emma's doorway. She'd left the light on. Makeup and hair things were strewn across her desk. But there was her book, the one from the library she'd asked him to pick up for her a few days earlier. He walked in and picked it up. It was thick and heavy. A hardcover science fiction novel. He was pleased to see she was already on page 250. So maybe she wasn't growing away as much as she was simply growing up. He set the book down, hating to leave it open on its back like that (ruins the spine!), but not wanting to be accused of snooping, and headed back downstairs.

"Last call for a walk," he called from the foyer. He waited.

"Enjoy," Amelia replied, absently. He gazed around the corner. She was stretched out across the cushions, the bright screen reflecting in her glasses.

"I may go for a drive," he said, changing his mind.

"Okay." Amelia did not ask to where or what time he'd be back. Frustrated, Perry grabbed his keys. He'd been looking forward to the weekend. But his daughter did not need him tonight, and apparently neither did his wife. He let himself out into the warm night and closed the door behind him.

When he pulled into the gravel driveway thirty minutes later, Perry turned the headlights off quickly. He didn't want to wake anyone. The windows of the big house were dark. In the rear of the property, he could see lights on in the cottage. He reached into the backseat for his reusable shopping bag.

Perry made his way down the walkway with his bag and knocked lightly. The barking was instant and voluminous. He jumped back.

Olivia appeared at the door, a look of surprise on her face. "Perry! Come in."

But Perry could not. Buster blocked the door and thrust his wet nose against Perry's leg and began his TSA-level sniffing. "I'm sorry," Olivia said, dragging him back by the collar. "Buster, leave it!"

Perry edged cautiously onto the threshold, clutching the bag close to his chest and wondering at Olivia's strange command. A guest, unexpected or not, was not an *it*.

"What a surprise," she said, releasing the dog. Perry closed his eyes, but only briefly. Buster, having found him unworthy of further inspection, had already turned back toward the living room. Perry winced as he watched the hairy dog clamber up onto the couch.

"Sorry to just show up," he said, suddenly feeling self-conscious. He didn't want to intrude. And he really wasn't sure why he was here. But he'd felt compelled to come.

The house was what he imagined someone like Olivia considered tidy. Books and papers stacked on tables. Toys strewn across the area rug in the living room. The kitchen surfaces teemed with fruits and vegetables he rather thought would be best preserved in the cool confines of the refrigerator, but clearly Olivia preferred all of her things to be out and visible. Still, aside from a few dishes he spied by the farmhouse sink, there was no evidence of her falling apart. Which for a fleeting moment he found disappointing. Except for her eyes. When he finally looked into them, they seemed rimmed in sadness.

"Luci is sleeping," she said, glancing toward the stairs. "Otherwise, she'd have loved to see you."

Of course she was sleeping. It was late, and Perry suddenly felt badly. "I didn't mean to just drop in," he began. "But I imagined you had your hands full both here and with Jake at rehab. I figured you may be running low on things."

He handed her the shopping bag. Olivia set it on the counter and peeked inside. "Bread, milk, eggs." She reached inside and smiled. "Blue cheese?"

Perry shrugged bashfully. "I remembered you liked it. From the picnic on the boat that day." At the mention of the boat they both fell silent.

"This is very thoughtful," she said.

"Well, Amelia and I were worried." Which wasn't completely true. Amelia was flat out on the couch back home with her blaring Bravo program, ignorant of her husband's errand.

Olivia began unpacking the bag. "Well, thank you," she said. "How's Emma?"

"Good. She's out tonight, in fact. With some friends."

Olivia raised her eyebrows. "That's wonderful. She must be feeling better."

Perry wasn't sure he agreed with "wonderful," but hearing Olivia's take on it was reassuring. "It's good she's getting back to normal," he allowed.

Behind her, Olivia's teakettle began to sing on the stove. She whisked it off and poured the steaming water into a mug. Tea. He had not thought of that! Perry wondered what kind she liked. "Would you like a cup?" she asked.

"Oh no. No thank you. I should go."

There was a pause and Perry knew it was his cue to leave. He'd brought the groceries. All appeared to be good here.

But as he watched Olivia return the kettle to the stove, he regretted not accepting her offer. "Well, thank you again, Perry. It was so kind of you to check in. Really." She followed him to the door and let him out.

"Good night," he said, as the screen door closed between them. She smiled. "Good night."

But Perry was not done. He hesitated. "Olivia. I wondered if I might share something."

She'd already stepped away from the door, but she turned back. "Oh?"

"It's about Jake." He looked at her carefully. This was not easy for him. "I know you two are engaged, and I want the best for you both."

Olivia pursed her lips uncertainly. Was he overstepping? It didn't matter. Jake had already done so. Upstairs was a little girl in a cast, and one town over was his daughter, still not quite herself.

"Jake is not the man you need him to be."

"Perry."

"Please. Let me finish. I love my brother. And I have no doubt that he loves you. But you have a daughter, and you are her only parent." Perry paused, trying to gather his words. How to explain all the years of Jake being Jake? "He has a history. Of being the life of the party, the fun one. The one everybody wants to be around."

Even through the screen door, he could see Olivia's jaw set. "I know that, and it's one of the things I've come to love about him."

"Well." This did not surprise him. All the women Jake encountered seemed to feel this way. "He may not mean to hurt people, but he does. Jake doesn't understand what it takes to be a parent. To put another life before your own. To *grow up*. You need someone who does."

Olivia said nothing, but neither had she closed the door in his face. Perry took this as permission to go on.

"There have been other women."

"We all have pasts, Perry."

He considered this. Perry's past was not at all like his brother's. And he doubted Olivia's was, either. "Well, you are nothing like any of them. You're a lovely woman, Olivia. With a lovely child. You both deserve someone who will take care of you. Jake may want to, but he doesn't know how. He lives for the present. For the thrill and excitement. For himself. And that gets him into trouble." Perry looked at his feet. "As we've seen."

Olivia let out a small whiff of air and pivoted away. For a moment, Perry feared she would tell him to get the hell out of there. To mind his own business. As she had every right to. But she turned back to him.

"I'm not stupid," she told him.

"I never thought you were."

"And I'm not naïve. Luci is—has *always been*—my first concern. I am not looking to Jake to rescue us or to take care of us. I can do that on my own. I always have."

Perry nodded. "I have no doubt."

"Then why are you telling me all this?"

Perry stared through the screen at her. Why was he? If Amelia had asked him, what could he possibly say? That some deep well inside him bubbled with the urge to protect Olivia and Luci? And what right did he have to assign himself that role, anyway? It was all so inappropriate, so unlike him. Perry shook his head, bashfully. "I really don't know."

"Well you should know this. I love your brother. I appreciate your concern, but Luci and I have got this." She paused. "You're right about some things. There have been times I thought Jake needed to grow up, to be more serious. Or—I don't know—more something."

She was getting flustered, and even in the growing darkness he could see her cheeks pinken. Perry felt badly. But he couldn't stop staring.

"And I know he's not a parent, and has no idea how to parent. But his instincts are good and his heart is, too. He is all heart." Her voice was sharp. But there was also a break in it that brought him sadness. Olivia knew.

"He is all heart," he agreed softly. "But his heart is aimed at pleasure. I have no doubt why he finds pleasure in you and Luci. But life is about the hard stuff, and I worry that someday, not far from now, he will tire. He will tire when he realizes that being a husband and a father figure are hard work. That living and working full-time in one place will bore him. And he will do something."

"What? What will he do, Perry?"

"He will disappoint you."

Olivia stared back at him, saying nothing. Perry felt a wave of something run through him. Something akin to guilt. Standing under the stars on the stoop of his brother's fiancée on a heady summer night, there was no shortage of reasons why it should.

Olivia stepped away from the screen, her back to him. "I heard what you had to say," she said, finally.

"I'm sorry" was all Perry could think of. He turned to go, but he could feel her standing in the doorway behind him.

As he stood on the step, an overwhelming fragrance met his nose. He paused, inhaling deeply. "What is that? Lilac?"

Olivia's voice was soft. "Heliotrope. Some people think it smells like baby powder or vanilla. Luci thinks it's more like grapes."

He inhaled once more. "I agree with Luci."

As he navigated the dark hills back home, Perry flicked through the radio stations, turning the volume up to drown his thoughts. It didn't help. He wondered how Emma was doing out with her friends, and if her head hurt. Idly, he thought of Amelia and whether she had noticed how long he'd been gone. And what it meant if she had not.

He wondered if perhaps he should discuss the matter of replacing the boat, or if it were too soon. For a brief moment, he allowed himself to think of Jake; of the terrible pain his mother had described him suffering, and the limp. And then he pictured Olivia's sad eyes as she stood on the other side of the screen door, his words fluttering between them like satin ribbons come undone.

For the drive home, these worries batted about his conscience like fireflies, until a dull ache spread across his forehead. *Enough.* He would not entertain any more of these thoughts, he decided. Mind over matter. But despite the growing miles between Olivia's cottage and his car, Perry could not escape the faintest scent of grapes.

Phoebe

The raspberries looked divine. Plump, red, robust. But they cost $6.99 a punnet. And her bank account had about that much in it. She set them down and eyed the bananas. The boys were sick of them, but the price worked. "I'm on a fucking banana budget," she muttered. Since moving in to her parents' house, she was cutting back on everything. They'd reviewed the savings account, and it was all but dried up. There was only two thousand dollars left in it. And she'd had to write a personal check for the electrician just the day before, since they'd exhausted the last bank installment. Phoebe was trying to remember if she'd thought to transfer the money from savings to checking so the check would clear, when she heard her name.

"Phoebe! Is that you?"

A river of dread ran down her spine. "Vic-toree-uh." Drat. She was on her way to visit Jake at the rehabilitation center, and she'd wanted to pop in to the grocery store to pick up a few quick things before she did. Now she was stuck.

"How are you? How is the new house going? We just miss you so much in the 'hood."

Phoebe very much doubted that. "Oh, well. Things are good." She nodded for emphasis. "Really good."

Victoria cocked her head. "Yeah?"

"Yeah." Phoebe chucked the bananas in the cart a little too forcefully.

"And how is the renovation going?" Victoria swept her long chestnut hair over her shoulder. "I am just so glad ours is done. It gets to be too much. The stress. The time. The money!" She barked out a laugh. "As I'm sure you're finding . . ."

"It's going fine, thanks. You know how it is."

Victoria leaned in conspiratorially. "Boy, do I. It's one thing to plan the reno, but as they say, nothing goes according to plan." She laughed as if that were hilarious. "Any hiccups yet?"

Phoebe would not give Victoria the satisfaction. "Nope. None so far," she lied.

"Because Don ran into Rob, and he was saying that you'd hit an electrical snag."

Phoebe grit her teeth and smiled. Damn Rob and his outgoing personality and honesty. "It's all getting taken care of."

But Victoria didn't seem to hear. "We had to redo our entire electrical system. Did I tell you that?"

"No, no, you did not." Phoebe was pretty sure she was about to.

"We went so far over budget that I finally said, 'Don.' I said, 'Don, what difference does it make now? We're already over, so let's just splurge and get that Viking range we wanted.'"

Rose, the loan officer, cleared her throat loudly in Phoebe's head: "Just because you're over budget doesn't mean you keep going."

"Is that so? Wow. And look, it all turned out."

Victoria grinned wildly, in that feral cat way of hers that Phoebe could not stand. "Oh, yes it did. We are so happy. Just couldn't be happier."

"Thrilled to hear that." Phoebe gripped the shopping cart

handles and pushed off. "Good to see you!" she said, before Victoria could say another word.

By the time she got to the checkout line, she realized she'd forgotten bread. Crap. She had planned to make sandwiches for the boys before she brought them to T-ball. Phoebe glanced across the store at the bread aisle, then back at her checkout line. The woman in front of her still had a ton of things on the conveyor belt, but the man behind her had her blocked in. Phoebe turned to him. "Excuse me, can I sneak by? I just need to grab something." She slipped past him, ignoring the imploring look, and made a dash for the bread aisle. Her usual favorite, the organic wholegrain oat, was six dollars a loaf. Phoebe groaned, and grabbed the regular kind, vowing not to look at the ingredients. With the loaf tucked under her arm she dashed back, squeezed past the grumpy guy once more with an apology, and unloaded her cart just as the woman in front finished paying. The victory was small, and yet Phoebe relished it. "Hello!" she said brightly to the checkout girl. She did not even mind it when the bagger left and went on break.

"Allow me," Phoebe said, taking her place at the end of the counter. She really needed to start bringing her own reusable bags. The environment and all that.

Phoebe tucked everything neatly into two bags, far less than her usual ten or twelve, but she prided herself on the neatness of it all. She glanced at her watch. And she was still running on time to meet Jake!

"That'll be fifty-seven thirty-five," the checkout girl said.

"Sure thing." Phoebe handed her her store savings card, then popped her bank card into the machine. "How's your day going?" she asked the checkout girl.

"Sorry," the girl said.

"For what?"

"Your card was declined."

"Declined?" Phoebe blanched. She squinted at the tiny screen, but it was all a blur. Her account balance had said three hundred dollars when she checked it that very morning! But she was so mortified she was not about to prolong this moment a second longer looking for her reading glasses. "I must've used the wrong card. Hang on." The man behind her in line cleared his throat.

She fumbled through her wallet. Her credit card was already at its maximum. That left Rob's American Express card, which he saved expressly for work expenses. He would not be happy, but she had no other choice. With shaking hands, she jammed it into the machine.

The checkout girl waited. "PIN code?"

Phoebe felt her chest tighten. She never used this card—crap! What was the PIN?

"Or you can choose credit," the girl said.

Her wave of relief was so strong, Phoebe's knees gave. "Credit," she practically shouted.

"Good to see you, Phoebe!" To her horror, Victoria pushed her cart up at the end of Phoebe's line. Involuntarily, Phoebe covered the credit card machine with her hand. The screen flashed, and a beeping sound went off.

"It cleared," the girl announced.

Phoebe tried to mask her relief. "Of course it did." Then, "Good to see you, *too*," she crooned at Victoria.

Hands still shaking, she turned out of the grocery store parking lot and toward the rehabilitation center. This couldn't be happening to her finances. She'd known they'd burned through savings. As it was, she'd transferred funds into her checking account three times in the last week to cover all the recent upstairs costs. But, clearly, she'd not stayed on top of balancing it all.

Something had to change. Perry was the obvious person to go to for help, but Phoebe did not want to hear "I told you so." She also wasn't sure what she needed. Sure, Perry was in a financial position to offer assistance. But Rob wouldn't want that, and to be honest, Phoebe really didn't either. This was their venture, and they'd have to figure a way out. At the very least, she needed to talk this through. Up until now, their financial strain had been a closely guarded secret she'd been keeping, and it was taking a toll on her. As she pulled into the rehab center, she resolved to talk to Jake. He may have been the least likely to offer monetary assistance, but he was a good listener. And he always had her back.

But as soon as she saw Jake, Phoebe had second thoughts.

He was seated on a table in the large OT room, gritting his teeth as his therapist manipulated his ankle. Even though he was gray with pain, he managed a small smile. "Hey, sis. How's it going?"

"Better than you, I'd say."

Jake put his hand up to the OT, signaling he needed a break, and lay back on the table. His forehead, Phoebe noted, was shiny with perspiration.

She had never seen Jake like this before. Their little brother had always been *all boy*, as Nana Elsie liked to say. He never stopped moving. First thing in the morning he snagged his bike from the garage and away he went, calling out to neighboring kids as he sailed down the street. It never failed: in his wake, children appeared, along with hockey sticks and baseball bats. Pickup baseball games, flag football, dodgeball—all of it ensued. Jake stirred people up, gathered them, brought them out of their houses and out to the curb. Anyone was ripe for the picking.

Once she had looked out the window and spied the mailman dodging a pack of kids as he raced for base, his mailbag slung over one shoulder and envelopes flying out behind him. In college it was the same; when Jake came home for break, all their old friends from high school started trickling through their front door. Beers were cracked. Card games started in the dining room and went long into the night. Touch football in the backyard. Their mother loved nothing more than a full house; Jane was known to plop herself down right in the middle of a raucous poker game. Edward, who liked a quieter house, would shake his head and take his book upstairs. But even he lingered in the doorway when the noise of political conversation filled his living room. When Phoebe's own friends popped over, they were always sucked in. More than once she and Perry stood on the outskirts of their own family room watching everyone encircle their brother as he launched into a story.

"Would any of them even notice if we left?" she'd wonder aloud.

Perry didn't dignify the question with an answer. But Phoebe already knew the answer. She and Perry were the opening act, and Jake the headliner. His pull was magnetic. They could hardly blame their friends.

Now, seeing him flat on his back on the table, there was no sign of the life force her little brother was. It made Phoebe feel unsettled.

"You all right?" She put a hand on his arm.

"He's doing okay," the OT said, as she sat back and studied him. "If he would do his exercises like he's supposed to, this wouldn't be so painful." She extended a firm handshake. "I'm Laverne."

"She's the grim reaper," Jake mumbled, as Phoebe introduced herself.

Laverne laughed loudly. "What you need, my man, is to get on board."

"What I need is to get out of here," Jake said. It had only been two days since he'd been transferred from the hospital to the rehabilitation facility, but already Phoebe could see the jitteriness in his eyes.

"What you need is to shut up and follow directions," Phoebe said. "Listen to these people. If they say stretch, stretch."

Laverne laughed again. "Your sister's a smart girl. She's right about that."

"Hear that?" Phoebe poked him in the ribs. "I'm smart. And right."

Jake sat up, and there was a small glimmer in his eye. "Yeah, yeah. Laverne lies. Don't believe a thing she says."

"Hey now. For that, we're getting you up on your crutches. Up you go."

Phoebe watched as Jake lifted himself gingerly from the table and swung his injured leg over the side. He winced, moving mere inches at a time to lower the leg to the floor. It hurt to watch.

"That's the way. Nice and slow," Laverne encouraged. "Use the crutches to support the motion, just as I showed you."

As awful as the recovery was, Phoebe knew that Jake could handle it better than any of the rest of the family. He was not prone to self-pity, as she and Perry could certainly be. Things happened, and Jake usually found a way to roll with them. But what he wasn't good at was relying on others, and now he would have to.

When he'd finished his session with Laverne, he settled back into his wheelchair and Phoebe pushed him out of the training room and down the hall. Sunlight spilled through the windows, reflecting off the sheen of the floor. "What I'd give to be out there today," Jake mumbled.

"Don't they let you outside?" she asked.

He shrugged. "They air us out, for short bits of time. But that's as you get closer to discharge."

She knew he felt like a caged animal in here. "Give it time. You're doing great."

When they got back to his room, a young woman in pink scrubs was setting a lunch tray on Jake's nightstand. Her face lit up when she saw them. Or rather, Jake, Phoebe realized.

"Hey there, Jake. Brought you extra fries. And more of the tapioca pudding you like." She winked at Jake.

"Thanks, Tiff. You're the best."

Phoebe tried not to roll her eyes when Tiffany fussed over the tray, opening the pudding for him and unwrapping the plastic spoon. "You let me know if you want any more. I'll sneak you some." There was that wink again. Phoebe fought the urge to ask her if she had something stuck in her eye.

Jake seemed embarrassed, but he thanked her again.

Tiffany tossed her hair and flashed him one more smile. "Bye for now!"

"Wait, where are you going?" Phoebe cried. She had no idea how to help Jake out of the chair, and she knew he was already drained from his OT session.

Tiffany halted, and looked Phoebe up and down. "To deliver lunches."

"You're not going to help him get into bed?"

"Oh, I can't do that. I'm not certified staff."

Phoebe scoffed. "Well, who is? He can't just sit here."

Tiffany glared.

"It's okay," Jake interjected. "Thanks, Tiffany. We'll be fine."

Tiffany smiled sweetly at Jake once more before leaving.

"Geez, Phoebs. Can you not alienate the staff? She's a nice girl."

"She's a moron, and you're engaged." Phoebe bent down and adjusted the footings of his wheelchair. "If you fall on my watch, I will kill you. Shouldn't Laverne be here for this?"

But Jake was already trying to lift himself out, balancing on one crutch. "Not unless I plan to take Laverne home with me, too," he grunted. "This is part of my rehab. I can do it."

She watched nervously as he lifted himself using the armrests. "How can I help? Do you want me to move the chair?" Oh, how she wished a therapist was there. She'd even take Tapioca Tiffany. If he fell now, with the rods and screws in his leg, *she* would need therapy.

Jake gritted his teeth as he balanced on his good leg. "Yes, back the chair up. Quickly."

Phoebe whisked the wheelchair back and stood close, arms out. "You've got this," she told him. She hoped she sounded more convincing than she felt.

Slowly, Jake managed to pivot so that his back was to the bed. She winced along with him as he leaned against it and slowly dragged himself up over the edge. At one point he caught sight of her expression. "Geez, Phoebs. Sorry this is so hard for you."

"Shut up and keep going!"

Ever so slowly he scooted back against the pillows. When he finally collapsed against them, Phoebe settled in the bedside chair. She swiped the glass of cranberry juice from his lunch tray and sucked it loudly through the straw.

"Jesus. Next time I'm coming when you're already in bed."

"You would totally suck as a nurse," he told her.

She laughed. "So, what's the plan?"

"A few more days, then hopefully I get to go home."

Which was exactly what worried Phoebe. "To where?"

Phoebe realized she was the problem. She was taking up valuable space in their parents' house, all because of the renovation. Space Jake could've used.

As it was, he couldn't possibly go home to his rental in Kent. His apartment was on the second floor of an old Victorian house off of Main Street, with a steep walk-up. Which left Olivia. Who had a tiny cottage on her employer's property, and a daughter who was also fresh out of the hospital after the accident. "I don't know." Jake closed his eyes and let out a long breath. "I don't want to be a burden to anybody, but I can't see doing the stairs at my place just yet. Maybe to Olivia's."

That's what Phoebe had been hoping he'd say, but it still made her feel bad. "I've fucked everything up," she told him.

Jake opened his eyes. "Hey now, I'm not done complaining. Why do you always have to make everything about you?" He was trying to make her laugh, but she couldn't.

"I'm serious. You should be going home to stay with Mom and Dad for a while. You need help. And you can't because I've already flooded their house with my own people."

Jake shook his head. "Phoebe, I probably wouldn't have gone there anyway. They already have Grandma to look after."

"See? Even that didn't stop me. I'm a horrible person."

Jake nodded. "It's been established." Then, turning to her, "Come on, sis. Don't beat yourself up. It's only temporary. Isn't it about the electricity or something?"

Phoebe slumped in her chair. "Or something." She needed to tell Jake. Everyone needed that person who, no matter what they said, wouldn't judge. Who wouldn't give unsolicited advice. Jake had always been her person.

With some effort, Jake pulled himself upright and adjusted his pillows so he could face her. "What's really up?"

Phoebe reached for his tapioca pudding and snatched it off the tray. Jake handed her the spoon. Between giant mouthfuls, she told him. About the budget, the hidden problems of the build, the tension between her and Rob. And the fact that they were "shit out of money."

When she had finished, both the tapioca and the horrid details, she burped.

Jake studied her. "Just so we're clear, are you *shit out of money*, or just *out* of money?"

Phoebe chucked the empty container at him, and he ducked playfully, then gripped his cast. "Ow! No sudden movements."

She jumped up. "Shit! Sorry." And then she started to cry.

"Phoebs, it's okay. I'm just joking." Jake grabbed her hand. "Listen, if I had any extra cash, I'd give it to you, no questions asked. But I just bought Olivia an engagement ring, and this hospital bill isn't going to be small."

She swiped at her eyes, and held her hands up in protest. "No, that's not why I'm telling you," she insisted. "I just have to tell someone. I don't know what else to do."

"You have to tell Rob," Jake said. "That's the first thing."

"He's going to stroke out."

"And so will you, if you don't tell him. Look, I know you think you're protecting him. But it's obviously taking a toll on you, and, from what you've told me, on both of you. You're stuck at Mom and Dad's. You can't get out of that situation until you finish the build. And you can't finish the build. What choice do you have?"

Jake was right.

"I hate to say it, but have you considered that maybe it's time to walk away?"

Phoebe jolted upright. "No. Not an option. It's our dream. We've nearly killed ourselves to get it done."

Jake regarded her sadly. "Phoebs. You're killing yourself trying to hang on to it. Is *that* your dream?"

Phoebe reached for her purse. "Well, thanks for listening. I really need to get back to Mom's and relieve her of the boys. I'm taking them to T-ball."

But he wasn't done yet. Jake snagged the straps of her purse just as she tugged it over her shoulder, and held on. "Phoebe. He's your husband." Jake was looking at her with too much sympathy, something Phoebe hated. People could disagree with her. They could dislike her. Hell, she didn't care if they hated her. But she would not tolerate an ounce of sympathy.

"Call me if you need anything, okay? Company. A cheeseburger. A bottle of bourbon. Whatever." She yanked the purse free from his hand, pecked him on the cheek, and headed for the door. "Thanks for the pudding."

"Tell him!" he shouted after her.

Olivia

She was beside herself. They'd been home from the hospital for almost a week, and Luci still hadn't spoken a word.

"It's normal for a traumatic episode to trigger a setback," Alison had explained at their last session. Olivia had called for an emergency appointment, even though Luci's schedule had been reduced to once a week for "summer hours."

"As prolonged as this?" Olivia couldn't accept it. It was one thing for Luci to be mute around others or in public places. But at home? With her own mother? It had become nearly impossible for Olivia to manage. Luci had reverted to gesturing and drawing, or worse, simply not expressing herself at all. And now that her arm was in a cast, Olivia felt stranded. They couldn't go to the beach or swim at the lake. And it wasn't like Luci had any real friends Olivia could call up for a playdate. Luci was hot and fidgety, and Olivia was at a loss as to how to fill their days.

As it was, Ben's art show was coming up, and she needed to put in more hours in the barn studio. She was behind on publicity and had taken to loading Luci in the car and taking her with her when she went to the printers to pick up fliers and advertisements, and then all over Washington, Kent, Roxbury, and New Milford as they delivered them to local newspapers and posted them in bookstores, coffee shops, and dance studios. Marge was a big believer in local word of mouth, and despite Olivia's attempt to bring the couple into the social media world, Marge still insisted she do it the old-fashioned way: in person and on foot.

"Honey, we live in the country," she reminded Olivia, gently. "People know us. They look for our events in lifestyle magazines and on coffeehouse bulletin boards. Then they tell their friends."

Personally, Olivia didn't think it mattered where they lived. Instagram and Facebook would save them all a lot of trouble, if Ben would just allow it. But she honored their wishes, and loaded Luci into the car to make their deliveries. If nothing else, it broke up the day and gave her a respite from speech therapy and doctor appointments. There was comfort in doing ordinary things.

The pediatric orthopedist gave Olivia somewhat more hope. "She's healing beautifully," she told them. "Seven more weeks and this cast will be off."

Just in time for summer and swim season to end, Olivia thought glumly, to herself. To Luci and the doctor, she quipped, "Great. Just in time for school!" She refused to wonder if Luci would still be silent then, as kindergarten started. Just in time to ruin her start to school and hopes to make friends. No, she would not project her doom and gloom that far ahead, she decided. Instead, she hurried Luci from the office, and straight over to the Sweet Spot ice cream shop, where she ordered Luci a strawberry cone, and a double scoop of coffee ice cream in a cup for herself. It wasn't like she'd be at the beach anytime soon, she figured, as she dipped her spoon into the creamy caffeinated depths.

But there was more to concern herself with that day. Jake was coming home from rehab. From the start, there was no question in Olivia's mind as to where he would go; he was her fiancé. But Jake saw it otherwise. "I can't impose on you girls," he'd insisted.

"The cottage is tiny, and you've got your hands full already with Luci and with Ben's upcoming show."

Olivia had waved her hand, as if swatting away a fly. "Ridiculous. We're going to be living together soon enough. And it's a one-level entryway, unlike your place with all those stairs. Plus, I get to take care of you."

It was what she'd wanted all along, really. To fall asleep and wake up next to the man she loved. Which they'd purposely held off on, solely for Luci's sake. Since they'd been dating, they'd agreed to no overnights unless Luci was "sleeping over" at Marge and Ben's. Which they'd managed to pull off a few times, though it never seemed enough. That was the hard part of "dating" as a single mother, the balance of personal needs with the respect and sensitivity to your child. *Kids come first* had always been her motto. And as hard as it was to uphold, especially on those nights she and Jake were nestled on her couch watching a movie, and she was so tired, and he felt so cozy, in the end she always managed to tear herself away and kiss him goodbye on the doorstep. It was a promise she'd made to herself as a parent, as much as to Luci. And one of the things she most loved about Jake was that whenever her resolve faltered, he was right there to prop her up. He was like that.

Now, however, they'd all be under the same roof. Perry's visit to her house the other night had been unexpected, but not nearly as much as his message had been. It didn't feel right, the two of them talking about Jake while he was stuck in recovery over at the rehabilitation center. A place he was dying to get out of, even though the thought of that worried Olivia just as much as her desire to spring him. What would he do when he was out? At least there he had a set schedule. There was PT and OT. There were doctor visits and people around to help with everything. Once he was home, he'd be bored stiff. Limited in both activity and independence. The thought of having to take care of him and get him to his appointments, to do the driving and cooking and housework alone, didn't bother her so much. But adding that on top of everything else she was juggling at the moment was beginning to feel daunting.

Perry's visit had been made with good intent, of that she was certain. If quirky, Perry was most certainly a noble guy. And Olivia could see in his eyes how conflicted he'd felt having to confront her like that, behind his little brother's back. On some level, that took guts. But she accepted his news with a healthy measure of skepticism. This seemed tinged with that age-old sibling rivalry the two of them had been nursing for many years. From the beginning Jake had shared with her the complicated nature of their relationship, and his regret at never quite understanding it. This had all started well before she entered the picture, she reminded herself, and as such she would not allow Perry's concerns to overshadow what she knew to be true of the man she wanted to marry. Jake's heart was pure, and there was no ego in the way he conducted himself. All along, she had trusted him unconditionally. Something she'd never done before with anyone, especially since Luci's father had walked out on her years before. Perry had his reasons for doubting Jake, just as Olivia had her own for trusting him implicitly. But though Perry did not change her mind, his visit had served to unnerve her. If anything, it seemed to have given voice to a growing doubt already within.

Something about the accident still didn't sit right. Initially, Olivia had been consumed with making sure that Luci and Jake were all right. Then came the order of recovery: the surgery, the discharge to rehab, the subsequent doctor appointments. It had been easy to get sucked into the grind and therefore ignore any sense of discomfort she harbored.

But at night, when Luci was safely asleep down the hall and she was alone with her thoughts, Olivia faced questions. About how the boat could've just crashed like that. Jake was the one adult on the boat; and the one adult she trusted her baby with. There was no doubt he was suffering from guilt as much as from his physical injuries. So much so, that she wanted to alleviate it for him in any way she could. But still—there was that lurking sense of dread she felt in the middle of the night when her mind wandered. That somehow he wasn't being straight with her. She'd pressed him in the hospital after the officers interviewed him, and he'd looked at her in a way that made her certain he was about to tell her something more. But he never did. Since then, a disquiet had simmered in Olivia's head every night she lay it on her pillow.

But then morning would come. When sunlight streamed through the gauzy curtains in the cottage, and Buster stretched at the foot of her bed, and like the fog outside her window her doubts lifted. In the light of day, there were certain truths Olivia relied on: Jake loved Luci. He loved her. And he would've done anything to keep both of them safe.

In that vein, she determined to welcome him home. She'd put him on the couch and make it as comfortable as possible. That would solve the issue of the stairs, as well as her concern about sharing a bed with Jake in front of Luci. Of course they would once married, but until they moved in together she thought it best not to. Especially now. Since the accident, Luci was fragile; as much as Jake needed her, Olivia wasn't sure if his being around would be helpful or prove more of a setback for her child. She couldn't risk the latter.

"What do you think about Jake coming to stay with us?" she asked, as they sat outside on the bench with their ice cream. Luci was working her tongue around the circumference of her cone, trying to keep up with the pink river of melting ice cream coming down its side. Olivia took the cone and tilted it, to help.

Luci didn't answer.

"It's kind of like a slumber party," Olivia explained. "But for longer."

Luci looked at her over the top of her cone, curiously. Olivia tried to imagine what questions might be batting around in her head.

"We can practice living together, which we're going to do when Jake and I get married. But there will be some things that take a little getting used to. Like having Jake's stuff in our place. Or Jake eating the food from our fridge, or maybe using the potty when he needs to."

Luci scrunched her nose. Any reference to "potty" always got her.

"We're going to be sharing our house." Olivia paused. "What I was wondering is if you're sure you can share Mommy time?"

Luci turned her attention across the street to a family walking by. Had Olivia struck a chord of anxiety? Or had Luci's mind already drifted to something else? Olivia was growing weary of guessing, of placing words in her daughter's mouth. This was a time when she needed to know, really know, what Luci felt.

Finally, Luci looked at her and nodded.

"So, you're okay with Jake coming to stay with us?"

When Luci placed her hand on Olivia's heart, Olivia's own skipped. It was the first time all week she was sure of anything Luci was trying to say.

"Okay, *ma chérie*. Let's go get him and bring him home."

Later, when the three of them pulled into the driveway, Ben was puttering outside the barn. *Stalling*, she thought to herself. His show was coming up, and one thing she'd learned was what a terrible procrastinator he became before a show.

He came around to the side of the car, a grim look on his face.

Jake's seat was already set as far back as it would go to accommodate his cast. Ben came around to the passenger side and held the door ajar. "Looking good for a broken man," he said, as Jake eased himself out of the car.

Jake held a hand out to Ben. "Thanks for having me. I really appreciate it." But Ben didn't take it.

He glanced at Olivia over the roof of the car. "It's what Olivia wanted. We'll make do."

The screen door squeaked on the front porch, and Marge sailed down the steps with Buster. But her greeting was also somewhat chilly. "You're here," she said. "Well, let's get you settled." Olivia glanced uneasily at Jake. This was not what she'd expected. When she'd asked them about Jake coming to stay, they'd seemed fine with it. Gracious, even. But this was not at all like them.

Ben grabbed Jake's duffel bag from the backseat of the car. "Oh, please let me get that," Olivia said, hurrying after him. But he was already tottering down the stone pathway to her cottage. Marge motioned for them to follow. Unsure what else to do, Olivia took Luci's hand and gestured for Jake to go ahead on his crutches.

As soon as they all arrived at the front stoop, Marge and Ben halted, blocking the door. "Say, we were wondering, could we borrow Luci for dinner?" Ben asked.

Luci, who seemed unsurprised by this, let go of Olivia's hand and ducked beside Marge.

Olivia eyed the three of them, suspiciously. "Now?"

Ben nodded. "We got some fresh watermelon from the farmer's market today."

Olivia didn't know what to make of the invitation. Marge

and Ben were acting strangely, and this transition with Jake was already filled with uncertainty enough. But Luci seemed eager to go with them. "We'll bring her back after dessert," Marge added.

Before Olivia could object, Ben set the duffel bag down and the three of them turned back down the path toward the big house.

"What was that all about?" Jake whispered.

When she opened the door, Olivia understood. From inside the cottage came the glow of candlelight. She held the screen door ajar for Jake, and a waft of summer hydrangea met them on the threshold. The table by the big window was set with a vintage blue-and-white tablecloth Olivia recognized from one of Marge's dinner parties, and bright red cloth napkins. Candles flickered on the hearth of the fireplace, and on the small kitchen island. "Those liars."

She followed Jake inside and spun around, taking it all in.

The candlesticks. The bowl of salad, the fresh corn. The still-steaming platter of barbecued chicken in the center of the table.

"Baby, this is something else." Jake made his way over to her on his crutches and stopped, his nose just shy of hers. As she met his eyes, Perry's words came back to her: "He will disappoint you."

Olivia pushed the memory away, and pressed her forehead to Jake's. "Welcome home," she said.

Emma

The morning of Amanda Hastings's party, Emma's mother thought it would be a good idea if they went to visit Luci and Olivia. Normally Emma would've agreed. Olivia was cool. Cool in a way that none of the adults she knew could ever be, even Uncle Jake. Olivia had lived in the city. She was an artist. But more than that, she understood teenagers. Even though they hadn't spent a ton of time together, Emma could tell. Like when Olivia asked about her friends, and Emma confided in her about Alicia being clingy but how she felt bound to her from their long childhood friendship. Olivia didn't judge or tell her to be patient with Alicia, like her mother did. Or remind her that Alicia was an honors student and a good influence, like her father did. Olivia nodded quietly and said, "Yeah, I had a few friends like that. What you need is to surround yourself with people who give back the energy you give to them. You know, the good stuff." Like Sully McMahon. When she was near Sully, Emma felt alive. When he tipped his head back and laughed at something stupid she said, it did something to her. It's like for the first time since high school started, she wasn't invisible anymore. Sully saw her.

———

When they turned into Olivia's driveway, Emma realized she'd been bracing herself. The whole ride there she'd felt carsick. But as soon as they pulled up to the big white farmhouse and the red barn, her spirits lifted a little. The barn door slid open and there stood Olivia, in a clay-stained apron with her hair pulled back in a red bandana.

Olivia's hands were wet and sticky, but she held her arms out wide. "You're here! Come in!" Then, "Yikes, don't let me get you all messy." But Emma was suddenly so happy, she stepped into her arms anyway.

Emma's heart sank a bit when Olivia told them Jake wasn't there. "He's at rehab, and Jane won't be driving him home for another hour or so. He'll be sorry you missed him!" Emma hadn't thought about that detail. Poor Uncle Jake; he couldn't even drive himself around.

"That's all right," Amelia said. "We really came to see you and Luci."

Emma sensed that her mother was somehow relieved. Did she blame Jake for the accident, like her father did?

Emma hadn't heard a thing from her uncle since the text in the hospital, and she was aching to see him. Not just to see how he was, but to let him know it was all right. That *she* was all right, and he needn't worry.

"Let me give you a tour," Olivia offered.

A clay-splattered art studio was hardly her mother's thing, but Emma was pleased to see her mother was wowed, too. "Olivia, this is incredible."

The inside of the old horse barn had been redone as a studio. The ceilings were high and vaulted. "That's the old hayloft," Olivia said. "That's where the office is now." She made quotation marks around "office" with her stained fingers. "And this little area, over here, is sort of mine. Jake and Ben set it up for me."

They followed her to the nearest corner, directly below the loft. Crowded workbenches ran along the adjoining walls, but there on the table, under an overhead lamp, was a slick earthen sculpture. "It's a little something I've been working on," Olivia explained shyly. "Though I haven't been able to get in here much lately."

Amelia gasped. "And here we are interrupting!"

"Oh no," Olivia said. "I'm glad for the distraction. I was getting frustrated and about to quit for lunch anyway." She went over to a trough sink and flipped the tap with her elbow. Emma watched as she scrubbed her hands. There was something so satisfying about the space: the light, the clay material, the sound of the rushing water. Olivia looked like her happiest self in the midst of it.

"May we ask what Mr. Rothschild is working on?"

Emma followed her mother's gaze to the largest worktable in the center of the barn. Beneath a white canvas tarp was some kind of statue, which made Emma think of a magician. There was a metal chair in front of it, and Emma pictured Mr. Rothschild seated before the statue, contemplating his next move. All around the tarped sculpture were smaller tables and benches, littered with tools. A plastic bucket of murky water. And dozens of torn white cloths, stained and crumpled on each surface. It looked like a creative mess.

"I'm afraid I can't show anyone yet," Olivia said, apologetically. "It's part of his upcoming exhibit. But I can assure you, it's brilliant."

Emma's mother looked disappointed, but Emma was glad she didn't press. She could do that sometimes.

"We brought something for Luci," Amelia said, swiftly switching the subject. Emma held up a floral gift bag, and Olivia clapped her hands together.

"How sweet! Please, follow me to the cottage. Hopefully she's reading."

But Luci must have sensed their arrival, because as soon as they left the barn, she was already trotting down the walkway toward them, Buster on her heels. He woofed loudly. "You missed your chance, buddy," Olivia told him. "So much for guard dog."

Emma bent to ruffle Buster's ears, and he licked her face. She waited for Luci to approach her. "Hi, Luci," she said, softly. Emma feared that seeing her would bring back bad memories for Luci.

To her relief, Luci smiled. Emma held out the gift bag. "I brought you a treat. I wanted to see how you were feeling."

Luci motioned them toward the front door and skipped ahead. "She's still not talking," Olivia confided, as soon as she was out of earshot.

"I'm sorry to hear that," Amelia offered. "Maybe given more time."

Emma didn't say anything, because her stomach flip-flopped. She didn't like to see Olivia looking so pained. But worse, she didn't like to hear that about Luci. Emma understood what had happened that day on the boat. Even though it was still raw, she was old enough and experienced enough on the water to know the danger was over. But even still, the memory woke her up at night, finding her in her sleep and causing her to sit bolt upright, soaked in sweat. She couldn't imagine what it was doing to a five-year-old.

Luckily, Luci seemed pleased to see them. She showed Emma her room, and Olivia made them all tea. When Amelia glanced at her watch and announced it was time to go, Emma was almost sorry the visit had ended so fast. She followed Olivia outside while her mother ducked into the powder room.

As they waited on the porch, Olivia reached for Emma's hand. "Jake feels awful about the accident. You know that, don't you?"

Emma blinked. Here was Olivia, whose own daughter had a broken arm and had now stopped talking altogether, and yet she was trying to make Emma feel better. As if, by extension, Olivia were somehow responsible, too. A terrible thought occurred to Emma at that moment: What if Olivia left Jake? She was the best thing that had ever happened to him. Emma had never seen her uncle so settled, so normal. So *happy*.

"It wasn't his fault," Emma said, quickly.

Her mother, however, had caught up to them. "It's why we call them accidents."

"But the boat," Olivia began. "And the neighbor's dock." She put a hand to her forehead.

Amelia spoke firmly. "Things that can be replaced. At least our girls are going to be okay." Her mother gave Olivia a hug, and Emma swore she could feel something pass between them. As if both were relieved of some invisible burden.

They were walking down the path when there was the crunch of gravel in the driveway. Jane's Volvo station wagon pulled up to the barn. "Oh good! He's back," Olivia exclaimed.

It was what Emma had been waiting for, and yet a wash of nervous energy ran through her.

Olivia grabbed her hand. "Come on! He'll be thrilled to see you."

Emma wasn't so sure, but she allowed Olivia's excitement to propel them both down the walkway. Jane was holding the passenger door open and Jake had just balanced himself on his crutches when he lifted his gaze and saw them. His eyes went straight to Emma's.

"Look who's here!" Olivia blurted out. Jane grinned. Emma hesitated; couldn't any of them see how hard this was? She cleared her throat.

"Hi, Uncle Jake."

He didn't answer at first, but stood there taking her in. Emma tried to read his expression.

"Come here," he said, finally.

Slowly, Emma walked around the car. It wasn't until she was right in front of him that she understood. Jake let one of his crutches fall to the ground with a clatter, and while balancing on the other he held his free arm out. Emma didn't hesitate. She pressed herself against him, wrapping both arms around his neck.

"God, I wanted to see you," he whispered in her hair. "Finally."

Emma couldn't speak. The lump in her throat was too big.

"What perfect timing!" Jane said. But Emma wasn't so sure. She turned her gaze toward her mother, fresh worry blooming in her chest.

"Jake," Amelia said. Emma turned, noting the cool tone in her mother's voice. But there was genuine warmth in her expression, much to her relief. "You look good."

Jake laughed. "What's left of me."

As they made small talk in the driveway, Emma couldn't keep her eyes off of her uncle. He looked like he'd lost weight. Gone was the flush of color in his cheeks, the deep rumble in his laugh. She hated the change.

"Baby, you must be tired," Olivia said, suddenly. She and Jane both extended their arms at the same time, then caught themselves.

"All this mothering," Jake joked. "I'm fine, but I am sore. I should probably head inside."

"Yes, we should go," Amelia agreed.

Hugs were exchanged and everyone agreed it was time to get going, though Emma could tell it was awkward.

Jake caught her eye as the women said their goodbyes.

"Hey," he said, as she went to hug him one last time. "About the accident . . ."

Emma stepped back, about to interrupt, but the look in his eyes stopped her.

"Look around," he told her, in a firm whisper. Emma glanced over her shoulder at her family, then back to Jake.

"This," he said, nodding his chin at the group of women behind them. "This is what it's all about now."

"But Uncle Jake," she began.

"No, Em. Everyone is okay. That's all that matters." He leaned in close, his eyes watery with emotion. "Do you understand?"

Emma bit her lip. "I think so."

On the way home, Emma said, "I want Dad to talk to Uncle Jake." She was tired of it. Every time she brought up his name, her parents got this worried look. Or made excuses to avoid him. First, they wanted her to recover. Then, they claimed he needed time to heal. But now he was in a rehabilitation facility, and Emma knew for a fact that other family members had visited him, if not her own parents. He was her uncle and they'd been through something awful together.

Her mother flicked her hair behind her ear and focused on the road. "I know you do," she said. "But your father is upset with Uncle Jake right now. And he's been worried that seeing your uncle might upset you."

"Well, now I have!" Emma barked.

Her mother shot her a look of surprise. "I didn't realize you felt so strongly. Let me talk to your father."

Emma slumped down in the seat. Jake was many things, but most of all he was loyal. Her family had to realize it wasn't his fault. After all, Olivia had trusted both of them to take Luci out in the boat. Emma was the one who'd helped her put on the tiny little life jacket. It was Emma's lap she'd been sitting on as they headed out into the center of the lake. And after seeing Luci today, she knew that every time Uncle Jake looked at Luci's broken arm, he, too, probably felt the same wave of remorse. Remorse in the form of a pink cast.

By the time the party rolled around, Emma had almost decided against going. Her dad had come home from work all hopeful looking, and asked her, once again, to play Ping-Pong. It had been years since they'd last played, and yet there he was asking, just like he had the other night when Alicia came over. The same night he'd acted all weird and nostalgic, as if she and Alicia would want to stay up watching Disney movies in their matching pink sleeping bags, like they used to. She felt bad for him; almost bad enough to stay home. But then she thought of Sully.

So she'd made up a story for her parents about meeting camp counselors at the Club—which wasn't exactly a lie. After all, she was hanging out with people from camp. What worried her far more than her parents finding out was what Amanda would say. She'd invited them. The problem was that Alicia's brother, Chet, wasn't with them.

Emma had begged Alicia, who in turn had begged Chet. According to Alicia, he wasn't exactly opposed to the idea, but hanging around with high school kids wasn't at the top of his list, and besides, he had plans to meet up with some friends at an outdoor concert. "He said he'll stop by after the show," Alicia reported back to Emma.

"After the show? When, like two o'clock in the morning?"

Alicia shrugged. "What do you want me to do? He said he'll try."

Emma was tempted to stay home. She wasn't stupid—the only reason they got the invite to begin with was because Amanda had hoped they'd bring Chet. But this was important. If Emma could produce Chet, Amanda would see her in a different light. Then, she might actually give Emma a chance to get to know her. The next time she had a party, Emma might be invited because she was Emma. Not because she was Emma whose friend was the sister of Chet. "Just text him and remind him," Emma told Alicia. "Every hour if you have to."

When they got to the party, to her relief Amanda wasn't even around. They walked around the back of the house, where music was blaring from the deck. Even in the growing darkness, Emma could see it was teeming with kids.

Almost immediately Emma spied Kyle and Sully, but when she waved, neither seemed to notice.

"What do we do?" Alicia asked. "Should we go find Amanda?"

"No!" Emma pulled her over to a corner of the deck. "Let's just chill here a minute."

Most of the kids held plastic cups and were standing around, talking in small groups. Across the deck Emma spied a keg set up by Mr. Hastings's outdoor bar. A senior, Mike Atwood, was standing behind it like he owned it.

"Want a beer?" Emma asked.

Alicia shrugged. "I don't know. Maybe later." She glanced around the deck uncomfortably. "It's so loud."

Emma deflated. She'd been counting on Alicia to hang out and have some fun, but now she was beginning to wonder if bringing her along was a bad idea.

"You're here."

When Emma spun around, she found herself face-to-face with Sully. "I am. I mean, we are." Emma nodded toward Alicia. She prayed Alicia wouldn't say anything embarrassing.

"Want a beer?" Before either girl could answer, Sully headed for the bar.

Mike Atwood would never know who Emma or Alicia were, but he tipped his chin amiably at Sully. "What's up, man?"

"Hey. Got any beers back there?"

Sully passed two cans of Pabst Blue Ribbon back to Emma and Alicia. Emma cracked hers open and took a deep sip. Alicia did the same and made a face.

"What?" Emma asked irritably. She really did not want Alicia to ruin this for them.

Alicia frowned. "It tastes like crap."

Sully smirked. "Yeah. Drink more and it won't."

From across the deck someone waved to him, and before Emma could thank him Sully was gone. They stood at the edge of the crowd sipping their beers. When Emma's was done, Alicia looked at her wide-eyed. "God, Em. Take it easy."

Emma shrugged. She turned to Mike at the bar, who was busy talking to some sophomore girls. It took forever, but finally she got his attention. She held up her empty can. "Got another? Please?"

He looked at her, and for a second Emma feared he'd say no. Sully wasn't with her this time. But he passed her another, and a thrill went down her spine.

"Now what?" Alicia asked.

"Now we have fun. Any word from Chet?" She watched as Alicia checked her phone.

"Not since the last time I looked, which was two minutes ago." Alicia looked bored. "Now what?" she asked.

Emma glanced around the deck. People were clustered in tight groups, laughing and talking. The second beer was definitely making her feel bolder. "Let's go inside," she suggested.

Stationed at the kitchen island was Amanda and a group of friends. They'd set up a blender, and there were pitchers of frothy green liquid and red Solo cups all around. Emma took a deep breath and approached.

Someone took the lid off the blender too soon, and the frozen green mix spiraled up and onto the counter. Amanda shrieked and ducked, and that's when she looked up and saw Emma.

"Oh, hi." To Emma's relief, she didn't ask where Chet was. "Want some?" When she saw the blank stare, she laughed. "They're *margaritas*." Emma held up her half-full beer in reply, but to her shock Alicia piped up behind her.

"I'll have one!"

And that's when things started to go bad. Half an hour later, they were seated on the couch between two junior guys who were playing poker. Alicia was on her third margarita and laughing too loudly at anything the guys said. She tried to join in the game, and at first they let her, but when she kept dropping cards, they started to look annoyed.

"Take it easy," Emma whispered in her ear. When Alicia turned, her cheeks were flushed pink and her hair had fallen down out of its ponytail and around her shoulders. She looked unusually pretty. "I don't want you puking," Emma said, tucking her hair behind her ear for her.

Alicia howled at this. "Me neither!"

Emma kept an eye out for Sully. A few times she spied him talking to others, and once she spotted him through the window, on the deck. Whenever he looked her way, she made sure to act like she was having a great time, paying special attention to the guys playing cards. It was lame, she knew. But the beer was making her feel floaty and silly. Someone had turned the music up even louder. Amanda and some of her friends were dancing on the deck. And that's when Emma saw Chet.

He was with his friend Taylor, outside, on the deck. Taylor came in first. She elbowed Alicia.

Alicia's head jerked toward the door. "Tay-loooooor!" she shouted, and then she tried to stand up.

Emma put her hand out. "Easy, there."

When Chet heard Alicia's voice, he looked their way. The look on his face was not a good sign, but Emma couldn't help it; she started to laugh. In fact, she couldn't stop. Beside her Alicia was already doubled over.

Chet did not find any of this as funny as they did. He pulled both of them up off the couch and out to the deck, where Alicia tried to join in the dancing. "What the hell is going on?" Chet barked as he watched his sister stumbling around.

"She really liked the margaritas," Emma stammered. "I tried to tell her to take it easy." She felt bad. Chet had shown up as they'd asked, but she'd let him down.

Chet put a hand on his sister's shoulder. "How many did you have?"

Alicia held up three fingers. "Four!"

"Jesus." Chet looked around uneasily. "I should take her home."

"No!" both girls said in unison.

"Well, she can't stay here like this," Chet said.

Emma couldn't let them go. The night was just starting to get good. "Tell you what, how about I get her some water and sit with her? You guys hang out a little while and have fun."

Taylor had his eye on the activity inside, and he seemed to want to stay.

But Chet didn't look so sure.

"I'll take care of her, I promise," Emma added.

"Like you have been?"

It stung, but she didn't blame Chet. If she didn't think fast, he was going to take them both home. Across the deck, Emma locked eyes with Sully. She motioned him over.

"Chet, do you know Sully?" she asked. To her relief, Sully took over.

"Hey buddy, good to see you!" Sully held up his beer. "Can I get you one?"

Emma watched gratefully as Chet allowed Sully to get them drinks. But he kept his eye on Alicia.

"I'm afraid my sister is having a little too much fun," Chet said. Again, he glared at Emma.

"Let me get her a chair," Sully offered. He returned with a deck chair he'd talked a girl out of and a bottle of water. *A magician*, Emma thought.

"She didn't have that many, man," Sully said for good measure. "I just don't think she's used to it."

"She's not," Chet grumbled.

Obligingly, Alicia sipped her water and seemed to settle down a bit. She glanced around at all the faces watching her. "I'm fine," she insisted. "I just needed some air."

Emma could feel the night being salvaged. "See? She's feeling better. Why don't you make the rounds, and then we can go." She could feel Sully's eyes on her, and she knew he was wondering at the way she was speaking to Chet.

To her relief, Chet finally agreed. By then, Taylor was already long gone. "Okay, but call me if she doesn't feel well. I mean it."

Emma kneeled dutifully beside Alicia and encouraged her to drink more water. She could feel Sully standing behind her. "Thanks for bailing me out. Chet's not too happy with me right now."

"So, you're tight with Chet?"

Emma stood. "Yeah. He's kind of like my big brother."

"Cool."

The liquid confidence the beer had given her seemed to dissipate in Sully's company. Emma glanced at Alicia. "Though he's probably never going to forgive me for this."

"He's just doing his job as big brother." He nodded toward Alicia, who was now slumped in her seat, eyes closed. "She seems like a sweet kid."

"She is." But before she could think of anything more to say, something else caught Sully's attention, and he walked away.

Emma sucked in her breath. God, she sucked at small talk. Maybe she should go get Chet, after all. Alicia was falling asleep. The night was over.

But to her surprise, Sully came back. This time, with two more chairs. She tried to hide her smile as he set them down. "Had to shake people out of these," he joked.

"I doubt that." When she sat, their knees touched, just like that first night in the boat.

"What's that supposed to mean?"

Emma looked up at the sky, letting the moment play out. "You're Sully McMahon. That's all."

He laughed, in that way that made his eyes crinkle. "So?"

"So people respond to that. Though I can't figure out why. I mean you're great and all. But not that great . . ." She caught herself, and tried to play it off as a joke.

But Sully wasn't letting her off the hook. He elbowed her lightly. "You think I'm great?"

Emma felt her face flush. She tried to think of something sarcastic to say, anything to downplay what had just tumbled out of her mouth, but when their eyes met she gave up. Sully held her gaze. "Sometimes, you can be kind of great," she said finally.

Then, before she could look away, Sully leaned in and pressed his lips against hers.

Emma closed her eyes. She had never been kissed. And she had no idea what to do. But she pressed her lips to his, aware of the fullness of his mouth and the sweet taste of beer. For a moment she feared she would burst.

Suddenly there was a retching sound behind them. They broke apart and looked over their shoulders just as Alicia sprang from her chair. She made it to the railing, where she bent over and threw up all over Mr. Hastings's brand-new hydrangeas.

Perry

He was in the middle of a meeting when the photo came through as a text message. It was bad enough he'd had to go into work on a Saturday morning, but because of the timing of the Super Bowl contract he'd had no choice but to call his entire team in for the morning. Perry had muted his phone, as he always did when working on something pressing, and he especially did not wish to be interrupted now. They were in the midst of a negotiation for the Super Bowl halftime show, and Spencer was trying to take over the meeting. This was Perry's largest client of the year, a repeat gig his firm had landed five years earlier and one he had every intention of hanging on to. And Spencer could go to hell for trying to take the helm. Perry hadn't worked his tail off with Bob Stanoppolis, balancing the general manager's ego and corporate wallet, for Spencer to step on his toes in the final hour. As Spencer cited the opt-out clause, Perry glanced briefly at his phone. It was Amelia, again. He didn't have time to look at the photo she'd sent. He swiped the screen to airplane mode and cleared his throat. "Thank you, Spencer, but I'll take it from here."

Forty-five minutes later the meeting was over. They'd reached an agreement, finally. Perry stood at the door, shook hands with the team, and listened to the usual winding-down banter at the close of a successful meeting. Someone was heading to the Hamptons to play golf for the weekend. Did he play golf? How was the family? He did not, and they were fine. Perry was impatient to get back to his desk; he knew nothing was a done deal until contracts were signed.

Bob Stanoppolis paused in the doorway and extended his hand. "Thank you, Perry. Another year in the basket. Let's hope the lead singer doesn't get shit-faced and fall off the stage."

Perry tried to ignore Spencer's exaggerated burst of laughter. He forced a smile. What Bob Stanoppolis didn't know was that the lead singer was the least of his problems. So much could go wrong: Pyrotechnics. Crowd control. Stage setup. These days, protecting against potential shooters and bomb threats was standard protocol. Bob should pray that the worst upset might be the lead singer yanking his pants down and face-planting into the audience. "To another year," Perry said, extending his hand.

To his chagrin, Spencer followed Perry out and down the hall. "Check, please!" he barked. He clapped Perry roughly on the shoulder. "Grab a celebratory drink?"

Perry did not drink on workdays. Spencer knew that, leaving his invitation as thin as his humility. "Can't," Perry said. "We need to go over those provisions."

Spencer flicked his wrist to check his watch. "Oh, yeah. About those, what do you say we tackle them in the morning?" Perry knew Spencer had no intention of looking over the provisions now or in the morning. Which was fine with him. Perry didn't need Spencer slowing him down. His phone buzzed again.

"Tomorrow morning, then," Perry said, moving on to his corner office. He was glad to be rid of him.

He tossed his notes on the desk and rubbed his eyes. If he ordered in takeout, he could get through half of the provisions tonight. Maura came to the door. "How'd it go?"

"Very well. A few changes and I'll have it on your desk for review tomorrow. I want to get it over to Hanley by midmorning."

Maura nodded. "I have two messages from Amelia. She said it was important. She's at home." Concern flickered across her face. Amelia never called Maura unless Perry was so deep into a project that he'd neglected to check his phone.

Perry retrieved his phone from his pocket and glanced at the screen. Three new messages. "I'll call her back."

"Can I order you something to eat before I go?" It was already an hour after her usual workday. Perry knew Maura had a forty-five-minute train ride home to Mount Kisco. He was famished, but he didn't want to delay her further.

"I'm fine, thanks."

"Thai or Chinese?" Maura wasn't about to budge.

Perry smiled. "Surprise me."

He opened his laptop as his phone buzzed again. Another message from Amelia. Perry sighed and opened the text. A grainy image filled the screen.

The first thing he saw was skin. A teenage girl in what appeared to be a bra and panties standing in someone's kitchen. She thrust a bottle of beer toward the camera at a precarious angle. To her left, a boy in a baseball cap was reaching for it. To her right, another had his arm slung around her bare waist. The girl stared back at him, her lips parted as if she was trying to say something. Dark makeup rimmed her eyes. Perry squinted. Emma's face stared back at him.

"No."

His phone buzzed in his hand. Amelia. Wordlessly, he accepted the call.

"Perry. You have to come home. It's bad."

Phoebe

I t was just after midnight when she tiptoed into the dark kitchen and was startled by a figure outside the window. Who would be out at this hour? But as she peered outside, she recognized the soft, moonlit shape of her mother in her nightgown. Jane stood outside on the patio, her back to the kitchen window. There was a small orange flicker against the night sky, and a smoky cloud rose up around her.

Phoebe tugged open the back door. "Mom?"

Jane spun around, hand to her chest. "Christ, Phoebe."

"Me? What are you *doing*?" Phoebe flicked on the lights.

Jane tilted her head as if contemplating how to reply, then blew a spiral of smoke from her lips. "Damn it." She tossed the cigarette on the flagstone, then ground it out with the pristine white toe of her Sperry Top-Sider. The look of her in the billowy nightgown and boat shoes only enhanced the ridiculousness of the whole scene.

"Since when do you smoke?" Then, "What if the boys saw you?"

Jane sighed. "The boys are asleep. Why aren't you?"

"Because I can't. At least I'm not skulking around out here with a pack of cigarettes like a teenager." Was no one in the family who they seemed?

"I'm sorry," Jane snapped. She bent, peeled the cigarette butt from the patio, and strode past Phoebe into the kitchen, where she dipped it in the sink then wrapped it neatly in a napkin like a little gift and tossed it in the trash. Clearly a well-rehearsed routine. "I'm just trying to unwind."

Phoebe plopped down on a kitchen stool and regarded her mother. "I feel like I'm meeting everyone in this family for the first time. Does Dad know you've taken up smoking?"

Jane scowled. "I haven't *taken it up*. And of course he doesn't know."

"Of course he doesn't. A bunch of liars, all of us."

"What's that supposed to mean?" Her mother went to the sink and rinsed her mouth out.

"Mom. Look at us." She put her head in her hands. It was the middle of the night. Across town her empty dream house sat in total disrepair. Another town over, Jake was hobbling around the confines of a tiny cottage on crutches while his brand-new fiancée's daughter was going through some kind of post-traumatic response to an accident he'd caused. And Perry—the rock of them all—could not bring himself to face his brother since.

Jane joined her daughter at the island. "We aren't exactly at our finest this summer, are we?"

There was a shuffling noise from the living room, and both women turned to see Grandma Elsie totter into the kitchen. "Well, hello, dears. Phoebe, what are you doing at your mother's house at this hour?"

Phoebe and Jane exchanged looks. Elsie's memory had been growing more inconsistent. "Flickering like a light bulb" was how Jake had described it, and there was no telling when she would be lucid and conversational, or forgetful and confused. "Hi, Nana. I'm staying here for a couple weeks, remember?" Phoebe reminded her.

"That's right. Your little visit."

Elsie went to the fridge and pulled the double doors open. Standing directly in front of them, she undid her bathrobe and tipped her head back. "Invigorating."

Phoebe tried to cover her smile as her mother intervened. "Elsie, is your room too warm? I can turn up the air-conditioning."

"My room? It's cold as a crypt."

"Well, would you like something to eat? I can make you a little snack."

"A snack!" With some effort Elsie retied her bathrobe and joined Phoebe at the island. Elsie was alert and delighted, as if she'd just arrived at a party. "Look at us! Nocturnal beasts, we are. Like a bunch of alley cats circling the dumpster." She giggled.

"Blueberry muffin okay?" Jane asked.

"Make it a double," Phoebe said.

They watched as Jane sliced and buttered the muffins, and set them on plates. She pushed them gently across the island like a bartender, and Phoebe and her grandmother fell into them. The summer-ripened berries were both tart and sweet on Phoebe's tongue, and mixed with the butter—heaven! Phoebe closed her eyes with pleasure. Even Jane, who shunned sweets, could not resist. She reached across the island and swiped a piece of Phoebe's.

"Hey!"

Elsie looked up, and dabbed a crumb delicately from her bottom lip. "You've got to be quicker, dear."

The women ate in silence, savoring the dim quietude. When Elsie was done, she stood. "I am going to lie down. And then, I hope, to dream."

Phoebe stood, too. "Let me help you back to bed, Nana."

Gently, she guided her grandmother across the house and into her room, where she helped her into bed and pulled the covers up.

How strange it was to take care of someone who had taken care of you for so many years. Her grandmother sat up pertly, holding the edge of her blankets like a little doll.

"Would you like me to turn the light out, Nana?"

"You used to be afraid of the dark, do you remember?" Elsie asked.

Phoebe did not, at first.

"Whenever I came to babysit you kids so that your parents could go out for an evening, you never wanted to go to bed with the lights out. Oh, the fuss you put up."

As Phoebe listened, the memories came back. The sense of worry in her chest at being alone in the dark. The unsettling feeling of going to bed in a house when her parents were not in it. "You would rub my back and tell me stories, about when Mom was a little girl."

Elsie nodded. "That's right. It helped you to sleep." She cocked her head, studying Phoebe closely through her watery eyes. "Are you having trouble sleeping, dear?"

Phoebe could not help it. Without warning, tears flooded her eyes and spilled down her cheeks. She hadn't slept well in weeks. She didn't know if she ever would again.

"Oh, honey." Elsie reached a shaking hand and pressed it to Phoebe's back, and Phoebe found herself leaning in to it like she was a little girl all over again.

"Nana, I've made such a mess of things."

"There, now. It can't be all that bad."

Phoebe grabbed the edge of her T-shirt and blew her nose into it. "Oh, but it is. That house we bought? I can't afford it anymore."

Her grandmother didn't answer, and at first Phoebe thought that the lightbulb was flickering again. But then she said, "It is just a house. Four walls. A roof. A door. The house does not matter."

But it *did*. It was the place she would raise her children, just as her parents had raised her. Where memories would take shape and form, into scratches on the floor from a favorite dog's toenails, into marks on the doorframe, counting the years by a child's height. Where birthday candles would be blown out and wishes made. Some that would never see the light of day, but were made nonetheless. Like Phoebe's own, as a little girl, when she biked up to the lake house and saw the young couple with the baby and saw her future.

"Nana, we need to finish our home."

"You already have a home."

At first, she thought Elsie was not understanding. "No, Nana, this is my childhood home. Rob and I can't stay here for good," Phoebe tried to explain.

Elsie's brow furrowed in frustration. "When your grandpa and I got married, we did not have a house. We lived in a tiny apartment in Yonkers. Our first real house was just a cottage, a little ranch in Westchester. But we raised all four kids in it." She paused, her watery blue eyes wandering softly across the ceiling as she remembered. "Later we moved. The house was bigger, nicer. But no matter where we lived over the years, the walls didn't make a difference." Here, she looked at Phoebe. "From the day we got married, we had our home. We had each other."

It was not her grandmother who was mixed up, at all, Phoebe realized. As she cried, Elsie clucked her tongue, her hand working across the plane of Phoebe's back in slow, rhythmic circles, the way it had all those years ago. It made Phoebe still. First her mind, then her tears. Until all that remained was the warmth of her grandmother's hand at the small of her back, and the dimly lit room, and the quiet breath.

When Elsie's hand slowed and she drifted off against her pillows, Phoebe found her own eyelids fluttering. It was cramped at the foot of her grandmother's bed, but Phoebe curled herself around Elsie's birdlike legs and nestled into the blankets. For the first time in months, she slept through the night.

Olivia

This was not how she'd envisioned their moving in together. She should've known better. The cottage was really meant for a single dweller, two at most. The notion of squeezing in one more had seemed cozy. What a foolish notion *that* had been.

The first floor proved to be a field of land mines. Luci's toys. A pair of flip-flops. Buster, the dog. And there was Jake—crutches splayed and balancing on one leg amid the hazards. The open layout had seemed like a good idea to move him into, but the quarters were so narrow that Jake had to keep his crutches tight against his sides as he navigated the couch, the kitchen island, the dining table. Olivia spent her days folded in half, seemingly forever bent over to retrieve a doll, a Lego, a shoe. To push a chair in, to shovel things into the closet. She felt like a snowplow, making her way in a repeat circuit around the cottage, forever clearing a travel lane for Jake. By day's end she wanted to scream, "Why can't you just sit?"

Jake, for his part, was not complaining. Worse, he was being a good sport. And it was driving her crazy. He wanted to do too much, and the fact was, he couldn't. Which was probably driving him crazy, too, but she was not about to ask.

There was a look on his face she had not seen before. It was in the tightened corners of his mouth and around his eyes when he spied the bags of groceries lined up in the hall. The ones he could barely get around, never mind pick up and carry, with crutches. Everything, it seemed, was a reminder to him of what he could not do to help. The everyday little things were the hardest, like taking out the garbage, bringing Buster outside to pee, unloading the car. When she was looking for her phone and realized she'd left it in the studio, he hopped up on his crutches before he got the look. "Don't worry. I'll get it," she'd say before running outside. She realized, with chagrin, that his desire to help was more burdensome than waiting on him.

Then there was Luci. Who wanted to do the impossible. She wanted to show Jake the green beans that were growing in the garden, the ones she and Marge had planted and made trellises for a few months earlier. But the garden was all the way across the yard, at the far end of the fence, in a muddy section. Or she wanted to go to the beach. "What can you possibly do at the beach?" Olivia wanted to ask. She couldn't imagine trying to keep her cast sand-free, let alone dry. Jake at the beach was simply not possible. In her worst moments, Olivia fantasized about tugging on her own swimsuit, sneaking out to the car, and just driving away. Just to steal an hour of sun and respite.

"Try some indoor activities," Olivia had pleaded with her daughter. As it was, with Jake on crutches and Luci in her cast, the outside world was rife with disappointment. Sand. Lake water. Sweating, which was no small thing when wearing a cast in summertime. Indoor activities it was. "How about one of your craft kits from Christmas?" Olivia suggested.

Luci listened, if begrudgingly. She got out a macramé kit that they all instantly realized required two hands. Same for her model clay. And the damn rainbow loom that a friend had handed down.

Olivia stood at the craft drawer she kept in the kitchen and stared at all of the art supplies with rage. Tiny beads. Fishing wire. Glitter. She slammed the drawer shut before the urge to pitch them out into the driveway overtook her.

"So, what's the plan for today?" Jake asked. He was half-reclining on their small couch, his bad leg propped up on her good pillows, his good leg dangling off the side. She knew he'd be uncomfortable and trying to adjust his position within minutes. After all, she watched him do this all day.

"The plan?" She drew in her breath. Ben's art show was upon them. Today she *had* to be in the studio. For a good several hours, uninterrupted. Initially, she'd been relieved to have Jake with her to help keep an eye on Luci. She'd even gone so far as to hope they could entertain each other, or at least provide distractions. But with Luci's ongoing muteness showing no improvement, she'd found herself hovering between the two. Translating and trying to connect the dots between them. Even with his deep well of patience, she could tell Jake sometimes grew weary from the effort it took to connect with Luci. And Luci was growing shyer around him, too. Which left Olivia awash with guilt and wildly distracted whenever she tried to steal an hour in the studio, so that instead she ran back and forth from barn to cottage to check in on them. Marge had offered to watch Luci, but Olivia couldn't take advantage. She was working for them, not the other way around. But at this rate, nothing was getting done.

"I was thinking of inviting Emma over," Olivia said.

"Emma? Why?" Jake looked alarmed.

"Because Luci likes her a lot. And I thought maybe she could use the money. That way you can do what you'd like, without having to watch Luci while I'm working."

"I don't mind watching Luci. Besides, you're only fifty steps away in the studio." Here they were again. Jake supported her work, but he still didn't get it. How many times would she have to explain that creating something wasn't like picking up a paint roller and starting in on the blank wall where you left off last? It required uninterrupted thought. A certain mindset. And time alone in your headspace once you finally got there. She couldn't just pick up her tools and "get it done."

She switched the subject. "Don't you have work to catch up on for the Audubon Center? Yesterday you said that you needed to spend time on your laptop. Make some calls," she reminded him. Jake had taken time off of work, at first, but he'd since made arrangements with his boss to work remotely until he could get back into the office.

"I guess," he said. But she could tell he didn't like the idea.

Olivia dialed Emma, but the call went straight to voicemail. She decided to send a text to Perry and Amelia, as a courtesy—she wasn't sure what was appropriate being the soon-to-be step-aunt, and since Emma didn't have a license and they were her parents, Olivia didn't want to step on any toes bypassing Amelia and Perry. But there was no reply from either.

"I really need to get into the studio," she said, finally.

Luci was upstairs, playing with her dolls. Olivia was worried about the amount of time she was spending alone, unlike other kids out enjoying the summer with friends.

But she had no other choice than to leave Luci with Jake. Olivia made tomato and mozzarella sandwiches and left them on a plate in the fridge. She washed and sliced strawberries and set them on the counter in a bowl. "Lunch is all set, whenever you're ready. Just call Luci down when it's time."

When she slid the barn door open, she was surprised to see Ben standing at his worktable. "Well, well. Come in."

"Am I interrupting?" she asked. Ben often worked alone, and she knew he preferred it that way.

"Not unless you consider walking in on an old man's doubt."

"Doubt?" She closed the door behind her and joined him in the cool recess of the barn. "Is this about the show? Don't tell me you get stage fright. I won't believe it."

Ben chuckled softly. "No, I have no nerves, though I don't like the meet and greets as much as Marge does. She's far more adept at that nonsense. I'm just not sure this one will finish."

Olivia came to stand beside him, and considered the sculpture. Ben had finished the galloping mare, and it was waiting to be boxed and crated for shipment to the gallery. This piece was a sudden last-minute addition, as Marge had warned her he was prone to do. "Just before a show, his wheels get spinning. Be prepared for eleventh-hour projects. Sometimes they make it in time, sometimes they don't."

Sure enough, Ben had done just that. Starting only a couple weeks ago, when Olivia had done inventory of studio materials, she'd noted the red clay was low in the bin and had asked if he wanted her to place another order. Instead of answering, he'd come to inspect the supply and removed a hunk of it. Shortly after, he'd had it on the table and begun playing around with it. When she'd come in later that evening, Ben was gone. But in his spot was a new project. A tree trunk, twisting up and away from the block of clay out of which it sprouted. She'd stood in the barn shaking her head in wonder for a long time before locking up.

Standing beside him now, she understood his concerns. The red clay needed to cure. And although the sculpture was a much smaller scale than he usually did, and with simpler material, Ben wasn't yet done.

"I've reserved six installation spaces for this show. This being the sixth." He set his tool down and stepped away, leaving Olivia alone with it. "It's not ready."

Olivia walked around it, considering its form. "It's lovely, Ben. You've captured the spirit of it."

Ben stood to the side, and lit up his pipe. "Bullshit."

Olivia turned to face him.

"Unless I finish it today, it won't cure by the show."

She turned back to the sculpture. The broad trunk at the base gave way to long limbs, then to branches, all suggesting subtle movement. The branches were so inviting, she fought the urge to run her fingers along them. But there was something about one of the larger limbs. The angle of it was perhaps too sharp.

"What do you see?" he asked, as if reading her mind.

Olivia let her breath out. Working for an artist was a tricky dance. Her job was to gather his audience and get his work out in the world, not critique it. But she wanted the chance to test herself. "The larger branch on the left?"

"What about it?" Ben sounded dejected, as if it had been something else that was bothering him. This was now another.

"I don't know, for sure." Olivia moved around the base, studying each angle. "It grows sharply away from the tree. Maybe it interrupts the continuity?"

Ben blew a ring of smoke out and walked back over. She felt a rise of hope.

"Maybe. I was thinking about the form, overall. She's too sinewy. I want grace, but also strength. She needs to look like she could bend in a wind."

Olivia was used to this; Ben assigned gender to his pieces, and she understood why. There were traits in every subject that an artist had to convey. The more you knew your subject, the more likely you were to grasp its essence.

"I need to give it time." Ben dipped a sponge in a stained bucket of water, and gently ran it over the tree. Then he covered the piece with canvas, where it would stay dark and moist until he returned to work on it tomorrow. She watched as he tidied his table, wiping down the work board with a towel, then picking up and cleaning each individual tool with another wet sponge. "I can do that," she offered.

Ben shook his head. "You," he said, "need to work."

Olivia turned for the stairs. "The mailings have gone out, and all the announcements we printed are posted around town. I've got another email blast to put together."

Ben turned. "Not that." He nodded toward the table in the corner of the barn. Her table, where her own work was shrouded in canvas. "That," he said. "I hope you don't mind, but I had a look."

Olivia paused on the stairs. "You looked at my piece?" She wasn't offended; she'd offered it to him countless times, hoping for some criticism or guidance. But she'd had so little time lately, she hadn't worked on it at all. There was no way she could sit down and work now.

"Unlike this," Ben said, nodding at his tarped work, "I think your piece is ready."

"But it's not done." Olivia was shocked. Ben had taken the time to inspect her work. But it was incomplete; there was no way it was near done.

"What's left to do?" he asked, watching her with genuine curiosity.

"Well, the right hand. The fingertips aren't even done. They're just clay stubs." She paused, closing her eyes, and she could see her mother's hands. The long, elegant fingers. How would she ever capture them?

"Then get it done."

Oliva glanced at her worktable in the corner, then up the stairs toward the office loft. There was desk work to finish up—work that could not wait—they were so close to the show. She needed to review details with the gallery owner, and go over the schedule for the installation, which would take at least two days before the show. Besides, even if all that were done, she wasn't in the mindset. Outside the studio, her cottage practically hummed in the distance. Jake and Luci would soon be done with lunch and looking to do something. They needed her. No one could work creatively like that. Ben, more than anyone else, should understand that.

"I know I need to spend more time sculpting," she admitted, trying not to see the disapproval in his expression. "But things are kind of crazy right now. I haven't got the time. Or the headspace."

Ben shrugged, and continued to clean up his work area. He took a bucket of dirtied water and went to the door, where he tossed it outside. "There is never a good time. That's life."

Olivia swallowed. "I know. But Jake and Luci need me right now."

"Yes. And so does your work."

Olivia tried not to let her frustration show in her face. This was where Ben was wrong. He was an artist, but he had Marge. He had her. What he did not have was a child, or a fiancé who was recovering from an accident and surgery. That was exactly what she had been hired to do: to protect his time, so that he didn't have to do anything other than focus on his work.

"I'm sorry," Ben said, "if it seems I am pushing you. I know you have much to concern yourself with. And I respect all of it. Deeply." He looked at her softly. "Do you want to sculpt?"

Olivia nodded, a plume of defense rising in her chest. "It's why I'm here."

Ben scoffed. "Then sit." His voice was angry.

"Excuse me?"

"Sit down with it, Olivia." He paused. "Sit still, and contemplate it. Look at it. Run your hands over it. Your work will speak to you. But you have to sit still with it so you can listen."

She waited, unsure of what to do. Olivia did not like being told what to do. But this was different; Ben was urging her. And she understood.

"Bah." He shook his head in frustration and made his way to the door. She feared he might slam the door, but he paused. "I have reserved six spaces at the gallery," he said gruffly. He jabbed his finger at his tarped sculpture in the center of the floor. "That is not ready."

Olivia understood: he had only five sculptures to show.

She waited until the door creaked closed on its hinges. Until Ben's footsteps on the gravel grew distant. From her position on the stairs, Olivia could see outside. The cottage was not on fire. There was no one crying for her attention or her help, at least not yet. She set the studio mail down on the bottom step. Quickly, before she could change her mind, she crossed the barn floor to her worktable and whisked the cover off her sculpture.

Olivia studied the clay length of the wrist she'd sculpted. It was narrow and long, both familiar and not at all a part of her. Much like her mother. Growing up seeing her mother's pictures, she was always struck by the elegance of her long fingers and slender wrists. Holding a glass of wine. A cigarette. And in one rare picture of the two of them together, holding Olivia on her lap. Her father, Pierre, often said with a note of sadness, "You have her hands." Now she placed her fingers gently on the sculpture and closed her eyes. The clay wrist was cold to the touch. But Olivia knew. All it would take was the warmth of her own hands. The strength of her fingertips. And it would yield in her desired direction.

Resigned, she reached for the canvas cover and draped it over the sculpture. If only her life could be shaped as such.

Emma

Her life was over. Not only was she a social pariah, but her parents were never going to let her out of their sight. Assuming they could stand to look at her to begin with.

The morning after Amanda Hastings's party, she awoke with a pounding skull. Her mouth was a desert. Emma reached for the glass of water by her bed and gulped it down. The sunlight streaming in the window was blinding, and she winced, pulling the pillow over her head. But something else was causing her head to pound; something that gnawed at the edges of her memory.

In small flashes, the night came back to her. She and Alicia had gone to Amanda's. As soon as they arrived, she'd felt uneasy. They'd stood, just the two of them, outside on the deck, sipping cans of beer. It got better when they went inside. Some of the other sophomore guys from her class were playing cards at the kitchen island. It was there Alicia had discovered margaritas. Boy, had she. At first Emma was glad, because Alicia was being such a bore.

After one margarita, she loosened up. After two, she got downright silly, and that's when the party started to get interesting. Then Chet arrived. Emma wasn't sure if her buzz came from the beer, or from Chet's arrival and the moment Amanda walked in and saw him talking to Emma and Alicia in her living room. Finally, Emma had some social credibility. And then, later, there was the moment, with Sully. Emma's insides went fuzzy when she recalled sitting with him on the deck. How close he was. The way he looked at her under the floodlights. It was different, different in a way that felt right and good. Until Alicia threw up over the deck railing.

After that, Emma's memory got disjointed. She remembered Sully had helped. Chet had not been happy, and at some point in the night he ended up picking Alicia up and carrying her to his car over his shoulder. Emma was embarrassed by the scene, but also invigorated. She was with Chet, a beloved graduate and college student. He would take care of Alicia. And handling it alongside him made it all seem okay.

But this was where things got dicey. Instead of going home with Chet and Alicia, Emma had decided to stay. That was where she had a feeling something went wrong.

After Chet and Alicia left, she'd headed back to the party. But it was winding down. She found Sully and Kyle with some of the others inside. The keg was kicked. Someone had broken out the hard alcohol from Mr. Hastings's bar and they'd started a poker game. Strip poker.

Emma's buzz had largely worn off at that point, and she knew she shouldn't press her luck. She'd guzzled a glass of water and tried to eat some pretzels. But then Sully invited her to play. Next to him, on the couch. His hand on her knee.

And then someone passed a bottle of Jägermeister around the table. Everyone was drinking from it. Why not? she'd thought. Emma tipped it back, then wiped her mouth on the back of her hand. It tasted like crap, and she'd had to force the nasty licorice-tasting liquid down. But the hot buzz that followed came fast, and when the bottle came back around the table she found herself taking another swig. The rest was all a haze.

As she lay in bed, trying to remember how she got home and what time it had been, there was a knock at her bedroom door. Emma sat up. Too fast, and the bed started to spin. "What?" she managed. She really hoped she wouldn't throw up.

Her mother poked her head in. "Hey, honey. It's eleven thirty. You feeling okay?"

Emma lay back down, shielding her eyes. "Sorry. Slept in."

Amelia pushed the door ajar and glanced around the room. She looked concerned. "What time did you get in last night?"

Emma closed her eyes. Was it lying if you really had no idea? "Sorry, I think I was a little late."

"What happened to Alicia staying over?"

Her stomach roiled and she rolled over to face the wall. "She was really tired and Chet was there, so she went home with him."

"Oh." This seemed to make her mother more concerned. "Did you two have a fight or something?"

"Mom. We're fine." Emma really wished her mom would stop asking questions. As it was, her head throbbed every time she had to speak. Lying, it turned out, hurt even more. "I'll text her later," she added for good measure.

"All right. Well, why don't you come down and have some breakfast. Or lunch, I suppose."

The mere mention of food made her head spin harder. Emma waited until her mother left. She did not, as Emma had hoped, close the door. Emma groaned and reached for her phone.

The second she turned her phone on, notifications filled the screen. One after the other, it vibrated and dinged in her hand. Emma sat up, squinting.

Her Instagram account was ablaze with notifications. Same with Snapchat. "Nice work" someone commented. Some of the names were kids from school, some she didn't even recognize.

"Girls gone wild," someone else said. A comment from Kyle: "Taking it off." Emma felt her stomach lurch.

There, at the top of her story was a picture. A picture of her, in just her bra and panties. With Sully on one side and Kyle on the other. Her eyes were half-closed and she held a beer in her hand. To her horror, there were 368 likes and 42 comments. As she scrolled through them, a wave of nausea washed through her. Hands shaking, she checked her Snapchat. Her photo was everywhere. But the one she noticed first: Amanda Hastings. Posted at one thirty-three a.m. On Amanda's story was the picture of Emma.

Then came the texts. One group text with so many people that the contacts alone filled her screen. "Who is that?" someone texted. "She looks like shit," another said. "Slut." Emma dropped her phone, ran to the bathroom, and threw up all over the tile floor.

She was still vomiting when her mother burst into the room, whimpering and holding her cell phone out in front of her as if it were radioactive.

"What *is* this?" she howled. "A parent from the Club sent this to me!" Then, seeing her daughter crumpled on the bathroom floor, she snapped back to mother mode and sank to her knees beside her. "Oh, honey."

Worse was her father. He came home early, clearly summoned. And then he paced. Around the kitchen. Up and down the stairs. Along the hall outside her room, while she lay in bed and nursed her hangover with glasses of water and Tylenol and toast, which her mother delivered every fifteen minutes. Emma listened to their strained conversations on the other side of her door. "How could this happen?" was all her father could ask. As though this was something that had been done to her by some outside force, and not something Emma was capable of doing herself.

She understood her parents were scared. But she was also offended. Was she so dull and meek in their estimation that it was unimaginable she could have made these bad choices herself? On some twisted level, though, it made her feel better. At least now she felt seen.

For once, her mother was the one who asked the questions. "Did you do anything other than drink? Were drugs involved? Did anything happen with a boy?"

Emma answered each one honestly. *No, no, no.*

The worst thing was Alicia hadn't called or texted once. Emma had tried to reach her: "Are you okay? I'm sorry I didn't come home with you." But there was no reply. She thought of texting Chet, but she was too humiliated. She cringed at the thought of him seeing the picture. She wanted to die when she imagined all the adults who might have: Her camp director. Her father's friends at the clubhouse. The neighbors she babysat for. Her parents must have realized the extent of her suffering because they finally stopped asking questions and left her alone. Since really, what more could anyone say?

Sometime later, her parents called her down to the kitchen. Dinner had been made, and it seemed they expected her to sit down and join them. She took her seat at the table and stared at her plate. "I'm sorry." It was all she could say. And it was the truth.

The look on her mother's face was mixed. "We know you are, honey. But all those posts, those comments . . . why do kids do that? I hate the internet. I just hate it."

As she looked at her parents' expressions, the fallout crystallized. Emma hadn't just scared them; she had disappointed them. She'd lied, she'd gotten drunk, she'd left her best friend and chosen to stay at a party with people who didn't even care about her. Now she was the punchline of a joke. Emma pushed her plate away.

Her mother picked up her fork. "What is going on with the drinking this summer, Emma? This is not who you are."

Emma turned to her father. This was his terrain: managing crisis. Coming up with a plan. Onward! But he had deflated to the point he'd become one with his chair. His glasses were smudged, his hair mussed, and he looked like he hadn't slept in days.

"I'm sorry," she said again. Then she speared a forkful of salad and popped it in her mouth. It was bitter on her tongue, but she took another bite and forced it down. Chewing and swallowing. That much she could manage. She was working her way up to trying a bite of chicken when her father finally cleared his throat.

"Emma." His voice was muted with sadness. When she looked up at him, he couldn't meet her gaze. "What happened?"

It was the question of the summer. What happened on the boat? What happened to their perfect daughter, the one with the good grades and the nice manners—the kid every neighbor asked to babysit their own kids?

That was the problem. Everyone in her parents' world saw that girl. They even adored her. But no one in Emma's world did. In her world, at high school—at camp—at the beach—that girl didn't matter. That girl was invisible.

It was the one thing she'd wanted that summer; she'd wanted to be noticed. Look at her now. She'd made her wish come true.

Perry

Crisis was Perry's professional specialty. It was what he did. And he did it better than anyone else.

Two summers ago, when a country-western concert had gone awry due to drunk and disorderly behavior that turned into a mob brawl, Perry's firm handled the fallout. They didn't just handle the insurance. They hired a legal team. And a publicity team. They managed the news reporters, the investigation, and the following medical claims. All of it. Though he was, of course, sorry for the injured, especially two children, and the property damage, Perry had compartmentalized his emotions and gotten to work. He relished the challenge of walking into his company boardroom and coming up with a strategy that addressed everything from lawsuits to financial damages to image refurbishment.

Just as he had during a crane collapse outside a minor-league baseball game three years earlier. There had been construction outside the stadium, and though it was shut down during the game and the spectators were partitioned off from the entrances in that location, the collapse had resulted in several injuries and the death of a security worker that day. As the news flashed on screens across the city, Perry was already in his office with his shirtsleeves rolled up. That was Perry Goodwin's relationship to crisis. It was tragic, but he had a job to do.

Now, however, when it came to his own flesh and blood, he was useless. The fallout had found them. He could thank social media for getting word out across the miles. All he could do now was attempt to manage the damage.

The first call came in on Monday morning. It was so early, Perry hadn't left the house yet for the train. "Mr. Goodwin, it's Jeff, the director at the clubhouse camp."

Perry set down his coffee. "Good morning, Jeff. I'm glad you called." Perry was ready for this call. "We appreciate the time off you gave Emma after the accident, but I'm afraid she may need to take another day or two. She's not feeling well." Perry hated lying. But he didn't want to get into the details with the camp if he didn't have to. Emma was great at her job, and the community families loved her.

"That's actually why I'm calling. As you know, the board of directors runs the summer camp. I'm not entirely sure what happened over the weekend, but they called to tell me there was some kind of incident. They would like Emma to take a few days off until it's sorted out."

Perry caught his breath. He was on the board. Hell, he was president. There was a regular board meeting scheduled but it wasn't until later that night. Which meant they'd called an emergency meeting, about *his* daughter, without him? He cut to the chase. "Is Emma losing her job?"

"I sure hope not. She's the best counselor I've got. But it's not up to me, Mr. Goodwin. I hope you understand." He paused, then added, "I'm hopeful this will all work out. Please tell Emma I'll be in touch when they reach a decision."

A decision. Meaning the Club was reviewing the incident at

Ted Hastings's house and Emma's behavior there. Both things that had nothing to do with the Club itself. Perry thanked Jeff and hung up. Emma hadn't been relishing the thought of going to work and facing everyone at camp. But this was far worse.

The second call came later in the day, when he was at work. It was the admissions office at George Washington University. Amelia, who was working from home to be with Emma, had received it. She called Perry, hysterical. "Somehow they found out about the photo. Perry, they kicked her out of the summer leadership program!"

Perry's stomach fell. "What? How did they even know?"

"I don't know—it's out there. The simplest search can cause it to pop up."

"There must be something we can do. Emma should call them back and try to talk to them. Surely they've had kids make dumb mistakes before."

"I spoke to the woman for almost half an hour. She was sympathetic, but firm. I believe her exact words were, 'At this time Emma's actions don't represent the mission of our program.'"

Perry wanted to throw his phone at the wall. GW was his alma mater, where some of the best memories of his life had been. The summer leadership program was something he'd told Emma about two years earlier, and she'd worked her tail off to get in. All those honors and AP classes since freshman year. All the clubs and extracurricular activities. It was what she'd talked about all year: going to Washington, DC, in August. Perry had already arranged time off from work to drive her down there. They were going to make a family trip of it. Best of all, Emma would get college credit for the program. Just a few weeks ago Emma had connected with the girl who would be her roommate: an international student from Korea whom she'd Face-Timed with to talk about what to bring. It was going to be the highlight of her summer. Now she wouldn't be going at all.

"How did she take it?" Perry asked his wife. He imagined Emma would be crushed. But then again, he'd been wrong about so much lately . . .

"She's numb, Perry. She's getting it from all sides. From friends. From us. The Wilders called from up the street and canceled her babysitting gig. They told her that the kids were sick. But then Emma heard that Mrs. Wilder asked another counselor at camp if she was free for the same night." Amelia let out her breath. "I'm so worried about her."

Perry was worried, too. But most of all he was angry. "I need to follow up with you later, honey. I have a call to make."

Ted Hastings's number was in his contacts, and he pulled it up now. Perry had been biding his time before placing this call, wanting to plan his words. He dialed. To his surprise, Ted picked up on the first ring.

"Perry, how are you?" If Ted understood the nature of the call, he gave nothing away.

"Ted, I wish I were calling under different circumstances, to be honest."

Perry waited for him to say something, to give some indication of empathy or camaraderie, but there was only silence.

"I'm calling about the party at your house this past weekend."

To his credit, Ted didn't deny it. "I heard about it. Janie and I were on the Vineyard visiting her sister. I want you to know we weren't aware of any party until after the fact, and it's not something we would ever allow."

Perry sat back in his chair. He was relieved to hear the acknowledgment. "Yes, well, I don't know if you heard, but my daughter, Emma, was at that party. And a photo of her in a rather compromising position was taken." Perry struggled to keep his voice steady. "Emma is not the kind of kid who finds herself in such positions. Ever. And unfortunately, this photo has had far-reaching consequences."

Ted paused, and Perry imagined him listening, father-to-father.

"What is it you're asking of me?" Ted asked.

The question threw him. Perry wasn't sure. He was asking for empathy, perhaps. For acceptance of responsibility, as well. But the sudden businesslike shift irked him. "Ted, Emma has lost admittance to a prestigious summer program as a result. And perhaps her job at the clubhouse camp."

"I was sorry to hear it."

Past tense. So, Ted had heard about the Club's review of Emma's camp job. Ted Hastings was in tight with the Club, a legacy member, in fact. And yet he hadn't reached out to either Perry or Amelia once.

"Ted. I don't know if you're aware that your daughter had a direct role in this, but the sharing of that photo has been very damaging. It continues to go on, and Amelia and I are reaching out to ask parents to talk to their kids and get this to stop. It's bullying."

"Perry. Come on. Kids will be kids."

Perry sputtered. "Yes, which is why adults need to be adults."

"I'm sure I don't need to tell you that Amanda is a good kid."

"I'm sure I don't need to tell you that hosting a party with underage drinking is illegal."

Perry could hear Ted's intake of breath. He didn't want to get legal, but if he had to he would. Ted Hastings could bet his legacy membership's ass he would. Why were some parents so reluctant to investigate their children's actions on social media? It was the worst kind of sticking your head in the sand.

"Listen, Perry. We're sorry to hear about the hot water Emma got herself into. But this has nothing to do with us."

"All of this happened at *your* house."

Ted Hastings's tone changed sharply. "Where your daughter clearly made some bad decisions. Look, I suggest you let this blow over."

Before Perry could say another word, the line cut out.

Perry dropped his phone on his desk. For more than fifteen years he'd known the Hastings. They'd attended the same clambakes at the Club every Fourth of July. The last night of every December they'd raised their glasses in the same neighborhood homes to toast the new year. He and Ted had watched their daughters learn to walk, to swim, to boat on the same lake. And yet all of it meant nothing.

Ted Hastings wanted no part of this. He wasn't going to talk to his daughter to find out what happened. Nor would he be asking her to take down her posts on the internet. Over all those years he'd considered Ted a friend, a good neighbor, a fellow dad. What a fool he'd been.

That night, the conversation still fresh in his mind, Perry changed out of his work clothes and into a golf shirt and shorts. Amelia was just coming in the front door with the mail when he came downstairs, his Club binder under his arm. "You're not still planning to go to that board meeting, are you?"

"If I stay home, people will only talk."

Amelia dumped the mail on the table. "Who cares what people think, Perry. It's just gossip."

"All the more reason to show my face. We need to confront this head-on." Why couldn't Amelia understand? Hiding out in their big house was no way to teach Emma to resolve her issues.

"Emma is still in her room," Amelia hissed. "She's been up

there all day, while other kids are going to the beach. To camp. Doing everyday summer things. And yet she's hiding out up there like some kind of shunned villager."

Exactly his point, if Amelia would only listen. "Which is why I'm going. Let me face it, first. The sooner we get this over with, the sooner she can get back out there herself."

"So she can suffer more? What we need is to get out of here. I was thinking we should take a trip. Maybe to Rhode Island? Get her away from it all."

Perry shook his head. "To what end? It will all still be waiting for her when she gets back. Better to get it over with."

Amelia looked stricken. "I disagree. You don't know what it's like to be a teenage girl. First the accident, and now this? She needs family time."

"Speaking of family," Perry said. "Don't tell my parents about this latest . . . *setback*."

"What? Why not? We aren't perfect, Perry. They probably already know."

Perry laughed, sadly. "Believe me—we'd know if they did. Besides, they all have their hands full with their own issues right now."

"Which is why I think they should know. This is tearing us apart."

Perry headed for the door. "It's tearing all of us apart. Olivia and Luci, too."

"Olivia and Luci? What do they have to do with this?" Something in Amelia's voice cooled. Perry turned around.

"The accident, of course."

Amelia studied him. "Perry, I don't know what's going through your mind, but why the concern for Olivia? You seem to be doing an awful lot for them."

Perry was stunned.

"Olivia told me you went to visit them and brought her groceries the other night. She thanked me. And I had to pretend I knew what she was talking about."

Perry paused in the doorway. "You said yourself, there's something vulnerable about them."

Amelia waited.

"What?"

"Did you bring her dog to the hospital?"

Perry nodded. "I didn't plan to. But things were so chaotic, and it's Luci's therapy dog."

"You hate dogs. You're afraid of them."

Perry felt caught, although he wasn't entirely sure at what. "It's true. But I guess the circumstances demanded it. Besides, it's not like anyone around here seems to need me."

"Of course we need you. But this isn't some crisis at work, this is *our* crisis. We need to handle this together."

Perry saw the hurt in her eyes. "That's the point. We have each other. Olivia is all alone."

"Funny. That's how I've been feeling lately."

"I was just trying to help her out."

"That sounds nice, but it's not your place. It's Jake's." Amelia pressed her lips together.

"And look what a fine job he's doing."

He was closing the door behind him when he heard, "Be careful, Perry."

Perry was already late, but he walked to the clubhouse anyway. Past the oversized houses along the water, past the lush green lawns and pillared driveway entrances. He'd worked his ass off to get into this neighborhood. The Candlewood Cove community. To be on the water, on the lake where he'd grown up. Where the air was crisper and scented with a hint of pine. Where he could think. But tonight, his thoughts ran wild.

The board members would already be seated around the big table in the dining room, waiting. Hell, they might well have started without him. The monthly meetings were attended by many of the community members, and despite the fact the meeting was held inside on this nice summer evening, he imagined the group was likely larger than warranted. It was unlikely there was a sole inhabitant of the cove who hadn't heard the news or seen the picture and didn't want to dip a toe in the ripple effect.

Jim O'Malley met him at the door. He looked at him with empathy. "Perry, good to see you. I wasn't sure if you'd be coming."

Perry had always liked Jim. He was a family man and a regular hand at the clubhouse, whether it was helping to get the docks in the water each year or manning the smoky grills at summer barbecues. "I'm here," Perry said, maneuvering around him in the doorway.

"Hey." Jim put a hand on his shoulder, and Perry paused. "How're you holding up?"

"I'm here," Perry said, again.

Jim grimaced. "Kids. They do the damnedest things. But she's a good girl."

As he crossed the special events room where they held their monthly meeting, Perry could feel others' eyes on his back. Bob Engel, the former president, waved him over from the bar, where he was sipping a glass of bourbon on ice.

"Perry. I wondered if I could have a minute."

Perry paused to shake hands. "Sorry Bob, the meeting is about to start."

"Ah, yes. I'm having a bite with Ginny in the dining room myself, so I'll be quick."

Perry hesitated. Bob was no longer on the board, but he still had sway. Over Bob's shoulder, Perry could see some of the other board members glancing their way. Did they know what Bob was about to say? Ted Hastings's seat was notably empty.

Bob got right to the point. "Look, it's come to everyone's attention that there was a get-together at the Hastings's house and things got a little out of hand."

"Yes. It's come to my attention that a board meeting was held this morning. Without me."

Bob grimaced. "I was sorry to hear about what happened with your daughter. But I'm sure you understand the board had to review this without your input. Conflict of interest, and all." He clapped Perry on the back. "I wanted to be sure we're all still on the same page."

Perry bristled. "Same page?"

"These things tend to pass, and the less fuss we make over them, the faster they do." He studied Perry.

"I'm not sure that I follow. What page are you suggesting I be on?"

"Hey, now. All I'm saying is that we can handle this within the community. I heard you used some legalese with Ted Hastings, and I really don't think we need to take things in that direction." Bob swirled his tumbler of bourbon slowly.

"Ted Hastings has a long history here. His father and grandfather were two of the Club's founding members. His family has done a lot for us." Bob paused. "You've had to work your way up here, but don't think I haven't noticed what a nice job you do as president. This Club has provided your family with a lot: a certain lifestyle, social connections, business networks. I'd hate to see anything change that." Bob sipped his drink thoughtfully. "We're all friends here, right?"

Perry glared back at him. "That was my understanding."

"Good, good. Say, we should play a round of golf. You around this weekend?"

But Perry was already making his way to the board's table. It was five minutes past start time, and he slid into his seat beside Madeline Whitcomb, the Club's secretary. "Shall we get started?" she asked.

Instead of returning to the dining room, Bob Engel lingered. Perry ignored this, half-listening instead as the meeting got under-way. Water tests were shared by the Candlewood Lake Authority. A review of building maintenance costs was submitted. The social chair gave an update on the lobster bake preparations. Perry made no notes, and asked no questions. It was eye-opening to realize the meeting could run itself without him. In fact, the whole Club, it seemed, could.

It was at the end of the meeting, during questions and com-ments, when things suddenly required his attention. A woman in a pink summer dress stood up in the front row. "My name is Amy Fuller, and my family just moved in to the cove. We'd like to apply for membership."

There was a buzz of welcome and greeting. But as Perry sat back listening, something about the woman's pink dress and the earnest look on her face did something to him. "Why?" he blurted out.

She hesitated. "Why? Well, because we have three kids. It seems like a nice close-knit community."

Across the room Bob Engel leaned against the wall. Perry couldn't help it, he started to chuckle. He felt bad for the woman, he could see she was confused. Hell, so was he.

He pushed his wheeled chair back and swung around toward the windows. Candlewood Lake stretched across the clubhouse beach like a navy ribbon. The clubhouse doors were wide open, and a brisk breeze swirled through the room. "Close-knit indeed," Perry said.

Beside him, the vice president, Dan Gibbons, shifted uncomfortably in his seat. Good old Dan, whom Perry regularly paired up with on the golf course. Who hadn't thought to give him a courtesy call either before or after their little emergency meeting. Dan smiled at Amy Fuller. "What you need to do is file an application," he told her. He turned to the social chair, at the end of the table. "Can you furnish this nice woman with one, please? And give her a list of members. She'll need a sponsor."

Perry slapped the table. "No need. I'll sponsor her," he said.

Dan turned. "You know one another?"

"No. But why not? This is what we do here in Candlewood Cove." Perry looked around the table, taking in the odd expressions from his fellow board members. Of course they'd all seen the photo of Emma. He cringed, imagining the women, and worse, the men, looking at his daughter in all her vulnerability. Emma had not just exposed herself. She'd exposed them all.

"Uh, thank you," the woman said. She sat down, clutching the application.

"You're welcome," Perry said, too loudly. "Happy to sponsor another fine family in our community." He stood up. "We take care of each other, right?" He turned to Mike Barberie. "Mike, remember when your daughter, Milly, fell off the dock a few years ago? Amelia dove in and pulled her out of the water, remember that?"

Mike nodded. "Couldn't forget it if I tried. That was a scary moment."

"Scary. Yes, it was. But we all jumped in to help, didn't we, Mike? Because that's what this community does when one of our own is in trouble."

Mike blinked, wondering where Perry was going with this.

"And Caleb Richter. Where's Caleb's dad?" Perry looked around the room for Brad. "I recall Caleb stole a canoe last summer." A murmur ran through the room.

"And we didn't press charges, did we? We figured out a way for him to return it and save face. We let him work it off raking the beach each morning. Isn't that right, Brad?"

Brad Richter didn't look pleased to be reminded of this, let alone in front of an audience. He crossed his arms. "My son worked it off, just as he said he would."

"Because we gave him a second chance," Perry reminded them, sharply. "Because kids make mistakes. Right, Brad?"

Brad Richter excused himself and exited through the side doors.

Dan Engel put a hand on Perry's arm. "I think now is a good time to wrap things up. Let's call the meeting to a close."

But Perry shook him off. "I'm not done here." Perry paused. His heart was pounding. "Our kids grow up here, and we keep an eye out for them. When they're swimming out to the dock, or out on the boat. Or getting in over their head at someone's house party where booze is being served to underage kids. Because around here we're family!" Perry's voice rang in his ears and echoed through the hall. The silence that followed was painful.

Across the room in the doorway, Jim was shaking his head, gently, as if to say, "Enough." But even Jim couldn't help him now.

Perry offered Jim a sad smile. "It's okay, Jimmy. I'm done now." To the woman in pink, glancing around nervously, Perry apologized. "You should apply for membership here. Everything you think you see?" Here, Perry turned and gestured to the ballroom. The view. The sunlight streaming in. "It's not real. But it's perfect."

Perry was halfway up his driveway, his head still spinning, when he saw someone standing on the front stoop. A boy, about Emma's age.

"May I help you?" He was in no mood to buy anything.

"Mr. Goodwin?"

Perry met him on the bottom step. "Yes?"

The kid looked like he would very much rather be somewhere else. "I'm Sully McMahon. I'm a friend. Of Emma's?"

The name was familiar, but Perry didn't recognize him or his name. But that didn't matter, because Emma was in no shape to have visitors. Especially some teenage boy.

"I came to see how she was doing," he added nervously.

And then Perry realized how he knew the boy's name. "Wait—were you at that party?"

Sully started to answer, but Perry was catching up. "You were in the photo. With my daughter. Weren't you?"

Perry felt his face flush as it did when he was angry. Only he was already angry from all the blows he'd endured that week. The blows that just kept coming. And here was another one, in high-top sneakers, on his front step.

"I wanted to say hello to Emma." The kid had balls, Perry had to give him that. He wanted to snap him in two. "To see how she's doing."

"How the hell do you think she's doing?" Perry hissed. He leaned in and watched with satisfaction as Sully leaned back. "Were you the one who got her drunk?" A worse thought popped into his head. "Did you touch her?"

Sully put his hands up. "No, no way, sir. I would never. I mean, we were all drinking. But I like Emma. She's a great girl."

"Damn right she is!" Perry got right in Sully's face so he could see the fear. "Get out. Get the fuck out of here before I call the cops."

The door flew open and Amelia appeared. "What's going on?"

Perry jerked back. "This is Sully. He's just leaving."

Sully reversed, his hands still up. "I'm sorry, Mr. and Mrs. Goodwin. I just wanted to say hi to Emma. I'm leaving now."

When Perry stormed inside and slammed the door shut, he looked up to see Emma at the railing upstairs, looking down at them. "Was that Sully McMahon?"

Amelia was wringing her hands. "He came by to check on you, honey." Then, "Who is he?"

"No one," Perry said, cutting across the marble foyer to his office. "He's no one at all."

Phoebe

Rose, the construction loan officer, did not look surprised to see her. But she also did not look happy. "The inspector has informed us that work has stopped on the house?"

"Sadly, yes." Phoebe fiddled with her wedding ring, something Rob told her she did when she was anxious. She was not there to beg, but she was also not there ready to give up. "I want to talk with you about options. Is there any way we can sell the property back to the bank, and then, using our equity, somehow complete the construction and buy it back?"

"We are looking at default. Our inspector went out yesterday. According to his report, the funding available is not sufficient to cover the cost of the project, and the time line for the building completion is also therefore at risk. From our perspective, we don't like to foreclose on unfinished homes. If foreclosure is our only course of action, we'd at least rather foreclose on a finished home. That said, we don't want to expose ourselves to further financial risk."

"Does that mean there's a way for us to finish the project and save it?"

Rose folded her hands. "If by 'save' you mean complete it, then yes. That is our goal as construction loan holder. But if you mean maintaining the house as your own, I'm afraid without additional outside funding or further investment on your behalf, then no. We would need to complete it as much as possible, and then go into foreclosure sale."

Without further sentiment, Rose opened an office file, the kind of file Phoebe had previously looked upon as a little manila door opening. Over the course of the project, there had been so many of them, and behind each manila door so much possibility. Files with architectural designs. Files with town hall permits. Files with loan payout schedules and inspector's reports. The contents of all equaling one thing: her dream house. But not this file. As Rose paged through a sheaf of contractual papers dense with text, Phoebe felt the encroaching shadow of a door closing.

"You and your husband will need to review the documents enclosed and sign. Then, upon return to me, the bank can move forward with foreclosure."

Phoebe couldn't think of a damn thing to say. It was all over.

Rose removed her glasses and rubbed her eyes, the most human thing Phoebe had seen Rose Calloway do since meeting her. "I'm really sorry, Phoebe. It happens, especially in this market."

An hour later, Phoebe left Candlewood Savings Bank with the file tucked beneath her arm. She got in her car and drove straight to Rob's office. He was in a meeting, and so she went into his office and shut the door. There were no tears left in her; she was as dried out as a husk.

Eventually, Rob came in. She waited as he set his laptop on the desk and removed his coat. It wasn't lost on her how businesslike his behavior was. She couldn't remember the last time they'd kissed. "What's the word?"

Phoebe drew in her breath. There were no words left.

She watched her husband roll up his sleeves and sit down at his desk, facing her. As if preparing for a brainstorming session. The look of determination on his face was more than she could bear. She shook her head.

"They can't help us?"

"Too much risk for the bank. It's over."

"What do you mean? Surely there has to be another way. They can extend the loan. Or offer us more capital. Something?"

Phoebe stood up and walked over to him. She ran her finger up and down the exposed part of his arm, just below the cuff of his dress shirt. Rob had beautiful hands. How long had it been since she'd reached for one? She did now.

"They're foreclosing."

For a long minute Rob said nothing. He turned his head and looked out the office window at the summer day outside. Phoebe had been prepared for anger or disappointment. For outrage— something. But not his silence. Confused, she wrapped her arms around herself, and stood, waiting. *Just get it over with*, she thought. *Just explode or yell or tell me what a fuckup I am.*

Finally, Rob stood. They were face-to-face, and when she got up the nerve to meet his eye she saw the last thing she'd expected. Relief.

"It's over, then."

The result was crushing. "You're okay with that?"

"Of course I'm not! We're losing the house. God knows what this is going to do to our credit or where the hell we're supposed to live. It's a fucking disaster. But the last few months have been pure hell, every step of the way holding our breath and tiptoeing around pennies and problems and worrying at night how to get it done. *That* was hell. And I'm sorry, but I'm glad it's over."

Phoebe spun around for her purse and tugged the folder out of it. "Here you go," she snapped, dumping it on his desk. "Now you can make it official. Sign it and put a fucking bow on it."

Rob held his hand out. "Phoebe, wait."

"After everything I've been through trying to get this project off the ground, and keeping it afloat. Mostly by myself, I might add. It's not just a house!" she cried. "It was my future!"

Rob leapt up, and for the first time his eyes filled with emotion. "Exactly! Which is how we ended up here."

"What the fuck does that mean?" Phoebe didn't care if anyone outside the door heard them. Rob was wrong. And ungrateful. She had done all of it for them, for their family. He didn't even care that they were losing all of it.

"Jesus, Phoebs. It was yours, all along. The boys and I just went along with it. I could live anywhere. Hell, I never thought anything was wrong with our old house if you want to know the truth. But I wanted you to be happy."

"So this is all my fault? The sill beams? The electrical issues? All those unforeseen overages that I had to click my heels for and hop through hoops just to scrounge up some more dimes? Do you have any idea how stressful that was? And yet I did it. Not for myself, but for our family."

Rob folded like all the winds had come out of his sails. "I made the sale. And I just got word—the company is promoting me to manager."

"You what?"

"The presentation went well. The company bought in."

"Oh my God." She crossed the room to him. "Honey. Why didn't you tell me?"

"Because it wasn't a sure thing until this morning. I had a feeling things were shaping up after the presentation yesterday, but

I didn't want to say a thing until I was sure. Everything has been such a mess lately. I couldn't handle another setback."

Phoebe kneeled down next to his office chair and grabbed his hands. "We should be celebrating!"

Rob smiled, sadly. "Phoebe. Come on. Do you know what a hole we've got to dig out of?"

"Wait." She sat back on her haunches. "You know what this means!"

"What?" He looked at her warily. "No, Phoebe. Please don't."

"It means we can save the house!" She leapt up. "How much did you say the sign-on bonus was? Wasn't it like fifty thousand?" She couldn't stand still; she was reeling with relief. She was talking so fast she almost didn't catch what Rob said next.

"No way."

"What did you say?" Phoebe stopped midsentence.

"I said no. There's no way. We haven't even sat down and figured out how much we're in the hole for yet. We still owe the subs and Dave. And we may also still owe the bank."

"But Rob, just listen . . ."

"Damn it, Phoebe!" Rob stood and punched his chair, sending it flying across the floor and crashing against the window.

Phoebe jumped back. "What's *wrong* with you?"

"With me?" It was his turn to yell. "I won't add more fuel to this fire. You have to let go!"

"How can you say that?" Phoebe backed away, her jaw trembling with anger. This was their chance to right the ship, to save the house. What was the matter with him that he wouldn't even consider it?

"Don't ask me again. I will go to the bank with you tomorrow and we will sit down and sort this mess out, but I will not put one more cent into that money pit."

Phoebe snatched her purse from the couch and stormed out of his office. This was their only chance, and he was going to kill it. She thought of what her grandma Elsie had said a few nights ago. About a good marriage being the only home you needed.

This was Phoebe's vision. For all of them. If Rob couldn't see what she saw, then maybe there was no hope for any future at all.

Olivia

Jake's new position at the Audubon Center didn't allow much sick leave or vacation time, and already he'd burned through all of it. The director, Tim Setterlin, had kindly offered to hold his position until he was "back on his feet," so to speak, but it was unpaid. Already, Olivia could sense the unrest Jake was feeling. The first hospital bill had arrived in the mail that she'd picked up for him the day before.

"How on earth are you going to pay that?" she'd wondered aloud. His insurance for his new job would cover some, but the bill was in the tens of thousands.

It was a rainy day, the first in as long as Olivia could remember. Normally she would've welcomed the sweet, clean showers; it had been so hot that summer, and God knew they needed it. But the weather made the cottage feel even more cramped than it already was, and they were all on edge.

"I've got some savings," Jake said, a little defensively. Then, "Maybe Tim will let me do some work from home. I feel well enough to do desk work," he insisted, as he hobbled through the house. But Jake's position as educational director was more hands-on. It required him to be in the field, working the nature center, giving tours. Aside from grant writing, which he'd already said was done in the off-season, there wasn't much desk work to do.

Olivia had her own work woes. Ben's show was a week away. The entire morning had been spent in the studio helping Marge wrap his pieces for shipment in giant sheets of Bubble Wrap, cardboard panels, and foam cases. Then each one was slipped into its own wooden crate and stapled together. It was precision work, and her fingers ached. A truck was arriving later that afternoon to pick them up for transport. Luci was sitting at the table making a watercolor. Olivia had had to cancel her speech therapy session, but really what was the point in her going? She still had not spoken.

"Careful," Olivia warned as Jake swung a crutch sharply around the edge of the couch. He did that sometimes, swept too far or hopped too long. Already he'd slipped once on a wet spot of hardwood floor in the kitchen and tripped on a throw rug. Both times she'd been the one to cry out when he did, imagining the metal pins shifting inside his screwed-together leg, but he'd righted himself and shaken his head, saying, "All good!"

Now Buster raised one eyebrow as he watched the base of Jake's crutches approaching. Buster was as trained as a therapy dog could be; his classes had involved exposure to wheelchairs, ramps, crutches, and medical devices of all kinds. He'd not once batted an eye. But since Jake had mistakenly pinned his tail with a crutch on the first day home, he was not having that again. As Jake approached, he hopped up on all fours and skittered away. Jake halted, with a look of dismay. "Buster. Buddy. Come on." Olivia turned her attention back to the cupboard. Frankly, she couldn't watch any of them anymore.

Behind her, Jake gave up on making it out to the kitchen. Instead, he pivoted to the couch and flopped down, grimacing. It had been like this lately. He was less patient and less ginger with himself, and it made for some painful outbursts.

"I'm starving," Jake said to no one in particular. "I want to make a sandwich, but I don't want to get in your way out there. And I don't want to ask you to make it for me."

"Babe, I'll make it."

But when she looked in the cupboard for bread, she realized they were out.

"Shit." Luci glanced up from her painting project. "Sorry, baby."

"What's wrong?" Jake asked.

"We're out of bread."

He peered over the back of the couch. "Tell me what you need and I'll make a list."

Olivia chuckled. "What *I* need?" They were all living together, at least for now.

"Sorry. You know what I mean." He was sorry, but he was also frustrated. Jake hated sitting still, and he hated not being useful. All through their relationship it had been he who'd done much of the caretaking. Showing up with flowers for Luci. Changing the oil in her car. Clearing out a corner of the studio with Ben, so that she had a place to work. "Not quite a room of your own, but you get the picture . . ." She focused on the memory now, used it as fuel.

"I have bagels. How about an egg and cheese bagel?"

Jake sighed. "Only if you and Luci want them, too. I'm not that hungry anymore."

She knew he was. But she also knew he hated to be a burden.

As she made them lunch, she glanced around. The house was a mess. The fridge was empty. And yet she had so much to do for the gallery show that she didn't have time to leave and go get groceries. Back in the city she could run downstairs and up to the corner market. Here, she had to get in the car and drive ten minutes minimum. What she needed was caffeine. She got a mug out of the cupboard, but then realized the coffeepot was empty. There was only a cup's worth of espresso grounds left. "Can you add coffee to the list?"

Jake was prostrate on the couch. "What list?"

"Never mind." She'd have to get to the store before the end of the day. Once she finished with Marge in the studio, that is. And there was dinner at Jane and Edward's at six. Jane had called the evening before to remind them. "We're looking forward to tomorrow night!" Jake's mother had chirped. Of course, Olivia had not remembered.

"Right, yes! So are we," she lied.

"I don't want to go," Jake had said.

"Why not? It'll be good for you to get out of here. I feel bad—there's so little room. You've been bumping into furniture and Buster. It'll be good to get you out."

Jake had made a face. "So I can go bump into someone else's furniture?"

She realized her mistake. "I didn't mean it like that."

"This isn't how I imagined our moving in together would be. You're doing everything, waiting on me hand and foot. All while juggling Luci and Ben . . ." Jake's hands were balled into fists. "I'm sorry, Livi. It's not fair to you."

She'd pressed herself up against his side, listening. When he finished, she ran her finger over his hands, until they relaxed, and then slipped her hand into his. "But wouldn't you do the same for me?"

Jake swiveled. "In a heartbeat."

"Well. There you have it."

They'd gone to bed, the sting of the matter somewhat dulled. But now, standing in the kitchen flipping eggs, with the rain pounding against the windows, it was back with fresh heat.

"Lunch is almost ready," Olivia announced. But she wasn't sure to whom. It wasn't like Jake was going to come out and help set the table.

There was a thumping sound from the table and Olivia looked over. Luci was pointing to her painting. "Are you done?" Olivia asked.

Luci shook her head, and pointed again.

"What is it?" Olivia asked. She'd just cracked the eggs into the pan. "I'm cooking, baby. I can't come over right now."

But Luci was determined to get her idea across, despite the fact Olivia was too far away to see what she was pointing at and therefore couldn't tell what it was.

"Luci," Jake said. "How about I help you?"

She nodded.

"Okay. Hang on while I get up."

"No," Olivia said, warily. She appreciated his wanting to help, but it was too much for him. In fact, all of it was starting to frustrate her. "She can hang on a sec. You stay put."

Jake paused. Luci clapped again. Something was upsetting her. "Is there a bug?" Olivia asked. Luci was afraid of bugs. But she shook her head. "Did you spill?" Again, she shook her head. Olivia flipped the eggs irritably. "Hang on."

This time when Luci clapped, she knocked a bottle of paint with her elbow.

Olivia looked up from the eggs just in time to see the paint tip. "Luci!" The container of tempera blue flipped over, then rolled off the table and onto the floor, where its contents exploded across the hardwood. Luci jumped back and squealed.

Jake hopped up. "What happened? Are you hurt?"

Olivia grabbed a roll of paper towels and rushed around the kitchen island.

The chair was splattered in blue. As were Luci's legs and socks. Her lips trembled like she might cry, and she hopped back, stepping in a puddle of it. "Careful," Olivia warned, bending to wipe it up. But Luci had already begun walking to the kitchen, leaving a fresh trail of blue footprints in her path.

Behind Olivia Jake was attempting to get up from the couch. He reached for his crutches, but one fell. It clattered to the floor with a crash and sent Buster scrambling across the floor again, this time right through the puddle of paint. "Please," Olivia cried. "Let me take care of it!"

She turned to Luci, who stood frozen in the middle of the floor. Tears had started. "Lu Lu, it's okay," Olivia pleaded. "Stay there." She continued to mop, on all fours. What she wanted to do was cry, too.

But Jake was already standing and making his way over. "Jake, please don't. I said I've got it . . ."

And then he caught his crutch on the edge of the rug. He felt it because his eyes widened in fear, but he was moving too quickly to catch himself in time.

"Jake!" Olivia screamed.

She leapt to her feet, dropping the paper towels, just as he crashed onto his side on the floor. His bad leg remained up in the air, but he took the force of the fall on his shoulder, and the noise that emanated from his chest was primal. "Oh my God." Olivia rushed to where he lay.

Luci started to howl.

Olivia knelt beside Jake, afraid to touch him. "Are you okay?"

Jake grimaced, rolling onto his back, groaning. "Fuck, fuck, fuck . . ."

"Your leg!" Olivia pressed her hands to his face, leaving a blue thumbprint on each cheek. "Did you hit it?"

"No," Jake managed. His voice was a whisper. "But it jolted. Everything."

Slowly, Olivia helped him to roll onto his back, where he lay catching his breath. "Don't move," she warned. "Let's assess the damage. Oh God, baby."

Eventually he pulled himself up to a sitting position. A sheen of sweat had broken out across his forehead.

"You're in pain," she said.

"I just want to go to bed."

Olivia glanced over her shoulder at the stairs. "We need to get you back on the couch. Here, let me help. Then we'll get ice."

Jake shook his head. He was angry and humiliated.

By the time she got him on the couch, the pan on the stove had filled the kitchen with smoke. The alarm went off, sending Buster running again. Luci hadn't moved from her trail of spilled paint. Olivia went to her, scooped her up, and carried her to the kitchen. She grabbed the burning pan of eggs with one hand and tossed it in the sink. Which only made Luci cry harder.

"It's okay," Olivia said, sitting her on the counter. "Shhhh." She stripped her feet of the wet blue-stained socks, and tossed them in the sink, too. Then she ran the water and washed Luci's hands, watching blue paint splash onto the ruined eggs. "Luci," she said, when she was done. She took her daughter's hands. "Luci, please. You have to start talking to Mommy."

It was wrong. Telling your child to talk only silenced them further. She knew it, and she chewed the inside of her cheek as the words tumbled out. But she said it again, her hands trembling with anger. She was squeezing Luci's hands, probably too tight, but she couldn't stop. "Please, talk to me," she pleaded.

Tears sprang to Luci's eyes and Olivia let go.

Luci spun away from her and ran upstairs. Buster, made uneasy by all the commotion, scampered up behind her. "Baby, I'm sorry!" Olivia cried after her. Everything was falling apart.

Jake grabbed a pillow and hurled it across the room. It hit a table lamp that wobbled precariously, but mercifully did not fall.

Olivia spun around. "What are you doing?"

"I can't take this anymore!" His cheeks flushed with effort and regret. "It's my fault. I didn't know what she was trying to say. Why won't she talk to me?" He was shouting now, and Olivia went very still.

"*You* want her to talk?"

"I'm sorry." Jake covered his face with his hands. "Jesus, Liv. I'm sorry. I didn't mean it like that. I know it's not her fault. Or yours."

Standing in the middle of the kitchen, Olivia felt her heart pounding back to life against her ribs. She would not cry.

"Olivia, please."

"NO!" she barked at him. "Not another word." This man she thought she knew, she thought she loved. He didn't understand any of it. And if he didn't understand it by now . . .

Frenzied, she paced the cottage, unsure what to do first. She needed to check on Luci. She also needed to get the hell out of there. Wreckage was everywhere. The sink was teeming with pots, paint, and the remains of their spoiled lunch. Without thinking, she ripped a hand towel from the nearest hook and headed for the spilled paint. She'd clean it up, get her child, and go. It was when she got to the table that she got a good look at what Luci had painted.

The page was splattered in blue flecks, but she could still make out the artwork. There were three people: a woman with brown hair, a little girl with brown pigtails, and a man, holding hands. And a brown-and-white spotted dog.

Holding back tears, Olivia set the painting on the only clear space of counter she could find to dry. Then she headed for the door.

"Where are you going?" Jake called after her.

"Nowhere." She shoved the screen door open. Out on the porch, she flopped against the cottage wall and slid down to the floorboards. There was nowhere she could go. Because everyone on the other side of the door needed her. She was tethered here.

Olivia closed her eyes and tipped her head back against the cottage siding. The rain was coming down sideways in sheets now. If it fell hard enough that it streaked her cheeks, was it really crying?

Emma

She did not want to go to her grandparents' for dinner. But her Grammy Jane was insisting they needed a family "gathering."

"None of us wants to go," her father admitted. "It's pointless to try to bring everyone together."

"Perry." Her mother didn't need to remind him to curb his ire for Emma's sake. Little did her grandparents know what had gone on with her in the last week. She was pretty sure none of the family did, if her father had had his way. While it had been fast-traveling news in their private community and among the teenage residents, Emma was pretty sure no one would have been rude enough to walk up to her grandparents in the local market and ask what they thought of their granddaughter's trending behavior. Emma cringed at the thought. Honestly, she wasn't sure which would be worse: their finding out or the fact that her father seemed determined to keep what his daughter was going through a big dark secret. Because, really, what did that say about her?

Something in her father had shifted since the accident, but even more so since the incident at the party. He was angry. Not so much at her. But at everything. And for the first time in her life, she was worried about her dad.

Suddenly her father hated the Club. His precious, prestigious

Club where he spent all of his free time in. Where he golfed, ran fundraisers, hosted balls for the adults and barbecues for the community. Her father was more tied to that Club than he was their own home. And now she, all by her well-behaved, perfect-GPA, boring little self, had gone and ruined it for him.

The clubhouse board had "postponed" her camp counselor position until it could be "reviewed." Whatever that meant. At first Emma was fine with it—the last thing she wanted to do was face those people. Amanda Hastings, whom she was pretty sure had taken that photo and first shared it—oh, she could imagine Amanda blaming the wildfire spread of the photo and the subsequent gossip on others. "What? I only showed it to like one person." It didn't matter. Amanda had lit the match and dropped it. Then stepped away to watch it burn.

Emma didn't care about Amanda Hastings. But she did care about her boss. She'd worked hard at camp, and she could tell he noticed and appreciated it. Most of all, she couldn't fathom facing her campers. While she doubted that any of the little kids knew (their helicopter parents surely would have shielded them from the sordid news of their beloved Miss Emma), she knew kids were smart. A favorite counselor doesn't just go missing. They would know something was up, and they would ask her point-blank. And the thought of looking into their earnest expressions and lying was almost as bad as their knowing. She loved those little campers. And even if they didn't know why she'd left, she'd left them. Without a goodbye. Or an explanation. She'd let them down.

Her parents had taken her phone away. "This is for your own protection," they'd told her, sitting at their kitchen island. "Until we get our arms around this." ("This" was what her parents were calling it now. "We have to deal with *this*. *This* cannot ruin our summer. I'm going to call GW University to discuss *this*." Emma wished they'd just call it what it really was—a shit show.) While they may not have meant it as punitive, having her phone taken away felt like it. Emma had no contact with the outside world. Which was fine with her at first. She didn't want any reminders of the firestorm on her social media accounts. But as the days passed, one blurring into the next in a level of hazy boredom she'd not known existed, she missed her phone. At odd times she'd find herself reaching for it, searching the house. Her fingers twitching with muscle memory at tapping the screen. Eventually she turned back to her first love: books. Books couldn't betray you. And books let you escape, without consequences.

Before her phone was taken away, she'd gotten one text from Alicia. "I can't believe what you did." Emma had it coming. She'd been a little hard on Alicia this summer. Alicia may have been boring and judgmental. She may have frowned at Emma's hanging out with Sully and the others. But that didn't make her wrong. Alicia was just being Alicia; her usual play-it-safe self. But she was also loyal. And patient. And, Emma prayed, forgiving. Because Emma had used her the night of the party. And then she'd turned her back on her friend, choosing to stay at the party just so she could have the chance to hang out with Sully. And look where that landed her.

Sully was the one question mark. After the accident he was one of the first people who reached out to her. But now—standing right next to her with his own shirt off in that damn photo she wished she could erase from her memory—he'd taken none of the heat she had. She'd heard her father shouting about it downstairs the night before when he came back from the Club meeting. "That McMahon kid works at the camp, too! Did you know that? But he hasn't been fired! No one's said a damn thing about him."

Emma wasn't stupid. Of course, her being photographed in her bra and panties was more lurid than a boy with his shirt off. But still—there was a double standard. The one her parents had taught her about and talked to her about her whole life. Women didn't get paid the same as men for performing the same job. But when something scandalous happened, women sure took the brunt of the blame. How many headlines of that nature had she heard in the last year, especially in the wake of the #MeToo movement? No matter what happened to a woman, there were questions aimed to disable her credibility: What had she been wearing? How much did she drink? Why was she even there in the first place? The implication being that somehow it always came down to her fault. This summer Emma had found herself in her own headline. And beyond the shame and guilt, it was having repercussions all over the board.

The picture had not hurt anyone, except herself. It might prevent her from working at the camp, a job she desperately missed. And it might keep her from attending the GW University summer program, which she'd worked hard for a long time to get into. As if those weren't bad enough, it had cost her what she thought might be her first real relationship. What a fool she'd been. She was the laughingstock of Lenox. Sully McMahon wouldn't want anything to do with her now.

Emma was wrong. The summer had not turned out to be promising; it had been one of ruin. Of keeping secrets to protect someone you loved. And of taking stupid chances for someone you thought you might. Look where it all had left her.

The realization kept her awake at night, tossing and turning in her bed until she had to sneak downstairs to her parents' liquor cabinet, where a few swallows would finally ease the sharp edges in her mind. So she could sleep just a little bit. And get through another day. Even if it meant numbing herself in order to do so.

Phoebe

She'd not spoken to Rob once since the day before in his office. And certainly not when he came home to her parents' house that night after work and sat down at the table as if nothing was wrong. They'd crossed paths, giving each other a wide berth all night. Business needed tending to. But she'd be damned if she was going to look at the man.

Jane had raised her eyebrows in the kitchen, as they washed dishes. "Is everything okay? How did Rob's presentation go?"

Phoebe scrubbed the pot in the sink, not looking up. "Rob has some news about that, in fact." She could include him without directly addressing him.

"Oh? Good news, I hope?" Jane asked, turning to face her son-in-law, who paused as he corralled Patrick and lifted Jed onto his hip before bath time.

He blinked like a deer in headlights, waiting for Phoebe to rescue him. Well, he could wait. "We got the deal. We signed the papers today," he said, finally.

"That's wonderful!" Edward stood and clapped Rob on the back while Phoebe banged the pot around in the sink. It almost hurt seeing her father's enthusiasm. He loved them all so much, and he'd be crushed if he knew the rift that had grown between them. But Rob had drawn a line in the sand.

That night she lingered on the couch downstairs, flicking aimlessly through television channels. She let Rob do the lion's share of putting the boys to bed. He didn't complain. Only once did he come out and looked over the upstairs railing. "Are you going to kiss the boys good night?"

Without comment, Phoebe had tromped upstairs, kissed their freshly shampooed heads (which almost made her cry), and tromped right back down to her spot on the couch, which was still warm. When she got bored, she fished her "House Ideas" folder from her bag and flipped through it. Pictures of tiles. Measurements for floor spaces. Crown molding. Appliance cost sheets. Page after page of things she'd lovingly collected that would now never come to fruition. When she grew too depressed to look at another image, and she was sure Rob would be asleep, she slipped wordlessly up into her dark room and under the sheets. She pressed herself to the edge of the mattress, which was hard to do when sharing a full-size, and kept her back to Rob. She almost jumped when he whispered, "How long is this going to go on?"

When she didn't reply—she just couldn't—Rob got up and took his pillow with him. He didn't come back. She'd lain awake, frozen with anger, most of the night. Her house was slipping away. They were completely out of money. How had they ended up here?

Now, as she helped her mother prepare for the big family dinner she'd arranged, Phoebe poured herself a glass of white wine and tried to focus, despite the fact that she was exhausted and had no idea where Rob and the boys were. When she'd awakened that morning after falling into a fitful sleep sometime around dawn, his car was gone, and she had no idea if he'd slept in the house or somewhere else. After breakfast he'd shown up and wordlessly collected the boys. "Where are you going?" she'd asked, starting to panic. Rob was never like this. "We're going to the field to kick the ball around." That was four hours ago, and she'd not heard a peep since. But her mother, who smelled strife and had the good sense to keep her beak out of it for now, was keeping her busy, if not entirely distracted.

For some reason, Jane had gotten it in her mind that the whole family needed to get together. Why, Phoebe could not imagine. It was the worst timing. Jake was barely up and able to hobble around. Olivia had apparently been back in therapy with Luci, who was still suffering the effects of the accident. She and Rob were miserable, even if the rest of them didn't yet know why. Phoebe kept her eyes peeled on the driveway, awaiting any sign of them. She had a plan for Perry. He might be the last person who could help her.

"How many are we again?" Jane tapped her chin. The menu was lavish and lovely, per usual. But her mother seemed distracted and tense.

"Let's see." Phoebe counted through the family aloud. As she did, just because she could, she named them by foible. "Well, we've got the homeless, the lame, the old, the mute. The eccentric, the repressed. And one starving artist rounds out the guest list. That's everybody!" She finished with an exaggerated clap. It was pure evil, but she couldn't help it.

Jane narrowed her eyes. "Phoebe."

"Mom." Then, "Don't even think about reaching for a cigarette."

By the time the ears of corn had been shucked and the chicken marinated, Perry had pulled in. Phoebe grabbed a bottle of beer from the fridge and raced for the door.

Perry's family had been her only hope for a somewhat normal evening, as stretched an expectation as that was, but she could tell the second they stepped foot inside that they were not going to be able to deliver. "What's wrong?" she asked, the second Amelia and Emma were out of earshot.

Perry looked askance. "Nothing. Why?"

"Never mind. Look, I was hoping to talk to you. It's about the house."

But Perry was peering over her shoulder in the direction of the kitchen. "Is Jake here yet?"

"What? No, not yet. But do you have a minute?"

Perry eyed the beer in her hand. "Is that for me?"

"Yes." She handed him the bottle, but before she could get a word in, he headed for the kitchen.

"I need to talk to Dad."

"Wait, I need to talk to you!" Phoebe trailed him impatiently, but Perry disappeared outside to the grill, where Edward was starting the chicken. Amelia already had her nose in a glass of wine. Emma stood forlornly by the counter beside Jane, taking instructions for mixing salad dressing.

"Where are Rob and the boys?" Amelia asked.

Phoebe blinked. What should she say? She had not received a single text from Rob. Unlike the rest of her relatives, it would be completely out of character for him to air any of their dirty laundry in front of her family, but they'd clearly reached an impasse. She realized, with a start, that anything was possible. "Out finishing up an errand. He'll be back soon," she lied.

Amelia nodded absently. "How's the house going?"

"Oh, you know . . ."

"Look. They're back." Amelia pointed outside to the patio. Rob was talking to Perry, and the boys were heading her way. When had they arrived? Was Rob telling Perry the dire news? He'd better not be. She wasn't giving up yet.

By the time dinner was set on the table, Phoebe's nerves had been lubricated by a second glass of wine. Maybe she could get through this dinner, after all.

No sooner had the chicken platter been set on the table than everyone took their places. Phoebe looked around at the miserable expressions around her. No one made a move to serve themselves.

Jane took her place at one head of the table and frowned. She had cooked and cleaned and assembled everyone together, and they weren't living up to their part of the bargain. "Isn't anyone hungry?" she asked. Then, when no one really answered, "Eat!"

Dishes clanked, platters moved, and serving spoons sank into dishes. Then followed the sound of chewing and sipping, and a discontented groan from one of the boys when salad was dished onto his plate.

"Well," Jane said, looking around at all of her people. "Isn't this nice."

Perry looked up. "Thank you, Mom. This is nice." But his face told another story.

Amelia cleared her throat. "So, Perry landed the Super Bowl contract."

"Is that so?" Edward beamed. "Congratulations, son. You worked hard for that."

Perry shrugged. "It's just work."

"Just work?" Jake stuffed a large forkful of chicken in his mouth. "Isn't that what you're telling me I should be doing more of?"

Jane flinched. "Jake, how is working from home going?"

"Oh, you know, working hard. Hardly working. Depends on the day."

Phoebe stole a glance at Olivia, who seemed on edge.

"It's not a real job, like Perry's. But it's something. At least I have more time now to spend with Luci and Olivia." He smiled at Olivia, but Phoebe could see that it didn't reach his eyes.

Perry cleared his throat. "Well, maybe if I was the golden child, I wouldn't have had to bust my rear so hard trying to please everyone else."

Phoebe snorted.

"Perry," Jake interjected. "No one could keep up with you. Four-point-oh GPA. Track star. George Washington scholarship. Jeez, I was lucky to eat at the same table as you."

Edward raised his glass. "Now, now. Your mother and I were proud of each and every one of you just the same."

Jane gulped her wine. "Well. Not always."

"And we still are," Edward went on.

Olivia cleared her throat. "Can someone please pass the chicken?"

"We just wanted you all to be happy," Jane went on, spearing a piece of her own. Then, "Phoebe, pass the chicken to Olivia!"

Phoebe was too busy glaring at Rob across the table to hear her. "Happy. Which is all I want for my boys."

"There's nothing happy about bankruptcy," Rob mumbled around a mouthful of food. Thankfully, no one else seemed to hear.

"You and Dad did make us happy," Jake insisted, glancing between his parents at either end of the table. "You guys gave us everything. This lake, this house. Your love and support."

"You were all lucky to grow up here and in a big family like this," Olivia chimed in, softly. "It's exactly what I always hoped for Luci."

Jane tipped her head appreciatively and laughed. "Oh, honey. We don't deserve either one of you."

Edward raised his glass again. "It's wonderful to have you." He looked around at each of his offspring, eyes crinkling. "Look at you all. Grown up and thriving."

"Some of us more than others," Perry quipped, raising his glass haltingly before tipping it back.

"Why do you say that?" Phoebe asked, setting her own down.

"Because you're still all coming to me. Jake needed a job. You needed money."

"I got my own job," Jake interjected. "In the end, I didn't need your help."

"Because I wouldn't get you a job, not after the last one I secured for you and you blew."

Rob set down his fork with a clatter. "You asked your brother for money? Phoebe, we agreed."

Phoebe swallowed hard. "We agreed on nothing. I'm just trying to save our house."

Edward opened and closed his mouth. "What's wrong with the house?"

"And you." Perry pointed across the table at Jake. "You're still living like life is one big party. Letting Emma drink. Encouraging her to be like you!"

Elsie took a spoon and clanged it against her water glass, silencing everyone if only for a beat. "Oh, I don't like this talk. I can feel our family tree shaking right up to its branches."

"Tree?" Patrick asked. "What tree?"

"Nana is right," Jane told them all. "Enough of this. Let's eat."

But Jake was still stung by the accusation. "I didn't let Emma drink!" he told them, looking severely around the table. "I would never."

Emma, who'd been pushing food around her plate, winced.

"Do you know what that cost her?" Perry asked. "Do you have any idea?"

"Dad," Emma mumbled. "Please stop."

Jake pushed his chair back. Which only made Olivia hop up to help him. "What do you want, honey? I'll get it for you."

Jane did the same. "It's okay—I'll get it."

"See?" Perry threw his hands up. "All the women, hopping up to help Jake. Poor, helpless Jake."

Jake wobbled, grabbing the edge of the table for balance. "I am not helpless."

"Enough." Jane raised her voice over the rest of theirs. "These petty jealousies! How many years are you going to nurse them?"

Perry turned to her. "Mom, you can't fix everything. Why must you force us together?"

Jane pounded the table and her bracelets rattled on her wrist. "Because we're a fucking happy family! Now sit down and eat."

Everyone stared at their plate, except for Patrick, who giggled nervously under his breath. "Grammy said . . ."

"Shush," hissed Phoebe.

Edward waited as his wife drew in her breath, sat down, and returned her napkin to her lap. "What do you all think of the avocado dressing?"

They ate in silence, the deafening sound of utensils scraping plates. When it was clear the meal was over, Jane stood up. "I'm getting dessert."

"I can help you," Olivia offered.

As soon as she said it, both Perry and Jake stood, though Jake teetered on his crutches. Jane held up both hands. "Stop. Phoebe and Rob, you help clear. The rest of you stay where you are."

Phoebe picked up plates, steering far around her husband as they passed. Jane returned with a steaming blueberry crumble right out of the oven. "Fresh from the farm," she said, dumping it on the table.

Edward grimaced. "Well. That looks lovely, honey."

Everyone had a small serving, though no one except the kids ate much. Phoebe had taken one bite of dessert, hopeful they could limp through just five more minutes and then she could beat it the hell out of there, when Rob started talking. "I'm afraid Phoebe and I have some bad news."

She swallowed hard. "Rob. Not now."

He looked across the table at her, his eyes heavy with sadness. "You have to be honest, Phoebe. If not with yourself, at least with the rest of them." He left it at that, and Phoebe felt all eyes upon her.

"Not in front of the kids," she said softly, eyeing Patrick and Jed across the room. They'd strayed from the table and into the kitchen, where they sat on the tile floor pushing around a green-and-white Hess truck, a relic from her own childhood.

"I can take the kids outside if you want to talk," Jake offered.

It was the smallest window, but Perry was determined to pry it open. "Because you know what's best for everyone else's kids."

Olivia stood abruptly. "How about I take all the kids outside for a bit?"

No one argued, and Jake watched her go in exasperation. "Come on, Perry. Enough."

"It's not enough until you understand. What you did out there on the lake—it's like some big secret. You don't remember what happened? I call bullshit."

"Be careful, Perry. You don't know what you're talking about."

"I'm talking about my daughter!" Perry roared. "Whose life has been turned upside down since your accident. How the hell are you going to be a parent when you almost killed the three of you out there that day?"

"He didn't do it!" Emma leapt to her feet with such force that her chair flipped over. It crashed to the floor, and everyone jumped. "It was my fault! I was the one who was driving the boat." She turned and bolted from the table.

"Emma!" Amelia called after her. There was the slam of the front door, and silence fell over the room. "Perry, we need to go after her."

But Perry had sat back down, hard, in his chair. "That can't be right."

"What did Emma mean?" Jane demanded.

Jake grabbed his crutches and jammed them under his arms. His face flushed red, eyes wild. "I was trying to protect her."

"Wait. You knew this all along?" Amelia asked.

Edward rose. "Okay, everybody, let's catch our breath. Please let's take a minute."

"Is that true? What Emma said?" Phoebe turned to find Olivia standing in the doorway, arms crossed.

All the anger drained from Jake's face at the sound of her voice. "Baby, I was going to tell you."

"But you didn't," Olivia persisted.

"Liv, please."

She started to laugh, a soft, sad laugh. "All this time. You lied to the police. You lied to *me*."

"Olivia," he pleaded. "I needed to protect Emma."

"From what?" Amelia snapped. "We should've known, Jake."

"From Perry!"

Jane put both hands to her forehead, her voice stern. "Jake. Not now."

"Then when, Mom?" He turned back to Perry. "The measuring stick you hold for all of us to live up to? It's *impossible*. You've done it to me my whole life. And I couldn't stand the thought of you doing that to Emma."

There was a collective intake of breath. Perry stared back at his brother, saying nothing.

Amelia reached for his hand, but he brushed it off. Then, slowly, he rose from the table and pushed his chair in.

"Perry," Edward said softly. "Hang on a second."

Perry was already moving away from the table.

Phoebe was the only one who dared to follow Perry out to the foyer, where he paused at the door. "Do you want to be alone?" she asked, gently.

He opened the door and looked across the yard. "I'm used to it."

She watched him walk across the yard at the pace of a much older man. The rainstorm had let up earlier, and a single ray of sun shot through the spongy sky. Phoebe looked up in time to see a bank of gray cloud swallow it.

Perry

He drove home but did not go inside. Instead, he walked through the rain around to the back of the house and continued across the puddle-filled yard. At the top of the stairs that led down to the lake, Perry removed his shoes. They were hand-stitched saddle-brown wingtips with brogue detail. His favorite pair, and a gift from Amelia last Christmas. He set them side by side on the top step, then removed his socks, which he carefully rolled and nestled, one into each shoe. At the rate the rain was coming down, he estimated the shoes would be filled with water in less than fifteen minutes.

At the bottom of the stairs, Perry stepped lightly across the grass and onto the dock. The boards were soaked and cold beneath his bare feet. He bent to roll up his slacks and continued to the edge. There, he sat and dangled his feet into the water. The rain had returned in soft, silver streams, breaking the glassy surface. He needed to sit and think.

He'd been wrong about so much. All these years he'd worked to provide his family everything, thinking that would somehow secure them a position of safety within their position of good standing. When it wasn't just the outside world he needed to shield them from, but also themselves. He was so busy proving himself—to his family, his neighbors, and yes, to Jake—that he hadn't noticed Emma needed him in a way he had not considered. He'd been wrong about his feelings for Olivia; they were not something to be ashamed of. And they posed no threat to his love for his wife. Good, strong Amelia, whom he'd strayed from not in infidelity, but in heart. Just as he had with Emma. They did not need things; not fast boats or high fences. They needed him. His attention and his time. Such foolishly simple things. And yet they were everything.

His feelings about Olivia had stirred in him a consternation, a kind of awakening. At first Perry feared he was falling in love with her. The urge to protect her from Jake may have come from a good place, but it was displaced. It was Perry's urge to protect himself from their past. A younger brother against whom he competed. Whom he compared himself to, and always came up short. Olivia represented another thing Jake had won. What Perry realized now was that she didn't need saving. And she certainly did not need him. Jake did not pose a threat to her. It was he, Perry, who'd felt threatened. And it was something he would have to come to terms with.

Perry sat until his wet hair was plastered across his forehead, his glasses blurred by rivulets. Until the gray sky turned charcoal, then opaque. Until his shirt clung to the skin of his back, his slacks soaked through. Then he climbed the stairs again, past his wingtip shoes, back across the yard, and got into his car.

When he pulled into the farmhouse driveway, he realized it would be for the last time. He had been here twice before. Once for the dog. Once to bring Olivia groceries. This time was different. This time he was here for something else. The thing he should've started with.

His headlights must have alerted him, because Jake was already standing on the small porch of the cottage, perched angrily over his crutches. The rain had picked up on the drive over and was coming down in torrents now. It didn't matter. Perry was soaked through and shivering with cold. Which somehow seemed fitting.

"What do you want?" Jake shouted from the stoop. The door to the cottage was closed behind him. He would not be inviting Perry in.

"I want to say I'm sorry."

Jake said nothing.

"I was mistaken about Emma. And about you, too. But you have to understand . . ."

Jake pointed one crutch at him. "No, Perry! You have to understand. Your whole life you've carried this chip on your shoulder. And I never understood it. But I always felt like it was somehow my fault."

Jake's voice cracked as he fought to be heard over the driving rain. Perry strained to listen.

"Maybe it was hard for you to fit in. Maybe you weren't as comfortable in your own skin as Phoebe and I were. I used to feel sorry for you. But not anymore. You've done it, Perry. You beat us all. You beat me! You've got the big house, the fancy job, the happy family. You've got it all. You win!"

Perry held up his hands. "I'm not trying to beat you. I'm trying to help you."

"Help me?" Jake tipped his head back and laughed. "By inserting yourself between me and Olivia? By scrutinizing every fucking thing I do? It's not a competition, Perry. It never was."

"This is about more than you and me, Jake. You're about to be a husband and a father."

Jake surged forward on his crutches and came at him quickly down the steps, stopping just short of Perry. For a second Perry thought he'd take a swing at him. "Then why can't you be fucking happy for me?"

"Because you don't get it. It's not just about you anymore!"

"I know that, Perry! Why the hell do you think I'm still here? Because I love her!"

Perry shuddered beneath the rainfall. "But do you love Luci?"

Jake glared at him from beneath the hood of his raincoat. "I'm trying to!"

It was the most broken, honest thing his brother had ever said.

Jake swung sharply away from him on his crutches, and stumbled. Instinctively Perry reached out between them, then stopped.

"Go home, Perry," Jake called back. "Go home to your own family."

Perry stood in the downpour as Jake struggled back toward the house, dragging his bad leg up over the front walk, one excruciating step at a time. Perry remained in the yard beneath the driving rain until the cottage door slammed behind his brother and the only sound remaining was water. He could not go.

A while later, the lanterns flanking the front door went on. His heart lifted. Olivia's figure filled the window, the oval of her face blurred by the showers. Could she see him out there?

As if in reply, Olivia placed her palm flat against the glass. The rain roared in his eardrums. Then she turned out the lights.

Emma

S he hadn't gotten far. Her mother found her down at her grandparents' dock, and whisked her wordlessly home. Emma was ready for the complete freak-out. For the long lecture. For all of it. After all, her father couldn't even look at her at the dinner table. But her mother didn't utter a sound when she got in the car.

"Where's Dad?" Emma asked.

At first her mother didn't reply, and Emma thought maybe she hadn't heard. Then she raked her hand through her wet hair and swung the car out of the driveway. "I don't know." It was the only thing she said the whole way home.

Back at the house, Amelia strode inside ahead of her and Emma followed uncertainly. She watched her mother toss her purse and keys roughly on the pedestal table in the foyer and head for the stairs. Halfway up, she stopped and turned around. "Hey." Her voice was sharp. Unlike her.

Emma looked up at her, afraid to say anything.

Amelia jabbed her finger in the space between them, her face distorted and red. "I love you."

It was the last thing she'd expected her mother to say.

"Do you know that?"

Emma felt herself sag in the middle of the foyer. "Yeah, Mom. I do."

"No matter what you do, nothing will change that. You got that?"

Unable to speak, Emma nodded.

"Good." Emma watched her swipe at a stray tear. "Okay, then. Let's talk in the morning."

As her mother disappeared down the hall from view, something inside Emma gave. The night had been a car wreck. And yet.

Emma wandered into the dark kitchen. Outside the rain battered the windows, but she left the lights out. She felt jumpy, and she itched for something to allay it. To take the edge off. She paused at the liquor cabinet, and continued on.

For the first time in ages she was hungry. Like starving. She'd barely eaten at her grandparents'. Let's be honest, she'd barely eaten in weeks. She tugged the refrigerator door open. Light spilled from the cavernous interior, and Emma blinked in its glow. Then she began reaching. For a block of cheddar. For the pitcher of iced tea. In a glass container she found leftover pesto pasta. In another, tiny meatballs. From the cabinets and drawers she grabbed a plate, a cutting block, utensils. Then she sat down and dug in.

When she'd emptied her entire plate, she shoveled more forkfuls of pasta into her mouth straight from the container. Who knew cold spaghetti could taste like heaven? As she filled herself, her thoughts meandered. She thought of Sully. Of the bravery it must've taken to walk up her front steps and be confronted by her father. The same way he'd stood up to the camp director that first day when he was late: not with disrespect, but with confidence. Not because he thought he was all that. But because it was the right thing to do. He wasn't like Amanda Hastings and some of the others. Sully McMahon cared.

Just as she cared about Alicia. Tomorrow, she would go to Alicia's house and apologize. Even if it meant facing Chet. Even if Alicia was still upset with her. There was something to be said for lifelong friendships. Just because you grew up together didn't mean you grew at the same pace, or even in the same direction. Sometimes you grew away from each other, and that was okay, too.

The last thing she thought about was something Great-Grandma Elsie had said at dinner that night, about family trees. Emma thought about her own family, picturing each one of them. All lined up together in a great big forest. Grandpa Edward was like an old oak, staid and sure. Just like Jane, though her branches were more colorful, her leaves a fiery red. Her mother was slender and delicate, maybe a white birch, who bent and flexed with the seasons, never breaking. Aunt Phoebe and Uncle Jake were probably the most alike, vibrant and full, with branches that shot skyward in every direction. Jake's toward all the places he had traveled to, the adventures he'd had, the people he'd collected along the way. And Phoebe's toward her husband and children, her leaves rippling with her big ideas and even bigger laughs, but always circling back, like vines, wrapping around her family and her home.

It was her father where Emma had trouble. She thought harder. If Perry Goodwin were a tree, he was unlike the others in his family. His trunk was straight and true. It rose dutifully out of the ground in one direction, due north. His leaves may not have been as frilly and soft, or as vibrantly colored, as the others in the forest. But Emma knew one thing: they were strong. They were branches you could climb on, and branches you could swing from. They provided sound shade on an unforgiving day, and respite from the rains.

As she sat alone in the dark kitchen and filled her stomach with food, Emma contemplated her own place in the forest. She was a sapling. A branch or two may have cracked. Hell, she'd broken more than a few. But saplings gave and flexed. Where one twig snapped, another unfurled. Always reaching toward the light. From now on, she'd try to grow toward the light. Alongside her fellow trees. Because underneath them all, where the soil was dark and pithy, their roots ran together. A complicated tangle of tuber and stem, root and rhizome coursing through shared earth. They were hers.

Suddenly a roll of thunder rumbled overhead and a flash of light filled the foyer windows, but it was not lightning. Emma watched the headlights cut through the dark, spilling across the marble floor and into the kitchen where she sat. Emma pushed her empty plate away. When the front door opened, and her father filled its frame, she ran to him. There was nothing she needed to say. Her father flung his arms open like branches, and she fell into their shelter.

Olivia

She and Luci lay side by side in the dark, exhausted. Jake was downstairs on the couch, unable to speak since Perry had left. They'd not talked much to each other on the way home from the disastrous dinner party, but Olivia had prattled on about things outside the window and what a nice dinner Jane had made . . . on and on, wondering what Luci had heard or thought about the whole unendingly awful evening. Olivia was pretty sure she'd managed to whisk her out before it got too ugly, but still—kids instinctively felt when things were wrong. They always knew. Now, side by side in the solitude of Luci's bedroom, was the chance to talk to Luci about it. But Olivia wasn't sure where to begin. "That was quite a dinner," Olivia whispered. "I'm sorry that some of Jake's family seemed mad. I hope it didn't upset you."

In the darkness, Luci slipped her fingers into Olivia's hand.

Olivia went on. "This is what it means to be in a family, Lu. Sometimes people laugh and play and talk together, and sometimes they argue. Just like with friends. Or with husbands and wives. Sometimes people who love each other get mad at each other." Olivia felt her throat tightening, as she spoke, and she had to pause.

"Are you mad? At Jake?" Luci's voice was so soft and the room so dark and her head so heavy, Olivia wasn't sure if she was hearing things. She rolled over, face-to-face, and from the faint hall-way light she could see the question in her daughter's eyes.

"Lu Lu!" She'd heard right.

"Are you?" Luci asked again.

Olivia pressed her hands quickly to her eyes, and smiled. "No, baby. I was mad, but I'm not anymore. Jake and I are having some quiet time now, and then we will sit together and talk. That's what you do when you love someone. Right?"

Luci nodded, but she still looked unsure.

"Tonight, I learned something I didn't know. That Emma was driving the boat before the accident."

Luci nodded again.

"It's important to tell the truth, Lu. Even when you love some-body and don't want them to get in trouble."

Luci rolled over on her side, nose to nose with Olivia. "I like Emma."

Olivia was so relieved to hear the whisper of words coming from her daughter, it almost didn't matter what she was saying. And yet it did. Now they could confront that day. Maybe not to-night, maybe not for a while. But Luci was talking. Some tied-up, knotted piece inside her had worked itself loose, and with it, fi-nally, came her words. And with those would come her thoughts, her worries, her feelings; *all* of her little self.

Oliva wrapped her arms around Luci and pulled her in close against her chest. "Sweet girl. You are safe and you are loved."

She must have fallen asleep because she awoke much later. Luci was curled against her, snoring lightly. Olivia stretched and gently rolled off the bed. She pulled the covers up around her child then pressed her lips against her forehead before tiptoeing out.

Downstairs, she found Jake splayed across the couch. His leg was elevated on a stack of pillows, one arm thrown across his eyes. He was sound asleep. Olivia took the blanket from the back of the couch and draped it over him. His eyes fluttered open.

He looked at her a long while, then reached for her hand. She let him take it.

"I'm sorry, Liv. I won't keep any secrets from you again, I swear."

She sat down beside him. "I know. I'm sorry, too. But you could have told me. I would've understood."

Jake struggled to find the words, and Olivia waited. "I felt so much guilt. I didn't want Emma to get in trouble, and as awful as it was to let you believe that I was the one who drove the boat into the dock and hurt Luci, I didn't know what else to do . . ." Jake's voice trailed off. He began to cry.

Olivia sat very still and rubbed his head, listening. Jake talked about the accident. About how Emma had begged him to drive that day. About how happy it made her. They were cruising gently along the shore, just as he'd told her to do, and they picked up speed. He'd cautioned her to slow down. But then there was a log in the water. A giant log, floating directly in their path. He was holding Luci on his lap, and he set her down in an attempt to reach for the wheel. But then Emma swerved. Which must've panicked her, because she also accelerated, and swung toward shore. The dock rose up before them. In the last second Jake had to decide. Whether to leap for the wheel, if there was even time, or grab Luci. "I grabbed Luci," he cried into Olivia's lap. "I tried to hold on."

As she listened, Olivia cried with him. When he finished, she took his face in her hands and kissed his forehead. Then his lips. Jake reached for her and she pressed herself against him as hard as she could and pulled him as close as she could. And she, too, tried to hold on.

Later, when she'd helped him upstairs and settled him into bed, she waited until his breath gave way to the rhythm of sleep. Then, softly, she padded downstairs. She plucked her raincoat from the hook and eased the door ajar. "Shhh," she said to Buster, who stirred from the living room rug. "You stay."

There was no need for her raincoat, after all. A warm gust blew her hair back and she looked up. The storm had ceased, and overhead dark clouds tumbled across the sky, flashes of stars appearing and disappearing behind them. She hurried across the driveway and tugged the barn door open.

Inside, she flicked on the lanterns. The studio was empty, the worktops clear. All of Ben's sculptures had been shipped out for the show. Since then, he'd cleaned off the tabletops and scoured the surfaces. Every tool had been polished clean and returned to its place in the rusty coffee cans that lined the workbenches. Olivia had never seen the studio so spartan, and it made it harder to ignore the one table in the corner. Her corner. Where her own work was shrouded in darkness.

It took no time to gather her tools: A small bucket she filled in the slop sink with water. A sponge. A handful of rags. And a metal rasp. She spread them out across her table, pulled her stool out from under it, and sat. Then she pulled the canvas off her sculpture, slowly.

The clay fingers rose into view first, their splayed fingertips opening to the light. Her eyes followed them down to the knuckles, the hand, the palm. Then the wrist, the very wrist she remembered from old photographs of her mother. She placed her own hands on either side of it.

It was time to work.

Phoebe

Phoebe was terrible at goodbyes. Whenever they'd lost a pet over the years, Phoebe grieved hard, often for weeks. On the occasion a friend moved away, she avoided driving past their house for weeks. Graduations were the worst because of their false premise: They were meant to be celebratory? All those memories and baby photos colliding with caps and gowns and speeches about the future and *the rest of your life*. It was like a funeral, for your childhood.

Phoebe's father had once told her it was because she had a big heart. Perry had suggested it was because she was stubborn; she didn't like change. Both were probably right.

But saying goodbye to a house was something she had not considered. Because a house was a some*thing*. Not a some*one*. And what excuse did she have for falling apart over that?

Granted, it was not just any house. It was her childhood dream, that little cottage on that little lane. And a dream it was, with its lakefront yard and fieldstone fireplace and leaded glass windows that creaked just so when you cranked them open . . . but she was getting off track, again. What she had eventually realized, the hard way, was if she did not let go of the house, she risked losing much more. Her marriage, for one. Rob, her best friend and college sweetheart, whose patience and good humor had been stretched as thin as their finances. Who had, if she were really honest, leaned away from the project from the beginning. But she was stubborn, like Perry said, and Rob loved her, and in the end her heart went out to the house. It should've stayed with her family, she realized now. But her heart was back, if a little battered and bruised.

Phoebe had been unable to go to the final bank meeting with Rose Calloway. After all, she and Rose were *not* friends, and she'd had enough soul-baring conversations with the woman to last a lifetime. Rose-the-loan-officer was one person she actually would not mind saying goodbye to. But Phoebe did go to a meeting. A much more important one, and one that proved even harder.

Since the first day, Dave had been her partner. Her GC. And yes, eventually her friend. Dave had steered her away from danger, and through highs and lows. It was not his fault that the build got away from them. It was hers, and to some extent Rob's, and they would have to continue to work through that together for some time. Because she and Rob had decided they would. And Rob was not going anywhere. Dave, however, was not someone Phoebe would likely see much of anymore. And the man deserved a proper goodbye.

Phoebe had called and asked him to meet her at the property. Along with some of the subs and the regulars on his crew who'd done the framing and the roof. Who knew her and her kids and her husband by name and face. She knew how they took their coffees. The names of their kids, and even some of their dogs. That's what happened when you worked together on a home with a crew. Your home became theirs for a while. In a strange way, it was like a little family.

Dave said he'd meet her, though she didn't tell him exactly

what it was for. They agreed on eight thirty. Which was why Phoebe arrived at eight sharp. She and the house needed time together first. The house, too, deserved a goodbye.

When she pulled into the driveway, Phoebe sat in the car for a while before getting out. She needed to let the memory soak in: the way she'd felt during the renovation each time she pulled in and saw the changes as the house grew and took shape; the intoxicating rush of adrenaline and hope.

On the walkway to the front door, she stopped one last time at the fifth stone, the one where the flagstone slab tipped upward just enough to grab the toe of her Keds sneaker every time. This time, she hopped over it. The front door creaked as she opened it, but she did not go in right away. Instead, she inhaled. The intoxicating scent of fresh-cut wood. The stretch of Candlewood Lake beyond the bay window. All of what she'd come to associate with *home* these last eight months. She swiped at the tears that pressed behind her eyelids. She would not cry yet.

One last time, she walked through the rooms. She ran her hands over the farmhouse cabinets that had been hung in the kitchen. And the plywood frames for counters that had not yet been laid. She wandered upstairs, peering into the new master bath where she and Rob would not shower. And into the master itself, where they would not lay their heads down to sleep at night. In the walk-in closet she reached her arms out and twirled one last time.

Last, she headed to the end of the hall, where two rooms overlooked the front yard. She walked through the first and stopped in the Jack and Jill bathroom that connected them. The black-and-white basket-weave tile had been laid on the floor, and she stood in the middle of it, looking left, into what would have been Jed's room, then right into Patrick's. That was where she came undone.

She cried for all the memories they'd never have, for the childhood dream unrealized. For the hell she and Rob had been through, and put each other through. For the mess of their finances, which would take years to repair. For the embarrassment of explaining to friends and family that they'd gone under—it was over.

And then she stopped. It was not because Dave's Ford pickup was rumbling down the driveway, though it was. And it was not because she was still unable to let go, because that would take time. It was because even though the house was over—she and Rob were not. In spite of all of it, they were still a family. They had fought, and they had resented. And for a while Rob had taken to her parents' couch, which everyone noticed and no one dared say a damn thing about. But they were making their way back to each other, one apology, one admission, at a time.

Phoebe dried her eyes with the tail of her shirt. She looked around and took it all in one last time. Then she went downstairs and out the front door. Where she met Dave, handed him a check large enough to pay off his crew and his labor, and hugged him hard. Rob's work bonus had covered most of it, and Perry had helped with the rest. Though that would have to be paid back, too. The bank was taking over, but the build would continue. Rob had talked them into keeping Dave on as manager. And when it was all said and done, the house would be put up for short sale.

When Rob had come home from the meeting at the bank and told her the news about the decision for a short sale, Phoebe's eyes had popped (she'd felt them). "Don't even think about it," he'd said. "Even if it's months away, we will not be in a position to buy it. Not then, probably not ever."

That was the thing about being stubborn and terrible at good-byes. You could never really admit you needed to say it. And you were never ready.

Phoebe got into her car and looked at the time. Per usual, she was late. The boys had a T-ball game, and she was meeting them there with Rob. Jane and Edward were going. As were Olivia, Luci, and Jake, who had just gotten his cast off. She started the car and allowed herself a final look at the front door.

A long time ago, when she was applying to colleges, her father had given her advice. At the time she was headstrong and eager to leave her small town of Lenox so she could elbow her way out into the big exciting world. Where exactly she was going didn't really matter to her at the time, as long as she escaped. Edward had cautioned her. "Never run away from something, Phoebe," he'd said. "Wait until you have something to run *to*."

As she rolled down the driveway one last time, Phoebe did not look in the rearview mirror. Not even once. She wasn't running away, she was learning to let go. And besides, right now she had everything to run to. And they were waiting for her at the ball field.

Perry

Perry knocked for the second time and stood outside the door, waiting. Why was it no one ever seemed to monitor the door when they were hosting a party? He checked his watch. He was on time. At least for another minute.

He was about to knock again when the door swung open. "Perry!" It was Olivia, and she was in one of those wildly patterned dresses she was so fond of. He blinked. "Come in, come in! The others are out back."

She led him through the cozy stone foyer and the living room. The house was like he'd expected: toys and books and food and kids and music. Loud and colorful, kind of like her dress. But he was a guest, and she was now family, so he supposed he needed to get used to it.

The sliding glass doors to the back lawn were wide open. Beyond them, there was a lot going on for his taste: groups of people he did not recognize talking and laughing, the smell of spicy barbecued food that was sure to set off his stomach, and one oversized hairy dog.

But as he looked more carefully around the yard, which probably could have benefited from a good mowing for the occasion, his gaze fell upon a few faces he recognized. Emma was playing with a group of children with that boy, Sully, from camp. Perry didn't exactly love seeing Sully spending so much time with his daughter, but what he did love was the look on Emma's face. She was back to her old self, but better. Happier. And if it meant putting up with Sully on occasion, Perry supposed he could muddle through. From the corner of the yard came a whoop of laughter, and his gaze landed on Phoebe and Jake, whose heads were bent together in some sort of private joke. At that moment Jake looked up and saw him. If there was any hesitation, Perry could not tell, because his little brother headed straight for him.

Jake's limp had not receded, something that pained Perry every time he saw his brother. Jake, who did not like to sit still, who was lithe and quick and graceful, now carried a distinct hitch to his long stride. But true to form, his smile remained in its place. "Perry. You made it." He clapped his big brother on the back before embracing him.

"It's a good house," Perry said, offering him a bottle of wine. Jake thanked him and dropped it into a cooler of indiscriminate beers, not bothering to take notice that Perry had just handed him another fine Shiraz, this time from a boutique vintner out of New Zealand. No matter. If someone opened it, Perry hoped they would enjoy it.

"Have you seen the view?"

Perry followed Jake to the far edge of the yard, where their parents conversed. The house was perched on a steep hillside, in a heavily wooded family community known as Deer Run Shores. But if you cocked your head and squinted, through the trees there was a slim glimmer of Candlewood Lake blue. Perry nodded in appreciation. "Congratulations," he said.

It had been one month since Jake and Olivia had married

and moved in. The wedding had been a simple affair at Ben and Marge's house, with drinks and appetizers in the garden. It was the same day that Jake and Olivia announced the purchase of the new house. Perry had been flummoxed.

"It's wonderful news," he'd told his little brother. And he'd meant it. "But how?" Jake's job at the nature center paid the bills, but would not have afforded them much beyond.

"Did you hear? Olivia's piece that was featured in Ben's show last month? It sold. And she's been commissioned for another."

Perry had not heard. Once again, this family who never seemed to stop talking about mundane details still managed to skip all the important ones. "Congratulations," Perry said.

"It's not a lot. But combined with my salary, it was enough for a deposit. The place is pretty small. But it'll be ours."

Now, standing in the backyard at the official housewarming party, Perry was pleasantly surprised. The place was very small. And much in need of updates. But it was bright like Olivia and felt friendly like Jake. Jake got Perry a beer, and excused himself to greet other guests. To Perry's joy, one of those others was Amelia. "Hi, honey. Don't you look handsome in your seersucker jacket." She pecked him on the cheek. It was then he noticed she, too, had brought a bottle of wine.

"Thank you. Wait, which bottle is that?" he asked. "I already brought one."

"Oh." Like him, Amelia coveted the wines they imported from their travels, and as such they reserved gifting bottles only for the closest of family and friends. One bottle was generous. Two was just plain crazy. She lowered her voice. "I can put this one back in the car."

"No, no," Perry said, slipping his arm around her waist. "It's all right."

"You sure?"

For a long time, Perry had not been sure of much. After the accident and the leaked photo of his daughter's first, but probably not last, bad choice, he had come to question everything he'd so firmly believed. That careful forecasting and prudence could secure them a safe station in the world. That crises could be managed. After that summer, those ideologies had been reduced to ash. But in the months since, as the smoke cleared, Perry had been unable to escape the notion of risk. And people's differing tolerance for it. Some avoided it like grim death. Others possessed an appetite for it; some, insatiable. Perry wondered at all his family had grappled with that summer. Sometimes the people you loved risked too much. To his surprise, he had been one of them.

For all he thought he knew about being a family man, his daughter had shown him there was much still to figure out. In the end, the very things he had strove for were not what he needed. Boats could be replaced. Docks could be repaired. Loyalties lost, however, could not. Perry had withdrawn as president of Candlewood Cove. He waited until they reinstituted Emma's camp counselor position, if only under pressure, and then he canceled the family's membership in full. He did not need to belong, at least not to the Club. What he needed he already had with his wife and daughter. And yes, his family, however unreasonable they could be. They still needed him, after all. And, as it turned out, it went both ways.

Still, it surprised him, the things that people willingly risked: Money. Marriage. Security. As such, Perry still subscribed to a healthy diet of skepticism, and caution still whispered in his ear. But how lovely, for a change, to scan a horizon for stars instead of danger. To race full-tilt down a dock on a summer day and jump into the lake. To put yourself out there, if only a little further, each day.

Perry still did not like parties and big crowds. And his family was still *so much themselves*. As he stood at the edge of Jake and Olivia's yard watching his wife and daughter mingle, he was nudged roughly in the thigh. When he looked down, he found himself staring into inquiring brown eyes. "Well, hello, Buster."

"He likes you."

Perry spun around to find Luci staring up at him with that strange and knowing look. She smiled—the same way she had on the Metro-North train that day, and again, in the hospital, when he'd read her the story about the mouse. But never before had she spoken to him. Was Luci's talking a new thing? Warily, he glanced around. "Buster likes me, does he?"

"He wants to show you something." To his further surprise, Luci held out her hand.

Perry wasn't sure what to do. He didn't know if he should alert Olivia, first, or follow the child. But he was also fearful of fumbling this, and embarrassing Luci. He paused, struggling to assess the situation.

"What does Buster want to show me?" he asked her.

"His new bike."

"How wonderful. I did not know Buster rode a bike."

Luci giggled, a bright trill that echoed her mother's, and Perry looked up just in time to see her staring at them. Olivia stood but a few yards away, and she drew her hand to her mouth. He watched as she grabbed Jake's arm and pointed in their direction. So, this was new.

But Luci was not aware of the many faces turning in their direction. "Come on." She tugged his hand.

Perry's gut stirred. Something told him this was not time to be squandered with assessment. Of this, he was suddenly sure.

"Ladies first."

Without further delay Perry followed the little girl, who trailed the big hairy dog, who smelled terribly, across the overgrown yard and into the garage to see about a bike. He sneezed once, then again. Some risks were worth it.

Acknowledgments

T his book is especially meaningful to me, as it takes place in a setting dear to my childhood heart. While Lenox, Connecticut, is a fictional town created for the purpose of this story, Candlewood Lake and the Litchfield Hills countryside surrounding it are as real as a Connecticut summer day is long. This area is home to many artists and families, and an attraction to visitors in search of a postcard-perfect New England summer day.

Candlewood Lake's storied past can be traced on the walls of the Sherman Historical Society and Old Store museum, in Sherman, Connecticut, where I grew up. I am thankful to this neck of the woods for allowing me to traverse its winding trails, dip my feet in its lakes, and hike its hillsides where my imagination could wander. It has inspired the settings for all of my novels and the characters who hail from them.

As always, I am ever grateful for the incredible team at Emily Bestler Books, and most notably, my talented editor, Emily herself. Your enthusiasm for this book buoyed me during the writing process. Thank you, also, to Lara Jones, associate editor extraordinaire who handles more details than this author can keep track of. To art director James Iacobelli, and cover designer Laywan Kwan: I couldn't be happier. Special thanks must be given to associate publisher, Suzanne Donahue, for her tireless support and zeal. To publicists Ariele Fredman and Gena Lanzi, who've ensured my books are seen, heard, and put on store shelves and who get me out on the road each summer to share them. To Michael Gorman, marketing manager; Sonja Singleton, production editor; and Rick Willett, copy editor, who each touched the pages and production of this book.

To the unsung industry book fairy godmothers: the reviewers, bloggers, book clubs, and readers. To Robin Kall Homonoff and Emily Homonoff, Suzanne Leopold, Lauren Margolin, Kristy Barrett, Andrea Peskind Katz, and all the readers who pick up my books and put out the good word. You do such important work for us authors and we are terribly grateful!

Family stories inspire my writing, and this book is no different. To Barry, Moe, Josh, and Jesse for your continued love and encouragement. To John Brown, for holding my hand and walking beside me. And always, my heart, to Grace and Finley: avid reader and writer, chaser of chickens and wrangler of rescue dogs, and two of the brightest, kindest, silliest, most interesting people I know. You are my stars, my sun, my harvest moon. You fill me up.